The demons of the Seven Deadly Sins

from the *Buch Granatapfel,*

1511

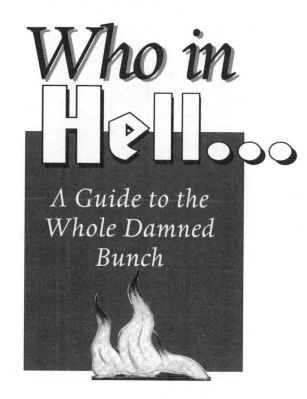

Who in Hell...

A Guide to the Whole Damned Bunch

SEAN KELLY

ROSEMARY ROGERS

VILLARD / NEW YORK

Library of Congress Cataloging-in-Publication Data

Kelly, Sean.
    Who in Hell . . . : a guide to the whole damned bunch / Sean Kelly and
        Rosemary Rogers.
        p.   cm.
    Includes bibliographical references.
    ISBN 0-679-76484-4 (alk. paper)
        1. Damned—Biography—Dictionaries.   2. Hell—Humor.   I. Rogers,
        Rosemary. II. Title.
    BL545.K45   1996
    920.02'0207—dc20   96-2527
    [B]

Interior design by Robert Bull Design

Random House website address: http://www.randomhouse.com/

Printed in the United States of America on acid-free paper

9 8 7 6 5 4 3 2

First Edition

In memory of Patrick Kelly,
who's in Heaven

PREFACE

THERE IS LIFE AFTER DEATH. Infallible, scientific polls and surveys reveal that 85 percent of Americans believe in it. However, in the words of the rousing old Negro spiritual, "Everybody talkin' 'bout Heaven ain't goin' there." So—what about you? Will *you* go to Hell? All right, then, but if *you* won't, who *will*? Your uncle? Your neighbor? O.J.? Madonna? Jimmy Swaggart?

"They are punished in hell who die in mortal sin," as we learned from the no-nonsense 1949 Revised Baltimore Catechism. Now, obviously, we are *all* sinners. But (the catechism further explains) to merit perpetual torment, our sins must be "mortal" ones—that is, both "grave offenses against God's law" and committed "with our full knowledge and consent." In other words, Hell is like capital punishment—reserved for deliberate, unrepentant malefactors in the first degree.

As might be expected, extreme liberals—known theologically as Pelagian heretics—argue that virtually no one is wicked enough to deserve Hell, whereas radical conservatives—aka Manichaean heretics—maintain that nearly everyone is utterly evil and certainly damned. Contemporary liberals blithely continue to commit the seven sins distinguished by Pope Gregory the Great as deadly: pride, wrath, envy, lust, gluttony, avarice, and sloth. But our up-to-date conservatives seem increasingly tempted to the four sins that traditionally "cry to Heaven for vengeance"—willful murder; the oppression of foreigners, widows, and orphans; injustice to the wage earner; and sodomy.

Thus it appears that even sins go in and out of fashion. It has been five hundred years since Dante described an Inferno full of alchemists, barrators, diviners, panderers, simonists, and usurers. Where in Hell, we may well ask, are the NRA lobbyists, urban renewers, strip-miners, paparazzi, on-line child pornographers, draft dodgers, infomercial producers, crack dealers, New Age gurus, tax cheats, self-help quacks, concentration camp commandants, and causers of gridlock? Whither, that is to say, are *we* bound?

Because, sooner or later, everybody dies, and then they have to go *some-*

where. Doubtless a righteous few—we call them saints—proceed directly to Paradise. Some of us—shabby, run-of-the-mill souls—will be sentenced to a term in the remedial torture chamber known as Purgatory. And the rest of us will depart for the place of "fire that can never be quenched," as the merciful Lamb of God so touchingly described it. After the Last Judgment, will stand-up comics be roasted? Must all smokers burn? Is phone sex, technically, "alone" or "with others"? Can George Steinbrenner plead insanity? Will St. Michael the Archangel give Clarence Thomas the benefit of the doubt? Is Woody Allen right about the certain damnation of all people who kid around with waiters? And, while we're on the subject, what about Woody himself?

Next time you scan the obituaries, try this experiment. After due consideration to the merits and vices of the recently deceased, give each of them a definitive thumbs-up or thumbs-down. Go ahead, play God. It feels divine.

INTRODUCTION

Hell is oneself.
Hell is alone, the other figures in it
Merely projections. There is nothing to escape from
And nothing to escape to. One is always alone.
                    —T. S. ELIOT, *The Cocktail Party*

Hell is other people.

                    —J. P. SARTRE, *No Exit*

S URELY HELL LIES IN WAIT." So reads sura 78, verse 21, of the Glorious Quran. Muslims believe that there are actually seven Hells, only one of which, the Flamer, is eternal. It is reserved for Infidels. *Jigoku-zochi,* a magnificent twelfth-century scroll, depicts the eight great Hells—each of which contains sixteen lesser Hells—wherein dead Japanese Buddhists must suffer until their sins are expiated. Of them, an eighteenth-century poet observed,

> *Judging by the pictures*
> *Hell looks more interesting*
> *Than the other place.*

"The doors of Hell are threefold, whereby men to ruin pass—the door of Lust, the door of Wrath, the door of Avarice. Let a man shun these three!" declares the Bhagavad Gita. There are twenty-eight underground torture chambers in Naraka, this triple-gated, seven-leveled inferno of the Hindus, but only six levels in the Adholoka, the Hell of the Jainas, and likewise six—progressively hotter—in the Hell of the Jewish Cabalists, known as Arka. (The uncircumcised inhabit its bottom floor.)

For Protestants who take their Bible literally, there can be no doubt about Hell's existence, nature, or origin: Jesus warns of "Hell, where the worm does not die and the fire is not quenched" (Mark 9:48) and of "the eternal fire, prepared for the devil and his angels" (Matthew 25:41). Indeed, for Christians, Hell promises to provide one of the joys of Heaven. According to the Angelic Doctor, St. Thomas Aquinas, in his *Summa Theologica,* "That the saints may enjoy their beatitude and the Grace of God more abundantly, they are permitted to see the punishment of the damned in Hell."

The traditional (1918) *Baltimore Catechism of Christian Doctrine* flatly informed generations of American Catholic schoolchildren that "Hell is the place in which the reprobate are condemned to suffer forever with the devils" and assured them that "all those who die in the state of mortal sin, even if they be guilty of only one such sin," proceed thence. The official, up-to-date 1994 *Catechism of the Catholic Church* likewise affirms that "immediately after death, the souls of those who die in a state of mortal sin descend into Hell, where they suffer the punishments of Hell."

Most creeds damn only unbelievers. But now that the Church has made salvation—or, at least, Limbo—available to well-meaning Protestants, pagans, and unbaptized babies, Catholic Hell may well have become exclusively Catholic—in George Orwell's words, "a sort of high class night club, entry to which is reserved for Catholics only, since . . . non-Catholics are too ignorant to be held guilty, like the beasts that perish."

Pope John Paul II, in *Crossing the Threshold of Hope,* affirms the existence of Hell but reminds us that "no man, not even Judas, can be said with certainty to be there."

Without certainty, then, we offer this directory of the damned. It consists of

1. The better-known devils—in whose existence, according to a 1989 Gallup poll, 37 percent of Americans believe. But be advised that we, like every demonologist since his time, have followed the definitive and exhaustive system of Dr. Johan Weyer (1515–1588), whose *Pseudo-monarchia Daemonum* turns out to have been an elaborate, satirical hoax.
2. Human souls who have been observed and identified in the Infernal regions by reputable eyewitnesses, such as Dante.
3. A subjective miscellany of famous and infamous ancient and modern sinners who seem to have died unrepentant.

In the cases of sinners of the latter two classes, we have supplied, whenever possible, their sins, as well as the dates of their damnations—by means of the designation DWH (DIed and went to Hell). Unless specified as B.C., dates are A.D.

An apology for the devil: It must be remembered that we have heard only one side of the case. God has written all the books.

　　　　　　　—SAMUEL BUTLER, *Higgledy-Piggledy*

At the end of things . . . the Blessed will say, "We have never lived anywhere except in Heaven," and the Lost, "We were always in Hell." And both will speak truly.

　　　　　　　—C. S. LEWIS, *The Great Divorce*

All folks who pretend to religion and grace
Allow there's a Hell, but dispute of the place;
But, if Hell may by logical rules be defined
The place of the damned—I'll tell you my mind.
Wherever the damn'd do chiefly abound,
Most certainly there is Hell to be found;
Damn'd poets, damn'd critics, damn'd blockheads, damn'd knaves;
Damn'd senators bribed, damn'd prostitute slaves;
Damn'd lawyers and judges, damn'd lords and damn'd squires;
Damn'd spies and informers, damn'd friends and damn'd liars;
And Hell to be sure is at Paris or Rome.
How happy for us that it is not at home!

　　　　　　　—JONATHAN SWIFT, *"The Place of the Damned"*

ABADDON

How many devils are there? The Talmud tells us, "If the eye could perceive the demons that people the universe, existence would be impossible. The demons are more numerous than we are." Martin Luther declares, "Everything is full of devils. They are in the courts of princes, in houses, fields, streets, in water, wood and fire." Feyerabend, a popular Lutheran theologian (the author of *Theatrum Diabolorum*), counted 2,665,866,736,664 devils. In 1467, a monk named Alphonsus de Spina (who was, incidentally, a convert from Judaism and the author of the first antiwitch tract, *Fortalicium Fidei*) did the orthodox Catholic math and concluded that there are really only 133,306,668 of the Infernal Host: precisely one-third of the glorious Heavenly host of angels—all members of the carping, dissatisfied minority who had rebelled against God and "rais'd impious War in Heaven" (in Milton's mighty phrase). They and their leader, SATAN aka LUCIFER, were (thank—literally—God) soon defeated and cast down into Hell. Thus were devils created, and the first of them (alphabetically speaking) is Abaddon, the "angel of the bottomless pit." He leads the legion of long-haired, armor-plated, scorpion-tailed devils—the "plague of locusts" so movingly described by St. John the Divine in the ninth chapter of the biblical book of Revelation. In his (1621) *Anatomy of Melancholy*, Robert Burton reported that Abaddon's title is "Captain of the Furies" and that he leads the warlike Seventh Infernal Order.

ABBAGLIATO   DWH circa 1300   SQUANDERING

In life, Bartolommeo di Folchacchieri was known by this nickname, which means "dazed and confused"—or just plain "stupid." Dante shared the sophisticated Florentine attitude toward the "silly" Sienese and comments sarcastically on Bartolommeo's "great wit" as he observes him and his fellow wealthy playboys—once members of Siena's notorious Spendthrifts' Club—scratching their leprous sores, deep in the Inferno's Eighth Circle. (See also CAPOCCHIO.)

ABDULHAMID II   DWH 1918   TYRANNY

If merciless totalitarianism and methodical murder entitle one to a place in Jahannan, the Muslim Hell, this remarkably despotic Ottoman sultan is surely among the damned. After losing a war with Russia in 1877, he dissolved the Turkish parliament, suspended the constitution, and ruled for the next forty years by means of a network of brutal secret police. In 1884, he instigated a systematic massacre of Armenian Christians. He was eventually overthrown by a progressive, liberal group known as the Young Turks—who undertook to complete the Armenian genocide.

ABDUSCIUS   🔥

A minor demon who specializes in uprooting trees.

ABIGOR   🔥

According to medieval demonologists, this fiend commands sixty of SATAN's legions and rides a winged horse. He is said to know the future as well as "the secrets of warfare."

ABIMELECH   DWH 1000 B.C.   USURPATION

This biblical (Judges 9) king of Shechem achieved the throne by murdering his holy father, Gideon, and sixty-nine of his seventy brothers. The Lord showed his displeasure with the usurper by ordaining that he be killed by a woman—the ultimate disgrace.

ABSALOM DWH 1020 B.C. TREACHERY

King David's charming, handsome, and favorite (third) son was a rebel and a traitor. He first "stole the hearts of the men of Israel," then waged a civil war against his father. After capturing Jerusalem, Absalom somehow contrived, while riding a mule, to get his big head stuck in the branches of an oak tree, and while hanging there he was righteously slain, much to David's sorrow.

ABŪ al ʿAbbās DWH 754 TYRANNY

A caliph, the founder of Islam's Abbasid dynasty, and another candidate for Jahannan, he methodically exterminated the Umayyads, the Alids, and all other claimants to power. He gloried in the name as-Saffah, the Blood-Shedder.

ACCORAMBONI, Vittoria DWH 1585 MURDER

The story of this beautiful Florentine adulteress and homicide inspired Elizabethan dramatist John Webster to write a sexy, violent (and commercially successful) revenge tragedy, which he entitled after her well-deserved nickname *The White Divel*.

ACCORSO, Francesco d' DWH 1293 SODOMY

Dante's old friend and mentor BRUNETTO LATINI names this Bolognese law professor as one of his distinguished companions in the windy desert that is the third ring of Hell's Seventh Circle. According to Brunetto, many of his fellow sodomites are—no big surprise—"clerics and men of letters." So great had been Accorso's fame as a teacher of law that he was invited to lecture at far-off Oxford University. The poet never explicitly names the "sin" for which these men are damned, on the assumption that his readers were aware of their "unnatural" sexual inclinations.

THE ACCUSER 🦇

A sometime biblical translation of the Hebrew word SATAN; but in his amusing digression on demons in *The Anatomy of Melancholy*, Robert Burton distinguishes between them. To SATAN he assigns leadership of the Fourth Order of fiends, the ones who tempt us to magic and other swindles; whereas, maintains Sir Robert, the Accuser (Greek *diabolos*) leads the Eighth Order and promotes the sin of despair. Whatever. Visionary English poet William Blake called the Accuser "the God of this world."

6 . . . . **A**

ACHILLES   DWH circa 1190 B.C.   LUST
 In the Second Circle of Hell, moaning and wafting about among the epicene ghosts of the lustful, Dante discovers, of all people, the wrathful and indomitable Achilles, mightiest of Greek warriors and hero of the epic poem the *Iliad*. (In its sequel, the *Odyssey*, we learn from Homer himself that Achilles is in Hades and that, although he is treated there with all due respect, he would prefer—he tells the visiting ULYSSES—to be alive, "even as a wretched farmer's hired man.") But the Italian poet had no Greek, and so read no Homer. All he knew of the Trojan War and its cast of characters he learned from fanciful medieval legends, according to one of which Achilles, during a truce, fell madly in love with Polyxena, a princess of Troy. This inappropriate—not to say treacherous—passion drained the hero of his superpowers and presented the Trojan prince PARIS with the opportunity to kill him—by shooting him in the heel, his only vulnerable spot. Thus, Achilles' "Mortal Sin," in Dante's eyes, was that he had "lost his life to love."
 We, who don't *need* to know Greek to read the *Iliad*, may speculate that, since "the anger of Achilles" is its very subject, the sulky Hellenic berserker might well be spending eternity even lower down in Hell, in Dante's Fifth Circle, to which the wrathful are condemned; it is even possible to imply from the intensity of his passion for his tent mate Patroclus that Achilles' afterlife takes place in the Seventh Circle, among the sodomites.

ACHITOPHEL   DWH 1020 B.C.   TREASON
 Called the Gilonite, he is doubly damned, as a traitor *and* a suicide. King David's trusted counselor, he first deserted him to side with his rebellious son ABSALOM, then hanged himself. In canto 28 of the *Inferno*, the deeply damned BERTRAND DE BORN compares his sin with that of Achitophel.

ADAM of Brescia, "Master"   DWH 1280   FORGERY
 The art of which he was a "maestro" was counterfeiting. Adam was found guilty of falsifying the twenty-four-carat gold coins of Florence—florins—and burned alive. (The coins he minted each contained three carats of alloy.) Dante reports (canto 30) that in Hell, Master Adam is shaped, for some reason, "like a lute."

ADRAMMELECH   ◆
 In *Paradise Lost* (6.365), Milton tells us this demon was once a "potent Throne"—that is, a member of the Third Order of the angelic hierarchy. He also did time as a Babylonian sun god (as which he is mentioned in II

Kings of the Bible) but is now the grand chancellor of Hell and president of its High Council. Something of a dandy, Adrammelech supervises SATAN's wardrobe and reveals himself to mortals in the form of a peacock.

ADRASTUS   DWH circa 1200 B.C.   TREASON

The king of Argos, he was the sole surviving member of the rebellious Seven against Thebes (see AMPHIARAUS, CAPANEUS, et al.). Adrastus eventually expired of grief over the death of his son, whom he personally led into a later, and equally futile, military expedition. His "pale shade" was seen and identified by Virgil's AENEAS during his brief tour of Hades in book 6 of the *Aeneid*.

ADRIAN IV   DWH 1159   SOWING DISCORD

Nicholas Breakspear was the first and only English-born pope. By his infamous papal bull *Laudibiliter*, he ceded Ireland to England, causing no end of trouble.

AEACUS   🐦

In the Hades of the Greeks, newly arrived souls were stripped naked and put on trial before a troika of judges, all sons of Zeus: Aeacus, MINOS, and RHADAMANTHUS, who determined whether the "shades" were to proceed to the eternal pleasures of Elysium or the perpetual torments of Tartarus. Aeacus—who was, incidentally, the grandfather of the hero ACHILLES—had been begotten by the father god on the mortal maiden Aegina. He was famous in life for his piety and honesty; Plato, in the *Gorgias*, describes his appointment to the Infernal Court, where he has jurisdiction over the European dead. (Rhadamanthus has Asia, Minos settles ties.) He appears in Aristophanes' blasphemous satire *The Frogs* and delivers a graphic description of the pains of Tartarus—hungry Hell hounds, hundred-headed snakes, lung-sucking eels, heaps of mashed kidneys and entrails—that eerily prefigures the sermons of televangelists.

AENEAS   DWH circa 1150 B.C.   BETRAYAL

The handsome and intrepid—if somewhat priggish—hero of Virgil's Latin epic the *Aeneid* takes a side trip to Hades while on his way from Troy to Italy, where he is to found the city of Rome. In the Underworld, he encounters, among other "shades," Queen DIDO, the mistress he ditched on his way to fulfill his noble destiny. In a later epic poem, *Orlando Furioso*, the Renaissance Italian Ariosto (1474–1533) places Aeneas himself deep in Hell—for his sinful betrayal of his beloved.

AESHMA DAEVA 🦊
A bad-tempered Persian demon who attacks cows.

AGALIAREPT 🦊
Grand general of Hell's second legion; on earth he holds sway over Europe and has the power "to discover all secrets and unveil mysteries."

AGAMEMNON   DWH circa 1190 B.C.   VIOLENCE
On his tour of Hades, ULYSSES is surprised to discover that his former commanding officer is already in residence there. Agamemnon, king of Argos, was not a sympathetic character. He began his military campaign against Troy by sacrificing his daughter to gain a favorable wind and ended it by kidnapping the priestess Cassandra during the victorious Greek forces' sack of the city. Upon his return, his ax-wielding wife murdered him in the bath—Ulysses marvels at the gory results of her hatchet work, still evident on Agamemnon's "shade" in the Underworld.

Rabelais reports that in Hell Agamemnon is employed as "a pot-licker."

AGARES 🦊
Grand duke of eastern Hell, he is also a language tutor, dancing master, and causer of earthquakes, and he rides a crocodile. He is one of the seventy-two demons King Solomon once captured and put in a jar.

AGNEL   DWH 13th century   THEFT
A little-known Florentine crook, possibly a member of the Brunelleschi family. Deep in Hell's Eighth Circle, Dante watches in horror as Agnel is attacked by an enormous snake—by the sound of it, a boa constrictor with six legs and feet—and squeezed so tightly he becomes fused with the serpent.

AGNIEL 🦊
One of the hundreds of fallen Watcher angels named in the apocryphal Book of Enoch (see AZAZEL). His divine assignment was to teach newly created humans the use of herbs and roots. But he succumbed to the wiles of a mortal woman and thus became a devil.

AGRAT BAT MAHLAT 🦊
In Jewish legend, the "queen of demons." Christian demonologists maintain that in Hell she is one of SATAN's four brides and on earth a guardian demon of prostitutes.

AGRIPPINA, Julia   DWH 59   MURDER

Ruthless Roman matron, sister of the emperor CALIGULA, she married first the emperor Domitius (whom she poisoned), then the wealthy Crispus (whom she poisoned), and finally her uncle, the emperor Claudius (ditto). She was the doting mother of the dreadful emperor NERO. After many elaborate attempts—one amusing one involving a collapsible boat—her son at last succeeded in killing *her*. Then she returned to haunt him.

AGUIRRE, Lope de   DWH 1561   ANGER

To this day his name is a byword in Spanish America for wickedness. The self-styled Wrath of God was a conquistador in Peru, where he suppressed the natives with more than usual cruelty before setting out to find the legendary El Dorado. Upon reaching the headwaters of the Amazon, Aguirre murdered the other leaders of the expedition, as well as several priests and his own daughter. He was duly arrested and, utterly unrepentant, executed by the Spanish authorities.

AHAB   DWH 843 B.C.   IDOLATRY

The seventh king of Israel, who "did evil in the sight of the Lord above all that were before him" (I Kings 16:30). What he did was set up an altar to the idol BAAL, at the insistence of his beautiful shiksa spouse, JEZEBEL. The Talmud itself quotes a folk saying that "Hell awaits one who always follows the advice of his wife."

AHI

The Hindu demon of drought.

AHRIMAN

In modern Farsi, this is the name of ANGRA MAINYU, the principle of darkness and evil according to the Magian (Zoroastrian) system.

ALASTOR

An ancient Greek prototype of SATAN, he was a wicked spirit who tempted mortals in this life and tortured them in the next. In Christian demonology, he has been demoted to the role of minor bureaucratic fiend, Executor of the Decrees of the Infernal Court.

ALBA, Fernando Alvarez, Duke of   DWH 1582   TYRANNY

A soldier and statesman of the old school, the duke waged, on behalf of his Church (Catholicism) and his State (Spain), outstanding programs of terror and slaughter, first in the Protestant Netherlands, which he ruled by the well-named Council of Blood, and later in Catholic Portugal.

ALBERIGO, Friar   DWH circa 1300   TREACHERY

Dante is understandably surprised to discover this member of the Manfredi family buried up to his eyes in ice in Hell—since he believes him to be alive and well in his native Faenza. In 1285, Alberigo, on the pretext of resolving a family feud, had invited two kinsmen to dinner, where, upon his signal ("serve the fruit"), they were assassinated. He explains to the poet that for this heinous sin against hospitality he was immediately transported to his eternal punishment, while a fiend took possession of his body in the world above. This monster was, incidentally, one of the corrupt JOVIAL FRIARS.

ALBERT of Mainz   DWH 1545   SIMONY

The selling of indulgences, as well as the holding of two dioceses, was (and is) contrary to Catholic canon law. But this German archbishop persuaded Pope Leo X to make an exception in his case, and he was permitted to hold two fertile bishoprics—in return for a huge contribution to the papal building fund. It was agreed that the money (which Albert borrowed from Fugger's bank) was to be repaid through the sale of indulgences, the proceeds from which Albert would split fifty-fifty with the Holy Father. It was to such simonic (see SIMON MAGUS) goings-on that Martin Luther took understandable exception.

ALCIBIADES   DWH 404 B.C.   TREASON

A handsome, arrogant, vainglorious Athenian aristocrat and onetime student of SOCRATES, he first betrayed his native city to the Spartan enemy, then betrayed Sparta to the Persians.

ALESSANDRO degli Alberti   DWH 1286   TREASON

Their father was a wealthy landowner, Alessandro was a Guelf, and his brother Napoleone was a Ghibelline; however, it was not politics but greed—their inheritance—that caused them to kill each other. Deep in Hell, frozen in the ice, they embrace forever and madly butt heads.

ALESSIO Interminei   DWH circa 1300   FLATTERY

Of this former citizen of Lucca, history has little to relate—but Dante apparently knew him personally and despised him as a flatterer. The poet may be settling a personal score as he observes Alessio in the Eighth Circle of Hell, up to his eyes in shit.

ALEXANDER VI DWH 1503 SIMONY

In the historic year 1492, the worst of the Renaissance "Bad Popes," Rodrigo Borgia, bribed his way onto the Chair of St. Peter in Rome. Among his mistresses were Vannozza Cattanei and Giulia Farnese. Among his ten known illegitimate children were CESARE and LUCREZIA BORGIA. He enjoyed an orgy—or a simple mother-daughter twosome—as well as the next man, but lust was the least of his sins. He had committed his first murder back in Catalonia at the age of twelve. As pontiff, his standard MO was to accept a large bribe, appoint a cardinal, then poison the new-made prince of the Church and reopen bidding for the position. This pope may be said to have single-handedly justified the Reformation. On his behalf, it must be admitted that he was a loving father—and he *did* have the killjoy SAVONAROLA executed.

Alexander died as he had lived—by poison—when he accidentally drank a deadly potion he had prepared for a couple of new cardinals. Lurid descriptions of his foul and bloated corpse abound in anti-Catholic literature. That he is in Hell there can be no doubt—even his successor, Pope Julius II, forbade the saying of a mass for the repose of Alexander's soul on the grounds that "it is blasphemous to pray for the damned."

ALEXANDER "the Great"

DWH 323 b.c. TYRANNY

In canto 12 of the *Inferno,* among the tyrants, Dante sees someone named Alexander. Some authorities identify this figure as the fourth-century despot Alexander of Pherae —a murderous brute who died and doubtless went to Hell in 358 B.C. But most scholars agree that the poet is referring to Alexander III of Macedon, aka the Great. A historic figure who achieved mythic status in the Middle Ages, Alexander may or may not have murdered his father, PHILIP (in 336), although Heaven knows the old man deserved it. He *did* cut the Gordian knot (in 333) and, to amuse

the courtesan THAÏS, burn down the Persian city of Persepolis, in 330. He *did* conquer the entire civilized world and may even have wept (in 325) at having "no more worlds to conquer." Like many a manly warrior since, he had numerous wives and mistresses and was deeply gay. Like many a successful general since, he came to believe he was divine.

The Roman satirist Lucian claimed to have visited Hell and seen Alexander employed there as a cobbler. Following his lead, Rabelais (via Pantagruel's returned-from-the-dead friend Epistemon), described Alexander the Great "earning a miserable living by patching old shoes, and being beaten by the cynic Diogenes for doing a bad job" (see also DIO-GENES).

ALI   DWH 662   HERESY

Mohammed (see MAHOMET) the Prophet's adopted son, later his son-in-law, and still later his successor, Ali is claimed as their founder by the Shi'ite sect of Islam. Brave, just, and learned, Ali was the fourth caliph and thus, by Dante's politically incorrect standards, a heretic. Ali long strove to placate or subdue the many warlike factions of Islam. He died, smitten by a poisoned sword, while at prayer—and thus, when Dante encounters him in Hell's Eighth Circle, his weeping face is "cleft from chin to crown."

ALICHINO

Despite its title, the *Divine Comedy* does not contain many knee-slappers. But Alichino does provide a moment of slapstick. He is one of the clumsy devils encountered by Dante in cantos 21 and 22 of the *Inferno.* (His name means "anchovy breath.") After saluting an officer with a trumpet-blast fart, Alichino belly flops into a bubbling tar puddle, in playful pursuit of a bribe taker's soul.

ALLEN, Ethan   DWH 1789   TREASON

Hero of the American Revolution, this feisty guerrilla leader of the Green Mountain Boys of Vermont famously called for the surrender of Fort Ticonderoga "in the name of the Great Jehovah and the Continental Congress!" But by 1780 he was, behind the back of that very Congress, negotiating with the British financial terms for the return of Vermont to the Empire. (Allen's motto appears to have been "Live Free or Sell Out.") As for his loyalty to "the Great Jehovah," in 1784, the sometime patriot published *Reason, the Only Oracle of Man,* a pamphlet in which he declared himself "no Christian" and denied the existence of a personal God. (As might be expected, his blasphemous book was itself a work of outright plagiarism.)

ALMAGRO, Diego de DWH 1538 CRUELTY

The greedy, bloodthirsty, and treacherous Spanish-born conqueror of Chile, he was once the friend but later the bitter enemy of FRANCISCO PIZARRO. That Almagro is in Hell we have on the authority of the poet Robert Burns. (For the curse in question, see BREADALBANE.)

ALOCER 🐾

A grand duke of Hell, he has a lion's head and is alleged to teach the liberal arts.

ALRINACH 🐾

One of Christian demonology's surprisingly few female devils, she presides over floods, earthquakes, storms, and shipwrecks.

ALUQA 🐾

Another female fiend, and a double threat, being both a succubus and a vampire. Aluqa invariably leaves her male victims feeling suicidally depressed, not to mention dehydrated.

AMAIMON 🐾

King of eastern Hell, he commands forty legions and vomits flame but is, for some reason, absolutely harmless between 3:00 A.M. and noon.

AMPHIARAUS DWH circa 1200 B.C. BLASPHEMY

Formerly a heroic companion of JASON, he was coerced by his wife (the usual story) into taking part in the ill-fated expedition by the Seven against Thebes. Worsted in battle, he fled the field—only to be swallowed up by a hole in the earth.

AMY 🐾

Once an angel of the order of Powers, he is now one of Hell's many presidents and an expert on astrology.

ANANIAS DWH circa 34 LYING

His shameful story is told in the Acts of the Apostles (5). Rather than selling all his possessions and giving the proceeds to the pope, St. Peter, like a good Christian should, Ananias hedged his bets, so to speak, and "kept back part of the price." Then, to compound the sin, he denied that he had done so—he had the cheek to lie to the Prince of the Apostles! Naturally, the Holy Spirit was quick to set Peter wise, and the Big Fisherman righteously confronted Ananias, whereupon the miscreant dropped instantly dead—proceeding directly, one can only assume, to Hell.

ANASTASIUS II   DWH 498   HERESY

Dante espies this pope's "great tomb" in Hell's Sixth Circle, among the graves of the heretics. There are two theories as to why: (1) In the interest of ending a schism, Anastasius had once granted an audience to a heretical deacon named Photinus, who had denied Christ's *divine* nature. (2) Dante simply confused Anastasius the pope with an identically named Byzantine emperor—Anastasius I (491–518), who subscribed to the Monophysite heresy, which denied Christ's *human* nature.

ANAXARETE   HARDNESS OF HEART

The Latin poet Ovid, in his *Metamorphoses,* tells the story of this pitiless virgin who drove her spurned suitor, Iphis, to suicide. The lovesick lad hanged himself in her doorway while she looked on, unmoved. Venus, the outraged goddess of love, instantly turned Anaxarete to stone. That her soul is in Hell, among those of other "ungrateful ladies," attests the Italian poet Ariosto, in his epic *Orlando Furioso.*

ANDRAS   🐾

A grand marquis of Hell, a provoker of discord, he is an especially picturesque demon, with a naked angel's body and an owl's head. Andras rides a black wolf.

ANDREA dei Mozzi   DWH 1296   SODOMY

Bishop of Florence in the time of Dante's youth, this nobly born prelate was an inept preacher and notoriously stupid—but he is in Hell for the sin of sodomy. (The poet puts it graciously, telling us that Andrea's "nerves" were *mal protesi,* that is, "sin-strained.") History relates that the public scandal of Bishop dei Mozzi's sexual predilections eventually caused the authorities—in this case, Pope BONIFACE VIII—to intervene. His Holiness quietly transferred the pederastic prelate from Florence to Vicenza. *Plus ça change . . .*

ANGRA MAINYU   🐾

The Zoroastrian principle of darkness, coequal with Ahura Mazda, God of Light. He mysteriously manages to be responsible for all the evil on earth, although he dwells eternally in the depths of Hell. It has been argued that the utterly malevolent Christian DEVIL has more in common with this wicked pagan entity than with the ambiguous Old Testament character SATAN.

ANIQUEL 🐾
One of Hell's seven grand dukes, who may be conjured in the form of a serpent.

ANNAS DWH 1st century   DEICIDE
According to the unerring Scriptures, at the time of the crucifixion of Christ, Annas was either high priest of Jerusalem (Acts 4:6) or co–high priest with his son-in-law CAIAPHAS (Luke 3:2)—or perhaps Caiaphas alone was high priest (Matthew 26:3, Mark 14:55, John 18:13). Anyway, in the *Inferno* (canto 23), Dante observes the pair of them perpetually crucified together.

ANTAEUS 🐾
Dante discovers that four giants, three from Greek mythology and one from the Bible, guard the entrance to lowest Hell, the Ninth Circle. Antaeus, whose mother was Tellus, the earth, once nearly bested Hercules in a wrestling match. Virgil bribes Antaeus with the promise that his poet-companion will speak well of him in the world above if he helps them across the yawning moat. The giant obliges.

ANUBIS 🐾
Jackal-headed Egyptian god of the dead.

APOLLYON 🐾
The Greek name (it means "the destroyer") for ABADDON, the king of the bottomless pit. Winged, scaly, and with a bear's feet, he makes an appearance in John Bunyan's famously edifying if somewhat tedious Christian allegory, *Pilgrim's Progress.*

ARAQIEL 🐾
Before his fall, he was a Watcher angel (I Enoch) who taught geography.

ARCHELAUS DWH 399 B.C.   TYRANNY
In Plato's *Gorgias,* this patricidal, fratricidal king of Macedon serves as an example of an "incurable" sinner, the incorrigible sort whose afterlife sufferings in Tartarus will be of no reforming benefit and thus (at least in SOCRATES' opinion) will never end.

ARCHERON 🐾
There has been a recent, unfortunate, revival of interest in the Gnostics, a second-century Egyptian sect whose creed was a synthesis, or hash,

of Christianity, Platonism, and various Middle Eastern mythologies. Like all "New Agers" since—Masons, Theosophists, Scientologists, et cetera—the Gnostics went in for secret passwords and cryptic technobabble and were shockingly elitist. (*Gnostics* actually means "those in the know.") They maintained that this material world of ours, being evil, could not have been made by Perfect God but was rather the "subcreation" of an evil spirit whom they named Demiurge and sometimes identified with the Hebrew deity Yahweh. (Like many highly spiritual sects since, the Gnostics were more than somewhat anti-Semitic.) In their system, the evil offspring begotten by the Demiurge (via the female principle Sophia) was Archeron, "the Tempter."

ARGYLL, Archibald Campbell, Duke of   DWH 1703   MURDER

He unsuccessfully sought the favor of the last Catholic king of England, James II, then traveled to The Hague and joined forces with the Protestant would-be usurper, William of Orange. After the "Glorious Revolution" of 1688, the vile turncoat was rewarded with a title. In February 1692, he conducted, and profited greatly by, the bloody massacre of the Macdonalds of Glencoe. (See also BREADAL-BANE.)

ARIOCH   🦞

A vengeful devil whose Hebrew name means "fierce lion," he makes a cameo appearance in Milton's *Paradise Lost* (6.371).

ARIUS   DWH 336   HERESY

No sooner had the Roman emperor Constantine declared Christianity to be the official state religion than a heresy broke out, which threatened not only the Church's unity but its all-important tax-exempt status. Arius, an eighty-year-old Libyan-born presbyter in Alexandria, had begun publicly to deny Jesus' divine nature! The emperor hastily convened the Council of Nicaea, at which 300 or so bishops gathered to produce the Nicene Creed ("I believe in one God, the Father Almighty," et cetera). When Arius wouldn't sign it, his writings were burned and he was both excommunicated and declared anathema. In this unholy state, he soon died. His dreadful heresy, Arianism, survives to this day, transparently disguised as Unitarianism. Dante did not catch a glimpse of Arius's tall, austere shade suffering among the schismatics in Hell's Eighth Circle—but there he must surely be.

ARNOLD, Benedict   DWH 1801   TREASON

His name lives on as an epithet for *traitor* in the United States—which nation might well have lost its War of Independence except for his 1775 capture of Fort Ticonderoga (with ETHAN ALLEN) and his brave and brilliant soldiering at the Battle of Saratoga, in 1778. Gravely wounded on that field, Arnold was posted to Philadelphia by his friend and supporter George Washington. There he began living (suspiciously) beyond his means. In April 1779, he married Peggy Shippen, a high-living socialite and Tory sympathizer. In May, the patriot-hero began secret negotiations to surrender West Point to the British for £2,000. When his contact, Maj. John André, was taken prisoner by American forces, he could not be—as was the custom of the period—exchanged for Arnold, because the latter had fled to England, leaving the gallant André to be hanged as a spy. This had the effect of making the turncoat's name forever odious to Loyalists as well. Arnold, said to be "away on other business," was unfortunately unable to serve on the all-American jury from Hell summoned by Mr. Scratch in Stephen Vincent Benét's classic story "The Devil and Daniel Webster."

ARUNS   DWH 1st century B.C.   WITCHCRAFT

The Roman Church has always had an almost superstitious hatred of the occult—including ESP, séances, witchcraft, Ouija boards, and every other form of "fortune-telling." Thus, the ultraorthodox Dante glimpses, in the crowded Eighth Circle of Hell, a certain Aruns—an Etruscan soothsayer who, according to the Roman historian Lucan, had in the year 48 B.C. correctly predicted Caesar's victory over Pompey at the Battle of Pharsalus.

ASDENTE   DWH circa 1300   FORTUNE-TELLING

Dante encounters this shoemaker of Parma with a reputation, during Dante's youth, for prophetic powers, wearing his head backward, among the damned soothsayers in canto 20. His Christian name was Benvenuto, but he was known by his nickname, Toothless.

ASHTORETH

The word itself is merely the plural form of AS-TARTE—and it means "goddesses"—but male chauvinist medieval demonologists understood it as the name of the demoness Astarte's "husband," whom they took to be the treasurer of Hell and grand duke of its western regions. Ashtoreth is the very devil who "finds work for idle hands"—that is, he specializes in tempting humans to the sins of sloth and irresponsibility while offering "the friendship of the powerful." He inspires us to daydream. He is especially powerful in the month of August, and his Heavenly adversary is the apostle St. Bartholomew. In the original *Faustbuch* (1587), Ashtoreth is identified as one of the "governors" of Hell, coequal with BEELZEBUB, PLUTO, and SATAN. His actual signature, affixed to a "pact with the devil," was introduced as evidence in a French court in 1634. He is sometimes called the Prince of Inquisitors. But he has terrible breath.

ASMODEUS (aka Ashmedai)

The king of demons in Jewish legend, he plots against the newly wedded. A former Seraph—an angel of the first hierarchy—Asmodeus is now chief of the Fourth Order of demons. In the fanciful Book of Tobit (which is, alas, non-canonical for Jews and Protestants) Tobias woos the beautiful virgin Sarah. Her seven previous husbands had all been slain by the demon Asmodeus on their wedding nights—but, aided by the Archangel Raphael, Tobias foils the demon and gets the girl.

Unfortunately, St. Jerome, in his translation of this charming love story, managed to slip in his own cranky opinions (via Raphael) about the virtues of marital abstinence, declaring, "The devil has power over those married people who abandon themselves to lust like horses and mules." Hence, among demonologists, Asmodeus was considered "the king of the wantons" and a tempter to the sins of vanity, jealousy, and lechery. Milton, in *Paradise Lost* (4.168), mentions his "fishy fume." As one of the infamous Devils of Loudun, Asmodeus possessed, in 1633, an Ursuline nun (Jeanne des Anges) and "filled her mind with shameful things"; in 1647 he inspired Sister Elizabeth of Louviers to some shockingly carnal antics. She it was who (postpossession) revealed that this fiend's Heavenly adversary is the fiercely chaste St. John the Baptist. In Alain Rene Le Sage's 1707 novel, *Le Diable Boiteux*, Asmodeus appears as a charming little lame demon who takes the hero to the top of a steeple, whence he shows him the miraculously roofless houses of the city, and all the naughty goings-on within them.

ASTAGORAS   🦁

A female demon, a storm bringer.

ASTARTE   🦁

To the Greeks and Babylonians (who knew her as Ishtar), she was a beautiful and enticing goddess of love. The Philistines called her ASH-TORETH, and made her a bloodthirsty goddess of war. And that's why we call them Philistines. She began her career as a demoness in I Kings 11:5; one medieval grimoire suggests she now resides in North America.

ATTILA the Hun   DWH 453   VIOLENCE

Widely known and loathed as Flagellum Dei—the Scourge of God—and reputed to be SATAN's own son, for twenty years Attila led his barbaric armies on rape and pillage sprees across both the Eastern and the Western Roman Empires. And not just for fun. He was running a sort of protection racket—in return for "tribute" paid by the people he conquered, he offered to defend them henceforth from . . . himself. Dante (who mistakenly believed that Attila had once razed his beloved city of Florence) placed the extortionist-warrior in Hell's Seventh Circle, "where the tyrants moan."

In person, Attila (whose name is Gothic baby talk for "Daddy") was short, squat, and swarthy, with a large head, small eyes, a thin beard, a flat nose, and a "truculent disposition," according to an eyewitness. But he was catnip to the ladies. In 452, he received a ring from the emperor's sister Honoria, along with a note begging him to rescue her from an unwanted marriage. The chivalric Hun was glad to oblige—and he claimed half the Western Empire as her dowry. He was persuaded to halt his march on Rome by a meeting with Pope Leo the Great. History does not relate the words with which the Holy Father convinced the Scourge of God to spare the Eternal City. Perhaps he informed Attila that Honoria was a promiscuous slut, which was, after all, only God's honest truth.

The last of Attila's many brides was the death of him. She was the delicious captive princess Ildico. (In his Hollywood biopic, *The Scourge of God,* she was portrayed by Susan Hayward. You get the idea.) Attila (as played by John Wayne) expired upon their nuptial couch, of a massive nose bleed. Fierce horseman that he was, he had died in the saddle.

AWAR   🦁

One of the five sons of the Islamic archdemon, IBLIS, Awar tempts mortals to sins of lust.

AZ ✦

An ancient (Zoroastrian) devil of lust.

AZARADEL ✦

According to the Book of Enoch, a Watcher angel by this name was assigned to teach men the motions of the moon, but he succumbed to the mortal wiles of Lamech's daughter NAAMAH—and thereby became a devil.

AZAZEL ✦

As a Hebrew devil, he lives in the wilderness and is the one to whom a "scapegoat" was ritually sacrificed on Yom Kippur, the Day of Atonement. In medieval (Christian) demonology, Azazel is described as having twelve wings and seven serpent heads, each with two faces. He is sometimes called the Spirit of Uncleanliness. In *Paradise Lost* (1.534), Milton describes him as "a cherub tall" and makes him the proud standard-bearer of the Infernal Host.

There exists in Hebrew lore an alternative (extrabiblical) version of the creation story, known as the Book of Enoch, in which Azazel plays a leading role. He was a leader of the *bene ba Elohim,* Watcher angels, who were commissioned by God to teach mankind the arts of civilization. (Azazel was to instruct mortals in the manufacture and use of weapons, and of cosmetics and perfumes.) Unfortunately, a few of these pure spirits, Azazel among them, beheld the seductive daughters of Cain "perambulating around and displaying their private parts, in the manner of harlots," and commenced mating with them, thereby becoming—and siring—demons. By God's command, Azazel was overthrown by the Archangel Raphael and buried beneath a heap of rocks in the desert.

In the Quran, Azazel is named as one of the angels damned by Allah for refusing to worship Adam—"Why should the son of fire fall down before the son of clay?" he asked (reasonably enough, it would seem). By Muslims he is sometimes identified with IBLIS.

AZZOLINO da Romano   DWH 1259   VIOLENCE

The Guelfs and Ghibellines were rival political parties in thirteenth-century Italy. Dante, a Guelf, discovered (not surprisingly) any number of Ghibellines in Hell—among them Azzolino, who is in the Seventh Circle, among the violent. He is immersed in a river of boiling blood. Known in life as the Tyrant of the March of Treviso, and excommunicated by Pope Alexander IV as "the most inhuman of the children of men," Azzolino was so infamous for his cruel atrocities that he was sometimes called a son of SATAN, by the Guelfs, that is, and behind his back, when he was well out of earshot.

Believing in Hell must distort every judgement on this life. However much a Christian may say that the central doctrine of the Church is the Incarnation and nothing else, he is led on inevitably to exclusive salvation, to Heaven and Hell, censorship and the persecution of heresy, till he finds himself among the brothel-owning Jesuits and cannon-blessing bishops.

—CYRIL CONNOLLY, *The Unquiet Grave*

BAL

The bull-horned fertility god of the other Semites, he was the archetypal "false god" of the Old Testament Jews, who believed him to be the son of DAGON and ASHTORETH. His worshippers were regularly denounced by Israel's prophets and slain by her righteous warriors. In the Book of Numbers, we read that Baal inspired the Israelites to enter into illicit relations with Moabite women and offer sacrifices to their gods (of which he was one). Jealous Jehovah was so angered by these goings-on that He instructed Moses to conduct a public execution, "hanging in the sun" all who worshipped Baal, destroying their towns and flocks, and enslaving their wives and children. (This perfectly justifiable act of war made Moses "one of the most detestable villains that in any period of the world have disgraced the name of man," according to the liberal atheist TOM PAINE.) As a medieval demon, Baal was General of the Diabolic Hordes, according to Peter Weyer, and one of his attributes was the ability to make men and animals invisible. Sorcerers who conjure him report that he can appear as a toad, a cat, a man, or sometimes as all three.

BAALBERITH 🦇

A Canaanite god and Old Testament demon, he is believed to have been, before the Fall, a prince of the Cherubs. He is now Hell's "Master of Ceremonies" and as such is called upon to notarize all "pacts with the devil." He is said to be especially powerful during the month of June. He it was who, in the seventeenth century, possessed Prioress Jeanne des Anges and many other nuns at the convent of Loudun, causing Jeanne to chew on her veil and spit the communion host in a priest's face.

BABI 🦇

The evil spirit of darkness, according to *The Egyptian Book of the Dead.*

BACHIEL 🦇

The demon who rules the sign of Pisces and governs eastern Hell.

BACON, Sir Francis   DWH 1626   BRIBERY

Even his fawning biography in the *Encylopaedia Britannica* admits he was "unattractive . . . cold-hearted . . . he cringed to the powerful, took bribes, and then had the impudence to say he had not been influenced by them." This Elizabethan noble, scientist, and philosopher abhorred nature, errors, and taxes. His opposition to royal taxes would have ended his political career had it not been for the support of his friend and benefactor, the earl of ESSEX, whom he repaid by persecuting for treason. Like NIETZSCHE, he felt that a good war "halloweth any cause," and, like VOLTAIRE, he thought it was better to educate one man than the masses. His scientific endeavors ranged from introducing the scientific (or inductive) method to proposing the eating of chopped mummies as a cure for head colds. Always one step ahead of his creditors, he was arrested for debt in 1598. This forced him to give up his gay bachelor life (at age forty-five) and marry Alice Barnham, whose substantial dowry he soon depleted. (In principle, Sir Francis disdained wives and children, calling them "hostages to fortune" and marriage itself "a noose.") In 1621, Great Britain's strict attorney general and national moralist was found guilty of taking bribes and using judicial verdicts to protect monopolies in which he had an interest. The subsequent disgrace ended his dream of becoming the living embodiment of Plato's "philosopher king." His fatuous statements "I have taken all knowledge to be my province" and "I bequeath my name to the ages" led some nineteenth-century scholars to the bizarre notion that Bacon was the author of

Shakespeare's plays. In reality, the lawyer-scientist disdained drama as "a thing of ill repute." He caught a chill during a scientific experiment (stuffing a hen with snow) and died, choking on his phlegm.

BAD

A well-named Persian demon who causes tempests.

BADUH

A frequently invoked Semitic demon who guarantees speedy delivery of messages.

BÁEZ, Buenaventura   DWH 1884   TREASON

He took part in the 1844 revolt by which the Dominican Republic became independent of Haiti but then sold out his leader, Juan Pablo Duarte, and spent the next thirty years trying to sell the new nation itself to France, Spain, or the United States. He served five terms as the republic's president; three of them ended in coups against his corrupt administrations.

BALAAM (aka Baalim)

A fertility demon from Phoenicia with two horns and a tail, he frequently (as in the Bible—Numbers 22) travels in the company of a talking ass. According to a far-fetched pagan myth, his enemy Mot once banished him to the Underworld, and the earth was barren until he was retrieved by his sister, the vengeful Anath. But the unerringly and literally factual Scriptures assure us that when the evil king of Moab commanded Balaam to put a curse on Israel, every curse turned into a blessing! Balaam reemerges in medieval French literature as a pathetic, quixotic creature and in later English literature (e.g., Dryden's *Absalom and Achitophel*) as a time-serving bureaucrat.

BALBERITH

An ex-Cherub, he is now keeper of the Infernal archives, with the power to tempt mortals to murder and blasphemy. After he was expelled from the Ursuline Sister Madeleine Bavent, this chatty fiend told all to the exorcist, Father Michaelis—describing in detail the inverted hierarchy of Hell. His spiritual adversary, he admitted, is St. Barnabas.

BALI

Hindu ruler of the Underworld. On earth he assumes the shape of an ass and lives in a dilapidated hut.

BALIDET

A minister of the demon king MAMMON, he rules the planet Saturn.

BALKIN

Goat-riding lord of the Northern Mountains, he commands 15,000 legions of dwarfs mounted on chameleons.

BAPHOMET

A devil much admired by the sorcerer ELIPHAS LÉVI and by the KNIGHTS TEMPLAR, he usually appears as a goat, with a pentagram between his horns and a caduceus between his legs. His name is a corruption of MAHOMET.

BARAKIEL

One of the Enochian fallen Watcher angels, he came to earth to teach men the secrets of astrology. He continues to be invoked by gamblers.

BARBATOS

A demon seer, he can tell the future, discover hidden treasure, and translate the language of bullocks and birds, but he may be conjured only under the sign of Sagittarius.

BARBAZON

He may be a fusion of the demon BARBATOS with a legendary French knight called Barbason. As a demon, he can take the form of a man or lion and read hidden thoughts. He promptly appears at the command of a conjurer. Shakespeare, who must have read of him in Scot's 1584 best-seller *Discoverie of Witchcraft,* refers to this fiend three times: in *King Lear, The Merry Wives of Windsor,* and *Henry V* (where the idiotic Nym declares, "I am not Barbason, you cannot conjure me!").

BARBINGER (aka Barbariccia) 🦅

A demon in canto 21 of the *Inferno,* described by Dante as sporting a curly red beard and leading a ten-demon "escort detail" of the Malebranche. He is called Captain by his men and wields a pitchfork, with which he prods a crowd of squirming "barrators"—bribe takers who in life trafficked in public office. In a quasi-comedic moment, one damned barrator briefly escapes from his eternal bath of boiling pitch, and some members of Barbinger's quarreling squad tumble into it themselves.

BARESCHES 🦅

A popular medieval demon, he acted as a pimp to clergymen. His fee (a bargain) was their souls.

BARKU 🦅

A demonic alchemist, he guards the secret of the philosophers' stone.

BARON 🦅

The demon to whom the vile sorcerer-alchemist GILLES DE RAIS sacrificed the hands and hearts of children, in order to discover the secret of the philosophers' stone.

BARRYMORE, John   DWH 1942
SLOTH

Prototype of the ham actor, the Great Profile indulged in such debauchery that he laid waste his considerable talents. His drunkenness was legendary even in Hollywood—his makeup, costumes, and hairpiece were often applied by film crews while the star was dead drunk. When asked what he thought of Prohibition, he replied, "Fortunately, I don't think of it." A cynical libertine, he once observed that "love is the delightful interval between meeting a beautiful girl and discovering that she looks like a haddock." His sins of pride, gluttony, overacting, sloth, and lust (he was kicked out of high school for frequenting a bordello) culminated in this final impenitence: his dying words, to longtime friend Gene Fowler, were "Tell me, Gene, is it true that you're the illegitimate son of Buffalo Bill?" In *Too Much, Too Soon,* the movie biography of his daughter, Barrymore was portrayed by his friend ERROL FLYNN.

BATHIN

A medieval devil said to be responsible for the disappearance of men and cities, he has no equal in Hell for his knowledge of herbs or his "agility and affableness."

BÁTHORY, Elizabeth   DWH 1614   MURDER

The Vampire Countess of Hungary, Báthory (with the help of her old nanny) graduated from merely torturing servant girls to "desanguinating" them—draining their blood—because she believed bathing therein would preserve her great beauty. The countess and her household staff murdered fifty girls for these cosmetological "blood baths" before they were arrested. Báthory's nanny and henchmen were duly executed, but she herself was spared (her cousin being the prime minister of Hungary). Her remaining days, beauty unpreserved, were uneventful—and unremorseful.

BATISTA, Fulgencio   DWH 1973   TYRANNY

A poor mulatto sugarcane cutter, Batista joined the army, rose in the ranks, staged a coup, and became president of Cuba, which, by the time of his second term (1952–1959), had become the most decadent and oppressed country in the Western Hemisphere. Besides American mob-controlled gambling and live sex shows, life under Batista included censorship, torture, and secret police death squads. Batista received an annual kickback from gangster Meyer Lansky's gambling casinos: $1 million Yankee, cash, delivered to him in a briefcase. The money was urgently needed for his many activities: shopping for clothes, gambling (using waiters to help him cheat), gossiping, eating (during meals he would vomit so he could continue gorging), and, most important, the salaries of his secret police. Batista dumped his frumpy first wife for a social climber who tried to get them admitted to the Havana Yacht Club—when the crude Batistas were blackballed, it was said to be "the only free election in Cuba." He enjoyed the enthusiastic support of the United Fruit Company as well as the U.S. government and its ambassador, Earl Smith, who continually undermined efforts by moderates to find a humane successor to him. Smith maintained that the dictator was a "bulwark against Communism." His cruel and corrupt regime ended when Fidel Castro came down from his mountain and entered Havana in 1959. Batista's army surrendered and deserted in droves. The dictator and his wife had taken off a few days earlier. In exile, in Portugal, he lived for another fourteen years before proceeding to Hell.

BAUBO

A sex-crazed female demon inhabiting the (Orphic) Greek Underworld, she has her head (literally) between her legs. Her name means "hole."

BAUDELAIRE, Charles   DWH 1867   DESPAIR

He called himself damned, a "poet maudit," and who are we to argue? Although he maintained that all his poetry was inspired by his erotic muses—Jeanne Duval (Black Venus), Mme. Sabatier (White Venus), and Marie Daubrun (the Green-Eyed Venus)—his contemporaries speculated that, despite his many bouts with syphilis, Baudelaire died a technical virgin. He was, at the very least, impotent, according to Mme. Duval. Baudelaire revealed something of his feelings about sex when he compared it to "torture or a surgical operation."

What is not disputed is his devotion to the DEVIL. "Dear Beelzebub, I adore you!" he declared; he regarded SATAN as the ultimate symbol of masculinity. "The neatest trick of the devil is to persuade you he does not exist," he said, and the opening line of his masterpiece, *Fleurs du Mal,* reads, "It is the devil who pulls the strings that move us." (A contemporary reviewer of the work declared, "Never has there been such a procession of demons, fetuses, devils, cats, and vermin.")

Baudelaire's extreme depression began when he was seven and his widowed mother married a virile young military man, the detestable Major Aupick. (Charles blamed his father's death on the age difference between his parents, calling himself "the chancy fruit of such a coupling.") All his life the poet obsessed about his mother, who, at the urging of the major, froze Baudelaire's inheritance. This caused him to despair frequently (and not just in verse) about money. He turned to pornography, hashish, and morphine, and made his first suicide attempt at age twenty-one, stabbing himself in the chest while sitting in a Paris café, having left a note that read, "I find the tedium of going to sleep and the tedium of waking up intolerable." He claimed to feel a kinship with fellow depressive poet EDGAR ALLAN POE, since they were both martyrs to a "barbarous realm equipped with gas fixtures." After moving to Belgium, where he loathed the boring people, the poet was taken ill and returned to Paris to die in his mother's arms. Only a handful of mourners attended his funeral, and they were dispersed by a thunderstorm.

BECCARÌA, Tesauro dei DWH 1258 TREASON

An abbot and papal legate (from Alexander IV) to Florence, he was accused of conspiring with the banished Ghibellines. Under torture, he confessed—and was beheaded.

BECHARD 🖘

An inferior sort of demon, he can be conjured only on Fridays.

BEELZEBUB 🖘

A god of the Philistines, he makes but one appearance in the Old Testament (II Kings, 1:2), but in the New Testament he is thrice called "the Prince of Devils" (Matthew 12:24–27, Mark 3:22, Luke 11:15). He is, according to Milton in *Paradise Lost*, "majestic though in ruin," SATAN's second-in-command, his prime minister and "nearest mate." He first functioned as Satan's spokesman, duping their fellow angels into joining the rebellion against God—acting as the original Devil's advocate, as it were. He seems to have started out in life as a minor scatological imp, in Phoenicia, where his name, Lord of the Flies, implies he was the spirit of the dung heap. In medieval lore, Beelzebub was somewhat comic and unusually verbose. He figures prominently in the legend of the Harrowing of Hell—his long debate with Satan over which of them should get credit for the crucifixion is rudely interrupted when the gates of Hell are blown open by Christ, and both devils are trampled by a mob of newly redeemed souls. Beelzebub is said now to rule Hell's northern kingdom and to specialize in temptations to gluttony and pride—hence his Heavenly adversary is the humble and abstemious St. Francis of Assisi. The Sufi master Gurdjieff claimed Beelzebub was his grandfather and an eccentric extraterrestrial who explained to him the history of the "terrestrial bipeds."

BEEZIT 🖘

One of the devils in charge of Africa, he employs hallucinatory drugs. As a giant locust, he costarred with Richard Burton in arguably the worst movie ever made, *The Exorcist II*.

BEHEMOTH 🖘

A demon whose first appearance is in the Book of Job, he or she is a combination water buffalo, elephant, and hippopotamus. Behemoth is seven miles in length, with a tail of cedar-wood and bones of bronze, and grazes daily over 1,000 miles of grass. At the end of the world, this devil-monster, the Great Beast, will be slain by the Jewish Messiah and become delicious food for the righteous.

BELETH

"A king great and terrible, riding a pale horse," Beleth visits earth rarely and reluctantly, and always accompanied by an orchestra that features a large trumpet section. To bring this about, the conjurer must remember to wear a magic ring on his left hand.

BELFANA

The devil of midwinter in Northern Italy; when he gets nasty, he turns into a ghost.

BELIAL (aka Beliar)

The prince of darkness, a lewd and lascivious demon of the Old Testament, throughout which "sons of Belial" is a synonym for *sinners*. His name means either "masterless" or "worthless." The wretched excesses of Sodom and Gomorrah are usually attributed to him; thus he is called "the fleshiest Incubus" by Milton, in *Paradise Regained*. Lazy and sensual, Belial is the spirit of bloodshed and destruction but mostly of fornication—which is sometimes known to the righteous as "the plague of Belial." In the old days, he habitually led the city of Jerusalem into general wickedness, demanding sacrifices and orgies in his honor. He it was who prompted Prince Manesseh to dissect the prophet Isaiah with a wooden saw. But he has been less successful in later years. When SATAN was preparing to tempt Jesus in the desert, he proposed to employ the manly temptations of money, glory, and praise—but it was Belial's idea simply to show the Savior a naked woman! And when he tried to convince the chaste (first-century) St. Juliana to marry, the holy virgin grabbed Belial by the throat, hit him over the head with a rock, triumphantly led him (on a leash) to the marketplace, and threw him in the sewer. The Guardian Demon of Turkey, he is especially powerful in the month of January. He is opposed in Heaven by St. Francis de Paul.

BELIAN (aka Belias)

A miniature demon, he tempts men to arrogance, women to wear fancy clothes, and children to talk during mass. His adversary is St. Vincent de Paul.

BELLO, Geri del DWH circa 1250 SOWING DISCORD

A first cousin of Dante's father, Bello took an active part in the Alighieri's family feud with the Sacchetti clan, once going so far as to undertake a "hit" disguised as a leper. He now resides in Hell's Eighth Circle but stalks away without speaking to the visiting Dante, who speculates that his kinsman may be angry at him for failing to avenge his murder.

BELPHEGOR

In the Old Testament he was called Baal-Peor, associated with carnality (he had a phallus-shaped tongue), and worshipped by the lusty Moabites. Curiously, Christian demonologists assigned to him the sin of sloth and made him the guardian demon of the city of Paris. Naive by nature, he once came to earth in search of a wife but, appalled by the wanton behavior of human females, fled back to Hell. This misogynist folktale, retold by Machiavelli and the basis for Ben Jonson's comedy *The Devil Is an Ass*, gave rise to a folk expression, "Belphegor's search," signifying a hopeless task, i.e., finding a needle in a haystack or an honest woman.

BENEDICT IX DWH 1056 LUST

The "boy pope" was all of eleven years old in 1032, when he assumed the Chair of Peter. His exploits with the ladies suggest he reached puberty soon enough. One contemporary wrote of him that he was "a demon from Hell in the guise of a priest"; there were even rumors that he employed demonic aid in his relentless seductions. He was deposed twice by antipopes and twice reclaimed the triple tiara. Then, in 1045, he took the uncharacteristically ethical step of resigning the papacy in order to marry his beautiful cousin. His severance pay consisted of 2,000 pounds (in weight) of gold—an entire year of the Peter's Pence collection from England.

BENG   

A Gypsy devil, Beng doesn't stay in Hell but lives in the woods, going out only at night.

BERIA, Lavrenti   DWH 1953   VIOLENCE

The chief of the dreaded Soviet secret police, the NKVD, Beria was for many years the trusted confidant of his fellow Georgian and monster JOSEPH STALIN—and was so close to the dictator that Stalin's daughter, in her memoirs, blamed Beria for some of her father's worst excesses. Beria ordered the "liquidation" of countless millions (including 15,000 Polish officers at Katyn) and oversaw the operations of the vast system of slave labor camps, the Gulag. Upon Stalin's death, he expected to be made chairman of the Party but was instead arrested and executed (he was shot while on his knees, begging for mercy) by Khruschev's command. His glowing full-page biography in the official *Great Soviet Encyclopedia* was then replaced by a glowing full-page description of the Bering Sea.

BERICH

A winged demon of gluttony who made his first appearance on earth in 1323, when a group of monks and laymen invoked him in a circle made of cat skin. He returned, along with 6,665 other demons, to possess Sister Madeleine of Aix-en-Provence.

BERTRAND de Born dwh 1215   TREASON

Dante encounters this soldier and troubadour in the Eighth Circle of Hell, decapitated, standing on a bridge, and swinging his head by the hair. The French warrior-poet thrusts his talking head forward to tell his sad tale: His body and head are separated to symbolize the father-son schism he created when he encouraged Prince Henry to retrieve land from his father, King Henry II. Although Bertrand was supported in the matter by the queen (Eleanor of Aquitaine), he likens himself to the Old Testament courtier ACHITOPHEL, who contributed to the rift between David and ABSALOM. Bertrand is the only person in the *Inferno* to use the term *lo contrappasso,* referring to the "law of retribution" on which Dante based his concept of Hell, in which "the punishment fits the crime."

BHAVANI   🦎

A Vedic demoness with protruding eyes and tongue, she wears a necklace of skulls and earrings stolen from the dead.

BHUTADAMANA   🦎

A spook-spirit in Indian Buddhism, Bhutadamana frequents tombs and has three eyes underlined in red, four arms, eight snakes, and a crown of skulls. He's all black—but he *shines*.

BIERCE, Ambrose   DWH 1914   ATHEISM

Author, journalist, and "the meanest man in San Francisco," Bierce wrote the masterful short story "An Occurrence at Owl Creek Bridge" as well as the satirical, anticlerical, blasphemous, and highly amusing *Devil's Dictionary*. His legendary drinking prompted him to describe himself as "an eminent tankardman," and he was outspoken in his hatred of God, who, in Bierce's view, had made the world in perverse opposition to the needs of man. He died somewhere in Mexico, in a vain attempt to find and join forces with the revolutionary Pancho Villa. An insight into his personal life: "Early one June morning in 1872 I murdered my father—an act which made a deep impression on me at the time."

BIFRONS   🦎

A European demon, Bifrons haunts cemeteries at night and "seemeth to light candles upon the sepulchres of the dead." We call him methane.

BILBO, Theodore Gilmore   DWH 1947   BRIBERY

Mississippi populist leader and virulent racist who served two terms as governor, Bilbo was a U.S. senator from 1935 to 1947 and known as "the most hated man in the Senate." The tiny (five foot two) demagogue always dressed in a white suit with red socks, suspenders, and tie. He proudly called himself a redneck and to establish his credentials gave interviews to reporters while urinating. In his book *Take Your Choice: Separation or Mongrelization,* Bilbo urged deporting blacks back to Africa. In 1946 the Senate barred him from resuming his seat, since he had been found guilty of bribe taking and mail fraud. One day while giving a racist harangue on the steps of the Mississippi capitol, he pointed to two small black children in the audience—Charles and Medgar Evers—and shouted, "If y'all don't watch it, one day these two li'l niggers are gonna try to get the vote and rep'sent you!" He got that right.

BILLINGSLEY, Sherman DWH 1966 FLATTERY

Founder-owner of New York's Stork Club, "the first speakeasy with carpet on the floor," this former bootlegger (convicted) from Enid, Oklahoma, was an outspoken hater of Jews, blacks, and homosexuals. He was simultaneously a puppet of gangster Frank Costello and head G-man J. EDGAR HOOVER (in whose honor Sherm invented a drink, the FBI Fizz). In his club, he installed two-way mirrors in the toilets and microphones under the tables to accommodate both of these valued clients. His refusal, in 1951, to serve a crab salad to the African-American entertainer Josephine Baker caused Billingsley to be censured, even in those conservative times. He died and went to Hell one year—to the day—after the Stork Club closed.

BILLY the Kid (William Bonney) DWH 1881 MURDER

The great Wild West cowboy outlaw was born in New York City. But it was only when his widowed mother remarried and the family moved West that the diminutive, harelipped, left-handed city boy fell in with bad company and set out on a killing spree that would total twenty-one corpses—one for each year of his legendary life. The Kid was captured once, tried, and convicted. The judge screamed, "You are sentenced until you are dead, dead, dead!" to which Billy replied, "And you can go to Hell, Hell, Hell!" After his escape (despite being chained hand to foot, he killed both his guards), he was shot to death (in the dark) by his sometime companion Sheriff Pat Garrett. Billy was holding two sixguns and a butcher knife at the time. His tombstone in New Mexico reads, "Truth and History. 21 Men. The Boy Bandit King. He died as he lived."

BISMARCK, Otto von DWH 1898 SOWING DISCORD

What can you say about the man who laid the foundation for two world wars? When the self-named Iron Chancellor came to power in 1871, he proclaimed his policy of "iron and blood" and resolved to unify Germany under Prussian leadership. (Austria and the rest of the country he considered "a putrid brew of cozy south German sentimentality.") His first acts were to dissolve the parliament—"Laws are like sausages, it's better not to see them made"—and expand the army. Bismarck's forces soon defeated Denmark (in 1864), Austria (in 1866), and France (in 1871). These victories were accomplished, the chancellor believed, with the help of phrenological analysis—he had conducted studies of the bumps on the skulls of his enemies. He then proclaimed the German Empire. The leading statesman of Europe from 1871 to 1890 (he created Realpolitik, "the art of the possible"), Bismarck was not above a little demagoguery. He once rallied a crowd of his countrymen with the cry "We Germans fear God but nothing else!" When the new kaiser, WILHELM II, took power, he dismissed the old chancellor, who retired to his estate in 1890. There he wrote two volumes of his best-selling memoirs, in which he orchestrated his own ongoing legend. In 1894, Wilhelm graciously invited Bismarck to his birthday luncheon, during which one observer said of the eighty-year-old Bismarck, "The look is of Faust, the thought of Mephistopheles" (see MEPHISTOPHELES).

Shortly before his death, the old man correctly predicted World War I, observing it would start with "some damn foolish thing in the Balkans." At the end, he anticipated the afterlife companionship of his long dead wife. And if Frau Bismarck is in Hell, he doubtless got his wish.

In the continuing tradition of Old World inbreeding, Britain's Princess Diana is Bismarck's eighth cousin five times removed.

BLACKBEARD   See EDWARD TEACH.

BLACK JIM   🐾
A demon by this name brought 10,000 fiends with him to dine at the house of sixteenth-century aristocrat Sir Guy LeScoop. In a pique, Sir Guy had foolishly "invited" Black Jim—he had invoked him after his human guests failed to arrive. He then had difficulty ridding himself of the devils. He pleaded with them to go to Hell and take the leftovers. Black Jim took the food and Sir Guy's son as well, prompting his host to call on St. Cuthbert. The saint retrieved the child, told Black Jim and company to finish eating, and chided them about their manners:

> Be moderate, pray, and remember this much
> Since you're treated as gentlemen, shew yourselves such.

BLUEBEARD   See GILLES DE RAIS.

BLUEBEARD II   See HENRI LANDRU.

BLUEBEARD, LADY   See BELLE PULSATTER.

BOCCA degli Abati   DWH circa 1270   TREASON
Upon encountering Bocca deep in the Ninth Circle, Dante uncharacteristically loses his cool, calls Bocca "a vicious traitor" and promises to

publish the details of his heinous perfidy. At the Battle of Montaperti, in 1260, Bocca, while pretending to fight on the side of the Florentine Guelfs, with a blow of his sword cut off the hand of their standard-bearer. The disappearance of their flag led to panic among the Guelfs and a smashing Ghibelline victory.

BOCKELSON, Jan (John of Leyden)   DWH 1536   HERESY

There is a striking similarity among the charismatic creeps who have declared themselves the Second Coming of Christ—from the twelfth-century TANCHELM of Antwerp to our own JIM JONES of Guyana and DAVID KORESH of Waco, Texas. They are semiliterate but eloquent; their paranoid interpretation of biblical prophecy leads them (in all humility) to proclaim their own divinity; they acquire harems; their well-armed and fortified communities are eventually besieged by the authorities; they and most of their dim but loyal disciples die horribly; all are thereafter (for a time) glorified as martyrs by those with a political ax to grind.

Bockelson—whose saga concludes Professor Norman Cohn's great book *The Pursuit of the Millenium*—was an Anabaptist of Münster, who ordained himself king "with power over all the nations of the earth." Thousands of his followers—men, women, and children—starved to death within Münster's walls (in Cohn's words, his "nightmare kingdom"), and the rest were slaughtered when the city fell to the surrounding army of orthodoxy. The "king" himself was captured, led about on a chain like a bear, and tortured to death with hot irons; his body was hung in a cage from a church tower. It was too good for him, but doubtless a more serious punishment awaited him in Hell.

BODENHAM, Anne   DWH 1653   SORCERY

A witch, Bodenham took over the practice of a local wizard, Dr. John Lamb, after he was dismembered by a mob for causing a storm. Proud of her profession, she wore a live toad around her neck, held hands with imps, and would frequently display her two blue "witchmarks," the nipples by which she suckled demons. Before her execution by the Inquisition, Bodenham had the presence of mind to drink a beer, spit on a priest, and wish a pox on her executioner.

BONATTI, Guido   DWH 1296   SORCERY

An astrologer, formerly of the city of Forlì, now and forever suffering in Dante's Eighth Circle. Bonatti's head is twisted backward in punishment for his unholy occupation, divining the future in an attempt to control it—which is, of course, God's prerogative. Bonatti wrote a popular astrology text and was the personal psychic adviser to GUIDO MONTEFELTRO.

BONIFACE VIII   DWH 1303   BLASPHEMY

He ascended to the papacy after "gaslighting" his predecessor, the ascetic old Celestine, by whispering through a hidden tube into the pope's cell, "Celestine, Celestine, lay down your office." He then locked up the senile ex–Vicar of Christ in the castle of Fumone, where he died of starvation and neglect. Triple-crowned for these efforts, Boniface took as his mantra "I am pontiff, I am emperor." He robbed and plundered, enriching his family while conducting simultaneous affairs with his mistress *and* her daughter. A cardinal said of him, "He is all tongue and eyes, and the rest of him is all rotten." His personal vendetta against the Colonna family led him to raze the city of Palestrina, killing 6,000 citizens and destroying both the home of JULIUS CAESAR and a shrine to the Blessed Virgin Mary. This is the sin that earned him a place in Dante's Eighth Circle of Hell. Boniface's feud with King Philip of France prompted him to issue his infamous papal bull *Unam Sanctam,* which claimed for the papacy all power, spiritual and temporal. His enemies—King Philip and the Colonnas—finally joined forces to topple the old sinner, by now a vigorous eighty-six. Approaching Boniface on his throne, they demanded that he resign, to which he responded, "Sooner die." He spent the following thirty-five days in solitary confinement and then . . . did. He is buried in St. Peter's, in a grandiose tomb of his own design. Even though he jested that he had as much chance of going to Heaven as a roasted chicken, he did pull off one final, blasphemous joke. When his tomb cracked open three centuries after his death, his body was revealed to be perfectly incorrupt—an honor usually reserved for the greatest saints.

BONIFARCE

The self-acknowledged name of an especially unpleasant demon exorcised from Sister Elisabeth Allier by Father François Fanconnet in 1639.

BORDEN, Lizzie   DWH 1927   MURDER

The girl who put Fall River, Massachusetts, on the map in 1892 was acquitted of axing her parents with the proverbial "forty whacks," despite mounds of evidence pointing to her guilt. Most latter-day criminologists have concluded without doubt that Lizzie was guilty—if with some justification. (Her wealthy parents were so parsimonious that the family lived in a downscale part of town and, on the day of the murder, dined on five-day-old mutton.) After the trial, Lizzie and her sister, Emma, came into an immense fortune and moved into a mansion. Suspicion was renewed when Emma departed, cryptically calling her living situation "intolerable." Lizzie went to Hell, leaving behind an estate of over a million dollars . . . and an incessant, intolerable rhyme.

BORGIA, Cesare   DWH 1507
INCEST, MURDER

The son of Pope ALEXANDER VI, he served as Machiavelli's model for tyranny, "the Prince." Cesare was feared by all, even his formidable father. At eighteen, *il Papa* made him a cardinal, and Cesare began a campaign of poisoning his fellow cardinals, whose wealth the pope would inherit. Cesare's recipe was unique—he would poison a hog, hang it by its hind legs, collect its dying drool in a basin, dry that to a powder, and add it to his victim's wine. He was less demure with his sister LUCREZIA's lover Perroto and with her (second) husband Alfonso. Cesare hacked both of them to bits. It was his custom to toss his own rape victims in the Tiber. His murder of his brother was said to have caused their father, the pope, great distress.

Made hideous by syphilis, Cesare took to wearing a black veil over his face but maintained his flamboyant lifestyle—he enjoyed, for example, fighting bulls in St. Peter's Basilica. He died quite valiantly, taking on a small army single-handedly, and endured twenty-three sword wounds before he expired. He went to Hell anyhow.

BORGIA, Lucrezia   DWH 1519
MURDER, INCEST

Glamorous daughter (and allegedly lover) of Pope ALEXANDER VI, she unquestionably had a passionate incestuous relationship with her brother CESARE. They had a child, Gionanni. The three members of this close-knit Vatican family sometimes unwound by presiding over a festival they called the Joust of the Whores, during which they threw chestnuts at nude dancers. The pope's devotion to Lucrezia was so great that one year he delayed the start of Lent so that meat could be served at her (third) wedding. (A commission had granted her brother's request that her previous marriages be annulled, on the ground that Lucrezia, widely known as the "greatest whore that ever was in Rome," was still a virgin.)

It must be said that the *Catholic Encyclopedia* staunchly denies her affair with her father, the pope, and that her dedicated patronage of the arts has caused some softhearted historians to maintain that many of the sins attributed to her actually belong to someone else.

BORMANN, Martin   DWH 1945 *(hopefully)*   MURDER

A thug's thug, he was a convicted murderer even before joining ADOLF HITLER's inner circle and rapidly rose to the post of head of the chancellery. The short (he only came up to Hitler's shoulder), bullnecked Bormann was despised even by his fellow Nazis as a sneak and a tattletale. After ousting Rudolf Hess as a traitor, expunging Hess's name from history books, and even rechristening his own son (formerly Rudolf), Bormann became Hitler's deputy. Bormann's main contribution to Western civilization was recording all of Hitler's words for posterity. It is believed he went to Hell in 1945 via suicide. But there *was* an unsubstantiated report that he and his wife, "dearest Mummy-Girl," were seen in Argentina in 1974.

BOSWELL, James   DWH 1795   FLATTERY

Because he was the literary type, Boswell is called a diarist instead of a gossip. He exploited his twenty-year friendship with a writer and wit to create his most famous work, *The Life of Samuel Johnson,* published in 1791. In his private diary, he dropped some 6,500 celebrity names and boasted of his sexual conquests, including one "Louise," with whom he was "lost in supreme rapture." Disliking intelligence in women, he preferred sex with prostitutes, usually on Westminster Bridge—so he could watch the Thames go by while humping away.

A former lawyer, Boswell left his native Scotland at age twenty-three to come to London—because that was where all the interesting people were. "I cannot help worshipping him," said Boswell of his subject, Dr. Johnson, who, flattered, tolerated the company of this toady. But Sam aside, Boswell was generally disliked. A near contemporary, Lord Macaulay, described him as a "bigot and a sot, bloated with family pride, a talebearer, eavesdropper, a common butt in the taverns of England." Many elements of his maladjusted personality—he never missed a public hanging and vigorously defended slavery—have been attributed to his unbalanced thyroid.

A grasping, manipulative, social-climbing sycophant and whoremonger, Boswell cannot be who Johnson was thinking about when he uttered his (alas, unoriginal) aphorism "The road to Hell is paved with good intentions."

BOTIS ✹

Another of the dukes of Hell, Botis is in charge of sixty legions. He generally appears as a hideous viper but can assume somewhat human form, albeit with buck teeth and horns.

BOULLAN, Joseph-Antoine   DWH 1893   HERESY

A defrocked Roman Catholic priest who used church funds to build his private château, Father Boullan maintained that he was the reincarnation of both St. John the Baptist and the prophet Elias, and that he had been sent to "exorcise" the Church. His religious philosophy—that salvation can be attained only through sexual intercourse with Archangels—was put into practice by his small but fervid cult, known as the Work of Mercy. Father Boullan claimed to have had sex with CLEOPATRA and ALEXANDER THE GREAT. Perhaps it was his use of excrement in the sacramental chalice that caused his assassination by a cabal of his fellow magicians, who found him heretical even by their standards.

BRANCA d'Oria   DWH 1275   TREASON

Although his dastardly murder of his father-in-law, Michel Zanche, took place in 1275, Branca was still apparently alive in Genoa, "eating and sleeping and wearing out his clothes," when Dante met him in Hell, in 1300. Like Friar ALBERIGO, Branca had been plunged into Hell immediately after his crime, leaving "a devil in his body."

BREADALBANE, Earl of   DWH 1752   TREASON

John Campbell, the first earl of Breadalbane, was, like his friend the DUKE OF ARGYLL, a greedy, double-crossing traitor and murderer. He went to Hell in 1717. His equally odious grandson, the third earl, refused to allow members of the Macdonald clan (his "tenants," whose land his grandsire had stolen) to emigrate to Canada. On this occasion, the poet Robert Burns composed his scorching satire "Address of Beelzebub," in which the Devil enthusiastically describes to the earl the welcome awaiting him "in my house at hame." His seat will be a hot one—"in the benmost neuk beside the ingle"—among his peers, the worst of history's despots, including HEROD and POLYCRATES and the bloody conquistadors PIZARRO and ALMAGRO.

BRIAREUS

One of the four giants guarding the entry to deepest Hell, Briareus was once a Titan who made war on Zeus, and for his pains was buried under a mountain.

BRUNEHAUT   DWH 613   SORCERY

This witch was executed by King Clotaire of the Franks. It was she who allegedly invented the infamous spell known as *nouer d'aiguillette,* which in English is called "ligature." By means of this *maleficia*—it involves tying knots in a strip of leather and/or in the penis of a (dead) wolf—the diabolical curse caster causes impotence in her victim. Christian theologian (and saint) Thomas Aquinas, in *Quod Libeta,* assures us that "demons . . . by their doings . . . can prevent carnal copulation."

BRUNETTO Latini   DWH 1294   SODOMY

Dante encounters this notary, scholar, and Guelf leader in the Seventh Circle of Hell, where he is running across the burning sands in the company of a band of known homosexuals. Dante had in life admired his fellow Florentine and mentor, whose encyclopedia, *Little Treasure,* describes an allegorical otherworld journey that may have inspired Dante's own poem. In their intimate infernal discourse, Brunetto (who pointedly ignores Dante's new mentor, Virgil) calls our poet a "sweet fig" and advises him, quite literally, to "follow his star." He then prophesies a great destiny for Dante—but one fraught with the enmity of his rivals. Brunetto also dishes his fellow damned sodomites, particularly the infamous bishop of Florence ANDREA DEI MOZZI, whom he likens to ringworm. Brunetto becomes overwhelmed by the stench of lust wafting off an oncoming group of sodomites and dashes away, recommending that Dante read one of his books.

BRUTUS, Marcus Junius   DWH 42 B.C.   TREASON

The man Shakespeare was to call "the noblest Roman of them all" had previously been discovered by Dante in Hell's deepest pit, being gnawed in the foaming jaws of SATAN, in the company of JUDAS and CASSIUS. History's three worst traitors squirm in perpetual agony in the three mouths of the Devil's three heads.

Brutus may, in fact, have been not just a regicide but a paracide—JULIUS CAESAR had reason to believe that he was Brutus's real father, and his last words to Brutus (as reported by the historian Plutarch) were not Shakespeare's "Et tu, Brute?" but rather (in Greek, no less!) "You too, son?" Aristocratic and anti-Republican, he had joined Pompey's (losing) side in the civil war with Caesar; nevertheless, the victor not only pardoned Brutus but appointed him governor of Gaul (in which capacity—if Cicero is to be believed—he extorted 48 percent interest on a loan to the city of Salamis). Plutarch insists that Brutus's motives for partaking in the Ides of March assassination were pure: "Even Brutus's enemies would say he had no other end or aim save only to restore to the Roman people their ancient form of government." He even convinced his coconspirator (and brother-in law) Cassius not to knock off MARC ANTONY while they had their knives out. Big mistake.

At the Battle of Philippi, Brutus's army defeated Octavian's—but when Cassius's forces were overcome by Antony's, Brutus had no choice but to kill himself.

BRUXAE

These demons transported witches to the Sabbats. Since *bruscus* is the Latin for "broom," it was (and is) believed that witches ride broomsticks.

BUER

Demonic teacher of logic and philosophy, Buer appears in the form of a starfish.

BULFAS

A devil prince who specializes in discord and battles.

BUNDY, Theodore ("Ted")   DWH 1989   CRUELTY

In a mere four years, Ted Bundy raped, mutilated, and murdered anywhere from eighteen to thirty-six women in four states. The monstrous horror of his crimes contrasted with the handsome, wholesome appearance of the man once named Mr. Up-and-Coming Republican. A chairman of the party once said, "If you can't trust Ted Bundy, who can you trust?" The first person not to trust him was his former fiancée, who detected aspects of Bundy's sexual quirks in the modus operandi of the Seattle murders—and also noticed that her boyfriend's sex drive had declined after the killings began. After his arrest, criminal psychologists, discussing his psychopathic personality, pointed to his rather intense inbreeding—he was, it seems, the offspring of his mother and his grandfather. In a strict religious household, Bundy had been brought up believing his mother was his sister, which, in fact, she was. After he started reading dirty books and was jilted by a college sweetheart, what choice had he, really, but to become a mass murderer?

During his trial, he acted as his own lawyer, and despite—or because of—the gruesome details that emerged, Bundy briefly became something of a folk hero. On death row, he convinced one of his female admirers to marry him. In his final interview before execution, he endeared himself to the Christian right by blaming it all on pornography.

BUNE

A ghoulish, three-headed devil who moves bodies from one grave to another, usually accompanied by BIFRONS.

BUOSO dei Donati   DWH circa 1300   THEFT

A member of the same great Florentine family as Dante's wife, Gemma, Buoso appears with two other noblemen in the *Inferno*'s Eighth Circle, where they are engaged in vivid shape-shifting—a punishment befitting their worldly dissembling and dishonesty. While Dante watches in amazement, Buoso metamorphoses into a serpent and, in the process, grows a pair of feet from his penis.

BURIEL

A prince of Hell who loathes all other demons, Buriel appears as a serpent with a woman's head and travels with an entourage of jesters.

BURR, Aaron   DWH 1836   TREASON

An ambitious soldier of the American Revolution, Burr introduced the party machine to American politics. In the 1800 presidential elections, he tied with Thomas Jefferson. Burr was named vice president, but he finished out his term as an indicted murderer, having killed his rival Alexander Hamilton in a duel. (Hamilton had termed Burr "tinctured with fanaticism," and each had—correctly—accused the other of womanizing. When he later learned that Hamilton had intended to hold his fire in the duel, Burr sniffed, "Contemptible, if true.") Burr next embarked on a grand scheme to take over the land west of the Mississippi, invade Mexico, and create his own Empire in the West. He involved some shady Europeans in the project, as well as Americans JAMES WILKINSON and Zebulon Pike, but he alone was brought to trial for "high treason, and for levying war against the United States." Acquitted but disgraced and impoverished (he took to borrowing money from his servants), Burr left for Europe, there to solicit funds for his next plan: the invasion of Florida. He was rebuffed by the British and by Napoleon—a particularly cruel blow, since the emperor was one of his role models. He returned home, to Staten Island, and at the age of seventy married Mme. Juval, the wealthiest woman in New York and a former whore. The marriage ended in divorce three years later, when Mme. Juval-Burr tired of her husband's philanderings.

BUTLER, Benjamin   DWH 1893   THEFT

He served as a Union major in the Civil War, despite entertaining such strong pro-slavery and states' rights sentiments that he had once backed Jefferson Davis for U.S. president. But after Lee's surrender, this pudgy, cross-eyed lawyer became the most hated man in Confederate legend, as both a stealer of silverware and insulter of Southern womanhood. Thus his two nicknames, Spoons and Beast. Butler, who introduced the concept of treating runaway slaves as "contraband of war," was a terrible soldier and worse administrator. During his notorious tenure as military governor of New Orleans, his carpetbagging civilian brother "Colonel" Butler made a fortune in illegal trading. After a gentlewoman of the city emptied a chamber pot over the visiting Admiral Farragut, Spoons issued orders that any woman who was disrespectful to the Union soldiers or the U.S. flag would be treated as a common prostitute. So the ladies of New Orleans took to turning their backs on him—causing him to remark, "These women know which end of them looks best." He jailed the publisher of the Confederate anthem "The Bonnie Blue Flag" and fined anyone twenty-five dollars for singing it. In 1883 Butler ran for president simultaneously on two different tickets—those of the Greenback Party and the Antimonopoly Organization of the United States. He lost.

BUTLER, Maj. Walter   DWH 1781   CRUELTY

A Loyalist to the Crown who opposed the American "War of Independence," Butler was the commander of the brutal Cherry Valley Massacre. He has the honor of serving as foreman on the all-American jury from Hell summoned by Mr. Scratch to judge the case of Jabez Stone in Stephen Vincent Benét's classic story "The Devil and Daniel Webster," announcing the not guilty verdict and observing that "even the damned may salute the eloquence of Mr. Webster."

BYRON, George Gordon, Lord   DWH 1824   PRIDE

I know this is unpopular; I know
'Tis blasphemous; I know one may be damn'd
For hoping no one else may e'er be so;
I know my catechism.
                    —"A Vision of Judgement"

He was, indeed, "mad, bad, and dangerous to know." The Byronic hero broods with guilt for some terrible sin in his past—in Byron's own case (his biographers agree), it was incest and/or buggery.

Compar'd to our unhappy Fate,
We need not fear another Hell.
—JOHN WILMOT, LORD ROCHESTER, "The Fall"

Confutatis maledictis,
Flammis arbribus addictis,
Voca me cum benedictus.
—Dies Irae, from the Mass for the Dead

CAACRINOLAAS

A mighty devil who holds the esteemed title grand president of Hell, according to some medieval demonologists.

CACODAEMON

A fiend so wicked that astronomers assigned his name to the twelfth house of the zodiac, whence (as everybody knows) all evil comes.

CAENEUS

A comely maiden of Thessalonica, Caeneus was raped one day by Poseidon, god of the sea. Puzzled and dismayed by her subsequent indignation, the god offered to grant her any wish. Caeneus, eager not ever to reexperience a sexual assault, asked to be changed into a man. And it was as a man that Caeneus died, murdered in a brawl that broke out at a centaur's wedding (an unseemly melee immortalized in a frieze at the Parthenon).

AENEAS caught a glimpse of this transsexual abuse victim while touring Hades and observed that he had once more become a she.

CAGLIOSTRO, "Count" (Giuseppe Balsamo)   DWH 1795   FRAUD

This flamboyant black magician (and ex-seminarian) of the eighteenth century was for a brief time the darling of English and continental noblemen and princes, a loveless and unfortunate lot for whom the count told fortunes and concocted love potions. Balsamo was born in Palermo. He and his beautiful fourteen-year-old wife, Seraphina, appear first on the world's stage—or in its written records—in 1769, when they chanced to encounter Casanova in a café. From the compulsive seducer's compulsively kept diary, we learn that they all got on famously—until Casanova found out that Balsamo had forged his signature on the check. (Casanova, by the way, is *not* in Hell, having repented of his sins on his deathbed and received the last sacrament.) The couple, now styling themselves Count and Countess, next appear in London, in 1776. There Balsamo formed a lodge of his own peculiar brand of Freemasonry, in which he was known as the Grand Copt. The count used an obscure ceremony (allegedly from ancient Egypt) called the Oracle of Prenestine Fates to make a series of astonishingly accurate predictions, which included winning lottery numbers and successful investments. His curses were successful too—he put a hex on Pope Pius VI, whom Napoleon soon banished. Because of his involvement in a scandal over a diamond necklace bought for (but never delivered to) Marie Antoinette, the count stood trial in Paris. In his successful defense, he stated, "I am a noble voyager." He was exiled from France. In Rome, Seraphina, who'd clearly had enough, denounced him to the Inquisition. He died in an apoplectic fit over being sent to prison. That Cagliostro is in the Eighth Circle of Hell there can be no doubt. The only question is whether he is among the sorcerers or the frauds.

CAGNAZZO

One of the slapstick comic devils Dante encounters in cantos 21 and 22 of the *Inferno*. His name means "dog nose."

CAHOR

A spirit known as the Genius of Deception, Cahor is considered charming, useful, and half admirable in Jewish folklore but rather otherwise by Christian demonologists.

CAIAPHAS   DWH circa 35   DEICIDE — to kill a god

High Priest (or co–High Priest, see ANNAS) of Jerusalem at the time of Jesus' crucifixion. As such, Caiaphas headed the Sanhedrin, the Jewish political-judicial council before whom (Matthew 26:3, Mark 14:55, John 18:13) Our Lord was tried and condemned to death. There is considerable scholarly debate as to whether the collaborationist Sanhedrin of Roman-occupied Palestine actually had this authority, but Mark's Gospel (intended for the Gentiles) goes to great lengths to make the Jew Caiaphas and not the Roman PONTIUS PILATE the villain of the tale. The saint and scholar the Venerable Bede wrote his *History of the English Church and People* at a time (731) when edifying visions of Hell were popular among his fellow monks. One of them, whose name Bede coyly declines to reveal, "saw Hell open, and Satan in the depths of the abyss, with Caiaphas and others who had slain Our Lord condemned like him to the eternal flames" (5.14). In 1115, Alberic, an Italian monk at Monte Cassino, published his own vision of Hell and confirmed that the high priest is in its "deepest pit," alongside HEROD and JUDAS.

CAIM

A demon with the head and wings of a blackbird, as a grand master of Hell he commands thirty legions. He enjoyed tormenting Martin Luther.

CAIN   MURDER

Cain the farmer, Adam and Eve's first-born son, murdered his shepherd brother, Abel, in a fit of jealousy, because Abel's sacrifice was manifestly more pleasing to God. Curiously, Jehovah—often cited as an example by advocates of capital punishment—did not instantly zap the Judeo-Christian tradition's very first homicide but rather threatened the direst retributions against anyone who harmed *him*. Islamic tradition explains God's rejection of Cain's offering: It seems Cain had disobeyed his father and refused to marry Abel's twin sister, Jumella, preferring to wed his own twin, Aclima. This incestuous-rebel concept appealed, for personal reasons, to Lord BYRON, and in 1821 he published a long poem titled "Cain, a Mystery."

As proof that Cain is in Hell, we can offer only the evidence of medieval iconography. Artists invariably portray him with a yellow beard, identical to the one adorning the unquestionably damned JUDAS.

A dreadful set of second-century Gnostic heretics styling themselves Cainites took him as their strongman hero, and Judas as their messiah. As might be imagined, they got up to all kinds of mischief.

CALCHAS   DWH circa 1300 B.C.   SORCERY

In the *Iliad,* Calchas was a Greek seer consulted about the most propitious time to launch the Argive fleet against Troy. Dante, in canto 20, locates him among the other soothsayers. Like the rest of them, he wears his head backward.

CALIGULA   DWH 41   IDOLATRY- worship idols

Gaius Julius Caesar Germanicus got his nickname Caligula (Little Boot) when, as a two-year-old, he first strutted his stuff before his father the emperor's troops. All historians agree that his adult behavior was singularly heinous, but some offer the excuse that he was nuts. As emperor, he famously expressed the wish that the people of Rome had but one head, so he could cut it off. Caligula declared himself to be divine—but somehow King HEROD ANTIPAS talked him out of erecting a statue of himself in the temple at Jerusalem. He did conduct an incestuous relationship with his sister but did *not* make his pet horse a consul. In addition to the pains of Hell, he has had to suffer a movie of his life made by *Penthouse* magazine.

CAPANEUS   DWH circa 1200 B.C.   BLASPHEMY

One of the Seven against Thebes, the mythic Greek warrior-rebels whom Dante, like his master Virgil before him, put in Hell. Although he knew full well that Zeus favored the Theban side, Capaneus defied the god and launched his assault on the city. He was struck dead by a thunderbolt, leaving his loving wife, EVADNE, a widow. Damned among the blasphemers in the *Inferno* (canto 14), Capaneus is an almost heroic figure, stretched on the ground, "sullen and disdainful," and still cursing Zeus.

CAPOCCHIO   DWH 1239   THEFT

His name, or perhaps nickname, means "blockhead." Capocchio was a swindler and an alchemist, burned alive for his crimes in Siena, which parvenu city was the butt of jokes among sophisticated Florentines like Dante. In cantos 29 and 30 of the *Inferno,* Capocchio joins our poet in a series of wisecracks about the Sienese ("than whom not even the French are sillier"), until he is suddenly pounced on, bitten in the neck, and dragged away on his belly by the rabid GIANNI SCHICCI.

CAPONE, Al   DWH 1947   TAX EVASION

Born in Brooklyn in 1899, the homicidal pimp known as Scarface, the crime czar of Prohibition-era Chicago, died of syphilis at his estate in Palm Island, Florida, and went directly to Hell. In 1931 J. EDGAR HOOVER and his fearless G-men succeeded in putting the odious Alphonse behind bars—

not, however, for murder, racketeering, bootlegging, or extortion but on an income-tax rap. And tax evasion *is* a sin, explicitly forbidden by the 1994 *Catechism of the Catholic Church* (pt. 3, art. 7, subsection 4, no. 2436).

CARDIGAN, Lord (James Thomas Brudenell) DWH 1868   VIOLENCE

The earl of Cardigan shamelessly used his wealth and aristocratic connections to buy (in 1832, for £40,000) command of the British Army's Fifteenth Hussars. A martinet, he horribly mistreated his subordinates—some of them older, abler men and veterans of Waterloo. In 1833, for unjustly court-martialing a popular officer, Cardigan was himself court-martialed and relieved of his duties. But within three years he had purchased command of the Light Dragoons. He resumed his bullying and flogging, and otherwise amused himself by seducing his fellow officers' wives. (He met his match when he ran off with a friend's bride, Elizabeth Johnstone. Captain Johnstone declined Cardigan's offer to duel, avowing that Cardigan had performed for him the greatest service one man might render another. Twenty years later, hours after Elizabeth's death, the sixty-year-old Cardigan would burst into the bedroom of his eighteen-year-old mistress, crying, "Darling, let's get married!")

At the age of fifty-seven, Cardigan was appointed commander of the Light Cavalry and headed off to the Crimean War in search of immortality. At Balaclava, he led the Charge of the Light Brigade into "the Valley of Death"—a vainglorious blunder summed up by an eyewitness French general as "magnificent, but not war." Cardigan's comment to his troops was "Men, it is a mad-brained trick, but it is no fault of mine." Although most of his soldiers were killed, Cardigan returned to England a hero, bragging publicly about his triumph. The only question raised in Parliament about the suicidal charge was: Had Cardigan been kind enough to his horses?

Then his second wife so disgraced the name of Cardigan by smoking and wearing her husband's "cherry bum trousers" that Queen Victoria had herself airbrushed out of her official portrait with the lord. Although he was elegized in the Warner Bros. movie *The Charge of the Light Brigade,* in which he was portrayed by ERROL FLYNN, his true immortality arises from having had a sweater named after him (see also LORD RAGLAN).

CARNIVEAU   🐾

In Heaven, Carniveau was a prince of the angelic order known as Powers. As a demon (often invoked by witches), he inspires those whom he possesses to the sin of "hardness of heart." His Heavenly nemesis is St. Vincent of Saragossa.

CARPOULET

In Amiens, in 1816, a Jesuit exorcist undertook to drive out the three demons possessing a young woman. The first fiend, self-identified as Mimi, went quietly. Zozo was the next to leave, smashing a church window in his flight. But the crafty Carpoulet (whose name seems to mean "chicken meat") took up lodgings in the girl's vagina, an area beyond the reach or understanding of any Jesuit.

CARREAU

Before his fall, Carreau was a prince of Powers. He is now reduced to inspiring mortals to acts of obscenity and shamelessness, which explains the outré behavior of Sister Seraphica, an Ursuline nun of Loudun, France, whom he possessed in 1633. (She had swallowed him in a drop of water.) Carreau's Heavenly adversary (as Sister explained, after her successful exorcism) is St. John the Evangelist.

CASSIUS DWH 42 B.C. TREASON

Whether or not he had a "lean and hungry look," as Shakespeare's JULIUS CAESAR says of him, the historic Cassius otherwise resembles the bard's portrait—Gaius Cassius Longinus was brave, vain, ambitious, literate, sharp-tongued, and bad tempered. Although he was a tribune of the plebeians, he sided with the Optimates—Pompey and the aristocrats—against Caesar in the civil war. Sometime after Pompey's defeat at Pharsalus in 48, Cassius met Caesar by chance and took the opportunity to surrender to him personally. The victorious new emperor not only pardoned him but promised him the governorship of Syria.

So what were Cassius's motives for planning the assassination of his merciful benefactor? It has been suggested that he was envious of the younger BRUTUS, who had been appointed to a more senior position. But maybe he just didn't *like* Caesar.

After the Ides of March murder, Cassius left town and claimed his Caesar-promised position in Syria, which province he proceeded to plunder most thoroughly before joining his forces to those of Brutus at Philippi. There Cassius lost his part of the battle and, mistakenly believing Brutus had also been defeated, played the Roman fool—i.e., committed suicide.

Dante encounters him in Dis, the deepest, darkest, coldest part of Hell, reserved for traitors. Only his head emerges from the grinding, foaming jaws of the giant, bat-winged, three-faced LUCIFER. Dante describes him as *si membruto*—still sturdy, or stocky—not lean and hungry at all.

CASTLEREAGH, Robert Stewart, Viscount DWH 1822 SUICIDE

Is this great British statesman in Hell? You bet. The curse of a genuine poet never fails. Percy Bysshe Shelley, in 1819, composed in "Peter Bell the Third," an elaborate satirical vision of Hell:

> *Hell is a city much like London—*
> *A populous and smoky city;*
> *There are all sorts of people undone,*
> *And there is little or no fun done;*
> *Small justice shown, and still less pity.*

The bard positively identified Castlereagh among the "caitiff corpses" dwelling there.

He was the marquis of Londonderry, an Irish landlord (a class well represented in Hell), a Tory, and an implacable foe of republicans, liberty, and Napoleon. As Britain's foreign secretary, he was instrumental in restoring the monarchy to France upon the defeat of same. But what Shelley most despised him for was Castlereagh's complicity in the 1819 Massacre of Peterloo, in which an unarmed mob of protesting English paupers was set upon by saber-wielding police. When a blackmailer threatened to expose milord as a sodomite, he killed himself by cutting his throat.

CATALANO dei Malavolti   DWH 1293   TREASON

This Bolognese monk, himself a Ghibelline, was elected *podestà*, co-mayor of Florence, on the coalition JOVIAL FRIARS ticket, together with a Guelf, Friar LODERINGO DI LANDOLO. As Dante believed, and historians have now established, both were agents of the pro-Guelf pope Clement IV.

CATHERINE de Medici   DWH 1589   VIOLENCE

Her detractors say she ordered the infamous St. Bartholomew's Day Massacre. Her defenders argue that she merely permitted it. She was the granddaughter of Lorenzo the Magnificent of Florence. Within a year of her birth, both her parents were dead of syphilis. In 1533, when she was fourteen, her uncle the pope arranged her marriage to the duke of Orléans, who in 1547 became King Henri II of France. The king's mistress was the celebrated beauty Diane de Poitiers, whose superb breasts were the subject of much art and comment. Catherine herself was short, stout, and pop-eyed. Her first son, Francis, was born in 1544. There followed, in the best Catholic tradition, nine siblings. This might have gone on indefinitely, but, in 1559, King Henri (an idiot) was killed while jousting, and young Francis (another idiot) ascended the throne. During his reign, after his death in 1560, and throughout the minority of his brother Charles IX (a *real* idiot, not to mention a sadist), Catherine sought to keep the peace between the kingdom's fanatically hostile Catholic and Protestant

(Huguenot) populations. This she did by managing not to choose between them. Then, on August 24, 1572 (the feast of St. Bartholomew), she came down rather firmly in support of the Papist position and ordered (or permitted) the slaughter of France's Protestants. In less than a week, 3,000 of them died at the hands of the Paris mobs; perhaps another 40,000 were martyred in the provinces. *Le Roi* Charles soon died (of guilt, it was said) and was succeeded by the third of Catherine's sons to assume the throne—this one yet another Henri, known as "the last Valois." He was a cross-dressing masochist and, like his mother, every inch a queen.

CATHERINE "the Great"   DWH 1796   LUST

No, she did *not* die in flagrante delicto with a horse. But being a strong-willed, intelligent, and powerful woman, she *did* have that kind of reputation. They called her the SEMIRAMIS or the MESSALINA of the North.

In 1745, Sophie Friederike Auguste von Anhalt-Zerbst of Austria, age fifteen, was imported to Russia, renamed Yekaterina Alekseyevna, and obliged to marry her cousin the future czar Peter III. He was a pigheaded, alcoholic boor, and impotent to boot. Nevertheless, his wife selflessly contrived to provide the nation with three male heirs to the throne—by means of three different lovers. One of these—Grigory Orlov, a dashing young army officer—eventually led a rebellion against Czar Peter, who quickly abdicated and was murdered in prison. Catherine assumed complete

AN IMPERIAL STRIDE!

power. Under the influence of French philosophers like VOLTAIRE, her regime was at first shockingly liberal—for example, she nationalized the property of the Church and even advocated education for women—until a Cossack-led peasant uprising in 1773 brought her to her senses and she became a properly ruthless tyrant, enforcing serfdom at home while expanding her empire by 200,000 square miles and, incidentally, wiping Poland off the map.

Catherine the Empress had twenty official lovers—boy toys she dallied with for a while before sending each one off, in turn, to become a loyal administrator in her far-flung empire.

CATILINE   DWH 62 B.C.   TREASON

Lucius Sergius Catiline was a bad guy. Politically ambitious and unscrupulous, he attached himself to the reactionary coup d'état of the odious general Sulla—in the course of which he murdered his own brother-in-law. As reward, he was appointed governor of Africa and there became extremely rich—although it must be said that he was eventually acquitted of charges of extortion, as indeed he was (in 73 B.C.) of charges that he had fornicated with a vestal virgin. Defeated (by Cicero) in the 64 B.C. consular elections, he formed a conspiracy to plunder and burn the city. Cicero got wind of the plot and in four passionate orations persuaded the Senate to sentence Catiline to death. The miscreant fled to Gaul and there raised a rebel army. It was easily defeated in a battle in which Catiline himself was killed.

CAVALCANTI, Cavalcante dei   DWH circa 1300   ATHEISM

Inhabiting one of the open graves to which the hedonistic and freethinking Epicureans are condemned, Dante discovers the father of his best friend and fellow poet Guido dei Cavalcanti. When the old man inquires pathetically about his living son's welfare, Dante realizes that the damned have knowledge of the past and the future but not of the present.

CERBERUS

In Greek (and Roman) mythology, it was understood that the way into Hades was guarded by this three-headed dog, and the dead were buried with honey-soaked cakes with which to bribe him. In the *Inferno*, Dante assigns this fierce, ravenous beast the task of watching over the gluttons. Virgil flings him a handful of mud.

CHARLES Martel   DWH 741   TYRANNY

The grandfather of Charlemagne, this Christian king of the Franks was in his lifetime lionized as the Hammer of God for his defeat of the invading Saracen infidels at the Battle of Poitiers, in 732. Nevertheless, one of his bishops, the great St. Eucher (with whom the king frequently quarreled), was granted a sure and certain vision of Charles burning in Hell. In the poem *Huon of Auvergne* (a French imitation of Dante's *Inferno*), King Charles sends the hero Huon off as his ambassador to Hell, the better to facilitate his own seduction of Huon's wife—for which sin His Majesty is eventually conducted to eternal damnation on a magic litter, a gift of SATAN himself.

The saintly person likewise named Charles Martel, met by Dante on the planet Venus (the Third Heaven of the *Paradiso*), was not this Frankish miscreant but a Hungarian prince who was a contemporary and acquaintance of the poet.

CHARON

The ancient Greek Hell, Hades, was on the far shore of the Styx, "the river of hate," which could only be crossed on a ferry conducted by the ancient, cranky Charon, who demanded a toll (hence the coins traditionally placed on the eyes or in the mouth of a corpse. As a character observes in Aristophanes' comedy of the Underworld, *The Frogs*, "Even Hell's gone commercial"). Those who arrived on the banks of the Styx without their fare were obliged to wait a hundred years for Charon's grudging transport. Dante, in canto 3 of the *Inferno*, echoes Virgil (*Aeneid* 6) in describing the ferryman as old, white haired and bearded, red eyed, and grumpy. But Dante goes further, calling him "a devil"—and a spirit named Charos remains to this day the "Angel of Death" in Greek folklore.

CHAUMETTE, Pierre-Gaspard   DWH 1794   BLASPHEMY

Almost everyone involved in the French Revolution is, of course, in Hell. But an especially nasty eternal afterlife must be the lot of this anti-clerical extremist and procurator general of the Paris Commune. Not only did he forbid whipping in the schools, suppress lotteries and prostitution, and improve hospital conditions for the poor, but, on November 10, 1793, he installed a naked whore upon the high altar in Notre-Dame Cathedral to be worshipped as the "goddess of Reason." Even the ghastly ROBESPIERRE thought this was going too far, and he soon dispatched Citizen Chaumette via the guillotine.

CHARLES / CLEOPATRA 55

CHAUVIN, Nicolas   DWH circa 1830   CHAUVINISM

To have a sin named after you (see CHEVALIER D' EON, ONAN, MARQUIS DE SADE, SIMON MAGUS, et cetera) pretty much guarantees your damnation. The man who gave his name to blind, fanatical patriotism and, by extension, to mindless zeal in any cause—i.e., "male chauvinism"—was a veteran of Napoleon's Grande Armée who was constantly, loudly, proudly, publicly, and boringly much devoted to his fallen leader and to France. He became a character in Cogniards's popular 1832 stage farce, *La Cocarde Tricolore,* one who proclaims repeatedly, *"Je suis Français, je suis Chauvin!"* Chauvin's name (like that of the great Protestant divine John Calvin) is a diminutive form of *chauve* and means "baldy."

CHEMOSH

The sun god of the Moabites and therefore an idol and "abomination" to the Israelites (who invaded and stole their land). As a Christian demon, Chemosh has a reputation for being a persistent possessor but easily exorcised.

CHORONZON

A demon allegedly conjured in the desert by the creepy twentieth-century Satanist ALEISTER CROWLEY.

CIACCO   DWH circa 1300   GLUTTONY

In the Third Circle of Hell, a rainy, muddy swamp where gluttons are punished, Dante meets an old acquaintance who identifies himself by his earthly nickname, Ciacco—"Piggy." Although gluttony is on the list of the Seven Deadly Sins, many (fat, bad-tempered) moral theologians have opined that neither it nor anger is an invariably "mortal" sin—that is, a sin deserving of eternal torment, a really serious sin like, say, lust.

CIRIATTO

One of the playful devils assigned to escort Dante through the bolgia of the Malebranche, Ciriatto has tusks, "like a boar."

CLEOPATRA   DWH 30 B.C.   LUST

The consort of both JULIUS CAESAR and MARC ANTONY, the queen of Egypt is characterized by Dante as *lussuriosa*—lewd, wanton, promiscuous (canto 5). As his guide Virgil explains, she is among those condemned to Hell for the sin of lust—for "making reason slave to appetite." This was the medieval Christian philosophers' objection to all, even marital, sex: "During intercourse there is an almost total extinction of mental alertness" (St. Augustine). "In coitus the mind is stifled under the weight of the flesh" (St. Albert the Great). "Sexual pleasure totally suppresses thought" (St. Thomas Aquinas).

Rabelais reports that Cleopatra is now an onion seller in Hell. But all other portrayals of her—Shakespeare's, Dryden's, Shaw's, even Elizabeth Taylor's—are based on her description by the Roman historian Plutarch. By his account, Cleopatra was no great beauty but an able ruler and diplomat, charming, witty, and intelligent. Unfortunately, she is surely damned, for having given (as the title of Dryden's drama about her phrased it) *All for Love.*

COHN, Harry   DWH 1958   TYRANNY

When Harry Cohn heard that BENITO MUSSOLINI refused novocaine at the dentist, the dictator became his idol for life. The Hollywood producer had his office redecorated so it was identical to Mussolini's, duplicating the thirty-foot walk to *il Duce*'s desk because, he said, "by the time they reach my desk, they're beaten." A former vaudevillian, Cohn made Columbia (which he always spelled "Colombia") into a major studio by his ruthless arrogance, imagination, and cruelty ("I don't get ulcers, I give them") and his simple philosophy of filmmaking: "If my fanny squirms, it's bad. If my fanny doesn't squirm, it's good." Cohn was such a lowbrow that he found even LOUIS B. MAYER too "hoity-toity" and once refused an invitation to the ballet, saying, "Watch those fags chase each other for three hours?"

Even after he dumped his first wife for not being pretty and remarried someone more attractive, he remained the biggest satyr in Hollywood, ripping clothes off young actresses while they were still signing their contracts. But he turned prudish when Kim Novak was having an affair with "Negro" Sammy Davis, Jr., threatening to kill Davis if he didn't stop seeing his big, blond star. And Cohn, a Jew who worked on Yom Kippur and smoked cigars in synagogues, wasn't any more tolerant of Jews. When asked, after the war, to contribute to a Jewish relief agency, he screamed, "Relief for the Jews! How about relief *from* the Jews? All the trouble in this world is caused by Jews and Irishmen."

Although he *did* have strong ties to organized crime, Cohn never, unlike the character based on him in *The Godfather*, woke up with a horse's head in his bed. But, as HEDDA HOPPER observed, "You had to stand in line to hate him."

COHN, Roy DWH 1986
SOWING DISCORD

If Roy's not in Hell, to Hell with it!

CONALLUS DWH 12th century
GREED

The most celebrated pre-Dante tour of Hell was that undertaken by Tundall, a twelfth-century Irish monk. Written in 1115, *Vision of Tundall* was eventually translated into fifteen languages, and manuscripts of the work (which ran some 250 pages) were illuminated by all the better illuminators of the Middle Ages. It is generally assumed that Dante was familiar with the text.

After suffering an apoplectic fainting fit, Tundall is escorted through Hell by his guardian angel, who allows his charge briefly to undergo a few salutary torments—for example, in the company of some other unchaste priests and nuns, he is devoured by a great iron-beaked bird and then defecated into a frozen lake.

The author is almost perversely discreet about naming names, but he does mention catching sight of Conallus and Fergusus, a pair of deceased monks whose punishment for greed is to be "devoured by Acheron." (Acheron is one of the rivers of Hades, and, by extension, as in the *Aeneid*, 5.137, a synonym for Hades itself. Hades was also the name of the lord of the Underworld, aka PLUTO, whom the medievals identified with SATAN.)

CORTÉS, Hernando DWH 1547
CRUELTY

His first voyage to the New World was postponed when the dashing young nobleman was injured escaping a married woman's bedroom. Cortés sailed for Hispaniola in 1504, when he was nineteen years of age. In Santiago he commenced an affair with the fiancée of the governor. In 1519 he led an invasion of Mexico, flying the banner of the Holy Cross—and, once ashore, he burned his own ships to prevent his troops from deserting him. He soon made a mistress of his captive Aztec translator, Doña Marina, and with her aid posed as a descendant of the god Quetzalcoatl in the court of the Aztec king Montezuma. He then took his host hostage. Although he grew wealthy and was even created a marquis, through his own recklessness Cortés fell from power in Mexico and, when he returned to Spain, was snubbed by the court.

COUGHLIN, Father Charles DWH 1979 SOWING DISCORD

"The floor of Hell," said St. John Chrysostom, "is paved with priests' skulls." If so, among the infernal flagstones is certain to be the clerical cranium of this Canadian-born American superpatriot. One of the original electronic evangelists, he began broadcasting his sermons from the Shrine of the Little Flower in Royal Oak, Michigan, in 1930. Originally a bleeding-heart Roosevelt supporter, throughout the 1930s the "radio priest" drifted to the political right until his (extremely popular) programs became outpourings of rabid, unabashed fascist propaganda. In 1942 his publication *Social Justice* was banned for violating the Espionage Act, and the Church pulled the plug on his show.

CRANMER, Thomas DWH 1556
HERESY

An archheretic, the first Protestant archbishop of Canterbury, Cranmer began his career inauspiciously enough—he was expelled from college for marrying his landlady's niece. But, luckily for him, the wench soon died, leaving him free to pursue his celibate theological studies. After his ordination, he chanced to meet HENRY VIII at a time when that lusty monarch was unhappy with his wife, Catherine of Aragon. Cranmer, ever eager to please, improvised on the spot a spuriously legal rationale for a divorce. Henry liked the cut of his jib and hired him. While on a royal mission to Germany, Father Cranmer met and secretly married. (It is said his wife, Margaret, traveled with him back to England packed in a trunk.) In January 1533, the king's mistress Anne Boleyn was pregnant. What Henry needed, fast, was an archbishop of Canterbury who would declare him legally free to marry her. Cranmer was the man for the job—and for the job of ecclesiastically yes-manning the king's subsequent spectacular series of divorces and spousal executions. After Henry's death, Cranmer browbeat the sickly boy king Edward into signing the infamous anti-Catholic Thirty-nine Articles into law, and, after Edward's demise, he conspired to place that unfortunate Protestant goose Jane Seymour on the throne of England, in place of the rightful (but Catholic) claimant, Henry's daughter Mary Tudor. Once installed, Queen Mary deposed the archbishop and ordered him tried for treachery and heresy. In prison, Cranmer six times recanted his heretical views, and he might have gone to Heaven at last, but at the stake he retracted his retractions and condemned himself to eternal perdition by denying not only the pope's power but also transubstantiation!

CRAWFORD, Joan

DWH 1977   CRUELTY

She began her career in porno two-reelers cavorting nude on a swing but stayed a movie star for a long time. Even in her fifties she was still chewing the scenery, playing a western desperado as well as a plucky hoofer, tap dancing in blackface. Her success was due more to her ambition than to her hammy acting, which once caused F. Scott Fitzgerald to complain, "She can't change her emotions in the middle of a scene without going through a sort of Jekyll and Hyde contortion of the face." Her children, besides being subjected to drill practice and wire hangers, were forced to curtsy to an endless succession of visiting "uncles" and the occasional "aunt." When she died, Crawford may have bequeathed her daughter Christine only a dollar, but she did endow the art world with her extensive collection of Keane paintings.

CRIPPEN, Dr. Hawley   DWH 1910   MURDER

A quiet, fastidious gentleman, Dr. Crippen was married to Cora, a vulgar, flamboyant, and bossy ex–music hall performer. (Her stage name was Belle Elmore.) Naturally, Dr. Crippen fell in love with his mousy nurse,

Ethel. After a January 31 party at their home, Cora disappeared. Dr. Crippen told the neighbors his wife had gone to California and soon let it be known that she had (alas!) died there and been cremated. Ethel moved in. Suspicions were aroused—especially those of Chief Inspector Drew of Scotland Yard. When Dr. Crippen and Ethel embarked on a romantic voyage to Canada, the policeman searched the house and discovered telltale bits of Cora in the coal cellar. Drew took a faster boat to Canada and arrived in time to greet and arrest the doctor.

The ensuing trial was a sensation. It was revealed that, having killed Cora, Dr. Crippen had professionally removed her bones and limbs and burned them in the kitchen stove. Her organs he dissolved in acid in the bathtub. Her head he had tossed overboard (in a handbag) while on a day trip to Dieppe. Throughout the proceedings and at his sentencing, Dr. Crippen showed no remorse, only concern for his beloved Ethel's reputation and prospects. After his hanging, Ethel's photograph, at his request, was placed in his coffin.

CROMWELL, Oliver   DWH 1658
TYRANNY

Fully justified, popular political revolutions have an unfortunate tendency to degenerate into civil wars, followed by despotisms. Certainly the English Puritan Revolution did. The uprising that overthrew the monarchy (in the person of King Charles I) soon became a theocratic "protectorate," that is, a dictatorship. The lord protector—a seventeenth-century politically correct euphemism for *tyrant*—was Oliver Cromwell, aka the Almighty Nose.

In the words of conservative historian G. M. Trevelyan, "Cromwell was the first ruler of England who was consciously an Imperialist." His "Roundhead" Imperialist army invaded not merely nearby Scotland but far-off Jamaica. But it was in Ireland that he did his best work, ruthlessly enforcing a policy of what would today be called ethnic cleansing. In the course of a three-year campaign, three-quarters of the island's arable land was seized from the Catholic Celts and one-third of the local population slaughtered. From conquered Dublin, in 1649, Cromwell wrote home a detailed account of his atrocities, together with this justification: "I am perswaded [sic] that this is a righteous Judgement of God upon these Barbarous wretches." It was generally believed—and not just in Ireland—that Cromwell had made a pact with SATAN and that, at his death, "the devil had come for his own."

He served his God so faithfully and well
That now he sees him face to face—in Hell.

CROWLEY, Aleister   DWH 1947
FRAUD

It isn't every twelve-year-old who crucifies toads, but what can you expect from a lad whose previous incarnations had included Pope ALEXANDER VI, COUNT CAGLIOSTRO, and ELIPHAS LÉVI? In the latter persona, he wrote a two-volume opus of diabolism, *Le Dogme et Rituel de la Haute Magie,* which would in the course of time be well thumbed by HEINRICH HIMMLER, L. RON HUBBARD, and JAYNE MANS-FIELD, as well as the members of the rock group Led Zeppelin. He bragged that he was "the Evilest Man in the World," and maybe he was. Crowley claimed to have conducted or-gies and Satanic rituals, raped women by means of astral projection, murdered someone named Raoul Loveday, and killed and eaten his native bearers on a mountain-climbing expedition. He certainly overate, shot heroin, and filed his teeth to points, so he could draw blood while kissing. His favorite light snack was his own semen. Both his wives ended their lives in mental institutions, and five of his mistresses—he was proud to say—killed themselves. His antics offended even the gross MUSSOLINI, who booted him out of Italy. A surviving band of the Beast's disciples may be found (no big surprise) in Southern California.

CUSTER, Gen. George A. DWH 1876 VIOLENCE

Native American author Vine DeLoria, Jr., has written a book called *Custer Died for Your Sins*. But the Martyr of Little Big Horn went to Hell for his own. The yellow-haired "Boy General" graduated from West Point last in his class—and only managed *that* by cheating on his exams. Although he distinguished himself as a Union officer in the Civil War, he was no abolitionist. Of black suffrage, he opined, "I would as soon think of elevating an Indian chief to the popedom of Rome." He was an adulterous whoremonger, a bribe taker, and a compulsive gambler. His bombastic, lying, self-serving autobiography was part of his planned campaign for the presidency of the United States. He wiped out peaceful Cheyenne villages and invaded the sacred Black Hills of the Sioux to further the interests of his paymasters, gold-mining speculators and the Northern Pacific Railroad.

"Did you ever hear the like?" said the Devil, and a hard note crept into his voice. "If there's one thing I can't stand," he said, "it's superstition."
—MERVYN WALL, *The Unfortunate Fursey*

Dives, when you and I go down to Hell
Where scribblers end, and millionaires as well . . .
. . . Who will look the ass?
You, or myself, or Charon? Who can tell?
They order things so damndably in Hell.
—HILAIRE BELLOC, "To Dives"

DAGON

A devil, the father of BAAL, Dagon was originally a Babylonian corn god, believed by the Israelites to be half man, half fish, *dag* being Hebrew for "fish." When the Philistines captured Samson, they imprisoned him in Dagon's temple; they also placed the head of King SAUL there, but when they did likewise with the stolen Ark of the Covenant, the statue of the idol fell to pieces. Much later, Dagon identified himself by name as one of the demons possessing a nun of the convent at Louviers. According to demonologists, Dagon is now employed as Hell's baker.

DAHMER, Jeffrey   DWH 1994   MURDER

After working his day job in Milwaukee's Ambrosia Chocolate Factory, Dahmer would cruise gay bars and bring his dates home to murder and dismember them. He would then freeze or fry their body parts. He killed a total of sixteen young men. His own lawyer likened him to Halley's comet, a killer that "comes around every seventy-five years and, thankfully, isn't seen for another seventy-five." Dahmer rationally explained his eccentric behavior: When he was attracted to people, he said, "I wanted to keep them with me as long as possible, even if it meant just keeping a part of them." In prison, while serving a 936-year sentence, he enjoyed baiting guards by reminding them, "I bite," and once posted a sign announcing a meeting of Cannibals Anonymous. Dahmer was murdered by a broom-wielding fellow inmate. His divorced parents then fought over possession of his valuable remains.

DALEY, Richard J.   DWH 1976   BARRATION

> Hell is a pocket edition of Chicago.
> —JOHN BURNS

Those damned for the sin of political corruption are known, in the Inferno, as "barrators." The Chicago mayor and Democratic party boss Daley was one. He took credit—probably correctly—for stuffing the Windy City's ballot boxes and thereby electing President Kennedy in 1960. (Kennedy staffers knew their man would win when the formerly standoffish Daley made a smiling beeline for JFK in the minutes following the first TV debate.) He was less supportive of LBJ's War on Poverty, sabotaging neighborhood programs so he could control federal funds and openly grousing during Martin Luther King's visit to Chicago. Daley's doughy face captured the world's attention when he hosted the infamous 1968 Democratic presidential convention and unleashed his charging, clubbing police on antiwar demonstrators. Journalists (even the avuncular Walter Cronkite), bystanders, and delegates were victims of the police brutality, which Daley defended with his famous malaprop "The policeman isn't there to create disorder. The policeman is there to preserve disorder." When Sen. Abraham Ribicoff of Connecticut denounced Daley's gestapo tactics from the convention floor, the mayor was shown on television mouthing, "Fuck you you Jew son of a bitch you lousy motherfucker go home." Norman Mailer summed up Daley and Chicago this way: "carnal as blood, greedy, direct, too impatient for hypocrisy, in love with honest plunder."

DALÍ, Salvador   DWH 1989   FRAUD

The Spanish surrealist painter was the second Salvador Dalí born to his father, Salvador Dalí. Maybe this explains his anger at his parents, which he expressed as a child by depositing his feces around the house and attempting to kick his baby sister to death, and as an adult by writing at the bottom of one of his paintings, "I spit on the portrait of my mother." (His mother had recently died.) Dalí, a superb draftsman, was an even more superb self-promoter and relied on his trademark look: flowing cape, skinny handlebar mustache, popping eyes, and the occasional brassiere and garter. In his autobiography, he flaunted his repulsive eccentricities, which included shaving his armpits, wearing his own brand of perfume (a mixture of fish glue and dung), and talking of himself in the third person. Luis Buñuel described Dalí the lover: "His seductions usually entailed stripping American heiresses, frying a couple of eggs, putting them on the women's shoulders, and, without a word, showing them to the door."

He supported FRANCO in the Spanish Civil War and was a devotee of HITLER as well. (In his later years, he confessed that Hitler "turned me on" and described fantasizing about their mustached coupling: "His flesh which I imagined whiter than white, ravished me.") In the 1960s Dalí embraced the American hippie culture (ignoring the politics and antimaterialism). Enthralled by Day-Glo and the accessibility of young boys and girls in the throws of free love, he claimed to have seduced both Ultra Violet and Mia Farrow. He eschewed drugs, however, explaining simply, "I *am* drugs, take me, I'm hallucinogenic."

DAMBALLA

A voodoo serpent demon.

DANAIDS   MURDER

Danaus, king of Argos, had fifty daughters. With daggers their father gave them, forty-nine of the young women stabbed their husbands to death on their wedding nights. In the Hades of mythology, they are condemned to carry water in sieves. Samuel Butler, in his *Notebooks,* claims to have met "a traveler who had returned from Hades," and there spoken to the Danaids. "The shades agreed that for the first six, or perhaps twelve months, they had disliked their punishment very much; but after that, it was like shelling peas on a hot afternoon in July."

DANDO   DWH circa 1000   BLASPHEMY

A wicked and sensual priest in the village of St. Germans in Cornwall, Dando rode to the hunt even on Sundays. On one such sporting occasion, his flask ran dry, and he swore to one of his attendants that he should "go to Hell" for a drink. A stranger joined the hunt and offered Dando a cup, saying it was the choicest brew from the place just mentioned. "If they have drink like this in Hell, I will willingly spend eternity there!" said the blasphemous priest. He, his horse, and the stranger vanished in a flash of flame.

DANGERFIELD, Thomas   DWH 1685   CALUMNY

The novelist Graham Greene often remarked on the similarities between the Cold War Red scare and the anti-Catholic paranoia in seventeenth-century England. In those days of secret agents and counterspies, plots and counterplots, Dangerfield was a rat disguised as a mole, a false friend, a false witness, and a planter of evidence. (See also TITUS OATES.)

D'ANNUNZIO, Gabriele   DWH 1938   LUST

As if being the poet laureate of Italian fascism wasn't bad enough, D'Annunzio was such a great lover that he often served his guests wine from the skull of a virgin he had allegedly deflowered and driven to suicide. He claimed to have seduced his first woman at twelve. He certainly began writing decadent, erotic verse at sixteen . . . and went completely bald at twenty-two.

He was a poet, playwright, artist, flying ace, gossip, and politician, who eloped with the daughter of a duke to gain a modicum of respectability. He arrived in Rome as a deputy and decided to join the Socialist party when he (mistakenly) thought a roomful of socialists had cheered him as he walked by. He swung back to the right on the eve of World War I, rousing his countrymen to the glories of war and denouncing the president of Italy, whose mouth, he said, "was filled with false words and false teeth." When D'Annunzio described in intimate detail his affair with the actress Eleonora Duse, his novel *Il Fuoco* (The Flame of Life) was denounced by one critic as "the most swinish ever written." (She, however, continued to star and invest in his plays, rationalizing, "I am forty—and in love.") D'Annunzio, who boasted that 1,000 husbands hated him, was a satyr who occasionally practiced safe sex, carrying his condoms in Napoleon's snuffbox. He was such an exhibitionist that he strolled naked through hotel lobbies and rode to the hounds in the buff—but he was phobic about rain, once bringing a hundred umbrellas with him on a brief trip to London. To maintain his image, he would pose as a mysterious woman in a flowing white cloak on a white horse and ride into his own castle at midnight— making sure he was spotted by the local townsfolk. He finally attained royal status in his sunset years when MUSSOLINI made him prince of Monte Nevoso.

DANTALIAN   🜁

A tempter demon who changes good thoughts to evil ones. Dantalian takes on many faces and likes to carry a book.

DASHWOOD, Sir Jeffrey   DWH 1781   BLASPHEMY

Nobleman and politician (chancellor of the exchequer), Dashwood organized the Hellfire Club for fellow English aristocrats with a penchant for Satanism and sex orgies. Under its aegis, Britain's finest (and once, so it was rumored, the American statesman Benjamin Franklin) dressed up as monks and conducted "black masses" in a former monastery, Medmenham Abbey. They were invariably attended by prostitutes dressed as nuns. (Dashwood's questionable sense of humor was evident in his younger years as well—at age twenty, he had masqueraded as King Charles XII of Sweden in order to seduce Empress Anna of Russia.) Once, John Wilkes dressed himself as a baboon in a devil's costume and hid under the altar during a Hellfire Club service. When the baboon emerged and jumped on Dashwood, the chancellor sniveled and prayed, "Oh spare me . . . till I have served thee better. I am as yet but half a sinner."

DASIM

A son of the Islamic archfiend IBLIS, Dasim is the demon of discord.

DATASCALVO and DUSACRUS

A pair of demons who possessed and then emerged from a pair of nuns in a seventeenth-century Munich convent; their arrival was cleverly timed for the Feast of the Holy Innocents—so they could curse at the holy relics.

DAVID, Father Pierre   DWH 1645   BLASPHEMY

This clergyman introduced dildos to the nuns of the convent at Louviers and convinced the misguided sisters to attend mass naked, "in the spirit of Adam."

DEBER

A demon whose name in Hebrew means "pestilence," he makes an appearance in Psalm 91 as "Deber that walketh in the darkness."

DECARABIA

A minor devil who produces birds and can always be conjured to appear within a pentagram.

DEE, John   DWH 1608   SORCERY

Known as Queen Elizabeth's Merlin, Dee was an official court astrologer with a government pension. The usually no-nonsense monarch ELIZABETH I regularly visited Dee's home in Mortlake, Surrey, for consultations—but whether Her Majesty made use of his healing crystals or his youth-preserving potion, the "elixir vitae," is not known. Dee teamed up with a seer, Edward Kelley, to convince spirits to appear in a "magic mirror," which also provided the two charlatans access to the fourth dimension. By means of this device, they learned Enochian, the language of

Hell, which devils have spoken since before the Flood. (A sample of its not too lyrical phrasing is *Odo cicale Quaa! Zodoreje, lape zodiredo Noco Mada, hoathahe Saitan!*) Kelley, who had no ears (they had been lopped off as a punishment for forgery), was, not surprisingly, a superb ventriloquist. Speaking through him, "spirits" correctly predicted such momentous events as the execution of Mary Tudor, the defeat of the Spanish Armada, and the cessation of Dee's rectal bleeding, but they also insisted the world would end on or by St. Patrick's Day, 1842. Kelley's spirit friends further recommended that he and Dr. Dee swap wives, which they promptly did—although Dee maintained that the arrangement was purely spiritual, "a covenant with God . . . between us four, all things between us to be common." Shakespeare is alleged to have modeled the magician Prospero in *The Tempest* on Dr. Dee, whose crystal ball and book of magic formulas are now in the British Museum.

DEKKER, Albert   DWH 1968   SUICIDE

A film actor (the mad scientist Dr. Cyclops was his signature work), Dekker was also a California state assemblyman. His odd suicide—he was found hanging from a shower rod, dressed in women's lingerie, hand-cuffed, with two hypodermic needles stuck in his flesh and obscenities written on his skin in red lipstick—hardly afforded him time for a last-minute act of contrition. Can it have been a coincidence that over twenty actors and actresses who costarred with Dekker died violent, tragic deaths?

DeLABARATHE, Angelle   DWH 1275   SORCERY

She confessed to the Inquisition at Toulouse that she had copulated with the DEVIL and borne him a son. Eyewitnesses testified that the boy had a wolf's head and serpent's tail, and lived to be fifteen, his mother having fed him a diet of dead infants. Mme. DeLabarathe has the distinction of being the first woman burned at the stake for having sex with the Devil.

de LANCRE, Pierre   DWH 1631   CRUELTY

This French inquisitor—that is, witchcraft judge, answering only to the king—condemned some 600 innocent people to the stake. He once accused all 30,000 residents, including the priests, in a Basque territory of being witches.

DEMOCRITUS   DWH circa 370 B.C.   ATHEISM

Dante, in canto 4 of the *Inferno,* puts Democritus in Hell because the brilliant and agreeable Laughing Philosopher of the Greeks was a materialist. He had maintained that the universe was created by mere chance and reasoned that "in reality there is nothing but atoms (particles of light) and space." Democritus also asserted, oddly enough, that semen is produced by all the organs of the body.

DEMOGORGON

A minor Roman god of the Underworld, Demogorgon has evolved into a powerful Christian demon, the mere mention of whose name can bring death and destruction.

de MONTFORT, Guy DWH 1272
VIOLENCE

On the bank of one of the Seventh Circle's bloody rivers, a centaur, acting as tour guide, points out to Dante the shade of this impetuous thirteenth-century statesman. His father, Simon, had been killed by Edward I of England. In revenge, Guy stabbed to death Henry III's nephew Henry of Cornwall—in church, at the very moment of the consecration! Naturally, the young victim's heart was put in a gold cup and placed on London Bridge, whence it miraculously continued to drip blood into the Thames.

deSHAYES, Catherine (La Voisin) DWH 1679   SORCERY

She was the head of a poison ring (although she failed in several attempts to poison her own husband), an abortionist, a fortune-teller, a marketer of breast-enlargement and antiwrinkle creams, and a maker of love potions (dried toad, semen, bat's blood, and graveyard dust) who did a bustling business supplying performers of black masses. When her friend Mme. MARQUISE DE MONTESPAN enlisted her aid in winning back the affections of King LOUIS XIV (the Spanish fly wasn't working), La Voisin devised a particularly perverted black mass. The naked marquise was the altar over which a debauched priest offered a mass to ASHTORETH and ASMODEUS, with baby's blood in the chalice. Louis tried to play down his connection with this sorceress, especially after rumors began to circulate that the bones of 2,000 infants had been found in her cellar. When she was tied to the stake in chains, she managed to toss the straw six times before the flames engulfed her. Her behavior shocked even twentieth-century diabolist and author Anton Szandor LaVey, who laments that, "the degraded activities of Voisin stifled the majesty of Satanism for many years to come."

DEVAS

In the Vedic period, the Hindu divine powers were divided into two classes, *devas* and *asuras*. In India, the devas were considered to be gods and the asuras demons; in Iran, it was the other way around; in Persian folklore, devils are still called *divs*.

DEVIL

According to Webster, "the chief evil spirit, a supernatural being subordinate to, and the foe of, God and the tempter of man." Our word *devil* is derived from the Greek *diabolos*, which means something like "false witness" or "slanderous accuser." In the Old Testament (as in the Book of Job), his name is SATAN, and he is not so much God's foe as his employee, the prosecuting attorney in the Heavenly court; in the Quran, his name is both 'aduw Shaytan and IBLIS.

Satan may be "the" Devil, but he is also "Prince of Devils"—that is, he rules over numerous other devils (or demons)—eternal spirits who were once his fellow angels and are now his wicked subjects and helpers. The most recent *Catechism of the Catholic Church* (1994) explicitly affirms the existence of both the Devil and devils (pt. 1, sect. 2, para. 5, II, 391–95) while conceding that "it is a great mystery that providence should permit diabolical activity."

We incline toward the view of author C. S. Lewis: "There are two equal and opposite errors about which our race can fall about devils. One is to disbelieve in their existence. The other is to believe, and to feel an unhealthy interest in them. They themselves are equally pleased by both errors, and hail a materialist or a magician with the same delight" (preface to *The Screwtape Letters*).

DIAB

A male Haitian voodoo demon whose symbol is a penis.

DIABLESSE

A female Haitian voodoo demon whose symbol is a vagina.

DIAGHILEV, Serge Pavlovich   DWH 1929
SODOMY

Born in Perm, Russia, Diaghilev began his career as a lawyer but soon took up art, music, and finally ballet, of which he became one of the great impresarios of the twentieth century. In 1909 Diaghilev formed the Ballets Russes in

Paris and announced himself to be in the vanguard of the cultural revolution, "the beautiful and illuminating resurrection," with his rallying cry
Etonne moi! (Astonish me!). At about the same time, he became mentor to
the nineteen-year-old dancer Vaslav Nijinsky, simultaneously making him
his star and his catamite. Diaghilev, a notorious woman hater, convinced
the previously heterosexual, beautiful, but dim dancer that the love of
women is "a terrible thing." Nevertheless, Nijinsky would sometimes steal
off to pursue female prostitutes, and, when Diaghilev did not accompany
him on a South American tour, he became enthralled with a hot-blooded
Hungarian hussy, Romola de Pulszka. When they married in Buenos
Aires, the scorned Diaghilev, in a fit of petulance, fired the dancer for what
he euphemistically called "breach of contract." Years later (after Diaghilev
had found another young lover and started dyeing his own white hair with
black paste), he summoned Nijinsky back to take the title role in what
would be his last ballet, *Till Eulenspiegel*. Shortly afterward, Nijinsky was di-
agnosed as a schizophrenic; he spent the rest of his life in a sanitorium,
neighing like a horse.

DIAKA

These unclean spirits are attracted to séances, where they pervert and
mislead mortals with a taste for psychic phenomena.

DIDO   DWH circa 1250 B.C.   SUICIDE

Both Virgil in the *Aeneid* and Dante in the *Inferno* condemn this beautiful queen of Carthage to Hell for the sin of suicide—although Dante mer-
cifully places her among the merely lustful, as one who "killed herself for
love." A Phoenician princess, she married a wealthy man named Sychaeus,
but he was soon killed by her greedy brother, the celebrated sculptor Pyg-
malion. Grieving and vowing to be true to her husband's memory, Dido
fled to Libya. Negotiating to buy real estate there, she was permitted by a
local joker to purchase "only as much land as could be covered by a bull's
hide." Cleverly, she sliced the hide into thin ribbons, with which she en-
closed several acres—upon which she then founded the city of Carthage.
(Thus, the expression "to cut a Dido" came to mean "to pull a fast one.")
Some years later, a ship bearing the handsome AENEAS washed up on her
shores, and the hero proceeded to tell her (as young men will older
women) the story of his life. He actually recited books 2 and 3 of the
Aeneid. Inspired by Venus, the goddess of love, to forget about poor old Sychaeus, Dido took Aeneas to bed and became for a while a very merry
widow. But, alas, Aeneas had a sacred destiny to fulfill. Despite her tearful
pleadings (and inspired by Mercury, the god of quick getaways), the hero

sailed off to found Rome. Mad with rage and sorrow, the queen slew herself with a sword. "Pious" Aeneas shed a manly tear aboard his ship upon looking back and seeing the light of her funeral pyre.

Aeneas encountered Dido again in the course of his (book 4) trip through Hell, where, a typical male, he was puzzled and hurt when she wouldn't speak to him.

DILLINGER, John   DWH 1934   VIOLENCE

After spending nine years in prison for holding up a grocery store, Dillinger talked his way out of the slammer wielding a bar of soap he had whittled into the shape of a gun and painted with black shoe polish. The escape made headlines around the world—especially since Dillinger used the sheriff's car in his getaway. As the original Public Enemy Number One, Dillinger enjoyed taunting FBI Director J. EDGAR HOOVER with postcards. America's favorite fugitive was rumored to have an enormous sex organ. He was certainly a sentimentalist, with tears streaming down his face when he held up a bank in Mason City, Iowa, and he liked to flirt with older women during his robberies. He was finally betrayed and gunned down by a team of FBI agents—never having a chance to pull his own gun. The publicity that followed made Hoover's G-man reputation; the director turned the anteroom of his FBI office into a Dillinger museum, displaying his death mask, last cigar, and hat.

A theory persists that it was an underworld fall guy, James Lawrence, who was killed by the FBI and that Dillinger, with altered face and fingerprints, escaped to South America. But then who would be the owner of the fourteen-inch (an estimated twenty inches erect) penis that was lopped off by an eager FBI pathologist and has long been rumored to be housed at the Smithsonian?

DIMME

A Sumerian female demon, Dimme specializes in slaying infants.

DIOCLETIAN   DWH 313   TYRANNY

A great maker of martyrs in Christian legend, this son of a slave and a bodyguard clawed his way to the top. As emperor, Diocletian opposed taxes, inflation, and Christians. His persecution of the latter began in 303—with his own recently converted wife and daughter. They relented and sacrificed to pagan gods, but his chamberlain, Peter, refused, so Diocletian had him cooked in a big pot over a low flame. The emperor was apparently able to invent new forms of torture for the faithful by the hour—and he denied tombs to those he executed, ordering their bodies to be thrown in the river. In later years, he suffered from acute depression and lost interest even in the grandiose martyr-making circuses and the elaborate baths he had built. When his subordinate Galerius forced him aside, Diocletian happily retired to his farm to grow vegetables.

DIOGENES   DWH 323 B.C.   ATHEISM

A philosopher of the school known as dogs—the Cynics—Diogenes lived in an earthenware bathtub, whence he rejected all theology and notions of an afterlife. In legend, Diogenes roamed Athens with a lantern, "looking in vain for an honest man," and suggested that humans live "with the animals, they are so placid and self-contained." ALEXANDER THE GREAT sought the wise man out and found him sorting through a pile of human bones.

Diogenes explained, "I am searching for the bones of your father but cannot distinguish them from those of a slave." Dante placed him among the noble pagans in Limbo, the First Circle of Hell, but surely the old cynic suffers in a deeper pit, for he was a champion of masturbation. He once declared, "If only it was as easy to banish hunger by rubbing the belly as it is to masturbate."

DIOMEDES   DWH circa 1300 B.C.   BLASPHEMY

A Greek hero of the war against Troy, a brave warrior, and a shrewd businessman, Diomedes appears encased in flame alongside ULYSSES in the *Inferno*. Virgil alone speaks to this pair of Greeks, since Dante, being an Italian, was a descendant of their vanquished enemies, the Trojans. A favorite of Athena, the impious Diomedes stole the Palladium (an image of the goddess) from Troy, thereby robbing the city of its good luck. He is said to have raised his prize horses by feeding them on human flesh and, fittingly, was himself eaten alive by them.

DIONYSIUS the Elder   DWH 367 B.C.   TYRANNY

In 1914, a British medium, Mrs. Willet, revealed that during a séance Dionysius had spoken with her, recounting his spying on prisoners of war and dubbing himself Ear. In mortal life, he was a king of Sicily whose despotism became proverbial—thus Dante discovers him among the tyrants (in canto 12). He was also a man of letters, and so sensitive to criticism of his bad poetry that he had his detractors killed. An ambitious warlord, Dionysius fought three campaigns against Carthage, while on the domestic front he made two political marriages. In a double wedding, he

8888888888888888888

88888888888888888888888888888

married both Doris and Aristomache, rotating conjugal visits and building a moat around both marriage beds. His paranoia was so intense that he killed his mother, his mother-in-law, and his barber (realizing the latter had an opportunity to slit his throat), and anyone who approached him had to disrobe. In an attempt to better himself, Dionysius once invited Plato to his court, but when they quarreled over a philosophical point, the tyrant, in a pique, attempted to sell the great philosopher into slavery.

DIS

He was once the Roman god of the Underworld (also known as PLUTO, the Romans' version of the Greeks' HADES); he is now (demonologically speaking) Hell's version of the Holy Trinity—at least he has three faces. (The middle one is red, the right yellow, and the left black.) The esteemed first-century Roman historian Plutarch wrote *The Vision of Thespius,* an account of a "near-death experience" in which the revived Thespius names Dis as the strict but fair judge of souls (see THESPIUS'S FATHER).

Dante sometimes employs the term Dis as a synonym for SATAN or LUCIFER, i.e., the Devil Himself.

DISNEY, Walt DWH 1966 SOWING DISCORD

Founder of an entertainment empire and creator (with the forgotten Ub Iwerks) of Mickey Mouse, Uncle Walt even supplied Mickey's squeaky voice in the first talking cartoon, *Steamboat Willie.* After a nervous breakdown in 1933, he changed his style temporarily—an unreleased cartoon of the period features Mickey as a mad scientist who cuts off Pluto's head and puts it on a chicken.

Politically, Walt was a proto-fascist—for example, he was a guest of Georg Gyssling, the Nazi consul general in Hollywood, at the 1940 party there in honor of an SS general and personal representative of ADOLF HITLER. In the 1950s, Walt testified before the House Un-American Activities Committee that he suspected Communist cartoonists in his studio were trying to use his beloved Mickey to spread Red propaganda. Disney always refused to hire Semites, and when one of his executives, David Swift, left to join Columbia, Disney bade him farewell in a stage Jewish accent, thus: "OK, Davy Boy. Off you go to work with those Jews." But Disney had a vision: He would bulldoze America and replace it with a plastic monument to itself, to which he would charge admission. *His* dream, at least, came true. Today, we all live in WaltDisneyWorld.

Despite rumors that his body was frozen in ice under the Pirates of the Caribbean exhibit, it's buried in Forest Lawn, where it perpetually spins in the knowledge his empire is now controlled by a man named Eisner.

DIVES DWH circa 40   CRUELTY

The prototypical plutocrat—Dives' very name is Latin for "rich." In a parable of Jesus (Luke 16:19–31), Dives prospers despite his gross, unsavory life, while his virtuous counterpart, the leper Lazarus, suffers and starves. Both die—but Lazarus spends eternity in Heaven, nestled "in the bosom of Abraham," whence he contentedly watches Dives down below, parched, suffering, and burning for all eternity.

DIVINE, Father DWH 1965
HERESY

George Baker was a four-foot-six hedge cutter from Georgia who announced he was the Messiah, having been around since Abraham. His religion, the Worldwide Kingdom of Peace, was headquartered in Harlem, and its members, who donated their labor to Father Divine, were forbidden to drink, smoke, go to the movies, or use the word *hello,* since it contained a swear word. Sex was also discouraged, except for Father Divine himself, who frequently seduced his "secretaries" with such original lines as "Mary wasn't a virgin" and "I am bringing your desire to the surface so I can eliminate it." He wore $500 silk suits and drove a Bentley. When (in 1931) a judge who had given him a six-month sentence instantly dropped dead of a heart attack, Father Divine told reporters, "I hated to do it!" Although he promised the faithful he would ascend to Heaven in an airplane, he merely died (at either 88 or 4,000 years of age), leaving an estate of $10 million.

DOLCINO Tornieli DWH 1307   HERESY

Fra Dolcino was a priest's bastard son and founder of the Apostolic Brethren, who held communal property and practiced communal sex. Pope Clement V had issued a bull outlawing the sect, and by 1300, the time of Dante's visit to Hell, Dolcino and his followers had taken to the hills of Novara, with the papal armies in pursuit. Most of the sect starved to death, but Dolcino and his mistress, Margaret of Trent, were arrested, tortured, and burned at the stake, together. Among the heretics in Dante's Hell (canto 28), MAHOMET offers him some unheeded advice.

DOMIEL 🐾

St. Peter's antithesis, Domiel is Hell's gate-keeper and a notorious letch.

DON JUAN   DWH 14th century   LUST

The career and eventual damnation of this legendary Spanish swordsman have been the subject of a Molière drama, *The Stone Feast,* in 1665; a Mozart opera, *Don Giovanni,* in 1787; *Don Juan,* an epic poem by BYRON, in 1819; a verse drama, *The Stone Guest,* by Pushkin, in 1839; *Man and Superman,* a philosophic com-edy by George Bernard Shaw, in 1903; a bril-liant silent film (starring JOHN BARRYMORE) in 1927; a swashbuckler featuring ERROL FLYNN, in 1948; and, most recently, a putrid Johnny Depp vehicle, *Don Juan DeMarco.* Juan Tenorio of Seville claimed to have seduced, in Italy, 700 women; in Germany, 800; in Turkey and France, 91; and in his own home-land, 1,003. In a duel, he slew the father of the last of these—then mock-ingly invited the murdered man's statue to a feast, whence the ghost of the outraged parent delivered our hero to Hell—a place he describes (in Shaw's version) as "the home of honor, duty, justice and the rest of the seven deadly virtues. All the wickedness on earth is done in their name."

Errol Flynn as Don Juan
(see also ERROL FLYNN)

DOUGLAS, Lord Alfred Bruce

DWH 1945   SOWING DISCORD

"Bosie," the *amour fatale* of Oscar Wilde, was shiftless, spoiled, stingy, capricious, greedy—and devastatingly blond. He was given to violent tantrums, bad poetry, and rough trade. His own mother summed up his life as "brandy, betting, and boys." Yet Wilde, financially ruined because of Douglas, still loved him deeply, with a passion modestly described by Douglas himself as "the love of an artist for a beautiful mind and a beau-tiful body."

Bosie was the son of a raging ho-

mophobe, the eighth MARQUIS OF QUEENSBERRY, and he delighted in taunting his father with his friendship with Wilde. Oscar once observed, "In your war of hate with your father, I am both a shield and a weapon." Douglas "outed" their relationship in order that "everyone could see Oscar Wilde and his boy." When his father sent him a letter demanding he break with Wilde, Douglas goaded the unstable marquis further with a telegram: "What a funny little man you are." This set in motion the libel and sodomy trials that ultimately led to Wilde's disgrace and imprisonment. (His conviction was assured after Douglas made certain letters public.) After his release from Reading Gaol, the virtually homeless Wilde asked Douglas (who had come into his substantial inheritance) for a loan. Douglas likened him to an "old whore," saying simply, "I can't afford to spend anything except on myself." In his later years, Douglas married, converted to Catholicism, denied he had ever been a homosexual, and (the marquis redux) wrote blustery letters to *The Times* and immersed himself in litigation—e.g., a libel suit against Winston Churchill. When publicly asked about his friend Oscar Wilde, he sputtered that he was the "lord of abominations."

DOYLE, Sir Arthur Conan

DWH 1930   SORCERY

Doyle felt his claim to immortality rested not on his best-selling Sherlock Holmes stories but on his specious historical novels and, more important, his experiments in spiritualism—particularly his epic work *History of Spiritualism*. The creator of the great scientific detective himself believed in the fourth dimension, reincarnation, the authenticity of photographs of cute female sprites (the Cottingley Fairies), and his friend Harry Houdini's ability to dematerialize and rematerialize. During one séance, Doyle tried, unsuccessfully, to convince Houdini that the British-accented voice of an invisible "spirit" belonged to the escape artist's mother—who, during her lifetime, spoke only Yiddish. After Doyle's own death, his fellow spiritualist Harry Price tried to call him up in a séance, whereupon a stranger, identifying himself as Flight

Lieutenant Irwin, appeared and attempted to absolve himself of any responsibility for a recent dirigible crash.

DRACI 🐾

Middle European water demons who assume the shape of plates floating down a stream. When women grab the plates, the draci suck them in beneath the waves, where they force them to nurse their young.

DRACULA (Vlad "the Impaler" Tepes)   DWH 1477   CRUELTY

This historical/legendary figure was, in fact, a native of Transylvania. His father, Vlad, Sr., was a brave warrior who died fighting the Turks, thereby earning his family the honorific Dracul, meaning "dragon." Vlad, Jr., inherited the title and signed his name alternately as Dracula and Draculya. He avenged his father's death first by nailing the Turkish ambassadors' turbans to their heads and eventually by slaughtering a total of 20,000 Turks. His enemies—Turks, Saxons, local criminals—were decapitated, boiled, scalped, and skinned; but Vlad's preferred mode of execution was to impale his live (sitting) victims on stakes. The Impaler liked to dine alfresco among his dying victims, and when one dinner guest complained of the stench, he ordered his guest impaled as well—but higher than the other impalees, to avoid their odor. But Dracula had his good points—he supported peasants' rights and was a law-and-order enthusiast. In modern times, the revisionist Romanian tourist board staunchly defends him in travel brochures: "The real Dracula fought for the cause of the Romanian people!" He was killed in battle in 1477 and buried near Bucharest. Years later, his grave was found to be empty, and thus began his reputation in local folklore as "undead."

Novels (and poems) about vampires were popular throughout the nineteenth century. The Irish author Bram Stoker came upon the legend of Dracula while researching in Eastern Europe for a new vampire story. Through his work, published in 1897, Vlad achieved true immortality.

DRAGONEL (aka Draghignazzo)   🐾

Another member of the slapstick ten-demon squad assigned by the flatulent devil MALACODA to escort Dante and Virgil in canto 21. His name means "Dragon Nose."

DRUJ 🐾

A collective term for female Persian demons.

DUERA, Buoso da   DWH 1270   TREASON

When the French army of Charles of Anjou was advancing on the Kingdom of Naples, Duera (having taken silver from Charles's wife), allowed the French to pass through Lombardy unmolested. This act of treachery earned him a place in the Ninth Circle of Dante's Hell, and the curious sobriquet Chatterbox.

DULLES, Allen Welsh   DWH 1969   SOWING DISCORD

The precocious son of a Presbyterian minister, at the age of eight Dulles wrote and published *The Boer War: A History*—then grew up to become an architect of the Cold War, as head of the CIA from 1953 until the botched Bay of Pigs invasion forced him to resign in 1961. Early in his career, Dulles had an appointment with LENIN, fresh from the Russian Revolution, who was looking to ally his country with the United States in World War I. The meeting never took place since Dulles stood Lenin up to join a lady friend for a quick game of "tennis." While his brother John Foster was secretary of state under Eisenhower, Allen was his undercover counterpart, infiltrating and destabilizing "unfriendly" governments. After he engineered the 1953 coup that brought Shah PAHLAVI to power in Iran, his public response to any probing questions was his trademark "ho, ho, ho." Unlike his sullen brother (nicknamed John Foster Dullard), Allen was a favorite on the Washington party and martini circuit, "the debonair spy." His love affairs were many and so open that he gave away the daughter of one of his mistresses at her wedding. (Whenever he embarked on a new affair, his wife, Clover, went to Cartier's to buy herself an expensive present.) In the late 1950s, he employed the most advanced aerospace technology to begin the U-2 spying missions. Dulles continued to promote these missions (even after photos revealed there was no real Soviet military threat) until pilot Gary Powers was downed and captured by the Soviets—and had the bad taste not to kill himself.

DUMAH   🦅

The angel of the silence of death. Once a mere Sumerian vegetation god, Dumah became (with his name mispronounced), the Hebrew demon TAMMÜZ.

DUMOURIEZ, Charles François du Périer   DWH 1823   TREASON

This French general won several brilliant victories in the north for the Revolutionary (Girondist) government of France, but on April 5, 1793, he defected to the Austrian enemy. His treachery discredited his associates and led to the June 2 expulsion of the Girondists from the Convention, the Jacobin takeover, and—ultimately—the Terror.

DUSII

Hairy demons who live in the woods and convince women to lie down with them—from their name (perhaps) derives a popular nickname for SATAN, "the Deuce."

DUVALIER, François (aka Papa Doc)   DWH 1971   TYRANNY

Dictator of Haiti from 1957 to 1971, Papa Doc exploited native superstition to convince Haitians that he was a god on earth. Duvalier dressed in black like Baron Samedi, the death god of voodoo, and the name of his dreaded secret police, Tonton Macoutes, means "bogeymen." He believed it himself, too, discerning the future by reading goat entrails, sleeping in a tomb, and keeping the shrunken head of an enemy on his desk. During his reign, half the children in Haiti died before they were four, and the chief national export was blood plasma, for which the donors were paid with bottles of soda pop. Papa Doc's foreign policy was equally odd: He once sent an envoy to JFK's grave to get dirt and a vial of air, with which he expected to control the U.S. government. When the movie *The Comedians* was released, Papa Doc, upset by what he felt was an unflattering portrayal, stuck pins in effigies of Elizabeth Taylor and Richard Burton.

DYBBUK

An unclean Jewish demon—a wicked spirit of the dead that sometimes possesses a living person's body, attempting to work out something uncompleted in his own lifetime. Dybbukim can be exorcised by a miracle-working rabbi (*ba'al shem*), who burns the ashes of a red heifer under the victim and/or blows a ram's horn. The dybbuk will leave the body through the pinky toe.

DYER, Gen. Reginald   DWH 1927   CRUELTY

In the Punjab city of Amritsar, on April 13, 1919, when British troops under General Dyer's command fired 1,605 rounds into an "illegally assembled" civilian crowd, 379 were killed, 1,200 wounded. At a subsequent inquiry, the unrepentant general explained that his objective had been "producing a sufficient moral effect, from a military point of view."

*Each place has its own advantages
—heaven for the climate, and hell for society.*
—MARK TWAIN

EARP, Wyatt DWH 1929
PANDERING

This hero of a hundred western movies and dime novels was actually just another corrupt cop. He was fired as the sheriff of Wichita for stealing the fines he collected, and in Tombstone he and fellow lawman Bat Masterson openly ran a whorehouse protection racket, so that they became known as "the Fighting Pimps." Earp ended his illustrious career in California, as a claim-jumping real estate salesman and movie studio hanger-on.

EBRONIUS DWH 8th century
USURPATION

He was a mayor of the palace of Neustria—that is, a mere civilian who nonetheless assumed political power—during the reign of one of France's late Merovingian kings. Saint and hagiographer (*The Golden Legend*) Jacobus de Voragine testifies that certain monks once encountered a boatful of demons rowing Ebronius to Hell.

EDWARD VIII

See DUKE OF WINDSOR.

EIBETH ZENUNIM

A demoness, one of SATAN's four Infernal brides.

EICHMANN, Adolf   DWH 1962   CRUELTY

The Nazi bureaucrat who meticulously supervised the transport of 3 million people to death camps was, before his trial in Israel, found by a panel of psychiatrists to be perfectly sane. He incarnated, in Hannah Arendt's brilliant phrase, "the banality of evil."

dishonorable because of overuse

ELIMI

A devil who cosigned the pact for the soul of the priest Father Grandier of Loudun, in 1634.

ELIZABETH I   DWH 1603   HERESY

Good Queen Bess had some admirable qualities. She was absurdly vain and bad tempered, but she was shrewd, brave, and sometimes witty. Unfortunately, by her 1559 Act of Supremacy, she declared herself to be the head of the Church, thus becoming a flagrant heretic; and by her Act of Uniformity that same year, she insisted that all her subjects become members of her heretical sect or suffer the considerable consequences, which included fines, torture, and beheading. Pius V, a patient pontiff, did not excommunicate her until 1570.

EMPUSA

A particularly foul female demon vampire.

EON, Chevalier d'   DWH 1810   EONISM

The sin—or syndrome, if you will—of eonism (aka cross-dressing) is named after this flamboyant French diplomat, secret agent, and drag queen. In 1755 King Louis XV sent him to infiltrate and spy on the Russian court. The chevalier opted to undertake his mission in women's attire and, for reasons of his own, continued to dress as a female even when posted to London. This naturally caused some scandal in British society—bets were placed on his true gender—and when the unamused king recalled Eon to Paris, he decreed that the chevalier had to continue to wear a dress in public in order to collect his pension.

EPHIALTES DWH 5th century B.C. TREASON

Dante makes the god Neptune's giant son Ephialtes a guardian of deepest Hell, where the great blasphemers are, because he had once piled mountains on top of one another in a doomed attempt to reach Heaven. In 480 B.C., a traitor by the same name betrayed the heroic Spartan forces who were defending Western civilization by holding the pass at Thermopylae against the army of King XERXES.

EPICURUS DWH 270 B.C.
ATHEISM

Although the specific vice of snobbish self-indulgence is known to us as epicureanism, in Dante's scheme, all materialists, those "who say the soul dies when the body dies," are classified as "epicureans" and condemned to suffer horribly in Hell's Sixth Circle, along with Epicurus himself. An Athenian teacher of philosophy, he had an open admissions policy—his classes, which he conducted in a garden, were attended by aristocrats, slaves, and women, even courtesans. He maintained that the cosmos, including human souls, is composed of whirling atoms, and that consequently there cannot be "life after death." Furthermore, this impious scoundrel held that we can acquire knowledge only through our senses, so that sensory pleasure (or at least the absence of pain) is the highest good.

EPP, Gen. Franz Xaver von
DWH 1947 CRUELTY

Founder of the SS, and altogether the sort of chap who gave Nazis a bad name.

Franz Ritter von Epp

ERESHKIGAL

Queen of the dead in the Sumerian Hell (which was called, if you must know, Ganzir).

ERINYES

As Dante passes through the Gates of Dis and enters the Sixth Circle and Lower Hell, he encounters these hideous hags, sometimes known as the Furies, or, euphemistically, the Kindly Ones. In classical mythology, they are the relentless avengers of crimes "against nature," as befits their origin—they were born of the blood spilled by the god Uranus, upon the occasion of his castration by his son Zeus.

ERIPHYLE

The wife of King AMPHIARAUS, Eriphyle nagged her husband into joining the ill-fated expedition against Thebes, having been bribed with a necklace. She in turn was slain by their son Alcmaeon, avenging his father's death.

ESCOBAR Y MENDOZA, Antonio   DWH 1669   HERESY

This Spanish Jesuit moral theologian first formulated the "end justifies the means" philosophy, which has resulted in centuries of well-founded distrust of his order. In themselves, Father Escobar reasoned, actions are amoral, the sole determinant of moral value being the *intent* of the agent.

ESSEX, Earl of   DWH 1601
TREASON

A profligate playboy, a self-aggrandizing and corrupt soldier, a flattering courtier and sometime favorite of Queen ELIZABETH I, Essex made a complete botch of his campaign to subdue Ireland, was recalled to England in disgrace, and there staged in the streets of London a pathetic and farcical rebellion against his queen, for which he was executed. In a 1939 film, he was played by—who else?— ERROL FLYNN (see opposite).

ESTERHAZY, Maj. Ferdinand
DWH 1923   TREASON

The behavior of many members of the blockheaded French military establishment and the bigoted Catholic intelligentsia throughout the "Dreyfus Affair" had Hell's welcoming committee working overtime. The Austrian-born (and phony Count) Major Esterhazy, whose evidence helped convict Dreyfus, was himself the spy who had sold military secrets to the Germans—for which treachery Dreyfus was sentenced to life imprisonment on Devil's Island.

Elizabeth I (see ELIZABETH I) *and Lord Essex*
(as portrayed by Bette Davis, who as far as we know is in heaven, and Errol Flynn; see ERROL FLYNN)

EURINOME　🦌

A devil known as the Prince of Death, according to authoritative demonologist Alex de Terreneuve du Thyme.

EURYDICE

Beloved wife of the poet-musician Orpheus, Eurydice is one of Hades' most celebrated occupants. After her death, so the story goes, her husband journeyed to Hades and with his music moved its stern lord, PLUTO, to tears and mercy. Orpheus was permitted to take Eurydice back with him, on the condition that he not look at her until they arrived in the land of the living. But, just at the gate of the Upper World, he looked back, and she rejoined the shades below.

EURYNOMOS　🦌

A hideous Greek "daemon" who dwells in Hades and there devours the flesh of the dead. His image is said to have once adorned the shrine to Apollo at Delphi.

EVADNE　DWH circa 1200 B.C.　SUICIDE

Notoriously devoted and faithful wife of the impious CAPANEUS, Evadne went too far when she threw herself on his funeral pyre and thereby perished.

EXAEL　🦌

Another of Enoch's fallen Watcher angels, Exael taught mortals the arts of mining, jewelry making, and perfumery, as well as "how to fabricate engines of war."

Fascilis descendus Averno:
noctes atque dies patet atri ianua Ditis;
sed revocare gradum superasque evadere ad auras,
hoc opus, hic labor est.
(The road down to Hell is an easy way:
the Devil's gates stand open night and day;
but to find your way back to the light of day,
that's work, the hardest work of all, they say.)
— VIRGIL, *Aeneid*

Fathers and teachers, I ask myself, "What is Hell?" I maintain that it is the
suffering of being unable to love.
— DOSTOYEVSKY, *The Brothers Karamazov*

Fear made her Devils, and weak Hope her Gods,
And Hell was built on Spite, and Heaven on Pride.
— ALEXANDER POPE, *An Essay on Man*

FAFNIR

An Aryan devil (his name means "gripper") who killed his father, assumed the shape of a dragon, and guarded the golden treasure of the Nibelungs until he was slain by the hero Sigurd. In his endless Ring Cycle, the composer RICHARD WAGNER called him Fafner.

FARFANICCHIO

An Italian imp whose name means "swaggerer."

FARFAREL (aka Farfarello)

"Coltsfoot," one of the playful Malebranche escort demons encountered by Dante (cantos 21 and 22).

FARINATA degli Uberti   DWH   1264   ATHEISM

This barrel-chested Ghibelline leader is burning in a fiery tomb with an open lid, condemned to Hell for the heresy of "epicureanism," Dante's term for materialism. Alive, he fled Florence for Siena and there oversaw the defeat of the Guelfs at the Battle of Montaperti. Although he convinced the victorious Ghibellines not to destroy Florence, the Guelfs of that city, Dante among them, despised Farinata and his descendants. In Hell, he and the poet briefly exchange insults about their respective families, and Farinata cruelly but accurately predicts Dante's exile (canto 10).

FAROUK I DWH 1965 GLUTTONY

When he was booted out of Egypt in 1952, ending a 142-year dynasty, Farouk was forced to leave behind his comic-book collection and some rare photographs of elephants copulating. He was corrupt and pro-fascist (he didn't declare war on Germany until 1945), and so disgusted the British that they sang an obscene ditty about him to the tune of the Egyptian royal anthem. After the war, he campaigned against both Israel and Britain, and offended even his own countrymen by taking a lavish honeymoon during the

penitential period of Ramadan. Most of his exile was spent gambling in Monaco, where he was renowned for being fat and getting fatter. He did venture to London in 1959; there his gluttony set the record for the biggest breakfast ever served at the Connaught Hotel. Farouk once poignantly observed, "One day there will be only five kings left: of hearts, spades, diamonds, clubs, and England."

FAUSTUS, Dr. Johannes DWH 1540(?) SORCERY

The man whose pact with the DEVIL is immortalized in works by Marlowe, Goethe, Berlioz, Gounod, and Mann was an actual person, B.A.,

Heidelberg, 1509. His career was first described in 1587 by Jonathan Spries, and the making of his biographies, called *Faustbuchs,* soon became a German cottage industry.

Georg (aka Johannes) Faustus was a student of magic, alchemy, and astrology who was once run out of town for "dastardly lewdness" toward young boys. The Protestant pastor of Basel, Jonathan Gast, was the first eyewitness to his diabolism. The pastor's suspicions, aroused by Faust's ability to serve out-of-season food, were confirmed when he saw the magician ride through the air on a beer barrel. Faust owned a genuine "Hell hound" and could take the shape of his horse. He made himself invisible in order to visit the Vatican, where—like the good Protestant he was—he slapped the pope across the face with a dead fish and stole his dinner.

On the stage, Faust's final moments on earth, as the Devil comes to claim his soul, make for effective tragedy. But according to folklore, the great necromancer was found dead in a pile of dung with his eyes stuck to the wall.

FENE

A Hungarian demon. A popular expression among the Magyars is "May Fene eat you!" (*Egye meg a Fene!*).

FERGUSUS   See CONALLUS.

FIDEAL

This evil water demon drags men underwater. His work is confined, primarily, to Scotland.

FILIPPO Argenti   DWH 1261   PRIDE

A Florentine knight who tries to attack his onetime political adversary, Dante, during his tour of Hell (canto 8). The poet, in a rare fit of pique, expresses his desire to see the sinner "dunked in the slop" of the river Styx. Filippo got his nickname because he was so rich and showy that he shod his horse with silver.

FILLMORE, Millard   DWH 1874   ILL COUNSEL

The thirteenth president of the United States and physical fitness buff is mistakenly written off as a mere bore—and a bland footnote to American history. But when Fillmore signed the Compromise of 1850, which included the Fugitive Slave Law, he dealt a definitive blow to the cause of abolition. Although he personally believed that slaves should be shipped back to Africa, most of his bile was reserved for Irish Catholics and immigrants, whom he blamed for his defeat in a gubernatorial election of 1844. As vice president, he moved into the White House after the death of his fellow Whig Zachary Taylor, but when he ran for president in 1856, it was as a candidate for the infamously bigoted Know-Nothing Party. In 1917, H. L. Mencken published the completely bogus account "The History of Bathing in the U.S.," in which he claimed the custom was unfashionable until Fillmore installed the first bathtub in the White House. Not only was the story believed at the time but to this day it is repeated in encyclopedias and Fillmore biographies—substantiating Mencken's assessment of the intelligence of the American public.

FISTOLO

A devil in Italian folklore.

FLAUROS

One of the spirits captured by King Solomon; he appears as a leopard and is both a liar and a killer. But, properly handled, Flauros will aid his conjurer against other demons and even destroy his enemies by fire.

FLEURETY

He is BEELZEBUB's lieutenant. One of the demons who controls Africa, Fleurety takes hallucinatory drugs, puts lust in men's eyes, and prefers to work at night. Extremely accommodating, Fleurety likes to perform any task demanded by a conjurer, hailstorms being his specialty.

FLIBBERTIGIBBET 🦇

A Shakespearean "foul fiend" who "begins at curfew and walks till the first cock; he gives the web and the pin, squinnies the eye and makes the harelip, mildews the white wheat and hurts the poor creature of earth" (*King Lear*, 3.4). As if that weren't enough, he is the spirit "of mopping and mowing, who . . . possesses chambermaids and waiting women" (*Lear*, 4.1).

FLOURON 🦇

In appearance either a winged man or a man riding a griffon, Flouron has power over the seas and may usefully be invoked by the drowning.

FLOYD, Charles Arthur (Pretty Boy)   DWH 1934   VIOLENCE

Midwestern prostitutes dubbed him Pretty Boy because he obsessively combed his greasy pompadour, *not* because he sometimes dressed as a woman to avoid the police. Floyd hated the moniker so much he killed two men just for calling him Pretty Boy—and his dying words were "I'm Charles Arthur Floyd!" His career as a Depression-era folk hero began when, on his way to prison for bank robbery, Floyd escaped by leaping through the window of a moving train. He soon became the Robin Hood of the Okies (in *The Grapes of Wrath*, Tom Joad defends Floyd: "Sometimes a fella's got to sift the law"). After a robbery, the outlaw would throw coins to his fans from his getaway car, and when he returned to his hometown to rob a bank, an audience gathered, his admirers cheering, "Give 'em Hell!" But he earned the enmity of J. EDGAR HOOVER, who called Floyd "a yellow rat who needed extermination." Finally trapped by FBI agents, Floyd asked, "Who the Hell tipped you off?" as one agent pumped bullets into him and another called Hoover with the good news. Floyd was a contemporary of that other Hoover nemesis JOHN DILLINGER, and all three are now united in Hell.

FLYNN, Errol   DWH 1959   LUST

The concept of statutory rape was unknown to Hollywood Lothario Errol Flynn until he was arrested for it. The underage "victims," who had, in fact, pursued the movie star, told all to the press, not omitting the swashbuckler's penchant for keeping his socks on during sex. Besides his legendary womanizing (the phrase "in like Flynn" sort of sums it up) and drinking, Flynn was always one step ahead of bill collectors. As he put it, "My problem lies in reconciling my gross habits with my net income." His home was equipped with one-way mirrors on the ceiling so Flynn could indulge his voyeurism. He described his guests as "pimps, bums, down-at-the-heels actors, gamblers, sightseers, process servers, phonies, queers—everything." But he was not without his romantic side: Smitten with costar Olivia de Havilland, he showed his devotion by leaving a dead snake in her panties (a trick he wouldn't attempt on leading lady Bette Davis, who, during the filming of *The Private Lives of Elizabeth and Essex,* made Flynn vomit and once knocked him out cold). In his later years, the former leading man was cast as a pathetic drunk on the lam from creditors, reflecting his real-life physical and financial deterioration. When he died at age fifty, the coroner said he had the body of an eighty-year-old. He is buried at Forest Lawn with six bottles of whiskey, placed in his coffin by his drinking buddies.

FOCACCIA degli Cancellieri   DWH 1293   TREACHERY
While his tailor-cousin Detto was making a doublet, Focaccia entered his shop and killed him, sparking the feud between the Black and White Guelfs of Pistola. Dante espies him up to his neck in ice (*fitta in gelatina*—placed in the cooler).

FOCALOR   🐒
Another of King Solomon's captive demons, Focalor has power over the sea, causes shipwrecks, and can appear as a sea monster; he can also destroy the exorcist during an exorcism.

FOMORE   🐒
The Irish demon who stole the magic harp of the gods.

FORCAS   🐒
A president of Hell, Forcas appears as a white-haired old man, a logician and rhetorician. He will make invisible all who conjure him; he can find lost objects; and he controls drugs and poisons.

FORD, Henry   DWH 1947   SOWING DISCORD
After he introduced assembly-line manufacturing and his affordable Model T auto (selling 16 million in ten years), this son of Irish immigrants' popularity was so great that he seriously considered running for president in 1923. He was a hero as well to ADOLF HITLER, who hung Ford's picture in his office as a tribute both to his industrial genius and to his prodigious anti-Semitism—Ford was a firm believer in and publisher (in his newspaper, the Dearborn *Independent*) of that infamous forgery *The Protocols of the Elders of Zion*—and he was the first American to win the Nazis' Supreme Order of the German Eagle. He also believed in both reincarnation and the power of the soybean, growing fifty varieties of the plant,

making it a staple of his every meal, and wearing clothes woven of that useful legume. Nor was his interest in horticulture confined to soybeans—years after his death, his marijuana crops were still growing wild.

FORD, Robert Newton   DWH 1892   MURDER

In 1882, the train robber Jesse James reluctantly added second-string gunmen Robert Ford and his brother Charlie to his outlaw gang. The sneaky brothers had been secretly deputized by Missouri Governor Thomas Crittenden, who offered them pardons and a $10,000 reward to bring in Jesse James dead or alive. So, in James's own home, while the unarmed Jesse was feather-dusting a picture of—accounts differ—either the racehorse Skyrocket or his hero, Stonewall Jackson—Robert Ford shot him three times in the back. While Ford tried to convince Jesse's wife, Zerelda (who, oddly, shared Jesse's mother's name), that it was just an accident, brother Charlie bolted out the back door to telegraph the news to the governor. And Jesse James became, in the words of Theodore Roosevelt, "America's Robin Hood." The Ford brothers went on the road with their show, "How I Killed Jesse James." They were booed and hissed off the stage, theater managers were forced to wear armored shirts, and the entire tour drove Robert Ford to drink. He opened a gambling casino and whorehouse in Colorado but was himself shot in the back by Edward O'Kelly, who became an instant hero and was sentenced to a mere two-year term for murdering "the dirty little coward who laid Jesse James in his grave."

FORNEUS   🐟

Once an angelic Throne, Forneus is now a marquis in Hell. He is said to take the material form of a sea monster and can be very useful to his conjurer, for he can "cause his enemies to love him."

FORTUNE, Dion (Violet Mary Firth)   DWH 1946   SORCERY

A devout Christian Scientist, in 1910 Fortune was a victim of a magical attack—her aura was torn and wasn't healed until 1919. This of course sapped her vitality and caused a nervous breakdown, but happily it resulted in her seminal work on the subject, *Psychic Self-defence*. She became a magician and witch, forming a splinter faction of the Order of the Golden Dawn, which provided her with a forum for her theories on the interrelationship between chakras and the endocrine system. The organization she founded, the Fraternity of the Inner Light, eventually replaced their magical practices with the Dianetic techniques of L. RON HUBBARD and merged into modern-day Scientology.

FRANCESCA da Rimini   DWH 1286   LUST

Dante meets Francesca and her lover among the windblown souls of the lustful and faints with pity over her (somewhat self-serving) version of their story: When a political marriage was arranged between this beautiful girl and the ugly Gianciotto da Verruchio, the groom sent his handsome brother Paolo to be his proxy in the prenuptial ceremonies, and it wasn't until her wedding night, when she looked upon her deformed husband, that Francesca realized a switch had been made. But Francesca and Paolo had already fallen in love, and—aroused, she explains to the poet, by a book recounting the romantic story of LANCELOT and Guinevere—"we read no more that day." Naturally, when Gianciotto discovered the affair, he killed each of them with one sword thrust and sent their souls swirling together into Hell. In this most famous passage from the *Inferno* (the last half of canto 5), Dante, with more than usual brilliance, has it both ways—condemning the poetic "courtly love" tradition while composing a perfect example of it.

The sordid facts of the case, incidentally, are that at the time of their murder, Paolo was a married man with two children and Francesca had a nine-year-old daughter.

FRANCO, Francisco   DWH 1975   TYRANNY

Aided by Nazi bombers, Moorish mercenaries, and the worldwide prayers of Catholics, Franco's Falangist forces defeated the merely elected Republicans in the Spanish Civil War, whereupon Franco graciously appointed himself dictator for life. His beloved Spain had the distinction of being the only fascist regime to survive World War II. During the war itself, Franco remained officially neutral—which irritated his onetime benefactor and ally, ADOLF HITLER. The Führer called Franco "Little Sausage" and griped he would "prefer to have three teeth pulled out" than meet again with the general. (The general, ever the military snob, dismissed Hitler as a "mere corporal.") In the 1950s, Franco remolded his fascist image into an anti-Communist one, thereby gaining the approval of (and plenty of financial aid from) the United States. Perhaps because Spain's artists (e.g., Pablo Picasso and Pablo Casals) despised him, the general developed his own creative side. He wrote an autobiographical screenplay, which he had produced, and personally cast a handsome actor to play himself. He watched the movie over and over, always in tears. He captured the world's attention with his long and lingering death, the arm (purloined) of St. Teresa of Avila by his side. During his protracted deathbed scene, his aide announced that a General Garcia had come to say good-bye. Franco innocently asked, "Why, is Garcia going on a trip?" He finally died (and went to Hell) on November 20, 1975—of Parkinson's disease, myocardial arrest, stomach ulcers with massive hemorrhaging, peritonitis, acute renal failure, thrombophlebitis, bronchial pneumonia, endotoxic shock, and irremediable heart failure.

FRANK, Jacob (né Leibowicz)   DWH 1791   HERESY

"The worst rogue in Jewish history," in the words of Bernard Bamberger (*The Story of Judaism*), Frank first claimed to be a follower of SABBATAI ZEVI but soon proclaimed himself the Messiah. The mystic religious rites of his Polish followers—who styled themselves Zoharists—consisted mainly of sexual orgies, but Frank was a militant Zionist. "The Resurrection," he proclaimed, "will be by the sword." Banned by the Jewish authorities in Warsaw, Frank sought the protection of the Catholics, on whose behalf he publicly debated members of the rabbinate and then submitted himself and his entire sect to baptism. King Augustus was his godfather. But when our hero announced himself to be the fourth Person of the Blessed Trinity, he ran afoul of the Inquisition and was imprisoned. The old reprobate ended his days in Vienna, having lived in splendor there as a court favorite of the dour and prudish empress Maria Theresa.

FREDERICK II ("the Great")   DWH 1786   TYRANNY

To the disgust of his gouty bully of a father, the king of Prussia, the youthful Frederick showed artistic leanings—his affectations included writing bad poetry, refusing to bathe, making coffee with champagne, and applying the occasional dollop of rouge. However, after the old man imprisoned Frederick in a fortress and had his best friend (and/or lover) beheaded outside the window, the young prince emerged with his "heart of brass." He became king in 1740, and the troops under his skillful command soon added one-third of Poland, as well as all West Prussia and Silesia, to his domain. It is interesting to ask, to what extent was their success due to the laxatives and enemas Frederick forced upon his officers? And what has that to do with Prussian discipline? An exemplary anecdote: During the Silesian campaign, the king discovered one of his officers writing a letter to his wife after curfew and ordered him to add the postscript "Tomorrow I shall perish on the scaffold." He did, indeed, have the man executed the following day.

Frederick is called an enlightened despot not because of his attitude toward serfs and Jews—"useless to the state," he opined—but because of his gushy sucking-up to French intellectuals such as VOLTAIRE. That particular liaison ended badly, however, when the poet dismayed Frederick by insulting his poetry and disgusted him by drinking too much chocolate. A teenage bout with syphilis had left him impotent and unable to consummate his marriage—which was fine by Frederick, since he despised his wife. At his request, he was buried with his pet dogs.

FREDERICK II, Holy Roman Emperor   DWH 1250   BLASPHEMY

King of Germany, Holy Roman emperor, and "Wonder of the World," Frederick II believed that there is no life after death—until he found himself in the circle of the heretics in Dante's Hell. Although officially excommunicated (by Pope Gregory IX), he joined the successful Sixth Crusade and at its climax modestly crowned himself king of Jerusalem. This act gave rise to rumors (which Frederick never denied) that he was the new Messiah, the Second Coming of Christ. For centuries after his death, German nationalist-religious wackos awaited and/or announced his glorious return to lead the Fatherland.

Dante (canto 23) refers to "the capes Frederick used"—a method of torture favored by the emperor whereby his enemies were wrapped in cloaks of lead—which were then melted to their bodies.

FRIENDS of St. Christina the Astonishing

After her *first* death, St. Christina's soul traveled to Hell and Purgatory; she saw friends in both places. Horrified, the saint returned to earth during her funeral mass, flew out of her coffin, and perched in the church rafters. She decided to stay on earth to liberate those in Purgatory but was unable, of course, to help those already in Hell.

FRIMOST   🦇

A minor but quite particular demon, Frimost can only be invoked on Tuesday nights, between nine and ten o'clock. When he appears, you must give him a white pebble.

FUMAROTH   🦇

In 1026, a woman in childbirth accidentally swallowed a demon by this name. The fiend was successfully exorcised by St. Bononio.

FURCAS   🦇

A demon and teacher of war, Furcas appears as an old man riding a horse and carrying a spear.

FURFUR   🦇

His specialties are carnal love, thunder, lightning, and winds. He occasionally appears as a deer with wings in a fiery lake. He never tells the truth, unless he's standing inside a triangle.

God had allowed him to see the Hell reserved for his sins: stinking, bestial, malignant, a Hell of lecherous goatish fiends. For him! For him!
—JAMES JOYCE, *A Portrait of the Artist as a Young Man*

GAAP

Bat-winged king of southern Hell, Gaap commands sixty-six demonic legions.

GADRIEL

Not SATAN but Gadriel (at least according to the Book of Enoch) was the Archangel turned devil who first seduced our mother Eve, thereby cuckolding our father Adam and plunging us all into a state of Original Sin.

GALEHOT   DWH 5th century   PANDERING

The adulteress FRANCESCA DA RIMINI cleverly calls the romantic book that led to her downfall "a Galehot"—for the love story therein was of Sir LANCELOT and Guinevere, queen of Camelot, whose sinful affair was facilitated by one Sir Gallehault, according to *Lancelot du Lac,* a medieval French version of the tale. *Galeoto* duly became an Italian (and Spanish) synonym for *pimp.* Curiously, Gallehault is a variant of Galahad, the name, in English, of the purest and noblest of King Arthur's knights—and Lancelot's son to boot.

GANELON   DWH circa 780   TREASON

Villain of the French national epic, *The Song of Roland,* Ganelon was count of Mayence and a knight of King Charlemagne, but, out of jealousy, he betrayed his rival Roland to the Moorish enemy. Dante, in canto 31, locates him in the deepest pit of Hell, and Chaucer (in the "Nun's Priest's Tale") compares him with the infamous traitors JUDAS and SINON.

GARNIER, Gilles   DWH 1574   LYCANTHROPY

A self-confessed werewolf, Garnier was captured and burned alive at

Dôle, France. A scavenger and beggar, he claimed to have killed many local children and then eaten their flesh—in one case, compounding his sin by doing so on a Friday.

GENGHIS KHAN   DWH 1227   CRUELTY

His army was described by the thirteenth-century historian Matthew Paris as "a detestable nation of Satan that poured out like devils from Tartrus so that they are rightfully called Tartars." His given name was Temüjin; his assumed title means "Lord of the Earth," "Ocean-Great King," or "Perfect Warrior"—you get the idea.

Genghis Khan was a brilliant if brutal general and creator of the Mongol Empire, which extended from Persia to Korea. His cavalry pillaged parts of Russia and India as well. Without discrimination, they massacred heathens, Christians, and Muslims. (In the city of Nishapur, not an infant, dog, or cat was spared—the only monument left standing when the Mongols departed was a pyramid of human skulls.) His tomb's location is unknown—those in the funeral cortege were put to death to make sure of that. But it is said his epitaph reads: "If I were still alive, people would not be glad."

GERYON   🦁

A three-headed Spanish cowboy with a two-headed guard dog, Geryon was slain by the hero Hercules. In Hell, he guards the usurers and other frauds—and is himself defrauded, by Virgil, into giving the visitors a swift and scary piggyback ride downstairs to the Eighth Circle.

GESTAS   DWH 33   THEFT

Christ was crucified between two thieves, to one of whom, the Good Thief, aka St. Dismas, He promised Paradise. We must assume that the Bad Thief, known in legend by the name of Gestas, went elsewhere.

GIACOMO da Sant Andrea   DWH circa 1300   PROFLIGACY

His fabulously rich mother married six times. He was a dilettante and playboy, and a member of the notorious Spendthrifts' Club of Padua. Giacomo once burned down several houses on his estate just for the fun of it, and when troubled by insomnia, he ordered his retainers to rip up silk tapestries, since the sound soothed him. In Hell, he is ripped apart by wild dogs.

GIANNI dei Soldanier   DWH circa 1300   TREASON

An influential Guelf of Florence who changed parties, joining the victorious Ghibellines and thereby earning Dante's (and, apparently, God's) everlasting anger.

GIANNI Schicci

DWH circa 1300   **FRAUD**

He is one of the few "insane" damned souls in the *Inferno*—Dante calls him "rabid" (*rabbioso,* canto 30, line 33). Naked and snapping his jaws, Gianni Schicci stampedes through the tenth level of deep Hell, behaving like a wild hog. In life, he was a gifted mimic who helped Simone Donati, the nephew of BUOSO, to inherit his uncle's money by impersonating the already-dead old man and dictating a new will to his lawyer.

GIRTY, Simon   DWH 1818   TREASON

"The Great Renegade" of American folklore, Girty deserted the Congressional Army to lead British and Indian raids. Cruelty was his most outstanding characteristic. He served on "the jury from Hell" in Stephen Vincent Benét's tale of the American Faust, "The Devil and Daniel Webster."

GOEBBELS, Joseph   DWH 1945   LYING

Raised a devout Catholic (with an overlarge head and clubfoot), Goebbels aspired to the priesthood—or, failing that, authorship—but settled for being HITLER's worshipper, propagandist, speechwriter, and spin doctor. As the Third Reich collapsed, he poisoned himself, his wife, and all five towheaded kids—Helga, Helmuth, Hedda, Hilda, and Holde.

GOERING, Hermann   DWH 1946   SUICIDE

In addition to being a bloated, vain, avaricious, duplicitous, bombastic, drug-addicted, murderous, sycophantic drag queen, HITLER's pet and chosen successor took poison in his Nuremberg prison cell the night his execution was ordered, thus escaping earthly justice but not—we trust —divine retribution.

GOLAB

Identified, in the mystic Hebrew Cabala, as one of the unholy Sefiroth, "the spirit of wrath and sedition."

GOMITA, Fra DWH 1296 BRIBERY

A Sardinian friar, Gomita was in the employ of Nino Visconti, governor of Pisa. The trusting Nino (whom Dante will later meet in Purgatory) long turned a deaf ear to charges of corruption against his chancellor, until it was proven that the good friar had accepted a bribe to allow some criminals to escape from prison. Gomita was hanged.

GOMORY

A popular medieval demon who allegedly procures the love of women.

GONG GONG

A Chinese demon in the form of a black dragon. An adversary of God, it was Gong Gong who let loose the great flood. Smelly springs and swamps are the excretions of his pet snake, Xiang Yao.

GORDAN

Cited, along with Ingordan and Ingrodin, as among the *genus demonorium* in the medieval manuscript known as the *Carmina Burana*.

GOWDIE, Isobel DWH 1670(?) SORCERY

In 1662, this wacky old dame voluntarily confessed to being a witch, and the details of her testimony—broomstick flights, thirteen-member covens, black cat familiars, and so on—formed our ongoing notions about witchcraft.

GRAFFIACANE

A member of the feckless squad of devils Dante meets in canto 21; his name means "lousy"—literally, "scratchdog," and might very well be a pun on Raffacini, the name of one of the priors of Dante's Florence.

GRAPPIN

This evil spirit tortured the saintly Curé D'ars for thirty years, taking time out for the occasional game of chess with his host. He would throw chairs around the curé's room and set fire to his bed, and he liked to terrorize visitors, especially visiting priests. At night, he would run up and down the stairs and rearrange the crockery.

GRESSIL

One of the demons who possessed Sister Madeleine at Louviers, Gressil confessed upon exorcism to being a former angel in the order of Thrones. He now specializes in temptations against purity—hence his Heavenly adversary is the most chaste St. Bernard.

GRIFFOLINO DWH circa 1270 FRAUD

Albero da Siena was the remarkably stupid but wealthy son of that city's bishop; Griffolino was an alchemist and all-round con man from Arezzo. For a substantial sum, the latter promised to teach the former how to fly. Griffolino was burnt at the stake after the disappointed (and bruised) Albero denounced him to his father as a magician. Dante, in canto 29, discovers him picking his scabs in Hell.

GRIMOALD

The demonic pet or "familiar" belonging to OLIVER CROMWELL.

GUERRA, Guido DWH 1272 SODOMY

Like another Guido (TEGGHIAIO ALDOBRANDI) and JACOPO RUSTICUCCI, Guerra was a nobly born, wise, and brave warrior on the side of the Guelfs of Florence. Unfortunately for his soul, he was also (like them) a homosexual. It grieves Dante in canto 16 to see the three of them rolling around like hoops across the burning sands in the Circle of Violence.

GUGLAND

A minor demon. You may conjure Gugland on any Saturday between 11:00 P.M. and midnight, and, if you feed him a piece of toast, he will gladly answer any question.

GUI XIAN

The souls of Chinese Buddhist suicides who cannot be reincarnated, and are therefore doomed to wander the earth as evil spirits.

GUILLEME

A demon who takes the form of a pale young man or a rooster. In the mid–fifteenth century, Guilleme was conjured by Bardonneche, the wife of Lorent Moti of Chaumont, for the purpose of cooling her husband's excessive sexual appetites.

Heaven is the work of the best and kindest men and women. Hell is the work of prigs, pedants, and professional truth-tellers.
——SAMUEL BUTLER, *Notebooks*

He saw a Lawyer killing a Viper
On a dunghill by his own stable;
And the Devil smiled, for it put him in mind
Of Cain and his brother, Abel.
——SAMUEL TAYLOR COLERIDGE, "The Devil's Thoughts"

HAATAN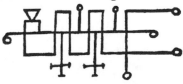
Demon of the sixth hour, who conceals treasures. His biography was written by Apollonius of Tyana.

HABONDIA
Professional witch-hunter PIERRE DE LANCRE reported that this is the name of the queen of both the HARPIES and the souls of the wicked.

HABORYM
Demon with three heads: a cat head reminiscent of the Egyptian pagan goddess Bastet on the left, a human head in the center, and a viper's head on the right. His name is a Hebrew synonym for SATAN. He is believed to be in charge of incendiarism.

HADES
The Greek name for the lord of the dead, as well as for his dark realm; the Romans (and Dante) called him either PLUTO or DIS.

HAEL
A demon who gives instruction in the art of letter writing.

HAGENTI
Demon-alchemist who assumes the form of a bull with the wings of a

griffin, oddly similar to St. Luke. Hagenti can turn metals into gold and, perversely, wine into water.

HAGITH

The demon commonly invoked to turn copper into gold.

HAHAB, HALACHO, and HAHABI

Demons specializing in fear, sympathy, and "the royal tables."

HAIG, Field Marshal Douglas   DWH 1928

CRUELTY

Scion of the celebrated Scots distilling clan, Haig distinguished himself at Oxford by his unusual stupidity and polo-playing skills. These, and family influence, qualified him for a military career. Late in 1915, he became commander of the British Expeditionary Force in France. Thanks to his absurd "strategy of attrition," his troops suffered 40,000 casualties on July 2, the first day of the Battle of the Somme—a rate Haig did not "consider severe." By year's end, 1,200,000 soldiers were dead on both sides of that field, and not an inch of ground gained. Haig was naturally promoted to field marshal and promptly oversaw the slaughter of 240,000 British and Allied soldiers in the mud at Ypres. At war's end, he was awarded £1 million by Parliament and made an earl. He died in bed and proceeded directly to Hell.

HAJIM Bey   DWH 19??   SODOMY

On the night of November 20, 1917, in the Turkish-occupied Syrian city of Deraa, Lawrence of Arabia was taken prisoner and "pawed all over" by the perverted military governor, then, by his orders, flogged and buggered—against (more or less) his will. "The citadel of my integrity had been irrevocably lost," wrote Lawrence of the incident, in his *Seven Pillars of Wisdom*—in which he decently cloaked the identity of the unnatural monster as "Nahi Bey."

HAKELDAMA

A demon who gets his name from the place where JUDAS was buried, Aceldama, the Field of Blood. In art, a large snake is seen emerging from his groin.

HAKIM, bi-Amrih al   DWH 1021   HERESY

The sixth ruler of the Egyptian Fatimid (Shi'ite) dynasty was known, with good reason, as the Mad Caliph. He was a somewhat arbitrary ruler—banning and/or mandating various foods and vegetables, and ordering all the dogs in Cairo killed. (Their barking bothered him.) But his constant persecution of Jews, Christians, and Sunni Muslims inspired visiting Isma'ili mullahs to proclaim him divine. Hakim agreed with their assessment—as, to this day, do the Druze.

HALPAS

A demon who assumes the form of a dove or a stork and speaks in a gravelly voice. Halpas keeps busy destroying towns by fire and water, visiting the wicked, and sending men to war.

HAMALIEL and HANAEL

Enochian demons who rule over the astrological signs of Virgo and Capricorn.

HAMAN

To this day, on the holy feast of Purim, Jews celebrate the execution on the gallows of this Persian villain—and of his ten sons—as well as the killing by the sword of "seventy-five thousand" (Esther 9:16) other anti-Semites.

HAN/HAM

A Norwegian storm demon who is in the shape of an eagle with black wings.

HARDING, Warren G.   DWH 1923   SLOTH

When Harding's future father-in-law heard of his engagement to his battle-ax daughter Flossie, he let loose with "That goddamned nigger!" giving credence to the persistent rumor that Harding was part black. Harding was, without doubt, handsome, with a flair for fashion and a taste for women, poker, and liquor. In the middle of Prohibition, the twenty-ninth president served a variety of wines and liquors in the White House and liked to ask his special guests up to his bedroom for a quick snort. Pushed into politics by Flossie, he was eventually nominated in the first proverbial "smoke-filled room." He then oversaw the most corrupt administration until that of

RICHARD NIXON. While still in the U.S. Senate, he became enamored of Nan Britton (who was twelve at the time), and their subsequent affair produced a daughter, who had been conceived on the couch in his Senate office. Nan followed Warren to the White House, where the lovers found a convenient trysting place, a five-foot-square closet outside the Cabinet Room.

Harding's only endearing quality was his honesty about himself. He once said, "I am not fit for this office and never should have been here." Speculation that Flossie poisoned him to spare him the embarrassment of an impeachment or in revenge for his affairs is probably incorrect.

HARISTUM
A demon who gives his followers the power to walk unharmed through fire.

HAROTH
Haroth is mentioned in the Quran, 2.102, as an angel sent to teach mankind the art of government. In Persian lore, it is said he fell in love with a mortal woman and revealed to her the secret name of God, for which sin he was buried head down in a pit near Babylon.

HARPIES

Winged bird women with two breasts, claws of steel, and bad breath, who were originally wind demons and/or vultures. Their name means "Snatchers." What food they don't snatch they make inedible by breathing on it. And they ruined a feast of AENEAS by targeting their bird droppings on the food, driving the hero and his men to near starvation. In the *Inferno* (canto 13), they shriek among the trees that cage the souls of the suicides and feed on the branches, causing them pain.

HARRIS, Frank   DWH 1931   LYING
Of this vulgar, American-born social climber, Oscar Wilde said, "Frank has been invited to every great house in England. Once." Harris's revenge was to publish a name-dropping, malicious—and posthumous—biography of Wilde. Harris's other claim to literary fame is his three-volume self-serving, cock-and-bull (that is, both pornographic and false) autobiography, *My Life and Loves.*

HARRISON, Rex   DWH 1990   VANITY
It was when actress Carole Landis committed suicide over this married (one-eyed) star that he gained the nickname Sexy Rexy. Michael Rogers, a

bartender at the Astor Bar, once reported that Rex left him a tip of four pennies. Richard Burton complained, "Rex Harrison used to joke that he was sometimes mistaken for Chinese because of his eyes, but it was always a Mandarin or some high-caste Chinese, he'd insist, as though it mattered."

HATFIELD, Anderson ("Devil Anse") DWH 1921 VIOLENCE

During the 1880s, Devil Anse was the leader of the aggressor Hatfield clan in the Hatfield-McCoy family feud, which began over rights to a razorback hog. The years of ambushes and shoot-outs in the West Virginia–Kentucky area were documented in bloody detail by the nation's tabloids and did much to gain hillbillies their ongoing reputation.

HATHORNE, Judge John DWH 1717 CRUELTY

This distinguished ancestor of author Nathaniel Hawthorne was one of three judges at Salem witchcraft trials in 1692. A proto-McCarthy, he was especially eager to have the suspects implicate one another and name their accomplices.

HATIPHAS and HAVEN

Demons specializing in, respectively, attire and dignity.

HATTO, Bishop DWH circa 913 CRUELTY

Tenth-century bishop of Mainz and counselor of Otto the Great, in a time of famine Hatto assembled the poor of the district in a barn, locked the doors, and burned it down, observing of its occupants, "They are like mice, only good at devouring corn." Shortly thereafter, he was attacked by an army of mice. He fled to a tower on the Rhine near Bingen, where the avenging rodents devoured him. The "Mouse Tower" remains a tourist attraction.

HAW-HAW, Lord (William Joyce) DWH 1946 TREASON

A fascist who hated Jews and jazz, Joyce formed the National Socialist League in England. His opening statement hailed the Nazis' "gallant achievement against International Jewish finance." He soon defected and was hired by German radio to make taunting broadcasts to England that began with his stentorian "Germany calling." He criticized the Anglo-French alliance, saying, "England will fight to the last Frenchman," and called Winston Churchill "the first honorary Jew in the world." Known as Lord Haw-Haw because the British public believed he was an embittered, stuffy aristocrat, Joyce became the second most hated man in England. In fact, the public hatred of him seemed to be directed as much at the British upper classes as at an anonymous traitor in Germany.

HAYMES, Dick   DWH 1980
SLOTH

Pig-faced crooner of the 1940s whose big hit was ironically "Little White Lies" and known by *le tout Hollywood* as Mr. Evil. The fourth husband of Rita Hayworth, Haymes ruthlessly exploited the star. He was a wife beater, drunkard, gambler, and lousy singer who fell out of favor with the American public when it was revealed he had dodged the draft during World War II, claiming citizenship of Argentina, a neutral country. A notorious deadbeat, Haymes caused Hayworth to lose her house, furniture, and, very nearly, custody of her children. He finally settled in Europe with his seventh wife, doing a lounge act, a fitting warm-up to Hell.

HEARST, William Randolph   DWH 1951   TYRANNY

He spent $7 million during the Depression to promote the career of his girlfriend, Marion Davies, requiring the newspapers in his chain to mention her name daily and banning the mention of any star, producer, or director who disrespected her. Most of Hollywood believed that he shot and killed director Thomas Ince in a jealous fit, but the incident was covered up, and eyewitness LOUELLA PARSONS became Hearst's Hollywood correspondent soon afterward. He bought one-fourth of the world's art to decorate his estate, San Simeon, where, although he and Davies lived in sin, the puritanical Hearst forbade their unmarried guests to sleep together. When visiting DOROTHY PARKER broke this rule, her host demanded she leave—which she did, but not before inscribing the following poem in the guest book:

> *Upon my honor*
> *I saw a madonna*
> *Standing in the niche*
> *Above the door*
> *Of a famous whore*
> *Of a prominent son of a bitch.*

HECATE

Early Christian tradition turned pagan gods and goddesses into either saints or demons. Accordingly, Hecate, a moon goddess of antiquity, a nocturnal "goddess of the crossroads" to the Greeks, became demonized by the Church because it was believed she was the patroness of the hated midwives. They identified her with the queen of the Underworld, PERSEPHONE, as well as with the murderous MEDEA, and appointed her queen of the witches. As such, Hecate has three heads and snakes in her hair; she dines on excrement. She roams the earth with her red-eyed Hell hounds, spying on humans and causing nightmares in children and dogs. Those seeking to appease her leave chicken hearts, honey cakes, and female black lambs outside their doors. Sorcerers, on the other hand, eat dog meat to conjure her up—during her month, November.

HECUBA   DWH **circa 1190 B.C.**   ANGER

She was the wife of Priam, king of Troy, who avenged the death of one of her sons by killing the children of Polymnestor. After her death, Hecuba was turned into a fiery-eyed dog.

HEDAMMU   🐕

Voracious snake demon who lives in the sea.

HEGEL   🐕

In the *Book of Magic,* Hegel is a demon who masters farming and agriculture with a working knowledge of metals.

HEIGLOT   🐕

Demon in charge of snowstorms.

HEL   🐕

The translators of the Bible into English rendered the Hebrew word *Sheol* as "Hades" and *Gehenna* as "Tartarus" or "Hell." The Anglo-Saxon verb *helan* signifies "to cover" or "to hide," and in Teutonic mythology Hel was the name given to the unprepossessing goddess-queen of Niflheim, the cold, dark, nine-level abode of the dead. In Norse myth, heroes (those who died in battle) were transported to feast with the gods in Valhalla— while everybody else went to Hel.

HELEL   🐕

In the Book of Enoch, Helel is the name of the leader of the giants called Nephillim, who were begotten by angels ("the sons of God" as they are called in Genesis), upon the daughters of CAIN.

HELEN   DWH **circa 50**   SORCERY

She was the girlfriend of the impious magician SIMON MAGUS and thought by the early Christians to be either a devil or a prostitute, despite her claim to be the reincarnation of HELEN OF TROY. Incidentally, in the movie *The Silver Chalice,* she was played by Virginia Mayo, wearing her lipstick over the lip line.

HELEN of Troy   DWH 13th century B.C.   LUST

She was not really "of Troy" but born in Sparta, the daughter of Leda and a swan—that is, the adulterous god Zeus in the form of a swan. Helen was acknowledged to be the most beautiful woman in the world, and her hand was sought by many, but she married Menelaus, Sparta's king. The Trojan War ensued when Helen was either kidnapped or wooed and won by a handsome visitor from Troy, Prince PARIS. Through the character of DR. FAUSTUS, the Elizabethan dramatist Christopher Marlowe called Helen's "the face that launched a thousand ships." Nor was her beauty confined to her physiognomy—she was captured after the fall of Troy, and the jealous Menelaus intended to kill her, but when she stripped to the waist, he changed his mind.

In the afterlife, according to Greek legend, fair Helen's ghost married that of the brave ACHILLES, but Dante (no romantic he) places her among the lustful sinners in the Second Circle of Hell.

HELIOGABALUS   DWH 222   LUST

Possibly the most sexually perverse of the Roman emperors—no small claim to infamy—this Syrian bastard was placed on the throne by rebellious eastern troops. He was a priest of the demon god BAAL and caused temples to this pagan idol to be erected in Rome. He was also a flagrant sodomite and transvestite. But he took three wives, one of them a vestal virgin. Fed up with such high jinks, his own Praetorian Guards finally murdered him (and his equally dreadful mother, Julia).

HENLEIN, Konrad   DWH 1945   TREASON

Head of the German Gymnastic Movement in Czechoslovakia, Henlein agitated throughout the 1930s for the "autonomy" of the Sudetenland, i.e., its cession to Nazi Germany; after the Munich sellout, Hitler appointed him governor of the territory. At the end of World War II, this Czech QUISLING committed suicide in Allied custody.

HENRI III   DWH 1589   VIOLENCE

"The Last Valois," Henri III was the third son of CATHERINE DE MEDICI and a transvestite who favored sweeping skirts, platform shoes, corsets, and makeup. He traveled everywhere with his parading "mignons." Henri was also an alchemist and sorcerer who gave private magic lessons at the Louvre and once procured a prostitute for his favorite devil. After NOSTRADAMUS predicted his death, Henri, strangely skittish for a mass murderer, would faint at the sight of a cat. He met an ignominious end, stabbed and killed by the monk Jacques Clément when he was sitting in the lavatory. The monk himself was soon killed by the king's soldiers, but his corpse stood trial anyhow.

HENRY VIII   DWH 1547   HERESY

Before he got English Protestantism in full swing, Henry attended three masses a day and wrote an essay condemning divorce. At the end of his life, he made a last-minute, unsuccessful stab at salvation by ordering a string of masses said for his soul and declared himself in his will exculpated from all his executions. His last words were a futile "Monks! Monks! Monks!" His debauchery ruined his good looks, so that, by the time he was forty, he weighed in at 400 pounds, suffered from putrefying leg sores, and had to be carried around in a sedan chair. Henry did manage to stay creative: He wrote a mass, the song "Greensleeves," and this riddle: What is it, that being born without life, head, lip, or eye, yet doth go roaring throughout the world till it die? (Answer: A fart.)

During his syphilitic reign, England's beloved Bluff King Hal had 72,000 people executed, invented a new form of torture called pressing, legalized the killing of Gypsies, and introduced death by boiling. Of his six wives, he executed two and treated himself to the most famous divorce in history, being the first husband to say "The Devil made me do it"—he claimed Anne Boleyn had tricked him into marriage by witchcraft. After his death at age fifty-six, his corpse was placed in a lead coffin, which burst open two weeks later; according to a witness, "All the pavement of the church was covered with the fat and the corrupt and putrefied blood foully imbued."

HERAMAEL

A demon who teaches the art of medicine and has comprehensive knowledge of diseases and their cures. Heramael is an expert horticulturist, knowing all plants and their curative powers.

HERENSUGUE

A seven-headed Basque demon who assumes the form of a flying snake.

HEROD Antipas DWH 39 LUST

Son of HEROD THE GREAT, he fell in love with his brother's wife, HERO-
DIAS, on a trip to Rome and proposed. She accepted, but the happy adul-
terers earned the condemnation of John the Baptist. After watching his
stepdaughter/niece SALOME perform an erotic dance, Herod quickly
agreed to give her the head of John the Baptist on a platter. Years later,
when he heard of Jesus and his popularity with the mob, the paranoid king
immediately assumed it was the Baptist come back to life. (Jesus, in turn,
called Herod "that old fox.") Following in the Herodian father-son tradition of toadying to the Romans, Herod also executed the father and sons
of JUDAS ISCARIOT for Zionist rabble-rousing. He was deposed and banished
by CALIGULA and, oddly, eaten by worms *before* he died.

HEROD "the Great" DWH 4 B.C. CRUELTY

When wizards told him that a rival king would be born in Bethlehem,
Herod had all male children under the age of two murdered. He wasn't so
kind to his own family either: He killed three sons, one wife, two brothers-
in-law, and a mother-in-law. Even though Herod kept kosher, he secretly
practiced polytheism, overtaxed the Jews, and burned Jewish insurrection-
ists alive. *And* most of his ten wives were not Jewish. He did restore the
Temple of Jerusalem to grandiose proportions, but when Herod was in his
prolonged death throes, rabbis happily removed his busts from the temple
along with the Roman eagle. Dying, he suffered from "a putrescent stomach, maggots in his private parts, foul breath, and a watery flow from the

bowels," symptoms formerly thought to be of
venereal disease but actually caused by arte-
riosclerosis. In medieval mystery plays, Herod
was the archvillain and the best part—the actor
playing him got to rave and rant and generally
steal the show. Thus Hamlet, in giving directions to the actors, asked them not to "out-
Herod Herod," that is, ham it up. And,
when designing the Nazi flag, Anton Drexler
chose red to compete with the flaming Communist banner, explaining, "We wanted something red enough to out-Herod Herod."

HERODIAS DWH 47 LUST

Wife of HEROD ANTIPAS, so wicked she was
reported to be a demon—and by the tenth century she was confused with Hell goddess

HECATE. In 936, a minor devil-worshipping cult arose around Herodias, claiming that she ruled one-third of the world. This upset the bishop of Verona, who promptly outlawed the sect.

HEYD

Norwegian sea demon who takes the form of a white bear.

HEYDRICH, Reinhard   DWH 1942   CRUELTY

The sole Nazi leader to resemble the "Blond Beast" of their fantasies, Heydrich rose in the ranks of the SS to become chief and is generally credited with initiating the "Final Solution to the Jewish Problem." While in pursuit of same, he was machine-gunned by Czech freedom fighters.

HICKOK, "Wild Bill"   DWH 1876   VIOLENCE

Before he was "Wild" Bill, he was "Duckbill," because of the convergence of his long nose and protruding lower lip. As sheriff, he took protection money from gamblers and pimps, perfumed his hair, and dressed in vulgar stage-western wear. He first learned he was a hero when he read a phony article about himself and his exploits in *Harper's Monthly Magazine.* He did kill seven men (including his own deputy), but his legendary stand against the McCanles gang actually consisted of Bill shooting the lone, unarmed Dave McCanles through a gingham curtain while the victim's son looked on. Western lore has made much of his brief fling with cowgirl-amazon-whore Calamity Jane (who may have given Wild Bill a dose of syphilis) and of the poker hand he was holding when he was shot in the back—a pair of black aces and a pair of black eights—the "dead man's hand." His tombstone notes his reunion with a Hell mate: "CUSTER was lonely without him."

HIEPACTH

A useful demon who can, in an instant, materialize a distant person.

HIMMLER, Heinrich   DWH 1945   CRUELTY

Since even HITLER didn't like him, the chicken farmer turned SS chief was forced to have conversations with a picture of the Führer that hung in his office. He did amuse himself by forming a secret cult around GENGHIS KHAN, which Mongol he believed to be a member of a lost tribe of Teutons. He further claimed through his cosmic ice theory that blond, blue-eyed Aryans were descended from the lost continent of Atlantis and that he, personally, was the reincarnation of Henry the Fowler, a Saxon king. Himmler also had more than a passing flirtation with the black arts throughout the 1930s, establishing a temple he called the Hall of the Dead, where he performed rituals prescribed by the Ordo Templi Orientis of

ALEISTER CROWLEY. In 1935, he established Ahnenerbe, the Nazi Occult Bureau. His less mystical side was evident in his extreme obsessive-compulsive behavior: He carefully recorded his shaves, baths, and haircuts and indexed all his receipts. When his parents used an official car, he deducted the mileage from his salary. *And* he did provide one million troops for the front, consolidate the concentration camps in what he called a "delousing" network, and invent successful new sterilization procedures. In 1945, General Himmler disguised himself as a private and took the vial of poison hidden in his gums. His last words were the fiendish affirmation "I am Heinrich Himmler!"

HINE-NUI-TE-PO

Female demon and ruler of the Maori Underworld. When a fellow demon, WHIRO, tried to rape her, she squashed him with her sexual organ.

HINIEL

A demon who was once an angel of the Fifth Heaven, Hiniel rules the north of Hell—on Tuesdays only.

HITLER, Adolf   DWH 1945   SUICIDE

Aside from exterminating millions of people, this fallen-away Catholic failed to do his Easter duty and committed suicide, assuring himself of a place in Hell. His charred remains were found by Russian soldiers, who laughed at his famous lone testicle. In some respects, it must be admitted that Hitler remained faithful to the Church's teachings: He kept his virginity and strongly opposed abortion (stating in *Mein Kampf,* "I'll put an end to the idea that a woman's body belongs to her ... the practice of abortion shall be exterminated"). But he also demonstrated several "New Age" virtues. He was a committed vegetarian (except for the occasional pig's knuckle), hoping for relief from his lifelong constipation problems, which obliged him to take 150 charcoal-based antigas pills a week. And he was *devoted* to astrology.

HIZARBIN

One of the numerous demons of the seas.

HOBBES, Thomas   DWH 1679   ATHEISM

The author of *Leviathan* is acknowledged to be "the Father of Materialism"—that is to say, he argued simultaneously against the existence of God and for the divine right of kings. With his last words, he called death "a great leap in the dark." We know where he landed.

HOBBIDIDANCE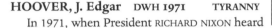

A fiend who makes his victims mute, the "prince of dumbness," according to Edgar in *King Lear*.

HOBGOBLIN

Originally a powerful devil. Beowulf calls his monstrous enemy Grendel a "Fiend of Hell, Grim Hobgoblin, Troll of Hell." But Hobgoblin has evolved into a diminutive nature sprite related to PUCK. During the night, the homely hobgoblin (who wears a suit of green leather) can shape-change and spoil milk—but he can also cure whooping cough.

HONORIUS I   DWH 638   HERESY

This pope was declared a heretic—at least on the subject of the Incarnation—by his successor Leo II.

HONORIUS III   DWH 1227   SORCERY

This pope wrote the standard how-to book of demon raising, known as *The Grimoire of Honorius the Great* or *The Black Book*. To conjure demons, His Holiness advocated the sacrifice of young goats and / or the ritual slaughter of a black cock, by tearing out his eyes, tongue, and heart.

HOOVER, J. Edgar   DWH 1971   TYRANNY

In 1971, when President RICHARD NIXON heard of Hoover's death, his first response was "Jesus Christ! That old cock-sucker!" Then he ordered the ex–head G-man's remains to lie in state in the U.S. Capitol. The FBI director (whose guidelines for agents forbade drink, debt, fornication, and acne) had compromising pictures of almost everybody in government, including Nixon. Hoover used the resources of his agency to dog the American Communist party (which consisted largely of undercover FBI agents), the "subversive" left, and minorities, but he pointedly ignored organized crime. According to current speculation, the Mafia had pictures of Hoover in his garb of choice, described by one eye-witness as "a fluffy black dress, very fluffy, with flounces, and lace stockings and high heels . . . and under the dress he was wearing a little, short garter belt."

Hoover *was* devoted to his mother, living with her until she died, but less solicitous of his lover of forty years, Clyde Tolson, whom he forbade to step on his shadow. Once, when the duo was at their weekly racetrack outing, the ailing Tolson fell, and Hoover refused to allow anyone to help him up, barking, "Let the dumb asshole get up by himself."

HOPKINS, Matthew
DWH 1647   CRUELTY

Having cast off all papish cant and superstition, the Puritans (of England and of New England) began discovering black magic, devils, and witches *everywhere*. Hopkins was a self-appointed (and highly paid) witch finder general of OLIVER CROMWELL's godly Commonwealth. "Finder, accuser, tormentor and executioner of hundreds, his reign of terror has caused his name to stink in the nostrils of all decent persons ever since," attests Montague Summers, in *The Geography of Witchcraft*.

HOPPER, Hedda   DWH 1966   SCANDAL

Her early years were blighted by poverty, a dysfunctional home life, and, especially, her ghastly name: Elda Furry. A runaway at age eighteen, she consulted a numerologist who renamed her the alliterative Hedda Hopper. She was a sometime actress who became a full-time calumnist; through her Hollywood gossip column, she became a much feared and flattered figure in the industry. For her items, she relied on a network of paid informers—including manicurists, janitors, and doormen. But the Queen of Gossip fiercely guarded her own privacy, fearful that the homosexuality of her actor-son—William Hopper, a regular on TV's *Perry Mason*—would be revealed.

She found her true passion in the 1950s as a Red baiter, marshaling her organization the Motion Picture Alliance for the Preservation of American Ideals to destroy the careers of actors Charlie Chaplin and Larry Parks and screenwriter Carl Foreman, who was fired in the middle of filming *High Noon*. The combination of leftist *and* foreign was unbearable to Hopper, who called Federico Fellini's 8½ "beneath contempt" and resigned from the Academy of Motion Picture Arts and Sciences (for the third time) when Simone Signoret won an Oscar, saying, "I never minded when the Democrats won, but I drew the line when Simone Signoret hit the jackpot. . . . Let her decorate her mantel with Picasso doves and the like."

HOSS, Rudolf Franz DWH 1947 CRUELTY

A devout Catholic, the father of five, and commandant of the concentration camp at Auschwitz, while "carrying out orders" Hoss introduced a more efficient lethal gas, hydrogen cyanide (marketed under the name Zyklon B). At Nuremberg, after Hoss testified about the 2,500,000 victims gassed or burned, he explained, "I am completely normal. Even when I was carrying out the task of extermination, I led a normal family life and so on."

HUBBARD, L. Ron DWH 1986 HERESY

He abandoned his early careers as a hypnotist and western writer (under the name of Rene Lafayette) at the seminal moment when he read *The Book of the Law* by ALEISTER CROWLEY. He then joined forces with a Southern California cult, Babalon [sic] Working, which, while unsuccessful in rousing the "goddesses of Babalon," did allow Hubbard to display his skill at curing sinusitis. He left the group, taking its $17,000 bank account, and formed the Church of Scientology, which by the late 1970s was worth billions, thanks to the generosity of its members and the sale of "electropsychometers"—crude lie detectors each of which is really a pair of cans wired to a galvanometer. Now wealthy, Hubbard took off on his yacht and indulged in his daily routine of drinking (eight rum and Cokes at a sitting), smoking (four packs of Kools a day), and dope (Benzedrine and testosterone injections) while surrounded by his "messengers": teenage girls in halter tops and go-go boots. He installed a disciplinary unit called the RPF, whose "detainees" were allowed only table scraps off the floor. He wasn't much kinder to his family, calling his son, Ron, Jr., a "fart in a hurricane"; both his ex-wives described him as a vicious wife beater. When he died, a Scientology commander assured his followers that L.

Ron, who immodestly traced his lifetimes back some 80 trillion years, had gone on to become an "operating thetan," without body mass and thus capable of astral travel. Possibly, but in a direction different than the commander had assumed.

HUICTIIGARA

Devil in charge of insomnia and sleepwalking.

HUMOTS

An accommodating demon who can transport all manner of books for his conjurer's reading pleasure.

HUMWAMA

Demon of the south winds and dark angel of excrement, Humwama has for a face a mass of animal entrails, and his breath smells like dung. Incense doesn't help.

HUS, Jan DWH 1415   HERESY

This proto-Protestant was a native of Goosetown, Bohemia. Just because there happened to be three popes at the time (1409), he began openly to criticize the Church and, what is worse, to promulgate the heretical views of the fanatical English reformer JOHN WYCLIFFE. One of the holy trio of popes (JOHN XXII) finally summoned Hus to a council, promising him safe conduct and lodgings with a friendly widow. But the joke was on Jan, who, upon his arrival to discuss "reforms," was excommunicated and burned at the stake.

If the kind of God exists who would damn me for not working out a deal with him, then that is unfortunate. I should not care to spend eternity in the company of such a person.

— MARY McCARTHY, *Memories of a Catholic Girlhood*

If there is any Hell more unprincipled than our rulers, and we, the ruled, I feel curious to see it.

HENRY DAVID THOREAU, "Slavery in Massachusetts"

If there is no Hell, a great many preachers are obtaining money under false pretenses.

— BILLY SUNDAY

If you want to know why God allowd the Devil to lead us astray, or if you wish to fathom the purposes of God Almighty, then your eyes ought to be in your arse.

— WILLIAM LANGLAND, *Piers Plowman*

I have also: the Bible of Hell; which the world shall have whether they will or no.
— WILLIAM BLAKE, *The Marriage of Heaven and Hell*

IABIEL

A nasty demon invoked to separate married couples.

IBLIS

The Islamic LUCIFER. Iblis was an Archangel who, being a hard-line monotheist, defied Allah's command to worship the newly created Adam and was damned. He is sometimes known as the Peacock Angel.

IDAEUS

The charioteer of King Priam of Troy, Idaeus is observed in Hades by Virgil's AENEAS, "still clinging to his chariot and weapons."

IGUMA　🐾

A nightmare goblin among the Basques, Iguma strangles people in their sleep.

INGERSOLL, Robert G.　DWH 1899　ATHEISM

"An honest God is the noblest work of man," declared the Great Agnostic, a prominent Republican who once toured America delivering lectures (at $3,500 a pop) in which he ridiculed Holy Scripture. After pointing out a series of apparent inconsistencies therein, he would defy God—if He existed—to strike him dead. For years, the Almighty was otherwise occupied, but He eventually got around to it, and we know what happened *next*.

INIAS　🐾

One of nine angels who were sharply criticized by a Church council in 745, Inias took umbrage and joined the demonic opposition. Invisibly, he infests churches—and farts loudly during sermons.

ISABELLA of France　DWH 1358　LUST

She was sixteen years old when her father, Philip IV of France, married her to England's exceedingly gay king Edward II. Isabella was soon complaining in a letter to her royal father that she was "the most wretched of wives," her husband being "an entire stranger to my bed." Her mood around the palace earned her the nickname the She-Wolf of France. When she was twenty (in 1312, an interregnum between her husband's affairs with Piers Gaveston and Hugh Despenser), she contrived to conceive a son by him and soon thereafter commenced a liaison of her own, with her husband's bitter enemy the Welsh baron Roger de Mortimer. Isabella was thirty-one when she helped Mortimer escape from the Tower of London and, taking her young son with her, joined her lover in France; three years later, she and Mortimer led an entirely successful invasion of England. Edward, sensibly, abdicated. He was murdered anyway. The new king, Edward III, may have been a mere teenager, but he was a Plantaganet. In 1330 he ordered Mortimer's execution and the banishment of his thirty-eight-year-old mother to a convent, where she died in her sixty-sixth year. Doubtless, she and Mortimer are now with PAOLO and FRANCESCA.

ISACAARON　🐾

One of the devils who possessed Sister Jeanne des Anges in Loudun and "filled her imagination with shameful notions."

ITURBIDE, Agustín de

DWH 1824   TREASON

The Catholic hero of Mexican independence was a staunch Royalist and dedicated his considerable military skills to crushing the nationalist, republican revolutions led by the radical priests Hidalgo and Morelos. Thus, Iturbide rose in the ranks (although he was briefly demoted, in 1816, for extortion and violence) as he continued the war against the remaining rebel, Vicente Guerrero. But a liberal coup d'état in the home country, Spain, inspired the deeply conservative Iturbide to switch sides. He allied the army with Guerrero's forces, and together they declared Mexican independence on August 24, 1821. Then, in 1822, the liberator crowned himself emperor, Agustín I. The post was to be hereditary. The United States (naturally) hastened to recognize his rule. The Mexicans did not. He was soon overthrown by General Santa Anna and went into exile. Upon his ill-advised return, he was captured by republicans and shot.

IVAN IV (the Terrible)   DWH 1584   TYRANNY

He had seven wives, one more than his contemporary HENRY VIII of England. At the age of three (in 1533), Ivan became czar upon his father's death (by poison), but his coronation was delayed until 1547. In the intervening years, he had little to do but order random executions and mutilations. His first wife died in 1560. He did away with his second wife—and her son—in 1569. In the meantime, he fought the twenty-four-year Livonian War in pursuit of a Baltic port. At its fruitless conclusion, the czar, in a fit of temper, killed another of his sons with a blow of his scepter. The prince's name was added to the *sidoniki,* long lists of his victims, which the very religious Ivan sent to monasteries with orders to pray for their souls.

IXION

Both ULYSSES and AENEAS caught glimpses of this miscreant during their visits to Hades, where he is bound to an eternally spinning fiery wheel. Zeus, the father of the gods, ordained this righteous punishment because

Ixion, while enjoying the hospitality on Mt. Olympus, almost seduced none other than Hera, the mother of the gods. When he discovered the pair on the verge of flagrante delicto, Zeus, thinking quickly, substituted a cloud for his goddess-wife. Upon it, it is believed, Ixion begat those randy half-horse, half-man creatures the Centaurs.

IYA

Among the Sioux, Iya is known as a malevolent spirit whose foul breath spreads illness.

Je me crois en enfer, donc j'y suis. C'est l'execution du catechisme. Je
suis esclave de mon baptisme.

*(I believe I'm in Hell, so I am. It's the fulfillment of the catechism. I am the vic-
tim of my baptism.)*
—ARTHUR RIMBAUD, *A Season in Hell*

JACK the Ripper   DWH circa 1892   MURDER

The Unknown Killer exists in most Western cultures; England's version
murdered at least ten London prostitutes, disemboweling two within an
hour. Suspects have included Prince Albert Victor (idiot brother of King
George V), a group of Freemasons, and Queen Victoria's personal physician, Sir William Gull. Sir ARTHUR CONAN DOYLE believed that the culprit
was a deranged midwife. The press originally called him Leather Apron,
until the publicity-hungry murderer signed one of his letters to the papers
Jack the Ripper—under his customary imprimatur, a bloody fingerprint.

When a vigilante committee was formed, his response was to send its
leader an organ derived from his most recent victim, with this note: "From
Hell, Mr. Lusk, sir, I send you half the kidney I took from one woman. I
preserved it for you. The other piece I fried and ate."

JACOPO Rusticucci   DWH circa 1260   SODOMY

Once a noble Guelf soldier, in Hell he introduces himself and his naked
companions (the very butch warrior sodomites) to Dante—then blames
his own homosexuality on his nagging wife.

JAHI   🐍

The Zoroastrian scriptures say Jahi brought menstruation into the
world after she mated with a serpent. The Hebrew patriarchs may have
evolved their notions of the uncleanliness and sinfulness of women from
Persian ascetics, who proclaimed all women "whores" because they were
descendants of Jahi.

JAMES I of England (aka James VI of Scotland) DWH 1625 HERESY

His mother was Mary Queen of Scots, which explains a great deal. When he arrived from Scotland to ascend the English throne in 1603, local pundits were fond of saying that Queen ELIZABETH I had been succeeded by Queen James. This strange king (who was alone in believing he had descended from King Arthur), had pop eyes, a jaw so narrow he had difficulty eating, a bulging tongue, and a crippling fear of pigs. He walked around endlessly in circles, touching his private parts. What's more, he was a Presbyterian and once shouted to an Anglican divine during a sermon, "I give not a turd for your preaching." Even more peculiar was his fondness for plunging his spindly legs into the bowels of dead stags to improve his muscle tone.

His various cultural innovations included the fork and the King James Bible (actually begun in Elizabeth's reign, and for which he reneged on paying the translators). He dismissed education for women with the explanation "To make women learned and foxes tame has the same effect—to make them more cunning." In general, he had little interest in women—including his wife, with whom he ceased marital relations upon his coronation—unless they were witches. James was obsessed with witches and in 1597 published his study of them, *Daemonologie*. He imported to England the hysterical witch-hunt he had instituted in Scotland and liked personally to supervise torture and interrogation, during which His Majesty took a special interest in demonic sexual practices. His Statute of 1604 was, until 1736, the legal basis for the prosecution of "witches" in Britain—and in the colonies, as at Salem, Massachusetts.

JASON   SEDUCTION

The mythical Greek sailor-hero who led the Argonauts to fetch the Golden Fleece. Jason's abandoning of his wife, MEDEA, as well as of his various sexual conquests (Hypsipyle and Glauce among them), earned him a place in Dante's Hell—not with the merely lustful but deep down, with the wicked seducers. Jason died old. As he was sitting on the beach under the rotting prow of his ship, the *Argo,* it fell on him.

JAZER ✺

The demon of the seventh hour, who compels love.

JEH ✺

In Zoroastrianism, Jeh is a demon-whore of lust and debauchery who mated with the chief of demons and then seduced and polluted Gayomart, theretofore the "perfect man."

JEQON ✺

A demon who tempted his fellow angels to rebel by showing them human women, "the daughters of men."

JEROBOAM   DWH 901 B.C.   IDOLATRY

In I Kings we learn of this "mighty man of valor" who was exiled by Solomon and settled with ten tribes in northern Palestine (Israel), where he devoted himself to worshipping golden calves as well as committing another crime curiously upsetting to the Almighty—"pissing against a wall" (I Kings 14:10). He gave his name to an excessively large bottle of wine.

JEZEBEL   DWH 840 B.C.   IDOLATRY

After she married the Hebrew king AHAB, this Phoenician princess lived in an ivory house and introduced eye makeup to the Hebrew women. She also promoted the worship of BAAL, thereby incurring the hatred of the prophet Elijah, who bested her pagan priests in a magic contest and then prophesied, "The dogs in the street shall eat Jezebel." She tried to seduce Jehu, the military leader who led a coup against her, but he in-

structed a group of eunuchs to throw her out a window. He then ran over her with his chariot, leaving her remains to be eaten by the dogs. After the doggie dinner, only the soles of her feet and the palms of her hands remained to be buried.

JIANG QING (Chiang Ch'ing)   DWH 1991   VIOLENCE

The third, ambitious wife of Chairman MAO TSE-TUNG, this failed actress engineered the torture, kidnappings, and mob violence of the Chinese Cultural Revolution. She used her Red Guards to purge "capitalist" influences in the arts while avenging old grudges against former directors, writers, and actors. Her slogan "hit them with a hammer" was often taken literally: One Western-trained concert pianist had his hands smashed. After Mao's death, when "the Empress" and the rest of the Gang of Four were arrested, posters sprang up over China urging, "Cut Chiang Ch'ing into Ten Thousand Pieces." During her long (1980–81) trial, she showed her flair for dramatics by stripping naked. Charges in the forty-eight-page indictment against her included riding in limousines, playing poker while Mao was dying, drinking saffron water, and watching the notorious movie *The Sound of Music* every night.

"JIMMY" (aka "Johnny")   LUST

In sermons by Catholic priests, Jimmy (or Johnny) is the pseudonym of "a young man, just about your age." Jimmy came from a "fine Catholic family." He himself was quite devout—he never missed Sunday mass or ate meat on Friday. (In some variants of the tale, he was considering a priestly vocation.) Jimmy was dating Mary, from an equally fine Catholic family. One night, however, they "parked." They committed an act of impurity. Immediately thereafter (a) their car was struck by a speeding truck or (b) snow blocked the exhaust pipe of their car, and (a1) they were both killed instantly and went to Hell, (a2) she was killed and went to Hell but he survived and went mad, or (b1) they both died of carbon monoxide poisoning, went to Hell, and were discovered in an impure embrace. "Perhaps he had time to make an act of perfect contrition. But I doubt it. I doubt it."

JINN (aka Genies)

Arabian demons who frequently disguise themselves as dust storms but, being made of flame, can assume animal form, eat, drink, procreate, and cause madness. Jinn eavesdrop around baths, wells, latrines, and ovens, and they appear with tedious frequency in the tales of the *1001 Nights*. The Quran concedes their existence and suggests that they, like humans, will face a final judgment.

JOHN, King   DWH 1216   CRUELTY

King John was not a good man.
He had his little ways.
—A. A. MILNE

The English king John "Lackland" is the legendary villain of the Robin Hood saga. He caused his father to cry himself to death, preferred his mistresses on the pubescent side, fathered eight illegitimate children, insulted the pope, and murdered his nephew Arthur, the rightful heir to the throne. After signing the Magna Carta, he died from an intestinal illness caused by gorging on eels.

JOHN XII DWH 964 LUST

This former gang member became pontiff at age eighteen. He used the Church treasury and pilgrims' offerings to support his gambling habit, raped a religious pilgrim in St. Peter's, turned the Lateran Palace into a brothel, and had simultaneous affairs with his mother, his sister, and his father's mistress. If all this wasn't enough, John made a pact with the Devil and offered a toast in his honor at the altar. This seemed excessive to the cardinals and bishops, who brought him up on

charges that included his rather open Devil worship. John's response was to threaten the group with excommunication, castrate his least favorite cardinal, and go hunting. His love life proved to be his downfall. According to Italian chronicler Liutprand, the pope was caught in flagrante delicto by an irate husband, who beat him to death with a hammer. He was twenty-seven at the time. Theologian St. Robert Bellarmine summed it up. Pope John, he wrote, was "the dregs."

JOHN XXII DWH 1334 AVARICE

At his death, he was the richest man in the world. To justify his wealth—24 million gold florins—Pope John tried to convince the faithful that Jesus did not live in poverty and executed 114 Franciscan monks who said that He did. John's definitive papal bull on the subject, *Cum Inter Nonnullos*, flatly declares it heretical to say that Jesus and his apostles owned no property. The florins that didn't come from his aggressive simony may have been manufactured rather than earned, since the pope was an excellent alchemist; he issued a papal bull against alchemy to eliminate the competition. This heretical pope claimed that God is the sole resident of

Heaven—according to him, even the saints and the Blessed Virgin would have to wait until the Day of Judgment to get in. He believed there was no one in Hell either, but found out different.

"JOHN XXIII" (Baldassare Cossa)   DWH 1419   BLASPHEMY

Not to be confused with the twentieth-century pope of the same name (who is in Heaven), this antipope was made priest one day and pope the next, having managed to avoid ever taking the sacraments. In the Vatican, he kept his brother's wife as his mistress but still busied himself seducing maids, matrons, and widows—and was known to be very partial to nuns. His court magician, Abramelin, was unsuccessful in saving him from being deposed by the Council of Constance, which narrowed down the charges against him from fifty-five to a mere five: lust, murder, rape, sodomy, and piracy.

JOHNSON, Margaret   DWH 1633   SORCERY

When she encountered a devil named MAMMILON, Johnson mated with him, thinking, as she lamely explained to her inquisitors, that he was an angel wearing a black silk suit.

JOLSON, Al   DWH 1950
VANITY

Even in an age not noted for racial sensitivity, his blackface act was offensive; even in a profession not known for humility, his egotism was outstanding. Asa Yoelson, born in Russia in 1886, made his American stage debut in Washington, D.C., in 1899. Once, at the height of his fame, when a music director ventured some mild criticism, Jolie, enraged, thrust a fistful of $100 bills in the man's face, screaming, "This is mine! Where's yours?" When Ruby Keeler, his third wife, performed, Jolson would often stand in the audience and begin singing to upstage her. His past-his-prime desperation for the spotlight inspired the creators of the film *A Star Is Born*—and its many remakes.

JOMIAEL   🦌

A Watcher angel turned demon, who descended to earth under the leadership of SEMYAZA.

JONES, Jim   DWH 1978   VIOLENCE

In 1953, Jones, a former hospital orderly, began to finance his religious vision of Utopia by selling monkeys door to door. But in practice, the community he founded never lived up to this early promise, and in the jungles of Guyana this guru in sunglasses joined 900 of his deluded followers in a mass suicide.

JOVIAL FRIARS

Friars of the religious order Ordo militiae beatae Mariae, which descended into total corruption soon after it was founded in 1261. The rule was so lax, the friars could marry and eat meat whenever they wanted, but they were forbidden to encourage actors. In Dante's Hell (canto 23), Jovial Friars CATALANO DEI MALAVOLTI and LODERINGO DI LANDOLO wear the gilded cloaks of the hypocrites, which are lined with molten lead.

JUDAS "Iscariot"   DWH 33

DEICIDE, TREASON

Dante places Judas in the deepest depths of Hell, a writhing morsel in the grinding jaws of SATAN himself. But in the sixth century, the Irish sailor-saint Brendan had seen the Bible's second most unpopular redhead (after CAIN) cooling off on an iceberg, enjoying, as Judas explained, his annual one-day respite from Hell.

Pious legend has it that he was the illegitimate son of an exotic dancer, born under the ominous sign of Scorpio rising, and had been an armed Palestinian terrorist (a Zealot) before becoming a disciple of Jesus. When he left the Last Supper midmeal, the other apostles seem to have assumed that he was going to give alms to the poor, even though they had always considered him stingy—in his role as treasurer, he had recently complained that Mary Magdalene had wasted valuable ointment on Jesus' feet. But, in fact, Judas had gone ratting to the authorities, and in exchange for thirty pieces of silver betrayed Jesus with a kiss—a gesture that has been called the "greatest archetype of human betrayal." Overcome with remorse, the deicide hanged himself, at which time, in the words of Scripture, "all his bowels gushed out" (Acts 1:18).

Revisionist interpretations of Judas do exist: A passage of the Quran insists that Judas had the same face as Jesus and was crucified in his stead; and in the film *The Last Temptation of Christ* he is portrayed as a hero, a man of passion with a New York accent.

JULIUS CAESAR   DWH 44 B.C.   VANITY

He claimed to be a direct descendant of the Trojan hero AENEAS, and, although he was called in his youth the Queen of Bithynia because of his homosexual proclivities, he married three times and indulged in numerous affairs, including one with Sevilia, the mother of his future assassin, BRUTUS. As an invader of surrounding countries, he proved a brilliant general, and as his own PR agent he wrote *Gallic Wars* to make sure everyone back home knew all about it. Although Caesar made a show of rejecting the crown, he favored the color imperial purple, toted the emperor's ivory scepter, and put his own face on coins. He cannot be held responsible for the Caesar salad, but since he combed his thinning hair forward over his (literally) oversize head, his vanity inadvertently created the Caesar hairdo, popularized throughout the ages by Napoleon, Peter Lorre, and Frank Sinatra.

Ketchum watched the building of the scaffold for his hanging outside his cell window. . . . On the day of his execution, the condemned man "leaped" up the gallows steps, the Times *correspondent reported. Black Jack helped in adjusting the noose around his neck and said cheerfully, "I'll be in Hell before you start breakfast." . . . The trap was sprung, and Ketchum's head was torn from his shoulders.*

—Carl Sifakis, *The Encyclopedia of American Crime*

KAFKEFONI

An evil angel, one of the Cabala's "unholy Sefiroth."

KAMSA

The Hindu archdemon, Kamsa ordered the slaughter of all boy children in a vain attempt to kill his newborn nemesis, the god Krishna. See also HEROD THE GREAT.

KASBEEL

Once an angel named Biqa, Kasbeel rebelled against God at the moment of his creation and was dropped into the abyss, where his new, Infernal name means "he who lies to God."

KASDAYE

The fifth Satan (so named in the Book of Enoch), Kasdaye is alleged to have taught humans the art of abortion.

KATERFELTO, Gustavus   DWH 1799   FRAUD

In London, during the influenza epidemic of 1782, appeared a tall, thin man in a long, black gown, invariably accompanied by a black cat. He claimed to have discovered the cause of the plague by means of an instrument known as a solar microscope. Naturally, his name has become a byword for "quack."

KELBY

A demon who appears in the form of a torch-carrying horse; probably related to the Celtic sea horse demon, and drowner of sailors, the Kelpie.

KEMUEL 🦋
A devil, formerly a prince of Powers, who now commands 12,000 angels of destruction. In Jewish legend, Kemuel is celebrated for his (failed) attempt to keep the Torah out of Moses' hands.

KETCH, Jack   DWH 1686   CRUELTY
A historic English executioner, notorious for his clumsy brutality. Ketch's name has become a byword, a synonym for *hangman*. After twenty-three years on the job, Ketch, in 1686, was fired for insubordination, and his position taken by a butcher named Rose. Within four months, Ketch was reinstated—and proceeded to hang his successor. He achieved lasting fame as the bogeyman puppet-hangman in the story of Punch and Judy.

KETCHUM, "Black Jack"   DWH 1901   MURDER
A remarkably stupid train robber of the Old West (he used to hit himself in the head with his own pistol when angry), Black Jack kept robbing the same train (the Twin Flyer) in the same place until he was captured and brought to trial in Santa Fe. *The New York Times* covered his botched execution (see quotation on page 131).

KEZEF 🦋
In Jewish legend, an angry "angel of destruction." In the wilderness, Kezef fought against both Moses and Aaron.

KHOMEINI, Ayatollah Ruholla   DWH 1989   HERESY
The grand ayatollah of the Shi'ites in Iran was exiled first to and then from Iraq for his Shi'ite-disturbing activities. From a suburb of Paris, he instigated—by radio—the overthrow of Iran's dreadful Shah PAHLAVI. Returning to his homeland in triumph and acclaimed political and religious leader for life, he established a militant theocracy—that is, a program of no fun but plenty of executions. His announcement that U.S. President Jimmy Carter was SATAN inspired his followers to seize the American embassy, taking seventy-nine hostages. The eight-year holy war he waged against Iraq was fought largely by children, many of whom died—with the ayatollah's assurance of a Heavenly reward. One of Khomeini's last official acts was to offer a large reward to any hero brave enough to assassinate a novelist.

KIDD, Capt. William   DWH 1701   PIRACY
The distinction between a (legal) privateer and (criminal) pirate was a fine one. But when Kidd, a wealthy British sea captain based in New York,

ran out of French victims and began attacking and looting British ships at sea, he was clearly out of line. Despite burying the evidence some-where—his famous "lost treasure"—he was ar-rested at Boston, transported, and hanged at Executioner's Wharf, Wapping.

KING, William Lyon Mackenzie
DWH 1950   SORCERY

Charisma-deprived leader of Canada's once-dominant Liberal party, this Presbyterian bache-lor was that chilly nation's prime minister from 1921 to 1930, and again from 1935 until his re-tirement in 1948. His many prudent political policies were—it has been re-vealed—the result of long nocturnal discussions with his (dead) mother, with whom he communicated via a Ouija board.

KINGSLEY, Charles   DWH 1875   SOWING DISCORD

Clergyman and author of the mawkish children's "classic" *Water Ba-bies,* this staunchly Protestant Victorian English advocate of "muscular Christianity" publicly accused the saintly Cardinal Newman—and Roman Catholics in general—of effeminacy, hypocrisy, and prevarication.

KISSINGER, Henry   WH 1973   HYPOCRISY

Some crimes are so heinous as to result in immediate damnation of the soul, even though the sinner's body (repossessed by a demon) continues to "live" on earth. Dante (in canto 33 of the *Inferno*) cites the case of the treacherous homicide BRANCA D'ORIA, who lived fifty years after his spirit was plunged deep into Hell.

However alive and well the esteemed statesman and wealthy consul-tant may appear to be on his frequent televi-sion appearances, the butcher of Cambodia was whisked to his eternal, exceedingly warm reward on October 16, 1973, at the very moment he modestly accepted the Nobel Peace Prize.

KITCHENER, Lord Horatio   DWH 1916
TYRANNY

The heroic incarnation of British imperi-alism, Lord Kitchener enforced England's civ-ilizing mission in the Sudan, Egypt, and India, but most memorably in South Africa, where his tactics included the wholesale burning of Boer villages and the herding of men, women, and children into "concentration camps," of which peculiar institutions he was the proud inventor.

KNIGHTS TEMPLAR DWH 1312   HERESY

A quasi-religious order of warriors founded in the twelfth century, in the wake of the First Crusade. Sworn to poverty and chastity, they made it their mission to guard Christian pilgrims in the Holy Land. Richly endowed by Europe's grateful rulers, the order grew, over two centuries, very wealthy—becoming, in a sense, the first international bankers. Financially strapped French king Philip "the Fair," with an eye to confiscating their vast land holdings, accused the Templars of sodomy and idol worship and had them all arrested. Under torture, many members of the order confessed to all manner of blasphemy, conspiracy, and buggery; in 1312, the pope declared them heretics, and the Templars, to the last knight, were burned at the stake. Nonetheless, in 1797, a French Jesuit, Abbé Baumel, published his opinion that a surviving cabal of anticlerical Templars had inspired and financed the French Revolution.

KNOX, John DWH 1572   HERESY

The founder of that dour and heretical sect—to this day the established church of Scotland—known as Presbyterianism was an ordained Catholic priest but with doctrinal doubts about the "Real Presence" of Christ in the Eucharist. In 1547 he allied himself with "a group of fanatical Protestants and political gangsters" (in the words of the *Catholic Encyclopedia*) whose most Christian motto was "No more mass. Death to the priesthood." So long as the heretical HENRY VIII ruled England, Knox was free to preach his mischievious tenets, but when the Catholic Mary Tudor ascended the throne, the courageous reformer fled to Switzerland, whence he issued brave calls to arms and a presciently antifeminist tract, *The First Blast of the Trumpet Against the Monstrous Regiment of Women*. He also found time to marry Marjorie Bowes, the mother of his two sons. Authorities agree that his second marriage (at age fifty-one, to sixteen-year-old Mary Stewart) was undertaken to spite Mary, Queen of Scots.

KOCH, Ilsa   DWH 1967   CRUELTY

The infamous "Bitch of Buchenwald" was the wife of Karl Otto, the commandant there. She was a nymphomaniac, a sadist, and a collector of kinky memorabilia—such as lampshades fashioned from the skin of her victims. After the war, Koch was sentenced to life in prison for her crimes and, despite official American pleas for leniency, finally hanged herself.

KONGO

In Japanese folklore, the "Sheriff of Hell," who leads a merry band of imaginative torturers.

KORAH   DWH circa 1400 B.C.   BLASPHEMY

The first scriptural evidence that Hell (Sheol, aka the pit) is below the earth and full of fire may be found in the sixteenth chapter of the Book of Numbers. While wandering in the desert, three princes—Korah, Dathan, and Abiram—rebelled against the leadership of Moses and Aaron. Moses summoned them "and their wives and their sons and their little children" (Numbers 16:27) out of their tents, and "the earth opened her mouth and swallowed them up. . . . They and all that appertained to them went down into the pit . . . and there came out a fire from the Lord" (Numbers 16:32–35). About this instance of (not untypical) divine overkill, the esteemed biblical commentator Matthew Henry observes, "This judgement . . . was severe upon the poor children, though we cannot particularly tell how bad they might be to deserve it, or how good God might be otherwise to compensate it; yet of this we are sure in general, that infinite justice did them no wrong."

KORESH, David   DWH 1993   BLASPHEMY

Just another typical false messiah (see JAN BOCKLESON or SABBATAI ZEVI), this gun nut and child-molesting peckerwood convinced a group of fallen-away Seventh-Day Adventists that the biblical Book of Revelation was all about him—and them. Koresh and most of them died in the ensuing confrontation with civil authorities. Since he did not return within three days of his demise, we can safely assume he is now most uncomfortably lodged among his peers in deepest Hell.

KRASNOV, Pyetor   DWH 1947   TREASON

An imperial Russian cavalry officer, Krasnov was so opposed to the revolution that he allied his Cossack troops to invading German forces in World War I. Defeated by the Bolsheviks at Petrograd, he was captured and (curiously) released by them; thereafter, he wandered Europe for thirty years in pursuit of his dream—a German-sponsored Cossack homeland. In 1944, at his suggestion, the Nazis established just such a state, in the Italian Alps. At the war's end, Krasnov surrendered there to the British; at Yalta, JOSEPH STALIN demanded the traitor's return to Russia, where he was duly hanged.

KRAY, Ronald   DWH 1995   MURDER

The "firm" of Ron and his twin brother, Reg, ruled the London underworld from 1957 until they were both jailed for murder in 1969. They began their professional careers as boxers but found their true calling in the protection racket. They operated a series of West End nightclubs, where they hobnobbed with such slumming luminaries as Frank Sinatra, Judy Garland, and Tony Bennett. Ron—doubtless a paranoid schizophrenic—was the less practical and more violent of the pair. He was convicted of murdering a man in a pub for implying he was a homosexual, whereas Reg Kray was given his life sentence for the murder of Jack (the Hat) McVitie, who owed them money. Ron married twice and divorced twice while in jail. The brothers' ghastly life story became a 1990 movie, *The Krays,* starring Gary and Martin Kemp.

KRUPP, Alfred   DWH 1967   SOWING DISCORD

Unspeakably wealthy grandson of the German industrialist Alfred "the Cannon King" Krupp, this Krupp supplied HITLER's forces with armaments and in return was authorized to plunder property and plants in all Nazi-occupied countries and to utilize as slave laborers the inmates of 138 Nazi concentration camps—including 1,000 French prisoners of war who were housed in dog kennels at the Krupp plant in Essen. Krupp was ordered to forfeit his property and sentenced to a twelve-year prison term by the Nuremberg war crimes tribunal, but in 1951 he was granted amnesty by the American high commissioner to West Germany. (The Korean War had begun.) At his death, Krupp was worth more than a billion dollars—but he could not take it with him to Hell.

KUNOSPASTON   🦅

A sea demon in the form of a fish, Kunospaston delights in shipwrecks.

KUSHIEL   🦅

A strict, prison guard sort of angel, Kushiel was assigned to preside over Hell.

KYTELER, Lady Alice   DWH circa 1330   WITCHCRAFT

A wealthy, thrice-widowed member of the Anglo-Irish ascendancy class, Lady Alice was the subject of the Emerald Isle's first witch-hunt. Her demonic incubus was ROBIN, SON OF ART.

La Fontaine heard someone express pity on the fate of the damned in Hell-fire, and said, "I like to think that they get used to it, and in the end are like fish in water."

—NICOLAS CHAMFORT

Listen, that's what Hell will be like, small chat to the babbling of Lethe about the good old days when we wished we were dead.

—SAMUEL BECKETT

LABARTU

A female demon with the head of a lion and the teeth of an ass, Labartu carries a serpent in each hand and travels with a pet pig. She attacks, and drinks the blood of, children, mothers, and nurses.

LABASH

This demon tried in vain to stop the prayers of Moses from reaching God.

LABATIEL

A fallen angel, "the Flaming One," Labatiel presides over the gates of death—a diabolical parody of St. Peter at the gates of Heaven.

LABEZERIN

A demon who claims to guarantee success in any enterprise.

LAIS DWH 4th century B.C. LUST

Several famous Greek courtesans bear this name, the best known being the daughter of ALCIBIADES. Princes, philosophers, and commoners sought her favors, but her high fee (10,000 drachmas) discouraged the statesman Demosthenes from doing so. She was killed by a posse of jealous Thessalonian wives.

LAMCHAMOR

The ruler of the sixth dungeon of Hell, with the face of a boar.

LAMIA ⚜

The Greek and Roman "bogeyman" was a woman—naughty children were once threatened with a nocturnal visit from Lamia. According to legend, she was a beautiful Libyan queen who caught the eye of the randy god Zeus. In a fit of jealousy, his wife, Hera, destroyed all Lamia's children. The poor queen went mad, and she took to enticing and devouring random mortal tots in the form of a serpent. In her honor, witches in the Middle Ages were sometimes called Lamiae, and, later still, the poet John Keats took her as a subject.

LANCELOT DWH circa 600 ADULTERY

The character of this arrogant, adulterous knight is a smutty twelfth-century French addition to the chaste and heroic legend of Arthur, the sixth-century Welsh Christian warrior king. An account of his dastardly seduction of his queen was the occasion of sin that resulted in the damnation of PAOLO and FRANCESCA.

LANDIS, Judge Kenesaw Mountain DWH 1944 TYRANNY

The Czar of Baseball, the game's original commissioner, was a publicity-seeking, dictatorial, arbitrary old bigot. One of his gems of wisdom: "The colored ballplayers have their own league. Let them stay in their own league."

LANDRU, Henri DWH 1922 MURDER

He used the Paris personal columns, in which he advertised to meet "a homely lady," to seduce and murder nine such, after bilking them of their modest savings. Landru romanced these lonely women with flowers and dinners, all the while maintaining a happy home life with his wife and an even happier liaison with his mistress. He meticulously recorded all his murders in a notebook, and when the police examined his stove, they found hundreds of bone fragments, teeth, and corset fastenings. He went to the guillotine whining, "This is not the first time that an innocent man has been condemned."

LANO DWH 1287 PROFLIGACY

A Sienese spendthrift who, after he squandered his inheritance, joined the local militia in the hope of being killed in battle, and succeeded.

LAODAMIA

Virgil's AENEAS sighted Laodamia in Hades, whence she had—so the story goes—voluntarily accompanied her beloved husband.

LARAOCH   🪶

The demonic ruler of the seventh dungeon of Hell, Laraoch has the face of a vulture.

LATURE DANO   🪶

An Indonesian demon of mottled black, white, and red, Lature Dano causes sickness, death, and bad weather.

LAWFORD, Peter   DWH 1984   DESPAIR

For reasons of her own, his mother (who recounted her story in the tellingly named *Bitch! The Autobiography of Lady Lawford*) dressed the young Peter Lawford up as a little girl. Maybe that led to his years padding about Hollywood in velvet fleur-de-lis slippers, an unregenerate alcohol and drug addict who chartered a private plane for his dealer during a stint at the Betty Ford Clinic. The debauchery of his later years limited his parental responsibilities to scoring and using drugs with his children, and cringing if they called him Dad instead of Peter. When dying, he suggested to his last wife that she wrap him in a sheet and drop him in a dumpster.

LECHIES   🪶

A demon-satyr who lives in the woods and sports long horns, a donkeylike head, a human torso, and a goatlike lower half.

LEIBENFALS, Lanz von   DWH circa 1940   SOWING DISCORD

Ex-monk and crackpot sociobiologist, Leibenfals inspired many of ADOLF HITLER's notions about race. His magazine *Ostara* mixed the erotic and occult in arguing that Aryans must rule the earth by destroying their darker, hairier enemies, who prey on blond women. His landmark book was titled *Theozoology, or the Accounts of Apes of Sodom and the Divine Election—An Introduction into the Earliest and the Most Modern World Philosophy and a Justification for the Orders of Princes and Aristocracy.*

LEMAY, Gen. Curtis   DWH 1990   SOWING DISCORD

Right-wing nut and SAC commander ("Bombs Away with Curtis LeMay!") he spent most of the 1950s waiting out a Communist air raid and in 1968 was George Wallace's vice presidential candidate on the American Independent party ticket. "What is the point of swatting flies?" LeMay ruminated during the Vietnam War. "Why not go after the manure pile—China?"

LENIN, Vladimir Ilich   DWH 1924   ADULTERY

The founder of the Bolsheviks and creator of the Soviet Union was also a husband—he married the long-suffering Nadezhda Krupskaya during his Siberian exile, in 1898, and she was with him until the end, nursing him through his bouts of shingles and various strokes. Nevertheless, he conducted a passionate and shameless affair with one Inessa Armand from 1911 until her untimely death in 1920. Since Comrade Lenin was an avowed atheist, it is most unlikely that he ever confessed and was absolved of this mortal sin.

LEO X, Pope   DWH 1521   SIMONY

Born Giovanni de Medici, the second son of Lorenzo the Magnificent, he was made a cardinal at thirteen. When he became pope, Leo rejoiced, "Since God has given us the papacy, let us enjoy it." And he did, traveling around Rome at the head of a lavish parade featuring panthers, jesters, and Hanno, the White Elephant. He served dinners with sixty-five courses at which little boys jumped out of puddings. His extravagance offended even some cardinals, who plotted an assassination attempt (foiled); the plan was to inject poison into his formidable hemorrhoids. Short on funds, Leo colluded with a German archbishop to sell indulgences, using the showy services of the monk JOHANN TETZEL, who entered German towns bearing the Bull of Indulgence aloft on a velvet cushion. Soon afterward, Martin Luther nailed his "Ninety-five Theses upon Indulgences" on the church door at Wittenberg, and the rest, as they say, is history.

LEONARD

A demon called the Knight of the Fly or Grand Master of the Sabbaths. A stickler for details, Leonard (in the shape of a three-horned, black goat) oversees black magic rituals.

LEOPOLD II   DWH 1909   CRUELTY

In a vision, the American mystic poet Vachel Lindsay was able to "listen to the yell of Leopold's ghost . . . hear how the demons chuckle and yell,/ Cutting his hands off down in Hell." King Leopold of Belgium had appropriated the rubber-rich "Belgian Congo" for his personal fortune, and his colonial regime of slave labor, rape, and mutilation there was immortalized in Joseph Conrad's version of Hell on earth,

The Heart of Darkness. It took an international outcry to force Leopold to relinquish control of what had become his private fiefdom. Despite his phobia about germs—he wore a bag over his beard—His Majesty had countless mistresses, until he fell in love for the first time with a cigar-smoking, sixteen-year-old prostitute named Caroline Lacroix. He married her a few days before his death, and, immediately after Leopold expired, she quietly left Belgium with his fortune in a suitcase.

LERAJIE

The Robin Hood of Hell, Lerajie wears a green archer's costume and carries a bow and arrows. Especially mean-spirited, he inspires quarrels and causes arrow wounds to putrefy.

LÉVI, Eliphas (Alphonse Louis Constant)   DWH 1875   SORCERY

This defrocked French priest single-handedly popularized the word *abracadabra* and revived the practice of magic in the nineteenth century. The gluttonous Lévi earned a living by giving lessons in the occult and "astral light," developing a large following despite his objectionable personal hygiene. At the pinnacle of his career in London, he conjured up the Greek magician Apollonius of Tyana, after twenty-one days of preparation, with four mirrors and two giant chafing dishes. When the cranky spirit finally appeared, wearing a gray shroud, he complained about the magic sword Lévi was wearing. Undaunted, Lévi asked him two questions, and the spirit's answer to both was a sonorous "death" and "dead." When Madame Lévi heard of the Apollonius episode, she surmised (correctly) that the spirit was a demon and both asked for and got an annulment. Immediately after he died, Lévi was reincarnated as ALEISTER CROWLEY.

LEVIATHAN

> *This is the black sea-brute bulling through*
> *the wave-wrack,*
> *Ancient as ocean's shifting hills.*
> —W. S. MERWIN

A demonic creature of the sea—a whale, crocodile, or serpent—whose name comes from the Hebrew word meaning "great water animal," the female counterpart to the monster BEHEMOTH. Leviathan may well have been the seven-headed dragon against whom St. Michael fought and of whom it is prophesied in Isaiah (27:1) that "the Lord . . . shall slay the dragon that is in the sea." She was originally, according to some demonologists, an angel of the Seraphim and, having been exiled from Heaven and become a devil in the form of a serpent, entered Eden and tempted our mother Eve. Leviathan is especially active during the month of February, inspiring men to the sins of envy and heresy.

According to the poet William Blake, Leviathan and Behemoth are now both occupied erecting pillars in Hell. But during the last century, a clever promoter almost succeeded in passing off an enormous skeleton made up of five fossil whales as the original, biblical Leviathan.

LIBBICOCCO

Libbicocco is one of the demons who guide Dante through Malebranche; his name means "grumpy." He casually rips the arm off a bribe taker.

LIEBTHENBUS

A demon who controls Africa and uses hallucinatory drugs.

LILIM

The succubi children of LILITH, they are also known as Harlots of Hell and Night Hags. It is their unwholesome habit to squat on top of sleeping men (especially monks), thereby causing them to have nocturnal emissions. The sound of their "filthy laughter" was once a nightly feature of monastic life. Devout Jews used to fend them off with amulets, and celibate Christians slept with their hands crossed over their genitalia, or with crucifixes tied over their lower parts, to protect themselves from the advances of these female fiends. After a night with one of the Lilim, no man can find satisfaction with a mortal woman.

LILITH

The First Lady of Hell, Lilith inspires the dying to impure thoughts, seducing sinners on their very deathbeds, so that when they embrace her, they've made the final move toward eternal damnation. In Jewish legend, she was the original wife created by God for Adam—and, some say, the mother of CAIN—but she resented Adam's insistence on employing the "missionary position" during sex. She suggested experimentation; he demurred. They quarreled, and Lilith grew wings and flew out of Paradise. To persuade her to come back, God dispatched three angels—Sanvi, Sansanvi, and Semangelaf—who found her flying over the Red Sea. Lilith refused to return to Eden, telling them, "It would be no Paradise to be the servant of man," and soon found a new (presumably more sexually open-minded) mate in the fallen angel SAMMAEL. The couple lived in a palace and produced a horde of 100 unclean children, the LILIM.

Some versions of her legend depict Lilith as a beautiful blond, but in the Hebrew tradition, she is a goggle-eyed, hairy-legged vampire (with a rotting back) who sucks the blood of men and steals newborn children. Her name was translated into English (Isaiah 34:14, Authorized Version) as "screech owl."

LILITU (aka Ardat Lili)

A Mesopotamian wind demon, a frigid, barren spinster, a "maid of desolation," who roamed the night drinking the blood of men. The goddess Ishtar, for her own mysterious reasons, sent this seductive demon to earth to lead men astray.

LITTLE PETE (Fung Jing Toy)   DWH 1897   CRUELTY

He was a notorious Tong warrior, leader of the Sum Yop Tong gang, which ruled San Francisco's Chinatown, specializing in slavery, opium, and murder for hire. Little Pete was considered impossible to assassinate, since he wore chain-mail underwear and a metal beanie, and lived in a windowless room with a vicious dog on either side of his door. When he did go out, it was with three bodyguards—one in front, one in the back, and one at his side—except for the fateful morning when he took only one bodyguard with him to the barbershop. While Little Pete was getting a shampoo, the bodyguard went out to buy a paper, and a member of the rival Chew Tin Gop gang jammed a revolver through his chain mail and put five bullets in his spine.

LIZZIE the Dove   See DANNY LYONS.

LJUBIA

A Lithuanian demon who sometimes causes the rivers to run dry, unless, naturally enough, a Lithuanian virgin is sacrificed to her.

LLOYD GEORGE, David   DWH 1945   SOWING DISCORD

Of his many adulteries (always with actresses and/or married women) Lloyd George's son later explained, "Father just couldn't help himself." A Liberal member of the British Parliament for fifty-five years, the Welsh Wizard was born in poverty but made himself financially secure (while serving as chancellor of the exchequer) by purchasing shares in Marconi, at a remarkably low price. (He was subsequently acquitted of wrongdoing by a committee.) In 1916, he seized power by stabbing his leader and mentor Herbert Asquith in the back—Asquith's wife, Margot, once observed, "Lloyd George could not see a belt without hitting below it." Allying himself with the Tories, he became prime minister just in time to unleash the murderous Black and Tan gangsters on the rebellious Irish and help formulate the disastrous Treaty of Versailles, which did so much to make World War II inevitable.

LOCUSTA   DWH **mid–1st century**   MURDER

She was a household servant—a nurse-practitioner, as it were—in the imperial palace; she was also an expert poisoner. AGRIPPINA employed Locusta's services in killing Claudius, and NERO did likewise against Britannicus. Locusta herself was put to death by Galba's command. Her name became a byword for the sort of woman who murders those committed to her care.

LODERINGO di Landolo   DWH **1293**   TREASON

One of the lax and liberal JOVIAL FRIARS placed by Dante in Hell among the hypocrites, Loderingo served as the Ghibelline *podestà,* a sort of mayor, of Florence and was supposed to act in that party's interests. But during his tenure, the Ghibellines were oppressed with particular savagery.

LOEB, Richard   DWH **1936**   MURDER

When Loeb, a college graduate at age seventeen, was propositioned by his homosexual friend Nathan Leopold, he said he would consent only if Leopold helped him murder a neighbor, fourteen-year-old Bobby Franks, "for fun." After the murder, Loeb rather audaciously assisted police and reporters in the investigation, until suspicion fell on the two young millionaires, and, under questioning, Loeb confessed. After fourteen years in prison, Loeb made improper advances to a fellow inmate, James Day. Day's response was to slash him fifty-six times with a razor. Showing his arrogance to the end, Loeb's last words were "I think I'm going to make it!" The following day Edwin A. Lahey wrote in the *Chicago Daily News,* "Richard Loeb, a brilliant student and master of the English language, today ended a sentence that began with a proposition."

LOKI   🐉

The SATAN of Teutonic myth, enemy of the gods and of mortal man, Loki had children that included his sons the Midgard Serpent and the wolf Fenris and his daughter, HEL.

LONG, Breckinridge DWH 1958 HARDNESS OF HEART

A tiny bureaucrat and open admirer of BENITO MUSSOLINI, Long served as assistant secretary of state under FDR, in a post theoretically responsible for war victim relief. But he adamantly opposed the admission to the United States of even refugee children from Europe, on the ground that there might be German spies in the group. His personal diaries were filled with invectives against Jews ("Jewish professional agitators"), Catholics, New Yorkers, and liberals, aka "the radical press."

LOUCHAR

A demon in charge of the seventh dungeon of Hell, with the face of a bear.

LOUIS XIV DWH 1715 LUST

The French Sun King was hot. He spent much of his seventy-three-year reign engaged in sexual pursuits: As his sister-in-law observed, "Everything was grist to his mill, providing it was female—peasant girls, chambermaids, and ladies of quality." When (in 1672), in the name of the True Faith, Louis went to war against the Protestant Netherlands, his queen and two of his three current mistresses followed him in the same carriage. His last mistress was the infamous MARQUISE DE MONTESPAN. His last wife (Madame de Maintenon) complained to her confessor about the seventy-seven-year-old Louis's incessant sexual demands, and the king, in turn, complained to his (deaf) confessor about her lack of enthusiasm.

His sexual appetite was surpassed only by his appetite for food—exacerbated by a tapeworm, which caused him to eat so voraciously that he was known to have as many as twenty-three artificially induced bowel movements a day. (He sometimes conducted business while upon the commode, which he called the *chaise des affaires*.) The enema fad, not surprisingly, reached its peak during his reign—every morning two *limonadiers des postérieurs* arrived at Versailles to administer enemas to the entire court.

Described by a contemporary as "superstitious and devout, in the Spanish style," when he heard of the French army's defeat at the Battle of Blenheim, Louis moaned, "How could God do this to me after all I have done for Him?" After the revolution, his heart was stolen from his tomb and sold to the dean of Westminster, the Very Reverend William Buckland, who proceeded to eat it for dinner.

LUCESME

A fiend who is invoked during witches' Sabbats with the words "Lucesme, pray for us."

LUCIANO, Salvatore Charles (Lucky) DWH 1962 MURDER

The *capo di tutti capi* and father of organized crime in America was first arrested at the age of ten and by eleven had started a protection racket, escorting the smaller Jewish kids to school for a penny. One kid who refused to pay was Meyer Lansky, and the two went on to form a crime syndicate that controlled bootlegging, drugs, and prostitution. Luciano disdained the old country mafiosi, calling them Mustache Petes, and brought the mob into the twentieth century. Mobster ARNOLD ROTHSTEIN once complimented Lucky on his natty suits but

suggested he might try a more "genteel" tailor. "What the Hell are you talking about?" sputtered Luciano. "My tailor's *Catholic!*"

While serving a fifty-year sentence in Sing Sing (for pimping), Luciano was mysteriously released for "services" rendered during World War II, which consisted of tightening security on the mob-controlled waterfront. In 1946, he moved his operations to the corrupt Cuba of BATISTA, but he died in Naples, where, going from bad to worse, he not only directed heroin smuggling but was writing a screenplay when he suffered a fatal heart attack (after ignoring his doctor's orders to refrain from sex with his teenage mistress).

LUCIFER

The eleventh-century Irish monk Tundall, whose *Vision* of Hell influenced Dante, describes "Lucifer, the first creature God made," as huge and black, with hundreds of multifingered, long-nailed hands and a cruel beak. In Dante's

scheme, he is six-winged, gigantic (1,720 feet tall), and "king of Hell." His name means "Light Bearer." He was the greatest of all fallen angels, a prince of the Seraphim who stood nearest the throne of God until he uttered his fateful line, "I will not serve." A legend has it that CAIN once asked Lucifer why, with all his power, he had not done humanity any good, and Lucifer responded, "Why hasn't Jehovah?" By some accounts, he's kept his "perfect beauty" and after all these years still blushes. He has dominion over Europe and Asia; the temptation in which he specializes is to the deadly sin of pride. (It has been suggested that his alternate name is "Morning Star" because the morning star is the last proud star to defy the sunrise.) Lucifer's been active with a lightning bolt, striking 400 church towers and killing 120 bell ringers in one thirty-year period. Although certain Gnostic sects regard him as divine, and both the prophet Isaiah and Milton saw him as a force for evil and good, his *is* the first name invoked in the liturgies of SATAN. His opponent in Heaven is the equally fiery St. John the Baptist.

LUCIFUGE ROFOCALE

The prime minister of Hell, whose name means "fly-the-light," controls wealth and worldly goods, "the treasures of this world," and can find hidden treasures. But he also inflicts disease and deformity

LUCIFUGI

Lower-class demons who, according to Fred Gettings, "may scarcely be considered sentient beings." Lucifugi live in the center of the earth.

LURIDAN

Luridan is a demon in Wales who, as a sideline, gave instruction in English, according to *Prophetical Poets in British Rhimes.*

LYCAON

He fed human flesh to the Olympian gods, for which prank Zeus changed Lycaon into a wolf.

LYDIA

In the Renaissance epic *Orlando Furioso,* an English prince named Astolfo visits Hell and there encounters an infinite number of heartless, "Ungrateful" ladies, among them Lydia.

LYNCH, Mme. Eliza   DWH 1886   EVIL COUNSEL

A refugee from the Potato Famine, she wended her way from Ireland to Paris and eventually to Paraguay as mistress to that tiny nation's repulsive dictator Francisco Solano Lopez. The Paraguayan Pompadour convinced Lopez he could lead an empire embracing Argentina, Uruguay, and Brazil, thereby precipitating the Paraguayan War of 1865–1870, one of history's most feckless conflicts. But the war, which reduced the male population of Paraguay by 90 percent, did afford Madame Lynch the opportunity to torture and assassinate her snooty in-laws. It was said that whenever she entered the cathedral of Asunción, tears streamed from the statue of the Virgin. But the Virgin of Caapucú lost her jewels to Eliza, who replaced the gems with paste imitations. Today, miraculously, Madame Lynch is revered as a saint by many and actually called the Joan of Arc of Paraguay. A life-size statue of her holding two crosses stands above her mausoleum, the tallest in Paraguay. Ironically enough, she was once played on South American radio by Eva "Evita" Perón.

LYONS, Danny   DWH 1888   MURDER

He was a member of the Whyos, a murderous, all-Irish New York street gang of the late nineteenth century—a hit man and a pimp. When Lyons stole Joe Quinn's girl Kitty to add to his stable, Quinn swore revenge, but he died in a shoot-out with our hero, who was then hanged. After his death, two of his girls, Lizzie the Dove and Gentle Maggie, quarreled over the right to mourn him, and Maggie stabbed Lizzie, who croaked (as she croaked), "I'll scratch your eyes out in Hell."

May I add that there are a lot of people who have their names on the church rolls, there are a lot of people who frequent the church building, who, in judgment, shall find themselves in Hell.

In fact, the church is a nice place to go to Hell from!
—Mississippi delta preacher, recorded by Alan Lomax,
The Land Where the Blues Began

Most Christians profess to believe in Hell. Yet have you ever met a Christian who seemed as afraid of Hell as he was of cancer?
—GEORGE ORWELL, *As I Please*

MCCARTHY, Sen. Joseph   DWH 1957   SOWING DISCORD
In canto 29, Dante reaches the tenth level of the Eighth Circle, where he beholds the falsifiers. They are writhing in filthy heaps amidst the stench of their own rotting flesh and the terrible sound of their own lamentations—some sprawled, some crawling, all clawing at their leprous sores and scabs.

MAGOT
Demon expelled from a noblewoman in the chapel of Notre-Dame in 1618.

MAHOMET (aka Mohammed)   DWH 632   HERESY
To the Christians who lived in fear of the forces of Islam, that religion's founder was known contemptuously as Mahound—a term employed to his sorrow by the novelist Salman Rushdie in his *Satanic Verses*. The prophet was, quite literally, demonized and on the medieval stage would emerge ranting from a fiery "Hell's Mouth" alongside SATAN and various other devils. (Curiously, Dante and his contemporaries believed the founder of Islam to have been an apostate Catholic cardinal.)

MAHONIN
By this name a demon exorcised from a lady of Auch (in 1618) identified himself. He claimed to be a former Archangel, now resident of a pond near Béziers.

MALACODA

A flatulent devil (his name means "evil tail"), Malacoda is kind enough in canto 21 to give Dante and Virgil directions to a bridge they must cross. Bad directions, of course.

MALIK

The stern guardian of the Islamic Hell, Jahannan (Quran 43.77).

MALPHAS

A demon who appears in the form of a crow. Malphas builds fortresses but destroys carnal desire.

MAMMILON

The witch MARGARET JOHNSON confessed, at her trial in 1633, to frequent but highly unsatisfactory sexual relations with a demon by this name.

MAMMON

An archdemon whose name is derived from the Aramaic word that means "wealth" or "profit," Mammon is a tempter to sins of avarice. He is alleged (in France) to be SATAN's special envoy to England, that "nation of shopkeepers." One of the rare evil spirits mentioned by name in the New Testament—Jesus observed, "You cannot serve God and Mammon"—he represents material greed and money itself. The poet Milton, casting aspersions on his dignity if not his virility, called Mammon "the least erected Spirit that fell."

MANI   DWH 276   HERESY

A lame and sickly Babylonian boy, Mani experienced a vision of his "angelic twin," who instructed him that he was the Paraclete, the Apostle of Light, with a mission to restore Christianity. After traveling to India, he arrived in Persia, where he successfully preached his heretical doctrines until being executed on the orders of the orthodox (Zoroastrian) king Bahram, who had Mani's head displayed on a stick. The dualistic religion called Manichaeanism holds that the material world is evil and that all pleasure is sinful. The faithful were vegetarians, considered wine an invention of the Devil, and were, of course, strict celibates. St. Augustine was a devout Manichaean for nine years.

MANSFIELD, Jayne DWH 1967 SORCERY

The fame and success of this talentless, cowlike "actress" can only be explained by the fact that she was a witch—an acolyte of Sandor LeVay's Hollywood "Satanic church," in which she served as a living altar at black masses. Mansfield has the distinction of being the most self-promoted and publicity-hungry star in Hollywood's history, but her later life seemed to echo the title of one of her movies, *The Girl Can't Help It*. When her star began to fall, she abused alcohol and her children, forcing her daughter to paint her toenails and pretend she was her sister. Her membership in the Church of Satan upset her boyfriend Sam Brody, and his attempt to wrest her away from the "church" landed a curse on his head. Unfortunately, Mansfield was decapitated along with him when his car collided with a truck. After her death, she made a return appearance in the Church of Satan and possessed a worshipper, causing him to go into convulsions and, more horribly, speak in her tinny voice.

MANTO SOOTHSAYING

Prophetess daughter of the prophet TIRESIAS. Dante condemns her to Hell (canto 20), despite the fact that she was alleged to have founded his birth city, Mantua. But he atones for this—or makes a very rare mistake—by also placing her in Purgatory (canto 32).

MAO Tse-tung DWH 1976 UNCLEANLINESS

That "cleanliness is next to godliness" we have on the authority of the eminent divine John Wesley (Sermon 93). But the chairman's personal physician Li Zhisui attests that Mao "stopped bathing after he moved to Zhongnanhai. He considered it a waste of time" (*The Private Life of Chairman Mao*, p. 100) and that "his genitals were never cleaned" (p. 364). Moreover, Mao never brushed his teeth, so that they "were coated with a heavy greenish film" (p. 98).

MARA

The Hindu demon of death and the archtempter of Buddhism. Mara's dangerous daughters are Raga (pleasure), Rati (desire), and Tanha (restlessness).

MARBAS 🦎
A demon who both causes and cures disease.

MARC ANTONY   DWH 30 B.C.   LUST
He had his faults. After the assassination of his mentor JULIUS CAESAR, he rose to power not just through his florid oratory ("Friends, Romans, countrymen . . .") but also by forging the dead emperor's papers. When his (third) wife Fulvia made trouble for his rival Octavian, Antony had the presence of mind to dump her and marry Octavian's sister Octavia. But we know that he is in Hell because we know (Dante tells us) that his beloved CLEOPATRA is there—and what's (hot) sauce for the goose . . .

MARCHOUR   🦎
Now a marquis of Hell (formerly an angel of the order of Dominions), Marchour manifests himself when conjured in the shape of a wolf or ox.

MARESIN   🦎
According to Robert Burton's *Anatomy of Melancholy*, Maresin is a prince of aerial demons, "the powers of the air." As such he causes both plagues and fires.

MAROU   🦎
A fallen Cherub, Marou is listed in the official record of the witchcraft trial of Father Urbain Grandier, in 1634, as one of the celebrated "Devils of Loudun" who possessed Sister Elizabeth Blanchard.

MAROZIA   DWH 944   BLASPHEMY
She was fifteen years old when she became the mistress of Pope SERGIUS III. After five passion-filled years, Sergius died, but Marozia had something to remember him by—a son. Sergius's successor, John X, was, by a happy coincidence, the lover of Marozia's mother, Theodora. Marozia kindly waited for her mother to die before having her papal boyfriend suffocated and her own child (John XI) placed in the Chair of Peter. But the story does not end happily. Another of Marozia's sons, Alberic, rose to power in Rome and had both his half brother the pope and their mother thrown in prison, where they died.

MASSIKIM   🦎
According to the Talmud, these Jewish demons were the products of Adam's sinful mating with LILITH.

MASTEMA   🦎
In the Hebrew apocryphal Book of Jubilees, Mastema is identified as

the "Prince of Evil," the cruel demon who hardened Pharaoh's heart against the Israelites.

MATA HARI   DWH 1917
TREASON

The prototype of the sensual temptress was born plain old Margaretha Zelle, the daughter of a bankrupt hatter in the Netherlands. She traveled to the Dutch colony of Java with her husband, Capt. Campbell MacLeod, in 1897. Her deep study of East Indian culture stood her in good stead when she began to perform sensational near-nude "exotic" dances in Paris nightclubs in 1905, having taken as her (Malayan) stage name Mata Hari. She became a craze, dancing in Spain and Vienna, and at La Scala in Milan. Her name and face adorned cigarette packs and biscuit boxes. But she couldn't resist a man in uniform. Before and during World War I, many of her lovers and confidants were German *and* French officers—and whether she was spying against the Germans or for them, the French authorities presumed the latter. She was executed by firing squad.

MAYER, Louis B.   DWH 1957   TYRANNY

The movie mogul who created the "star system" and headed MGM, arguably the greatest studio in Hollywood history, was an immigrant from Russia who started his career dealing in scrap metal and cotton waste. He was the highest paid executive in the United States from 1937 to 1944, and he viewed his contract players as his children—he would cry real tears when one asked for a raise. He also really believed the sentimental view of America his movies promoted. "I worship good women, honorable men, and saintly mothers," he declared, and he once screamed at a misbehaving Mickey Rooney, "You're Andy Hardy! You're the United States!"

So long as the German film market was a lucrative one, Mayer found it convenient to deny the rising Nazi menace. But the war came home to him when his brother Rudolph was taken prisoner by the Japanese. In an extraordinary display of power, Mayer called his buddy Archbishop Spellman in New York, who in turn called the pope, who contacted MUSSOLINI. Mussolini got HITLER on the horn, and the Führer quickly wired Tojo. Within days, Rudolph Mayer was on a plane to Los Angeles.

Louis Mayer was a generous financial supporter of Red-baiting Sen. JOSEPH MCCARTHY. Said he, probably forgetting he was born in Russia, "The more McCarthy yells, the better I like him. I hope he drives all the bums back to Moscow."

In his later years, worried about mortality, Mayer began lessons in Catholicism. But his daughter Irene dissuaded him from conversion, saying, cruelly, that a fat, short Jew pretending to be Catholic would be laughed out of Hollywood.

MEDEA   WITCHCRAFT

Dante implies mysteriously that the damnation of her ex-husband JASON is Medea's "revenge on him" (canto 18). According to the Greek myth, Medea was a sorceress who fell for Jason, helped him to obtain the Golden Fleece, then facilitated their escape from her angry father by cutting her brother to pieces and scattering them behind for Dad to pick up. As Jason's queen, she murdered first his mistress Glauce and then her own children. In her youth, she had rejected the advances of Zeus, thereby winning the affection of Hera—after Medea's death, the goddess married her to the studly ACHILLES in Hades.

MEDUSA   🦇

At the Gates of Dis, the entrance to the Sixth Circle and Lower Hell, Dante encounters Medusa but has the presence of mind not to stare and so is not turned to stone. A mortal but snake-headed demoness of the Gorgon class, she had been slain long ago by the hero Perseus.

MELCHOM   🦇

A minor but essential demonic functionary, the "paymaster of Hell," according to Weyer.

MEPHISTOPHELES (aka Mephisto)   🦇

His name first appears in 1587, in the original *Faustbuch*. It seems to be derived from the Hebrew words for "destroyer" and "liar." A fallen Archangel, Mephisto proudly claims to be one of the Maskim—the seven rulers of Hell. He first achieved literary fame courtesy of playwright Christopher Marlowe, in whose 1604 tragedy *Dr. Faustus* he acts as the magician's dignified servant and gloomy adviser—a sort of infernal Jeeves. In

Goethe's (1832) *Faust*, he is a witty and cynical fiend who acts as SATAN's lawyer. The long, philosophical, and quite unstageable drama ends ignominiously for Mephisto—he allows the soul of Faust to escape to Heaven while he makes clumsy passes at a group of shapely female angels.

MERIDIANA

A succubus, said (by the learned scholar Walter Mapes) to have been the lifelong mistress and helpmate of Gerbert of Aurillac, otherwise known as the learned and celibacy-enforcing pope SYLVESTER II.

MERIRIM

One of the diabolical powers of the air, Meririm is most powerful at noon. He sometimes boils the oceans.

MESMER, Anton DWH 1815   HERESY

The Swabian doctor who discovered—or invented—"animal magnetism" became briefly the toast of Paris, curing all manner of mental and physical illnesses by inducing a trance state in his patients and then immersing them in a large bathtub filled with purportedly magnetized water; they tied cords around themselves while Mesmer used a wand to

point to the afflicted areas (and a band played in the distance). Ben
Franklin investigated, and reported to LOUIS XIV that Mesmer was a quack.
The Vatican (in 1856) officially declared him a heretic.

MESSALINA   DWH 48   LUST

MESSALINA.

As a cruel joke, CALIGULA
arranged the marriage between
his allegedly simple fifty-year-old
uncle Claudius and the gorgeous
fifteen-year-old Messalina. She
bore him a daughter, Octavia,
and, in 41, a son, Britannicus. That
very year, Claudius became emperor, and Messalina became
. . . a nymphomaniac. Her affairs
were indiscreet and indiscriminate—she chose as her lovers
slaves, courtiers, gladiators, actors, the handsomest men in
Rome and sometimes, just for a
change, the ugliest. She challenged a notorious prostitute
named Scylla to a fucking competition. The whore gave up at
dawn, but Messalina humped into
the morning, returning to the palace (in Juvenal's words) "tired but not sat-
isfied." Not until Claudius learned that his beloved wife had undertaken a
bigamous marriage did he react, by ordering her arrest. Despite her own
mother's pleadings, Messalina refused to kill herself and in the end was
stabbed by an officer of the guard. Claudius was at dinner when he was
told of her death. He asked for more wine.

Apparently a glutton for punishment, he took as his next bride JULIA
AGRIPPINA.

MINOS

In pagan (Greek and Roman) mythology—and, curiously, in Dante's
Christian scheme—Minos is the judge of the dead in Hades; he assigns in-
nocent souls to Elysium and condemns the guilty to Tartarus. Virgil, in the
Aeneid (book 6), gives a description of proceedings in his court. He was a
demigod, son of Zeus and the mortal maiden Europa, and king of Crete.
Although his legend is one of bloody murder—he had constructed the

labyrinth in which Athenian maidens were sacrificed to a half-man, half-bull monster—he was reputed to be both wise and just. In Dante's scheme, Minos stands at the gate of the Second Circle—the entrance to Hell proper. The poet goes so far as to call him infallible as judge of the dead (canto 29). It was his custom to wrap his serpentine tail around the guilty and with it fling them to perdition. (An accurate portrait of this judicial appendage may be seen in Michelangelo's painting *The Last Judgment.*)

MISHIMA, Yukio (Kimitake Hiraoka)   DWH 1970   SUICIDE

This celebrated Japanese writer took the name Mishima—"mysterious devil bewitched with death"—as befit his fascination with ancient Japanese martial arts and ritual suicide. His boyhood hero was St. Joan of Arc, until he found out she was female. He had his first orgasm gazing on a picture of the martyred St. Sebastian. Oblivious to his rather open homosexuality, his wife and mother doted on and competed for him, although a survey revealed that most Japanese women would rather commit suicide than have sex with him.

Mishima evolved a political movement that was a mishmash of fascism and samurai philosophy. He formed a private army with himself as general and his lover, Morita, as second in command. His ultimate political statement was public suicide by disemboweling. Mishima and his little army seized control of military headquarters in downtown Tokyo, but police helicopters drowned out his final speech, and he botched the disemboweling part, although he had been rehearsing for weeks.

MISROCH   🦅

Grand steward of Hell.

MITHRANDJRUJ   🦅

The Zoroastrian "demon of lies."

MOLECH   🦅

Prince of the Land of Tears. As a demon, Molech appears in *Paradise Lost,* "besmeared with blood of human sacrifice." As a god (of the Phoenicians, aka the Ammonites), he is first mentioned in Leviticus 18:21; we are told the backsliding Israelites sacrificed by fire their firstborn children to him. In the interest, perhaps, of ecumenism, King Solomon

(I Kings 11:7) built a temple to Molech—near the entrance to the place known as Gehenna—that is, Hell. Demonologists believe him to be at his most powerful during the month of December.

MONKER ⚜

In Islamic lore, two black, blue-eyed demons, Monker and Nakir, examine and judge the dead, then assign them to Paradise or Hell.

MONTEFELTRO, Guido   DWH 1298   EVIL COUNSEL

He advised BONIFACE VIII to break his papal word. Penitent, Montefeltro joined the Franciscans, and, at his death, witnesses beheld St. Francis himself appear to fight a (losing) battle with a "black angel" for eternal custody of his soul.

MONTESPAN, Marquise de   DWH 1707   SORCERY

No wonder she relished her role as mistress of King LOUIS XIV: The marquise de Montespan had an annual allowance of 800,000 gold louis, not including money paid for her gambling debts (she once lost a million in a card game), on clothes, or to support the six illegitimate children she bore the king. When she strutted proudly before the king's Germans troops, they excitedly cheered her on, "Königs Hure, Königs Hure" (King's Whore, King's Whore). So who can blame her for panicking when the lascivious king started looking elsewhere? First Montespan sneaked an aphrodisiac—dried cockerel's testicles—into the king's food, then availed herself of the services of La Voisin (see CATHERINE DESHAYES). In the black masses she prescribed, the accommodating (read naked) marquise would serve as altar, holding a cross between her breasts and a chalice between her thighs. Even the king was shocked by news of this debauchery and ordered everyone involved executed—except madame the marquise, who was quietly shipped off to the convent of St. Joseph in Paris—of which institution she eventually became the mother superior. There she indulged her gluttony, becoming so fat that an ungallant aide, Prima Visconti, reported that "her legs have become as wide as my body."

MORDRED   DWH circa 300   TREASON

King Arthur was once seduced by a wicked but beautiful witch, the Orkney queen Morgawse, otherwise known as Morgan le Fay. She happened to have been his sister. Their son became a knight—Sir Mordred, the villain of Camelot. In Arthur's absence, Mordred declared himself king, and in a battle fought on Salisbury Plain on the Monday after Trinity Sunday (attests Sir Thomas Malory), the Once and Future King and his nephew–illegitimate son slew each other. Mordred is, Dante assures us in canto 32, in deepest, freezing Hell, quite at home among the worst of history's traitors.

MORRISON, Jim   DWH 1971   FRAUD

If singing flat were a mortal sin, which it is not, Morrison would be damned for it. But his eternal funeral pyre burns for unrepentant drug abuse, indecent exposure, and stealing his only catchy tune, "Hello, I Love You," from the Kinks, as well as for sorcery, spitting on his fans, gluttony, simulating masturbation onstage, and continuing to wear leather hip huggers after getting fat.

MOSCA dei Lamberti   DWH 13th century   SOWING DISCORD

In the Ninth Bolgia (canto 28) Dante encounters this Florentine troublemaker, who instigated the Guelf-Ghibelline feud. On earth, his family was wiped out; in Hell, his lying tongue is torn out, and his sly hands are cut off. The poet adds to his agony with an insult.

MULCIMER   🦇

A clever devil—the architect of Hell.

MULLIN   🦇

A demon in the Royal Satanic Household, serving as the first gentleman of the bedchamber.

MURIEL   🦇

The demon who rules over the astrological sign of Cancer.

MURMUR   🦇

A former angelic Throne, Murmur is now a count of Hell, commanding thirty legions. He it is who first takes charge of a damned soul and subjects it to a "third degree." He is also alleged to be most musical.

MUSSOLINI, Benito   DWH 1945   TREASON

Lower than all the lustful, the thieves, the liars, and the killers in Hell—in SATAN's very jaws—the traitors are to be found. The strutting bully who styled himself Il Duce (and who began his political career as a socialist) formally allied his fascist government to HITLER's, forming the Axis in October 1925 and joining, in May 1939, a Pact of Steel. But the Nazis invaded Poland unilaterally, and the Germans picked up all the loot when France fell. Determined to "pay Hitler back in his own coin," Mussolini had his forces invade Albania without alerting his Nazi allies. Hitler had a fit, predicting—correctly—that German troops would have to waste precious time and manpower extricating the Italians from their defeat. Consequently, when he launched Operation Barbarossa against the USSR, he didn't bother informing his ally Mussolini of his plans. When he heard the news, the betrayed Duce ranted—correctly—"We have just lost the war!"

Now and forever, writhing together between the Devil's teeth, the two are reunited and howl at each other, "Traitor!"

MYRRHA   INCEST

The beautiful daughter of King Cinyras of Cyprus, Myrrha was smitten with lust for her own father and went incognita to his bed. She escaped his righteous wrath when she was transformed by the gods into a myrtle tree, whence the spice myrrh is derived. (Myrrh was reputed, among the ancients, to be an aphrodisiac.) Dante (canto 30) has this pagan girl among the deeply damned for her sin of deception. But he does not include the lusty daughters of the holy Hebrew patriarchs Lot and Noah, who (Scripture informs us) pulled exactly the same incestuous prank.

No Devil; no God.
—JOHN WESLEY

No Hell, no dignity.
—FLANNERY O'CONNOR

Nema. Olarn a son arebil des.
—First words of *The Devil's Creed*

NAAMAH

In Jewish tradition, Naamah is the wife of CAIN's descendant Tubal. Demonologists say she is the most oversexed of SATAN's four wives and list her among the ten evil Sephirath. Satan is grateful for her many infidelities, which include relations with angels, other demons, and mortal men—whom she seduces in their sleep, afterward sucking their blood. She gave her name to the anemone, the "flower of blood," and is the mother of the great demon ASMODEUS.

NABERIUS

When magicians conjure up Naberius, he flutters around the magic circle in the form of a crowing cock, teaching the art of rhetoric in a hoarse voice. In Hell, Naberius has the rank of marquis and the ability to regain lost favors or honors to those who invoke his aid. He appears to suffer from a form of St. Vitus' dance.

NAGA

An Indian demon who is human above the navel but a snake below.

NAGRASAGIEL

A prince of Hell who served as Moses' tour guide of the infernal regions, as recounted in the Hebrew *Midrash Konen*.

NAKIR  See MONKER.

NAMON
One of eight demons who possessed Sister Jeanne Fery of Mons in 1835. They made her cough up hair balls.

NAMTAR
This plague demon inflicted Ishtar with a ghastly disease when she visited Aralu, the Babylonian equivalent of Hell. Later, acting under orders of the demon queen Allatu, Namtar sprinkled Ishtar with the waters of life, restoring her to her former beauty.

NAMUCI
Tenacious male demon in India whose name means "he who never lets go."

NANTUR
The demon of writing, a jinni of the eighth hour.

NAPOLEONE degli Alberti   DWH 1286   TREASON
Brother of ALESSANDRO.

NARI
Slavic demons who take the shape of birds.

NASR-ED-DIN
A Muslim demon and one of Hell's great jokesters.

NAT
A Burmese evil spirit.

NATASCHURUS and NABASCURUS
Demons expelled from a pair of nuns in seventeenth-century Munich.

NATHURAM
The ghost of a notorious libertine who, even dead and in Hell, has prurient interests. To pacify Nathuram, women in certain sections of India sing lewd songs and make obscene gestures.

NEBIROS
Demon alleged by demonologists to be in charge of North America.

NEBUCHADNEZZAR   DWH 6th century B.C.   TYRANNY
King of Babylon who conquered Jerusalem, destroyed its great temple, exiled the Hebrew king, ended the kingdom of Judah, and, in the coup de grâce, castrated thousands of Jewish prisoners. The prophet Daniel

worked in his court and correctly predicted that Nebuchadnezzar would go mad, be deposed, and "eat grass like an ox."

NELCHAEL

A fallen angel who, in Hell, gives lessons in mathematics and geography to his fellow demons.

NELSON, Lester "Baby Face"   DWH 1934   MURDER

The man who succeeded JOHN DILLINGER as Public Enemy Number One was a homicidal maniac whose bank robbery MO was to enter, spray the premises with a machine gun, and demand loot from a lucky survivor. Jealous of Dillinger's reputation, Nelson determined to surpass him in public esteem by robbing a bank a month—but was dissuaded by seventeen G-man bullets.

As much as he hated his "sissy" Christian name, Lester, this killer hated his nickname Baby Face more. He insisted that he be called Big George—which is odd, because George wasn't his name and he was only five foot three.

NEPHALIM

The demon responsible for asthma.

NEPHILIM

These are the gigantic offspring of fallen angels and the daughters of CAIN (mentioned in Genesis 6), who built the Tower of Babel. Even though the Nephilim were supposedly eradicated in the Flood, there exists today in Chicago the Satanic Church of the Nephilim Race, which claims that demons are matter in the purest form.

NERGAL

A former angel of the Chaldeans, Nergal is now the chief of Hell's secret police, reporting directly to BEELZEBUB. Nergal is a ruthless, crouching, lion-headed demon who on earth spreads pestilence.

NERO   DWH 68   TYRANNY

When he married his boy-girlfriend, a eunuch named Sporus, Nero said it was because he/she reminded him of his dead wife Poppaea. This sentiment was somewhat misplaced, since Nero had killed the pregnant Poppaea with a kick to the stomach. He also killed

his first wife, Octavia, as well as his mother (and former lover), JULIA AGRIP-PINA. Her final words were the (understandably) unmaternal cry "Smite my womb!"

According to Tacitus, Nero "inflicted the most exquisite torture on Christians," blaming them for the fire he himself started as an excuse to begin remodeling Rome. His political enemies didn't fare much better: Nero sewed them into the skins of wild beasts and threw them to the dogs. Worst of all, he forced the public to witness (and applaud) his ghastly performances as a singer, poet, musician, and charioteer. He was fond of entering talent shows, which, since the judges knew what was good for them, he always won. No wonder theories persist that he was "the Beast" predicted in Revelation 13:18.

NEWELL, Patrick   DWH 1975   SORCERY

This New Jersey teenager squashed hamsters in Satanic rituals. Newell daydreamed of going to Hell and becoming captain of a team of devils. To this end, he convinced his friends to kill him by binding his hands and feet and throwing him in a pond.

NEWTON, Florence   DWH 1661   WITCHCRAFT

When a neighbor failed to share her beef, Newton bewitched her, causing her to vomit needles, pins, horse nails, wool, and straw. She was arrested and confessed merely to giving her neighbor the evil eye—but in prison, successive attempts to teach her the Lord's Prayer failed, because she never remembered to include "and forgive us our trespasses."

NGO Dinh Diem   DWH 1963   TYRANNY

When the U.S. government installed this Catholic mandarin as ruler of South Vietnam in 1954, they hired a press agent to convince Americans and Vietnamese that Diem was a nationalist. Unfortunately, Diem proceeded to torture and kill his political opponents and even forbade Buddhist monks to fly ceremonial flags on Buddha's birthday. When the monks protested, his secret police opened fire and killed nine of them. Diem encouraged the ascendancy of his sister-in-law, Madame Nhu, who was such a tyrant and prig that she banned all romantic songs. After he was finally killed in a U.S.-backed coup (approved by President Kennedy and called, oddly, an "accidental suicide"), U.S. officials freely—and finally—acknowledged that Diem had been a "terrible character."

NICHOLAS I   DWH 1855

TYRANNY

The grandson of CATHERINE THE GREAT, Nicholas was reactionary and despotic even by the standards of Russian czars. After usurping the throne, he brutally suppressed a Polish revolt, expanded the army and secret police, and spent the rest of his reign persecuting serfs, liberals, and minorities. Depressive, anal-compulsive, and paranoid (he referred to a war he had started as "my cross"), he forbade beards, "dilettante philosophizing," and fireworks. Nicholas had the distinction of being wrong about everything. Even his last words, to his heir, were "Now I shall ascend to pray for Russia and for you."

NICHOLAS III   DWH 1280   SIMONY

A papal cheapskate. Nicholas made a fortune off the Inquisition but did not—as was the custom—split the profits with the executioners. Dante buries him (head down, with his feet on fire) among the simoniacs and accuses him of nepotism, describing in detail (canto 19) how Nicholas, thwarted in his scheme to marry his niece to the king of Sicily, conspired in the insurrection and massacre known as the Sicilian Vespers.

NICOLÒ dei Salimbeni   DWH 1311   PRODIGALITY

An ostentatious "foodie" who only cooked with expensive spices, Nicolò was a member of the Brigata Spenderecci, or Spendthrifts' Club, which consisted of twelve young men who spent lavish amounts of money to rent a palace for their sumptuous monthly banquets. They ate exotic meals and flung their gold and silver utensils out the window after every course.

NICKNEVEN

A demonic hag of Scotland who was once queen of the fairies—some scholars think Nickneven lent her name to the demon Old Nick.

NIETZSCHE, Friedrich   DWH 1900
HERESY

Early in his philosophic career, Nietzsche declared himself a disciple of the pagan god Dionysus and insisted that God, idealism, Christianity, and morality were dying—or, in God's case, already dead. The Devil, on the other hand, is alive and well. Representing the creative force of love, feeling, and joy, he is the "most ancient friend of wisdom." The Devil expressed his gratitude by afflicting Nietzsche with syphilis and raving madness.

Raised in a household of five women, Nietzsche was a lifelong bachelor and explicit misogynist ("Do you go to a woman? Bring a whip!"). Nonetheless, he lusted after Lou Salome, the mistress of his friend the poet Rilke, as well as Cosima, the wife of his enemy RICHARD WAGNER.

His fateful preaching in *Thus Spake Zarathustra*—"Dead are all the Gods: now do we desire the Superman to live"—definitely reached the wrong audience. Thanks to the efforts of his literary executor, his Nazi sister Elisabeth, Nietzsche became Hitler's pet philosopher.

NIHASA
A Native American demon.

NIJA
The pagan Polish god of the Underworld.

NIMROD   PRIDE

Dante (canto 31), following St. Augustine, believed that the biblical giant Nimrod (Genesis 10:8–12) had built the Tower of Babel. In Hell, he helps guard the gate at the mouth of the Ninth Circle and, as might be expected, speaks gibberish. Nimrod, "a mighty hunter," was the ancestor of the Assyrians. For some reason, no dew ever falls on his tomb in Damascus.

NINHURSAG
A demon queen.

NINKASI

A demon queen who wears horns.

NINNGHIZHIDDA

A demon queen who carries a magic wand.

NISROCH

An eagle-headed deity of the Assyrians and (according to Milton—*Paradise Lost* 6.447) a former prince of the angelic order of Principalities. After Sennacherib's defeat, Nisroch joined SATAN and became Hell's cook; he is said to make liberal use of spices. He tempts mortals, through the pleasures of the table, to sins of gluttony.

NITIBUS and NITIKA

Demons mentioned in *The Nuctemeron* of Apollonius, they rule over, respectively, the stars and precious stones.

NIXON, Richard M.   DWH 1994   WRATH

> *And I saw the dead, small and great, stand before God; and the books were opened; and another book was opened, which is the book of life; and the dead were judged out of the things which were written in the books, according to their works.*
>
> —Revelation 20:12

There are seven Deadly Sins: pride, wrath, envy, avarice, lust, gluttony, and sloth. With the last three of these, Richard Nixon was not even

charged—having been in life notoriously sexless, puritanically abstemious, and always *very* busy. As an experienced defense attorney, he next pled innocent to avarice ("I am not a crook") and pride ("Pat wore a good Republican cloth coat"). But on the evidence, he was sentenced to the Fifth Circle of Hell (where the wrathful are covered with slime and burning with rage), because there are no "expletives deleted" from the book of life.

NOSTRADAMUS DWH 1566 SORCERY

This French astrologer predicted, by means of pyromancy (divination by fire), the Great Fire of London, the French Revolution, Napoleon's campaigns, both world wars, and, some say, the Watergate scandal. After an early career compiling jelly recipes, he went to work in the court of CATHERINE DE MEDICI, casting horoscopes, reading moles, and, if rumors were true, becoming the queen's lover. (He truly prophesied to Catherine that all her sons would become kings of France— but neglected to mention that they would reign in rather rapid succession.) His book of rhymed prophecies, published in 1555 and inspired by his indulgence in absinthe, became a classic of occult literature. It was consulted by both sides during World War II. Nostradamus was buried (upright) in 1566. In 1791, when the soldiers who opened his grave found his skeleton with a plaque reading "1791" hanging around its neck, they fainted.

NYBBAS 🦅

A master mimic and jester, Nybbas is master of the revels in Hell and in charge of the pleasures therein.

O Lord, Thy people know full well
That all who cannot . . . speak or spell
Thy various names,
Shall be forever broiled in Hell
Among the flames.
　　　　—ALGERNON SWINBURNE, "The Cannibal's Catechism"

On the whole, he had enjoyed himself very much down there in Hell, and he
insisted that the devils were not such bad fellows after all.
　　　　—FRANÇOIS RABELAIS, *Gargantua and Pantagruel*

OATES, Titus　　DWH 1705　　BEARING FALSE WITNESS

This bandy-legged, baboon-faced son of a Baptist concocted, in 1678, a "papist plot" to assassinate King Charles II of England. The Jesuitical conspirators, he claimed, included the duke of York, five lords (who were beheaded), and Archbishop Plunket (who was drawn and quartered). On his false testimony, thirty-five innocent Catholics died, hundreds were driven into exile, thousands were imprisoned. When the duke of York assumed the throne as James II, he ordered that Oates be pilloried, flogged, and imprisoned; but the fiend was granted amnesty and a pension by the revolutionary Protestant regime of William and Mary.

OBIZZO, d'Este　　DWH 1293　　TREASON

Dante sights the marquis of Ferrara immersed to the eyes in a river of boiling blood (canto 18). A Guelf nobleman and cruel tyrant who treacherously assisted the army of Charles of Anjou, he was murdered by his bastard son, AZZOLINO DA ROMANO.

OG

A wicked biblical (Deuteronomy 3:10–11), antediluvian giant (but not, apparently, one of the NEPHILIM), who survived the Flood either by walking beside the ark or by riding on its roof.

OIELLET 🦟

Once an angel of the order of Dominations, from Hell Oiellet tempts monks to break their vows of poverty.

OIGNES, Mme. d'   DWH 1213   SIN: ???

Thomas of Cantimpre, thirteenth-century author of a treatise on miracles, *On the Nature of Things,* described the life and sanctity of the recently deceased Belgian Marie d'Oignes, a phenomenally pious, wealthy, married virgin. She possessed, he tells us, "the gift of tears," that is, she wept unceasingly, leaving a snail-like trail on pavement. (She perspired copiously as well, but her sweat, testified her holy confessor James de Vitry, smelled like incense.) One cause of her tears was the death of her mother, to whom she was most devoted. But when she was favored with a vision of her mother burning in Hell, she naturally stopped mourning at once.

OLIVIER   🦟

This fallen Archangel now encourages cruelty toward the poor.

ONAN   ONANISM

Genesis 38 features a typically edifying biblical episode: God, in His mercy, slew Judah's firstborn son, Er, for being "wicked." The grieving patriarch naturally ordered his second son, Onan, to "go in unto thy brother's wife." Onan went in all right but then pulled out and "spill[ed] his seed on the ground," which displeased the Lord, wherefore He slew him also. Now desperate for *somebody*'s seed, the twice-widowed bride (whose name was Tamar) proceeded to disguise herself as a prostitute and seduce Judah himself. By her whoremongering father-in-law, Tamar, in the fullness of time, gave birth to Perez, of whom, St. Matthew is at pains to establish (Matthew 1:1–16), Jesus was a direct descendant. But in vain do we argue that Onan's act of coitus interruptus was necessary, in order that sinful mankind be ultimately redeemed. St. Augustine argued, sensibly enough, that the sin for which Onan was slain was the practice of birth control. Not until 1710 did a Puritan physician in London (Bekkers) refer to masturbation, "the loathsome sin of self pollution," as "Onania." Thomas Aquinas had long ago realized that masturbation "is a worse sin than intercourse with one's own mother"; and in our time, Pope Paul VI, in *Persona Humana* (1975), affirmed that "masturbation is an intrinsically and gravely disordered action."

ONI-NO-NEMBUTSU   🦟

Oni are a class of Japanese horned demons, gigantic in stature. They are available in pink, red, or blue-gray models and may from time to time be converted to Buddhism. This particular specimen is associated with greed and hypocrisy. His name means "demon as monk."

ORBAN   DWH 15th century   CRUELTY

Don Quixote himself described artillery as "those devilish engines . . . whose inventor I am persuaded is in Hell, receiving the reward of his diabolical invention." The name of artillery's inventor is known only to God and/or the Devil, but certainly among the damned is one Orban, a treacherous Hungarian gun maker whose enormous cannon was employed by the infidel Turks in their (1453) siege of Constantinople. The Holy Roman Empire was ended by a machine that fired hundred-pound stone balls and took one hundred men two hours to load.

ORCHARD, Harry   DWH 1954   MURDER

Convicted in 1905 of the murder of the ex-governor of Idaho, Orchard claimed to have done it on the orders of labor leader William D. "Big Bill" Haywood. At Haywood's subsequent trial, it was revealed that Orchard was not only a killer but a liar, fink, provocateur, and paid agent of the union-busting Pinkerton agency. He died in jail.

ORGEUIL   🐾

A demon who, along with BONIFARCE, was exorcised from Sister Elizabeth Allier in 1639. He claimed to have entered her body on a crust of bread.

ORIAS   🐾

A self-help demon who transforms men and gives them titles.

ORIGEN   DWH 254   HERESY

By consensus the greatest of the early Greek Fathers of the Church, Origen argued that Hell is not necessarily eternal—that in God's mercy, everyone, even damned souls, even the Devil himself, might someday repent and be saved. For these views, he was posthumously excommunicated and damned by the synods of Constantinople in 543 and 553, and likewise declared anathema by synods in 680, 787, and 869.

OSCEOLA   DWH 1838   VIOLENCE

When, in 1815, the duly constituted, piously religious, and highly civilized U.S. government instructed the indigenous Seminoles to leave Florida, this malcontent refused and, with a band of like-minded miscreants, fled into the Everglades, whence they waged a highly successful two-year guerrilla war against the federal army until a brilliant and honorable general, T. S. Jesup, lured the wily Osceola into the fortress of St. Augus-

tine under a flag of truce—then bravely arrested him. Osceola, quite unrepentant, soon died in jail.

OSIRIS

Osiris is a pagan god, ruler of the Egyptians' dim afterlife
Underworld. The poet Milton (*Paradise Lost* 1.478) affirms
his new Christian-demonic status.

O YAMA

SATAN, in Japanese.

Parting is all we know of heaven,
And all we need of hell.

— EMILY DICKINSON

PACKER, Alferd   DWH 1907   MURDER

He led five prospectors into the San Juan Mountains, but he returned alone to Salt Lake City, claiming his party had deserted him. While he was drinking and gambling at a local saloon, looking more prosperous than usual, Packer was approached by an Indian chief, who observed, "You're too damn fat." After the bodies—rather, the skeletons—of his companions were found, Packer confessed to killing and eating all of them. He was the first person in U.S. history to be convicted of cannibalism. His judge screamed, "Packer, you depraved Republican son of a bitch, there were only five Democrats in Hinsdale County, and you ate them all!"

PAGAN BABIES

Until recently, giving money to the foreign missions to "ransom pagan babies" was a feature of Catholic parochial school life. St. Cyprian said it: *"Salus extra ecclesiam non est"*—There is no salvation outside the Church. But does this mean that everyone who dies unbaptized goes to Hell? Perish the thought.

The early Fathers, such as Tertullian and Gregory of Nazianzus, opposed infant baptism, on the ground that children are (obviously) innocent of sin. The first theologian to propose that unbaptized newborns would burn in Hell was St. Augustine, early in the fifth century. His odious notion of a sadistic, baby-burning God was immediately ridiculed by the great ORIGEN—and, well before Dante's time, the existence of a happy afterlife state for unbaptized children (St. Thomas Aquinas called it *"limbus infantum"*) was well established. The reformer John Calvin, however, was a strict Augustinian; as a consequence, the only "Christians" who continue to condemn "pagan babies" to an eternity of Hellfire are the boobs who get their Old-time Religion from the blow-dried flimflam men known as televangelists.

PAHLAVI, Mohammad Reza
DWH 1980   TYRANNY

His army officer–father, Reza Khan, usurped the peacock throne of Persia in 1925 and declared himself Shah Pahlavi. His pro-Nazi policies led, in 1941, to an Anglo-Soviet invasion of his oil-rich domain, followed by his abdication. He was succeeded by his son Mohammad Reza Pahlavi, *our* shah, briefly deposed in the mid-1950s by nationalist premier Mosaddeq, but restored to office through the good offices of the CIA. He felt, he said, "a Supreme Being guiding me." Among his "reforms" were the change of his nation's name to Iran ("land of the Aryans") and the creation of Savak, his infamous secret police. At one point, Amnesty International estimated there were between 25,000 and 100,000 political prisoners in Iran. Newspapers were forced to publish a daily glowing report about the shah and avoid mention of his lifestyle: fast cars, poker (he once lost $1,500,000 in a game), and busty blond hookers. "Women," said he, "are important only if they are beautiful and charming." In 1979, his corrupt regime was overthrown by Islamic "fundamentalists" under the direction of the AYATOLLAH KHOMEINI.

PAIMON

A great king of Hell, answering only to LUCIFER himself, Paimon commands 200 legions. He appears to mortals as a young woman—or a man with an effeminate countenance—riding a camel. Paimon is conjured for his ability to teach art and science, and he enables magicians to subject people to their will.

PAINE, Thomas   DWH 1809   ATHEISM

A lifelong propagandist in radical causes, Paine published popular and resoundingly effective pamphlets in support of the American War of Independence (*Common Sense*), the French Revolution (*The Rights of Man*), and religious liberty (*The Age of Reason*). As might be expected, he was thoroughly disliked—smelly, unkempt, and frequently drunk. Found guilty of libel in England, imprisoned in

France, he died in poverty back in the USA—and was denied burial in consecrated ground. His earthly remains were lost on their way to England for reburial.

PAN

An ancient pagan nature spirit—half man, half goat—whose hairy legs, horns, cloven feet, and outsized phallus suggest his relationship with later Christian "devils"—in fact, demonologist Collin de Plancy, in his *Dictionnaire Infernal,* calls Pan "the prince of the succubi." The oracles of Greece, when silenced by the crucifixion, uttered as their last words "Great Pan is dead." FRIEDRICH NIETZSCHE, as might be expected, elevated Pan to a symbol of creativity, fertility, and sexual license.

PANDER   DWH circa 1190 B.C.   PANDERING

In the *Iliad* (book 5), he is merely a truce breaker. But in the medieval legend of the affair between the Trojan prince Troilus and his beloved Cressida, Pander serves as the lovers' go-between—that is to say, pimp.

PANZRAM, Carl   DWH 1930   MURDER

A rapist and murderer who killed 21 people, sodomized 1,000, and, during a stint in the army, even stole government property. Before his hanging, Panzram's last words were "I wish the whole human race had one neck and I had my hands around it."

PAOLO

See FRANCESCA. Dante's encounter in Hell with this adulterer and his paramour (canto 5) is one of the *Inferno's* most celebrated passages.

PAPUS

A demon nicknamed the Physician.

PARACELSUS   DWH 1541   SORCERY

Philippus Aureolus Theophrastus Bombast von Hohenheim, known to posterity by his professional name of Paracelsus, was an alchemist, doctor, and psychic healer. (Our word *bombast* comes from his original name; he had a penchant for rant and bluster and getting red in the face.) Paracelsus theorized that the essence of life resides in a substance called *mummia,* which could be extracted by a magnet made of blood, excrement, sweat, and hair. Fortuitously, this same magnet could be used to extract "nervous fluids" from the body. He further taught that mermaids, once married, attain immortal souls and recommended *zebethum occidentale* (finely powdered human feces) for eye ailments. Recently, Prince Charles urged British physicians to return to the precepts of Paracelsus.

PARIS DWH circa 1190 B.C. LUST

His guide Virgil points him out to Dante, among the "thousands" of shades who died for love and must therefore spend eternity in Hell's Second Circle: Paris, prince of Troy, whose abduction of the beautiful HELEN caused the Trojan War. Archaeologists have established that there really was such a city, such a war, and perhaps even such a rapacious playboy prince—the Hittites knew him as Alexander of Ilious. But Dante was not a stickler for distinctions between myth and history; his Hell is populated by Greek demigods, Semitic demons, Roman emperors, popes, and Florentine businessmen.

PARKER, Dorothy DWH 1967 DESPAIR

". . . work is the province of cattle, And rest's for a clam in a shell, So I'm thinking of throwing the battle—Could you kindly direct me to Hell?" wrote this wit in her youth. In her old age, warned that she would die within the month if she continued drinking, Parker sighed, "Promises, promises."

PARSONS, Louella DWH 1972 SCANDAL

It was said in Hollywood that the last time Parsons kept silent about anything was after she witnessed her boss, WILLIAM RANDOLPH HEARST, murder director Thomas Ince. She was rewarded for her zipped lip with a gossip column in the tycoon's newspapers. Eventually she had 40 million readers, and her power became so great that buddy Walter Winchell once suggested renaming the movie capital Lollywood. At Christmastime, list in hand, Parsons would pull into a succession of stars' driveways, pop open her trunk, and remain in the car while the loot was piled in. In the 1950s, when Marlon Brando actually *wanted* an Oscar (for *On the Waterfront*), a Columbia executive suggested that he call Parsons and "make nice," to which Brando snorted, "Screw it, I'm not going *that* far."

PASIPHÄE BESTIALITY

The wife of King MINOS of Crete, Pasiphäe took a shine to a bull, by means of which she became the mother of a monster, the Minotaur—"a monument to her polluted passion" in Virgil's memorable phrase (*Aeneid* 6.37).

PAUL IV, Pope DWH 1559
SOWING DISCORD

When this former inquisitor general was made pope, he extended the powers of the Grand Inquisition and gladly paid for new instruments of torture out of his own pocket. By his papal bull *Cum Nimis Absurdum* he created one of the first Jewish ghettos and forced Jews to sell all their property, refrain from commerce (except to sell secondhand clothes, *strazzaria*), and wear yellow hats at all times. He hated women almost as much as Jews, forbidding any to come near him, and perpetuated the Church's rift with England when he refused to communicate with the new queen, ELIZABETH I. As he was dying, Paul ordered the Inquisition to begin persecution of "actors, buffoons and sculptors who create shoddy crucifixes." One of his last acts was to create the Index of Forbidden Books, which in time grew to include the works of Rabelais, Erasmus, and Boccaccio. And when he did die, joyous mobs tore down his statue and kicked it around the streets of Rome.

PAZUZU

He's the demon prominently featured in *The Exorcist* and known as the "Dark Angel of the Four Wings." Besides wings, Pazuzu has horns, talons, the tail of a scorpion, and a rotting serpent penis. He likes to sharpen his teeth and is the younger brother of HUMWAMA.

PEARCE, Alexander DWH 1824
CRUELTY

A convict from County Monaghan, Ireland, Pearce escaped from an Australian prison with seven other fugitives and wandered deep into the bush. Starving, they began to bicker until one convict uttered the fateful line "I could eat a piece of man." Weeks passed. And then there were. . . only two, Pearce and another convict, each eyeing the other warily—until Pearce finally ate him. Captured, Pearce confessed, but British authorities, even factoring in the barbarity of the Irish, found his story hard to believe and assumed he was lying to cover up for his escaped mates. But after Pearce ate another convict—this time not out of hunger but miffed because he couldn't swim—authorities finally had the Irish cannibal executed. For some reason, Pearce and his story aroused the interest of American phrenologists, and his skull was shipped from Hobart to Philadelphia, where it is currently on display in the Academy of Natural Sciences.

PEARY, Robert Edwin   DWH 1920   FRAUD

Recent studies suggest that the admiral's famous "discovery" of the North Pole may have taken place some sixty miles south of the place. But whether or not he was first to the Pole, he was surely the first to pass around naked pictures of Eskimo girls, including candid snaps of his fourteen-year-old Inuit mistress, the mother of one of his children. These nudie shots made it into his books, all in the interest of what Peary termed "ethnographic" studies.

Matthew A. Henson, his black aide (and former valet), did all of Peary's trading, hunting, and translating, and once saved the explorer's life by rescuing him from a raging musk ox. If the expedition *did* reach the Pole, Henson was the first person to set foot there, since he was carrying the ailing Peary at the time—which didn't prevent Peary from referring to Henson as "my colored boy" or dismissing him from his service.

A. E. Thomas, the collaborator on Peary's memoir, *To the North Pole,* acknowledged the book was "dull." He went on to say that "Peary was a dull man, and it was impossible to get much lively human material out of him."

PENEMUE

One of Enoch's Watcher angels, Penemue taught humankind the art of writing with pen and ink.

PERCHTEN

Demonic creatures in the Alps.

PERÓN, Juan Domingo   DWH 1974   TYRANNY

Perón was the first, but sadly not the last, military dictator in postwar Latin America. He based his political ideology on FRANCO, HITLER, LENIN, and MUSSOLINI, and rose to power thanks to his wife Eva, whose immense popularity deflected attention from the fact that Perón was destroying the economy and having his critics killed. When Eva was dying, Perón, repulsed by the deathbed odor, would reluctantly visit her with muslin draped over his face. But after she died, he enlisted the services of a master embalmer so that "Evita" went on to be the most famous corpse of the twentieth century. While millions of Argentinians, mourning at her open coffin, declared her a saint, the widower consoled himself with his fourteen-year-old mistress. But Perón, quickly realizing the political potential of his dead wife, fostered the cult around her. (Nineteen years later, he had Eva's body exhumed so she could join him and his new wife for supper.) He made her birth and death days national holidays, removing Catholic feast days (including the Immaculate Conception!) from Argentina's calendar to make room for them. This may have prompted his excommunication in 1955—Vatican action that was not taken against Hitler or Mussolini.

PERSEPHONE (aka Proserpina)

She is the kidnap victim–wife of DIS / HADES / PLUTO, king of the classical Underworld. In the *Odyssey*, Persephone is addressed as Iron Queen; the Romans named her Proserpina; Dante calls her "queen of timeless woe." The pomegranate is sacred to her. Her mother was the earth goddess Demeter (aka Ceres), her father an obscure country god, one of her mother's brief flings. When the gloomy god of the Underworld fell in love with her, he asked Zeus for Persephone's hand. Zeus, ever the diplomat, answered with a wink. Taking that as a yes, Dis / Hades / Pluto kidnapped the young girl. But her grief-stricken mother retaliated by letting nothing grow while Persephone was in the Underworld. So Zeus proposed a compromise—henceforth, Persephone could spend two-thirds of the year (spring and summer) with her mother. This fails, however, to make her existence less wretched. She can have no children by the god of the dead and pities herself as well as the ghosts with whom she shares her husband's company.

PETER   DWH 5th century   THEFT

In the *Dialogues* of Pope Gregory the Great, we read that one Stephen was granted a vision of Hell in which he beheld Peter, a dishonest steward of the pope's family, sunk in filth and weighed down with iron.

PETER "the Great"   DWH 1725   TYRANNY

He is damned for his many mortal and oversize sins—if Hell can hold a

force of nature like Peter the Great. He banished his dull first wife and ambitious sister to a nunnery and had his son and heir, whose biggest crime was drunkenness (inherited from his father), executed. He kept fourteen torture chambers going twenty-four hours a day and was constantly violent to his family, friends, and the nobles at his court. Peter was idiosyncratic: The six-foot-seven czar wore boots to bed, was afraid of bridges, collected dwarfs, and liked to snatch wigs off people's heads. But he did "open Russia to the West," starting by shaving his beard and ordering the facial hair off all who ruled with him—this in defiance of Russian tradition and his predecessor IVAN THE TERRIBLE, who said, "To shave the beard is a sin that the blood of all the martyrs cannot cleanse." Peter built an army and navy, industry and harbors, all without foreign aid, and developed a new society and economy for Russia. His death at age fifty-three was no doubt hastened by the fact that he plunged into icy waters two days after he passed a kidney stone.

PEY

A demon of the Tamils, Pey drinks the blood of the dead and wounded warriors.

PHAEDRA   BEARING FALSE WITNESS

She was married to King THESEUS but found herself fatally attracted to her stepson, Hippolytus, who, though close to Phaedra in age, prided himself on his "virgin soul." Hippolytus rejected her, and in revenge Phaedra hung herself, leaving a letter falsely accusing him of violating her. Theseus believed Phaedra and banished his son, putting a curse on him, which was fulfilled when a sea serpent attacked his chariot and dragged Hippolytus to his death.

PHAETON

A demon who possessed Sister Mary of Jesus in the convent of Louviers in the 1640s.

PHALAG

A demon who rules the planet Mars.

PHALDOR

One of the demons of the eleventh hour in Apollonius of Tyana's *Nuctemeron*, the genius of oracles.

PHALEG

A demon who, according to one Dr. Rudd, ruled over the planet Mars from 430 to 920.

PHIALGUS

One of the demons of the fourth hour in Apollonius of Tyana's *Nuctemeron*, the genius of judgment.

PHARMAROS

A demon who teaches pharmacy, herbal lore, and practical medicine and can diagnose illness.

PHARZUPH

Demon of lust and fornication—in Hebrew legend, Pharzuph successfully tempted the patriarch Abraham to coit with his daughter-in-law. In Christian lore, he especially enjoys tempting members of the hypocritical clergy. (His Hebrew name means "two-faced.")

PHILIP of Macedon   DWH 336 B.C.

TYRANNY

So deep was his respect for Greek culture that in 340 (breaking a treaty he had signed in 346), Philip invaded and conquered Athens. By all accounts a military genius and a drunken lecher, he was ignominiously assassinated by an agent of his jealous wife, Olympias—to whom he was spectacularly unfaithful but by whom he was the father of ALEXANDER THE GREAT.

PHILIP II of Spain   DWH 1598
CRUELTY

Philip was a champion of Catholic Christendom; more people were executed by his Inquisition than had been killed by the Romans during the entire Christian persecution. He married often, once England's queen "Bloody" Mary. Upon her death, he pursued Queen ELIZABETH I, who was decidedly uninterested. Undaunted, the middle-aged king went on to marry his fourteen-year-old niece, whom he then outlived.

In Protestant legend, he is a monster—the villain who was foiled when his England-invading Armada was wrecked by the hand of God. In truth, he was a devout man, not without charm, but paranoid.

"His smile and his dagger were very close," wrote the official court historian. Philip maintained his sense of the macabre, sleeping next to an open coffin that contained a skull topped with a crown of gold.

PHILOTANTIS
Infernal assistant to BELIAN, a demon of sodomy and pederasty.

PHLEGETHON
He started out in classical mythology as one of Hell's five rivers—the flaming one. In Judeo-Christian tradition, Phlegethon became a mighty devil, coequal in power with ASHTORETH, BEELZEBUB, BELIAL, and LUCIFER.

PHLEGYAS   BLASPHEMY
He impiously burned down the temple of Apollo, just because the god had raped his daughter. When AENEAS meets Phlegyas in Hades, he advises the hero "not to scorn the immortal gods." For some reason, Dante makes him—not Charon—the bad-tempered ferryman on the river Styx. He ferries Dante and Virgil between the Circle of the Wrathful and the City of the Impious to the entrance of Dis.

PHLOGABITUS
One of the demons of the third hour in Apollonius of Tyana's *Nuctemeron*, the genius of adornments.

PHOENIX 🦌
A former angelic Throne, now a marquis of Hell and a celebrated patron of poetry and letters.

PHUL 🦌
A demon identified by PARACELSUS as lord of the moon and of water—that is, of the tides.

PICOLLUS 🦌
Dressed in his customary seventeenth-century costume—wide cuffs and flowing cloak—this demon closely resembles the Victorian Mr. Punch. However, the *Dictionnaire Infernal* claims Picollus is a devil who was revered by the ancient inhabitants of Prussia.

PIER da Medicina   DWH circa 1271   SOWING DISCORD
A noble from the neighborhood of Bologna whom Dante seems to have known personally and, we may assume on the basis of his damnation, one who instigated strife between local families.

PIER della Vigne   DWH 1248   SUICIDE
Wandering in the gloomy Wood of the Suicides, Dante snaps a bleeding twig off a barren and blasted tree, which screams, being in fact the damned soul of a poet, Pier della Vigne. He was a pampered favorite in the court of FREDERICK II but fell from grace and was imprisoned. He took his life by dashing his head against the wall of his cell. He and Dante chat, providing the latter an opportunity to parody the hypersophisticated, complex wordplay of the "Sicilian school" of verse composition.

PILATE, Pontius   DWH 39   DEICIDE
The Roman prefect—governor—of the colony of Judea from 26 to 36 had the misfortune to be the one before whom Jesus was tried and convicted, and by whose order he was executed. The historian Josephus portrays Pilate's regime as authoritarian and insensitive to local customs and taboos. In the New Testament, Pilate is vilified as timid, vacillating, equivocating, vainly attempting to pass the buck and move the trial of Jesus to another jurisdiction. Historically, Pilate was removed from office by Vitellius, governor of Syria. Traditionally, he is then believed to have committed suicide, in Rome, by order of the emperor CALIGULA. The river Tiber would not accept his body, which somehow ended up in a Swiss Alpine lake.

Dante makes no mention of seeing Pilate in Hell, where he must surely be, but in folk belief, he, like JUDAS, is released from the inferno one day a year to sit and cool off on an iceberg. A nineteenth-century mystic named Anna Katharina Emmerich traveled back in time and conversed with Pilate's wife, Claudia Procles, who confided that after the trial she was so disgusted with Pilate that she left him and went to live in a vault in the house of Lazarus. This must be true, because Claudia is revered as a saint by the Eastern Church.

A fourth-century marvel of anti-Semitism, the apocryphal *Acts of Pilate*, places the blame for the crucifixion squarely on the Jews.

PILLARDOC

The patron demon of pawnbrokers, Pillardoc once had an aerial fight with ASMODEUS over the soul of a handsome young Parisian. Pillardoc won.

PINOL, Martin

One of the Devil's names in Spain.

PIZARRO, Francisco DWH 1541 CRUELTY

When he heard about the kingdom of Peru, Pizarro metamorphosed from swineherd into soldier. He was bent on acquiring the legendary gold of the Incas for Spain, the Catholic Church, and himself—not necessarily in that order. Outfitted in shining armor, Pizarro landed in an ancient and most advanced society and did not disabuse the Incas of the notion that he was the son of their white-skinned god, Viracocha. The conquistadors then captured the Inca ruler, Atahualpa, and demanded a huge ransom of gold and silver in exchange for his life. Pizarro took the ransom *and* his life, presumably finding some comfort in the fact that he forced Atahualpa to convert to Christianity before he killed him. He soon killed the rest of the Indians but still found time to cheat and execute his comrade-in-arms ALMAGRO. Three years later, Almagro's men killed Pizarro. Today his skull and bone fragments reside in the cathedral at Lima.

PLUTO

This is the Latin name for the Greek HADES, or DIS—the lord of the Underworld. It means "rich"—as in *plutocrat*. Thus, Dante assigns Pluto the task of guarding the souls of those damned for greed and prodigality. In the first of the German *Faustbuchs,* Pluto appears as a genuine devil, "a prince of Hades."

POE, Edgar Allan DWH 1849 DESPAIR

Ever true to his southern heritage, Poe married (in 1835) his thirteen-year-old cousin. It has been suggested that her untimely death (in 1847) caused the poet's morbid sexual obsession with female corpses, but death had always obsessed him. It was his lifelong habit, when denied anything he wanted—money, usually—to threaten suicide. He was also a racist, a junkie, a sponger, a self-pitying snob, and a drunk. His gloomy, hobbyhorse-rhythm verse (e.g., "The Raven") was briefly popular with the American public (whom he affected to despise) and later with the French, in particular the equally impotent pseudoper-

vert CHARLES BAUDELAIRE. Perhaps, as some wag once put it, "it gains something in the translation."

POL POT WH 1976

CRUELTY

In the frozen darkness of the Ninth Circle, in the area called Ptolomaea, among those damned for betraying their own kin, Dante discovers several suffering souls who are not yet dead (see Friar AL-BERIGO and BRANCA D'ORIA). Alberigo explains, "This zone is very special, for it often happens that a soul falls here before the time that Atropos [fate] should send it."

In 1973, the United States, despite its public support for the repressive regime of Lon Nol, began to bomb his country, Cambodia (see HENRY KISSINGER, RICHARD NIXON). Aside from civilian deaths on the ground, the only result of this action was the overthrow of Lon Nol, the fall of Phnom Penh (in 1975), and the ascendancy of Pol Pot and his Communist guerrillas, the Khmer Rouge. The capital city was promptly evacuated, its citizens sent to the countryside for "reeducation." For the next four years, Pol Pot waged a campaign of genocide against his own people. Millions died of disease and starvation; millions more were executed in the notorious "killing fields."

Although, with the blessing of the United Nations, a demon inhabiting his body still walks the blood-soaked earth of Kampuchea, the soul of Pol Pot joined the murderous traitors in Ptolomaea sometime before 1980.

POLK, James K.   DWH 1849   TYRANNY

One of the first acts of Polk's presidency was to declare, on the flimsiest possible pretext, war on Mexico. It netted the United States a million square miles of Mexican territory, including California and most of Texas. Historian Kenneth C. Davis calls it "America's most naked war of territorial aggression." It was also unconstitutional, and one senator suggested at the time that if an ambitious man wanted a career of duplicity, "he could not select a better example in all history than to follow in the footsteps of our President."

Not that Polk, our eleventh president, was immoral. He was married to a fellow teetotaler, Sarah Childress, and in their White House card playing, wine drinking, and dancing were banned. They were, for obvious reasons, childless. Curiously, Polk was only baptized on his deathbed, at the age of fifty-four. (He expired of chronic diarrhea.)

POLYCRATES   DWH 522 B.C.   TYRANNY

He and his brothers blasphemously seized control of the island city of Samos during a religious ceremony. Then Polycrates eliminated his brothers. He prospered by means of his one-hundred-ship pirate fleet, which controlled the Aegean Sea. The miraculous return of a ring, which he had tossed into the sea, presaged his downfall—on a state visit, he was crucified by his host. The antityrant Scots poet Robert Burns assures us of Polycrates' damnation.

POMPADOUR, Madame (Jeanne-Antoinette Poisson)   DWH 1764
VANITY

Soon after Louis XV's young mistress the duchess of Châteauroux died, the freshly divorced Madame Pompadour was presented at court as the new *maitresse-en-titre*. For the occasion, she wore a forty-pound petticoat. During five years in the palace attic and fifteen in a regal apartment, she wielded such enormous influence in domestic and foreign affairs that she was virtually Louis's prime minister. VOLTAIRE knew and admired her. But she was tormented by her sexual frigidity—an unfortunate malady in a mistress. To cure it, she sought the aid of the quack Count ST.-GERMAIN. He prescribed a diet of chocolate, truffles, and celery. In vain. Louis complained, "I have acquired a cold sea bird," and so, in time, Madame Pompadour began procuring young girls for the king's bed. Her expenses, by her own conservative accounting, totaled 73 million gold louis. Yet she bemoaned the rich food and late hours of court life, likening it to the trials of the early Christians, "a perpetual struggle." She put on rouge moments before she died. At her funeral, a little ditty hit the streets of Paris: "Here lies one who was twenty years a maiden, seven years a whore, and eight years a panderer."

POOKA

An evil, or at the least mischievous, spirit who frequents the roads of Ireland. The pooka appears suddenly, in the form of a jet black animal—horse, dog, goat, and even (according to the poet Yeats) eagle. In Wales, he is *pwka,* in Iceland, *puki.* See also PUCK.

PRAESTIGIATORES

A class of demons who perform miracles on behalf of magicians versed in black magic. Their prince is SATAN.

PREMINGER, Otto   DWH 1986   SCANDAL

His 1953 movie *The Moon Is Blue* earned a C—condemned—rating from the Catholic Legion of Decency because the words *virgin* and *pregnant* were actually spoken on-screen. Called Penishead by his many detractors because of his (shaved) bald pate, Preminger postured as Hollywood's vanguard director because his sanctimonious films dealt with "issues." However, as Dwight Macdonald points out, "No one is more skilled at giving the appearance of dealing with large controversial themes in a bold way, without making the tactical error of doing so." This was nowhere more evident than in *Hurry Sundown,* a turgid Uncle Tom melodrama that earned Preminger another C rating, this time for being "superficial and patronizing." It was summarily reviewed by *Esquire:* "To criticize it would be like tripping a dwarf."

Kenneth Anger reports in *Hollywood Babylon,* "It is surely fortuitous, but Otto Preminger holds the record for the highest number of suicides among his leading ladies."

PRISCIAN   DWH circa 500   SODOMY

Dante places the ancient Latin grammarian Priscian with BRUNETTO among the homosexuals in the Seventh Circle—which is curious, because nothing is known about Priscian's sexual habits. Either the poet assumed pederasty was perpetually rampant among academics or, as many Dante scholars believe, the sodomy referred to is a metaphor for some "intellectual" violation of the natural order.

PROCEL

He can assume the form of an angel or a duke and will teach the conjurer all sciences, but Procel specializes in geometry. He speaks mystically of hidden things and can simulate the sound of running water. He also has the ability to make bathwater hotter or colder.

PROCRIS

AENEAS in Hades glimpses the shade of this unhappy wife of King Cephalus. They were a couple with, in the words of Elvis, "suspicious minds." To test her chastity, the king disappeared for eight years, then came back in disguise and seduced her. Aha! said he. Determined to catch him in a dalliance, she secretly followed him on a hunting trip. He heard a rustle in the bushes, launched his javelin, and wounded her mortally.

PSEUDOTHEI

A class of demons who seek to usurp the name of God with a view to being worshipped. Their prince is BEELZEBUB.

PTOLEMY   DWH 2nd century B.C.   TREASON

The frozen pit at the bottom of Dante's Hell is reserved for traitors; one area is Caina, named for CAIN and reserved for those who betrayed their families, another is Ptolomaea in (dis)honor of Ptolemy, a biblical (I Maccabees) captain of Jericho who invited his in-laws to a feast and there murdered them. He is to be distinguished from Ptolemy, the Alexandrian astronomer, mathematician, and geographer who placed the earth at the center of the solar system—a "system" not disproved for 1,400 years. In the *Divine Comedy,* Dante follows Ptolemy's cosmography but might have condemned him to Hell—for writing a book on astrology and thereby making respectable that form of pernicious and most ungodly superstition.

PUCCIO dei Galigai (Sciancato)   DWH circa 1290   THEFT

Limping Puccio was a Florentine nobleman and Ghibelline whom Dante places among the thieves (canto 25), even though he was a gentleman crook, committing "beautiful and graceful thefts" in broad daylight, indifferent to witnesses.

PUCK

His name may be a variant of the Celtic POOKA, although Irish nationalists deny this. In the linguistic Middle English period, Puck was the Devil: William Langland calls Hell "Puck's pinfold." But, in the course of time, the old gods became "fairies," who devolved to "pixies," and such is the much diminished, mischievous Puck whom we encounter in Shakespeare's *Midsummer Night's Dream.* See also HOBGOBLIN.

PULSATTER, Belle   DWH circa 1908   MURDER

A midwestern strong woman, Pulsatter used the personal ads to attract her victims—lonely single men—to her remote Indiana farm. In 1908, when her farmhand set fire to the place, police discovered the skeletons of nine men, along with those of Belle's own children. She herself was never found, having taken off for parts unknown, but her ultimate destination was Hell.

PURSON

He appears as a huge king with the head of a lion, riding a bear and holding a viper. Purson is always preceded by a trumpet section and has the ability to divine the past, present, and future as well as the whereabouts of hidden treasures.

PURSUS

A demon who sees the future.

PURUEL

A fiery and pitiless fallen angel who prods and torments the souls in Hell.

PUT SATANACHIA

Commander in chief of Hell; he has power over mothers.

PUTIFAR

A demon who possessed Sister Mary of the Holy Sacrament in the convent of Louviers in 1647.

PWCCA

The Welsh name for SATAN.

PYRRHUS   CRUELTY

The son of ACHILLES, Pyrrhus murdered King Priam of Troy and his son, then sacrificed Priam's daughter to the shade of his father. His cruelty inspired Boccaccio to call him *e crudelissimo omicida e rapacissimo predone,* "most cruel murderer and rapacious pillager." But perhaps the Pyrrhus Dante beheld in the river of blood is the former king of Epirus (DWH 272 B.C.), his namesake and fabled descendant, who was a fierce enemy of imperial Rome. His too costly defeat of the Romans at Asculum, in 279 B.C., inspired the phrase *Pyrrhic victory.*

PYTHON

A demon who is a giant serpent. Although he is the "Prince of the Spirits of Lies" (according to Francis Barrett, *The Magus,* 1801), Python can predict the future.

Queequeg, said I, rather digressively; Hell is an idea first born on an undigested apple dumpling; and since perpetuated through the hereditary dyspepsias nurtured by Ramadans.
　　　　　　　—HERMAN MELVILLE, *Moby-Dick*

QANDISA

A water-dwelling demoness of Morocco, Qandisa seduces handsome young men and thereby drives them mad.

QEDESH

A Syrian goddess of prostitution, the lady of Kadish is portrayed as a full frontal nude, riding a leopard. Canaanite temple prostitution was ended by King Josiah in 622 B.C.

QUANTRILL, William　DWH 1865
CRUELTY

Ohio born, a failed schoolteacher turned horse thief, Quantrill served in the Confederate army in Missouri and then, with the rank of captain, became the leader of an autonomous guerrilla band, Quantrill's Raiders. On August 21, 1863, these Bold Chevaliers of the Lost Cause rode into the town of Lawrence, in the free state of Kansas, where they shot and/or burned 150 civilians. Donning, with distaste, blue Union uniforms, they proceeded to Baxter Springs, there to surprise and slaughter 90 of the hated Yankees. The legendary outlaw heroes Cole Younger and Jesse James rode with the Raiders and, like their captain, saw no reason to discontinue lives of murder and looting after the war. Quantrill was killed while "raiding" a town in Kentucky.

Other Confederate "raiders"—such as "Bloody Bill" Anderson—are doubtless in Hell as well, but this book has too few *Q*'s and quite enough *A*'s.

QUEENSBERRY, Marquis of (Sir John Sholto Douglas) DWH 1900
CRUELTY

A man's man. Hunter, brute, boxer (he laid down the rules of boxing still in effect today), adulterer, homophobe, wife abuser—and so vocal an atheist that eventually his seat in the House of Lords was denied him. Suspecting that England's foreign minister had unnatural designs on his son Percy, he followed the statesman around London wielding a dog whip. At the height of Oscar Wilde's trial, which he precipitated, he encouraged Wilde's catamite, his dreadful son ALFRED DOUGLAS, to go to the South Sea Islands, "where there were plenty of beautiful girls." On his deathbed, one of the "Screaming Scarlet Marquis' " last acts was to raise himself and spit in Percy's face because the lad had expressed sympathy for the imprisoned Oscar. In his will, he specifically ordered that there be "no Christian mummeries or tomfooleries over my grave."

QUEMEUL   🦁   See KEMUEL.

QUESNEL, Pasquier   DWH 1719   HERESY

A Jansenist priest, banished from Paris, Quesnel died in Amsterdam. One hundred and one sentences of his work *Reflections Morals* were condemned by Pope Clement XI.

QUISLING, Vidkun   DWH 1945   TREASON

The name of this Norwegian Nazi collaborator has become a synonym for *traitor*. Typically, he was a bleeding-heart liberal (working for Russian relief and the pinko League of Nations) before he wised up and realized HITLER was right. He acted as advance man for the about-to-invade Nazis, then proclaimed himself leader of his occupied homeland. Although hampered by a massive "resistance" within Norway (financed by outside agitators, the Allies), Quisling managed to export a thousand Jews to the camps. After Norway's liberation (ironically, by the Russian army), our hero was tried and executed.

*Readers are advised to remember that the devil is a liar. There is wishful think-
ing in Hell as well as on Earth.*
                              —C. S. LEWIS, *The Screwtape Letters*

*Represent to yourself a city involved in darkness, burning with brimstone and
stinking pitch, and full of inhabitants who cannot make their escape . . .*
                              —ST. FRANÇIS DE SALES, *Introduction to the Devout Life*

*Round and round the shutter'd Square
I stroll'd with the Devil's arm in mine.
No sound but the scrape of his hoofs was there,
And the ring of his laughter and mine.*
                              —MAX BEERBOHM, *Enoch Soames, Nocturne*

RABISU

An evil spirit in Assyrian demonology, Rabisu sets humans' hair on end
when he possesses them.

RAGAMUFFIN

A member of LUCIFER's Infernal
Council in the account of the "harrowing of Hell" described in William Langland's poem "Piers Plowman."

RAGLAN, Lord (Fitzroy Somerset)
DWH 1855   CRUELTY

When he was made British commander of the Crimean War in 1853, Raglan
hadn't seen action since 1815, when he
had served as secretary to the duke of
Wellington at Waterloo. This might ex-
plain why he left for Turkey without any
maps and persisted in calling his allies,

the French, "the Enemy." It was he who gave the suicidal order to charge to the doomed Light Brigade. He watched the slaughter from his yacht, a safe distance away. Still, he had a sleeve named after him—a singular honor, especially since he was missing one arm.

RAHAB

The ancient Hebrew demon of chaos, Rahab rebelled in Heaven by refusing God's order to "separate the waters" during the creation. He later attempted, in vain, to help Pharaoh follow Moses through the miraculously parted Red Sea. He is the evil angel of insolence and pride.

RAHU

The Indian demon Rahu drives around in a chariot drawn by eight black horses. He constantly pursues the sun and the moon, with his jaws open. Whenever he succeeds in swallowing one or the other, there is a total eclipse.

RAHUMEL/RAMUEL

An Enochian demon who rules the North, on Tuesdays.

RAIS, Gilles de   DWH 1440   SORCERY

The legendary bogeyman of medieval history, de Rais is the first of many serial spouse murderers to be called Bluebeard. He killed six wives—but he also did in 200 children for his sexual gratification and abducted and slew 150 women as sacrifices to the Devil. Their skeletons were dug up in front of his private chapel, which was facetiously named the Holy Innocents. It was in this chapel that de Rais held black masses, séances, and demon raisings—and took stimulants. In his spare time, he curled his hair and dyed his beard blue. Because his busy lifestyle had put him in debt, he experimented in alchemy and was so successful at it that his court was more lavish than the king's. De Rais was also a marshal of France, patron of the theater, and guerrilla leader of courage and skill, a companion-in-arms of Joan of Arc. Testimony at his trial combined (obviously) fact and fiction, but the verdict was preordained, since those who judged him had already seized his land. He was condemned to burn at the stake for heresy, invocation of demons, sodomy, sacrilege, and murder. He admitted his guilt to most of the crimes but blamed it all on parental overindulgence.

RAKSASAS

Black Indian demons who wear wreaths of human entrails.

RAND, Ayn   DWH 1982   ADULTERY

Her best-selling novels, which are basically forums for her philosophy of objectivism, all feature long-winded but hunky male "individualists." Rand and her lover of nineteen years, Nathaniel Branden, formed the Nathaniel Branden Institute to promote her books and theories. When Branden's wife, seriously ill, phoned her husband at the novelist's home during their trysting time, Rand shrieked, "How dare you! Do you think only of yourself?" Rand's own husband, Frank, her precious "cubby hole," was considerably more stalwart about the affair, as well as his wife's occasional outbursts of violence. When her lover left her for a younger woman, she physically attacked him, screaming, "My life is over!" then banned Nathaniel Branden from the Nathaniel Branden Institute. Rand, Russian born, was a rabid anti-Communist and a "friendly" witness to the House Un-American Activities Committee, before which she complained that the 1943 MGM movie *Song of Russia* showed Russian people smiling. But even HUAC wouldn't let her denounce the movie she found still more subversive, *The Best Years of Our Lives.*

Currently Rand is enjoying a renaissance on the Internet, where websites and newsgroups chat earnestly about her books in cyberspace.

RASPHUIA

A demon of the first hour, a necromancer and sciomancer.

RASPUTIN, Grigory Yefimovich   DWH 1916
LUST

The son of Siberian shamans, Rasputin claimed to have had a vision of the Virgin when he was eighteen and entered a monastery. Mary's influence did not deter him from conducting orgies there, in the course of which his young followers worshipped his (considerable, by all accounts—see below) phallus. From those evening sessions of monastic naughtiness (which would always end in meditation and prayer) came his nickname, which means "the debauched."

Rasputin was thirty years of

age, a filthy, hairy, wandering *starets*, when he arrived in St. Petersburg. Even his enemies have conceded that Rasputin was a natural wizard, with enormous psychic abilities, so it wasn't surprising that, after meeting the royal family, he held total sway over the dim-witted czar and czarina. They ensconced him in the royal apartments, where he was called at varying times the Czar above Czars, the Mad Monk, or the Holy Devil. He transferred his sexual attentions to ladies of the aristocracy, frankly admitting that he preferred them to peasant women because they "smelled better." Russian princes, resenting his enormous power in their fast-crumbling empire, attempted to assassinate him. In one evening, Rasputin was poisoned, beaten, raped, shot four times, and thrown, bound and gagged, into an icy river. He survived.

After he was finally killed, one of his murderers cut off his thirteen-inch penis and gave it to a former lover. She took it to Paris, where eyewitnesses described it as resembling a "blackened overripe banana."

RAUM

A demon count, a destroyer of cities—in cases of theft, Raum infallibly identifies the guilty. This evil spirit appears in the form of a crow and will steal money and give it to the conjuring magician. While he can create love and reconcile enemies, he has the power to destroy cities, dignitaries, and reputations.

RAVANA

The ten-headed demon and twenty-armed evil prince of the Kingdom of Lanka. Ravana abducted Sita, the wife of Rama, and is frequently depicted with an ass's head.

RAZANIL

The demon who presides over onyx, the magical stone.

REAHU

The Khmer people give this name to the demon who chases the sun and moon in an attempt to swallow them.

REMY, Nicholas   DWH 1612   CRUELTY

This French attorney general's forensic philosophy was simple: "Whatever is not normal is due to the Devil." Openly admitting to "irregular" judicial practices, Remy claimed, in his monumental work, *Demonolatreiae*, to have burned 900 witches and personally tortured twice that number. His assertion that witches shape-shift into cats when they enter a home led to the Great Cat Massacre.

REOCH, Elspeth, of the Orkneys DWH 1616 SORCERY

When she first met the Devil, Reoch was twelve; eventually she bore him a child. At her trial, she testified that the Prince of Darkness dresses in tartan plaid.

RHADAMANTHUS

A son of Zeus, together with MINOS and AEACUS, Rhadamanthus judges the "naked souls" of the newly dead in Hades, sending them to Elysium or Tartarus. Plato, in the *Gorgias,* maintains that Rhadamanthus has jurisdiction over all Asia. According to Virgil, he is the sternest—or, as we would now say, most "conservative"—of the triune tribunal: He punishes first and listens afterward.

RHODES, Cecil DWH 1902
SOWING DISCORD

When he learned that a British territory had been named Rhodesia, Rhodes chirped, "Has anyone else had a country named after them?" His triumph was made possible by the African king Lobengula, who granted Rhodes the diamond and gold rights that became the basis of his immense power and fortune. (In 1890, he controlled 90 percent of the world's diamond production.) Lobengula's generosity didn't prevent Rhodes from hiring an assassin to murder the African. In a rare moment of conscience, he later hired the king's sons as gardeners but would occasionally ask them, "What year did I kill your father?" Besides his name, Rhodes's other legacy to the continent of Africa was apartheid, which he introduced in 1894 with the Glen Grey Act. Rhodes believed himself to be the founder of a new, male, Anglo-Saxon world order. His famous scholarships were available only to men from the "truly white" countries of Britain, Germany, and North America (although he regarded the American Revolution as a failure since it had opened the country to Irish immigrants).

RIBESAL (aka Rubezal)

A demon who is the prince of gnomes. Ribesal lives on the summit of Mt. Risemberg, covering it with clouds and causing tempests.

RICHARD III   DWH 1485

TYRANNY

Although he *was* responsible for the deaths of King Henry VI, Prince Edward, Prince George, and his nephews, he did *not* have a hunchback. In fact, according to the countess of Desmond, Richard was always the "handsomest man in the room." But he did have a full set of teeth at six months of age and was rumored to practice alchemy. It was Shakespeare, in his effort to make Richard an archetypal villain, who made him deformed, not fit to "court an amorous looking glass." He became king in 1483, the year that saw three kings on the English throne. He died in battle from a skull fracture caused by an ax. His crown, found hanging on a thorn bush, was picked up and worn by Henry Tudor. Richard's body was stripped, put on public display to assure the populace he was dead, then buried in an unmarked grave.

RICHELIEU, Cardinal (Armand-Emmanuel du Plessis)

DWH 1642   AVARICE

The shrewd, merciless villain of Alexander Dumas's novel *The Three Musketeers* was prime minister to King Louis XIII of France. A forward-thinking statesman, Richelieu made great contributions to international espionage and domestic secret police. "Secrecy," he said, "is the first essential in affairs of state." His favorite secret agent was a monk named Père Joseph—François-Joseph du Tremblay—the original Gray Eminence. Richelieu (while stoically enduring his own hemorrhoids) also undertook to supervise the king's health: In one six-month period, the cardinal ordered 47 bleedings, 215 laxatives, and 312 enemas for His Majesty. At court, he set a new, elegant tone, stressing table manners and absolutely forbidding tooth picking.

The cardinal, unlike many clergymen of his day, adhered to his vow of chastity. In fact, he simply hated women: He may have had his archenemy Marie de Medici in mind when he observed, "As men employ their abilities for good, so women use them for evil," but another of his *pensées* combined snobbery *and* misogyny: "He who marries a woman not of his class commits a mortal sin." He seems to have been less successful in keeping his priestly vow of poverty. He left an enormous estate, 1.5 million livres, part of which his will designated as a pension for his cats.

RIMMON

Once a storm god of the Syrians, Rimmon has been demoted to the role of a physician practicing in the Infernal regions. Because he never has any patients, he has time to function as SATAN's ambassador to Russia.

RINALDO dei Scrovegni   DWH 1289   USURY

In the Seventh Circle of Hell, the usurers sit in burning sand, weighed down by money bags around their necks. One of these bags bears the family crest of the Scrovegnis of Padua; significantly enough, it features a fat sow. Dante chats briefly with its wearer, Rinaldo, who was an archetypal Scrooge—a miser as well as a moneylender, who died clutching his strongbox.

The artist Giotto, a friend of Dante's, painted the frescoes for the Scrovegni Chapel in Padua, which Dante is known to have visited—leading some commentators to think that the poet's inclusion of Rinaldo is a bit of an in-joke.

RINIER da Corneto   DWH circa 1270   THEFT

A highwayman of Dante's day who is said to have "held all the Maremma in fear of him."

RINIER dei Pazzi   DWH 1268   THEFT

Another highway robber, who acted on orders from FREDERICK II, robbing and despoiling churchmen. Rinier and all his descendants were put under perpetual excommunication by Pope Clement IV in 1269.

RINTRAH

A demon of wrath, but, according to demonologist Fred Gettings, he's also creative—in William Blake's *Song of Los,* Rintrah "gave Abstract Philosophy to Brahma in the East."

ROBERT "the Devil"   DWH 16th century   SORCERY

His mother, the duchess of Normandy, grew tired of fruitlessly praying to God for a son. Finally, she prayed to BEELZEBUB and got . . . Robert! The infant, who tore out his nurse's hair, grew up to be a bandit chief who slit the throats of nuns. It has been said that when he found out who his father was, he became a hermit and would eat only food that was chewed and wrenched from the jaws of a dog.

ROBESPIERRE, Maximilien

DWH 1794   CRUELTY

Robespierre, the French Stalin, rationalized that "terror is an emanation of virtue" and virtuously ordered the execution of more than 20,000 of his countrymen and women—including Queen Marie Antoinette, condemned to the guillotine on the bizarre charge of having sex with her eight-year-old son. He accomplished this indiscriminate massacre by means of a Committee [an early example of newspeak] of Public Safety. He denied, however, being a "radical" and affirmed his belief in God by staging the Festival of the Supreme Being in the Tuileries.

His unhappy life was tormented by constipation and fits of vomiting, which affected his complexion and led to his famous nickname, the Sea Green Incorruptible. When he was finally captured during the Thermidor Reaction, he attempted suicide—but only managed to shatter his jaw.

In addition to his other crimes, Robespierre introduced what has become a terror to most Americans: the metric system.

ROBIN, Son of Art

The alleged demon lover of alleged Irish witch ALICE KYTELER. Under torture, Lady Alice's maid Petronilla testified that she had witnessed sexual relations between her employer and this incubus, who took the shape of a shaggy dog or "three Negroes." The self-effacing Robin, she said, had described himself to her as "one of the poorer demons."

ROCKEFELLER, John D.   DWH 1937   BLASPHEMY

The founder of Standard Oil, who enjoyed passing out dimes to the indigent, was a devout Baptist and the author of this blasphemy: "I believe that the power to make money is a gift from God."

ROCKEFELLER, Nelson   DWH 1979   ADULTERY

Grandson of John D. (see preceding entry), four-time governor of New York State, and last of the moderate Republicans, Nelson was—indirectly, at least—responsible for the deaths of forty-three inmates and guards in a riot at Attica prison, and the circumstances of his sudden death seem to preclude the possibility that he was able to make an act of perfect contrition.

RODERICK (Don Roderigo)   DWH 711   LUST

The last Visigoth king of Spain, Roderick raped Cava, the queen's lady-in-waiting. Outraged, Cava's father betrayed Spain to Islamic invaders, who brought smallpox into the country. Roderick was defeated by Moslem forces at Río Barbate, and after the battle he disappeared; only his horse was found by the river. But witnesses came forward to testify they had seen flocks of demons carry him off to Hell.

ROFOCALE   See LUCIFUGE.

ROGERS, Lela   DWH 1977   SOWING DISCORD

She was the mother of movie musical star Ginger and, remarkably, the only serious (female) girlfriend of J. EDGAR HOOVER. Lela was one of the first woman recruits in the United States Marine Corps, where she edited the monthly *Leatherneck,* an experience she felt prepared her to be a founding member of the Motion Picture Alliance for the Preservation of American Ideals. It might have been nepotism that prompted her daughter's studio, RKO, to hire Lela to ferret out Communist propaganda in screenplays, but she triumphed in the job. The House Un-American Activities Committee declared her "one of the leading experts on Communism in the United States." Lela cut a dramatic figure testifying before the committee, proudly telling the valiant story of how her daughter, filming the World War II movie *Tender Comrade,* refused to utter the subversive line "Share and share alike—that's democracy."

ROMENA, Aghinolfo da   DWH 1300   FRAUD

A counterfeiter. Dante implies (in canto 30) that Romena was burned at the stake, a customary punishment for this crime against the state.

RONOBE/RONOVE 🦋

A demon who teaches foreign languages, rhetoric, and art. In Hell, Ronobe is a fine earl, but, conjured up on earth, he is an overweight monster.

RONWE 🦋

A marquis of Hell who appears as a humanoid.

ROSENBERG, Alfred DWH 1946 SOWING DISCORD

After traveling by foot from Estonia to Germany, Rosenberg arrived at the doorstep of fellow anti-Semite Dietrich Eckart and introduced himself thus: "Can you use a fighter against Jerusalem?" Eckart could, and the two co-wrote articles in the Munich weekly *Deutsche Republik,* placing full blame for World War I and the Russian Revolution, not to mention the crucifixion, on the Jews. They further hinted that Jews, along with equally despised Masons, were currently plotting to take over the world. Rosenberg became a member of Hitler's inner circle, and, although the Führer found his writings monumentally dull, he liked his enthusiasm—especially when Rosenberg compared Nazism with "an accomplishment of the human soul that ranks with the Parthenon, the Sistine Madonna, and the Ninth Symphony of Beethoven." The Third Reich was horrified when HERMANN GOERING, who enjoyed spying on his colleagues, found a set of love letters from Rosenberg to a young Jewess.

ROSIER 🦋

By use of sugared words, Rosier tempts men to fall in love. His Heavenly adversary is St. Basil, who during his lifetime would have none of that.

ROTHSTEIN, Arnold DWH 1928 CORRUPTION

Known along Broadway as Mr. Big and The Brain, Rothstein was an immensely powerful mobster, bootlegger, and gambler, but he lives in infamy as the man who fixed the 1919 World Series and won $270,000 betting against the "Black Sox." Rothstein had just put his money down on Hoover to beat Smith when he was shot in the stomach (by either Nigger Nate Raymond, Titanic Thompson, or Hump MacManus) over a $320,000 poker debt. When asked by the police to name his killer, the dying Rothstein answered, "My mudder did it." The character of Meyer Wolfsheim in F. Scott Fitzgerald's *Great Gatsby* was based on Rothstein: "A small, flat-nosed Jew raised his large head and regarded me with two fine growths of hair which luxuriated in either nostril."

RUBIROSA, Porfirio DWH 1966   LUST

In tribute to his prodigious sexual member, patrons of New York's El Morocco, indicating the tall pepper mill, would ask for the rubirosa. Before becoming the darling of international society, Rubirosa had been shot in the kidney by the French Resistance for being a Nazi sympathizer who sold phony visas to Jewish refugees. After the war, he married heiress Doris Duke, who presented him with a seventeenth-century Paris town house as a wedding gift. By the time he married another heiress, Barbara Hutton, seven years later, his price had gone up. Rubirosa's lawyers asked for $3 million, payable in advance, but finally settled on $2.5 million. In addition, Hutton gave "Toujours Pret" a 400-acre sugar plantation and thirteen polo ponies. The marriage lasted fifty-three days.

RUBICANTE

One of Dante's demon guides. His name means "red with rage."

RUDOLF II DWH 1612   SORCERY

This Holy Roman emperor oversaw, indeed justified, the decline of the Holy Roman Empire. He himself was neither Roman (although he was the hereditary king of Hungary, Bohemia, and Austria) nor holy. But he was the emperor. And he was nuts. Dismayed by the wars between Protestant and Catholic factions, he retired to a palace in Prague, there to study the occult arts and, rumor had it, sell his soul to the Devil, for all the good it did him. By the time of Rudolf's death, his brother Matthias was ruling the empire.

RUGGIERI degli Ubaldini, Archbishop DWH 1295   TREASON

A Ghibelline of Pisa, Ruggieri plotted with COUNT UGOLINO to take political control of the city and incidentally to banish Nino dei Visconti, Dante's dear friend. To the archbishop's surprise, the count then turned on him, accused him of entertaining Guelf sympathies, and imprisoned him—with his two sons and two young grandsons—in a tower where they all starved to death. Part of Ruggieri's Hell (canto 33) is that he shares his space there with Ugolino.

RUGIERI, Cosimo   DWH 1615   ATHEISM

He was court astrologer to CATHERINE DE MEDICI. As a sideline, Rugieri made wax images of young girls that enabled admirers to win their affections, or kill them. The queen hired him to spy on her son Francis, but instead Rugieri became a double agent, spying for Francis on the queen. Dying, Rugieri affirmed his atheism, and soon after his death a biography was written about him titled *The Appalling Story of Two Magicians Strangled by the Devil in Paris during Holy Week.*

RUMAN

An Islamic angel who has his office in Hell. Ruman requires all who appear before him to document their sins.

RUSH, Friar

This demon was sent from Hell in the seventeenth century, on a mission to keep German monks in a constant state of inebriation.

RUSSELL, Lord Bertrand   DWH 1970   ATHEISM

It is astonishing, not to say scandalous, that a man of Russell's intellect continued throughout his very long life to deny the existence of a just God. In his *Sceptical Essays,* he wrote, "The infliction of cruelty with a good conscience is a delight to moralists. That is why they invented Hell." Now the philosopher who spent his life in pursuit of certainty knows whether he was right.

Saint Augustine continued, "And if, Lord, you pour an animated soul into them, they will burn eternally in Hell, according to your adorable decrees."
—ANATOLE FRANCE, *Penguin Island*

She believed herself hopelessly damned, and strove to hide herself from the sight of Hell by overwhelming Julian with caresses. In short, nothing was wanting to the happiness of our hero.
—STENDHAL, *The Red and the Black*

SABNAK

The demon who causes bodies to decay.

SACHER-MASOCH, Leopold von   DWH 1895   MASOCHISM

This Austrian author's many autobiographical novels celebrate the sexual joys of pain—of being humiliated, dominated, degraded, whipped, and otherwise tortured—to which source of pleasure his name has been given. It has always been a teaching of the Church that such activities, unless undertaken in a religious spirit—that is, under clerical supervision—are morally wrong.

SADE, Donatien-Alphonse, Marquis de   DWH 1814   SADISM

Despite an adolescence and young manhood of considerable depravity, the Jesuit-educated Sade, being a well-connected aristocrat, managed to avoid serious prosecution until he was arrested on a complaint from his even better connected mother-in-law and imprisoned in the Bastille (from 1777 to 1790). Denied the usual outlets for his creativity, Sade was so bored he took to writing pornographic novels—which detail and describe every possible and impossible sexual act with a cold, compulsive, French philosophical thoroughness—among them *Justine, or The Adversities of Virtue, Juliette, or Vice Rewarded,* and *The 120 Days of Sodom.*

When the Bastille—that hated symbol of oppression—fell at the onset of the French Revolution, Sade was liberated. He rose to such prominence in the new regime that he was able (ironically enough) to spare the life of his mother-in-law, arrested during the Reign of Terror.

But his fortunes declined under Napoleon. Sade's smutty satire against the empress Josephine, *Zoloé et ses Acolytes,* resulted in his commitment to the insane asylum in which, grown monstrously fat, he died—still protesting his hatred for the God in whom he did not believe.

ST.-GERMAIN, Count   DWH 1784   SORCERY

He was promoted around the French court by MADAME POMPADOUR, who partook of his rejuvenation potion, the "elixir vitae," as well as his wrinkle creams. The count was wooed to the German court by FREDERICK THE GREAT, who publicly claimed him immortal and privately used him as a spy. St.-Germain convinced his followers that he never ate and had been born 2,000 years earlier, the offspring of an Arabian princess and a salamander. He claimed to speak eleven languages, including Sanskrit; reported chatting with the queen of Sheba and being a guest at the wedding at Cana. Actually he was a Portuguese Jew who had once made a living dyeing silk and leather. During the last 200 years, several people have popped up claiming they were St.-Germain, including the nineteenth-century windbag occultist Bulwer-Lytton.

SALEOS

Yet another demon of lust.

SALMIEL

A fallen angel who took an intense dislike to Moses and, according to his legend, makes an annual demand on his master SATAN for Israel's destruction.

SALMONEUS   BLASPHEMY

In Tartarus, the torture chamber of Hades, AENEAS beheld this former Greek king paying a "brutal penalty" for his impious behavior (*Aeneid* 6.774–87). Motivated by either a strange sense of humor or utter madness, the torch-waving Salmoneus had driven his chariot through his city, claiming to be Zeus himself and demanding "the honor due the gods." Unamused, Zeus nailed him with a real thunderbolt and sent him directly to Hell, where he continues to reel and tumble in "the blast of whirlwind."

SALOME   DWH 1st century   LUST

Daughter of Herod Philip and HERODIAS, Salome danced before her stepfather, King HEROD ANTIPAS, at his birthday party; then, for payment, demanded (and got) the head of John the Baptist (Matthew 14). That she performed a striptease, the Dance of the Seven Veils, is the invention of Richard Strauss, who composed the opera *Salome* about the event. (It was based on Oscar Wilde's play of the same name; a charming photograph exists of Oscar himself dressed as the title character.)

SAMMAEL

A Sumerian demon whose name means "the bright and poisonous one." Described as redheaded and virile, Sammael is, according to Enoch, the chief of demons. He is sometimes identified, in Hebrew demon lore, with LEVIATHAN, the Great Serpent who tempted Eve and by her begat CAIN; he may also have been the "angel" who wrestled with the patriarch Jacob. And he is the "Sam Hill" invoked in American cussing.

SANDERS, George

DWH 1972   DESPAIR

Hell holds no terrors for this actor, who specialized in playing cads, Nazis, and world-weary sophisticates. On earth, he married both Zsa Zsa and Magda Gabor. He left a suicide note reading, "Dear World, I am leaving you because I'm bored."

SARAKNYAL

A leader of Enoch's fallen Watcher angels.

SARDANAPALUS DWH **7th century** B.C. SUICIDE

Mentioned in the Bible as Ashurbanipal (Ezra 4:10), Sardanapalus was a voluptuous—and, according to the poet BYRON bisexual—Assyrian tyrant. Defeated in battle, he was persuaded by his favorite concubine to construct, ignite, and perish upon his own funeral pyre—into which she then lovingly leapt.

SARGATANAS

A favorite of medieval demonologists, Sargatanas is the brigadier major of Hell, a skillful picklock, and a stealer of minds and memories.

SASSOL Mascheroni DWH **mid–13th century** MURDER

A member of the Toschi family of Florence who murdered his own cousin for financial gain. Young Dante may have watched as he was rolled through the streets in a barrel of nails, then beheaded.

SATAN

His Hebrew name means "accuser" or "adversary," although Milton translated it as "Arch-enemy" (*Paradise Lost* 1.81). It is generally agreed that Satan was created the mightiest of the angelic order of Seraphim — although St. Thomas Aquinas begs to differ, arguing in the *Summa* for Satan's cherubic origins. He certainly had twelve wings and the title regent of God. He first appears by name in the biblical first book of Chronicles, in which he "provokes" King David to take a census. Next, in Job, he is "one of the sons of God," sent by Him to try Job's famous patience. He plays the same role, prosecutor in the Heavenly court, in his final Old Testament mention, Zechariah 3:1: "standing at [the Lord's] right hand to resist him." In the New Testament, however, he is simply "the Devil," the evil spirit who tempted Christ until ordered, "Get thee hence, Satan" (Matthew 4:10) and who later "entered into Judas" (Luke 22:3).

Satan is usually pictured with the goat horns, hairy legs, and cloven hoofs of the Greek nature god PAN, wielding the trident of the Roman sea god Neptune. There has recently been some loose, multicultural pointy-headed academic talk about his relationship to a shockingly phallic Egyptian serpent god named Sata.

SATANACHIA

A grand general of the Infernal spirits, Satanachia is often conjured because he is said to exercise an irresistible power over women.

SATHANAS

A demon, mentioned by Chaucer, who seems to have specialized in the clergy:

> Hold up thy tail, thou Sathanas, said he
> Show forth thine arse and let the friar see
> Where is the nest of friars in this place . . .
> Out of the Devil's arsehole then did drive
> Full 20,000 friars in a rout
> And through all Hell they swarmed and ran about.

SAUL, King   DWH circa 1000 B.C.   WITCHCRAFT

The first king of Israel was selected by the holy prophet Samuel, acting on God's personal recommendation (I Samuel 9:17). But within two years, the prophet was publicly accusing Saul of "witchcraft" (15:23) and privately anointing David as his replacement. Defeated in a battle with the Philistines and disgraced, Saul killed himself. For good measure, King David later hanged his seven surviving sons (II Samuel 21:9).

What sin, what "witchcraft" had Saul committed thus to incur God's wrath? In the course of his war with the neighboring pagan Amalekites, he disregarded *explicit* instructions from the Almighty (via Samuel) to "utterly destroy all they have, and spare them not, but slay both man and woman, infant and suckling, ox, sheep, camel and ass" (I Samuel 15:3). Oh, he took care of the women, infants, and sucklings all right, but, in his headstrong way, he spared the life of the Amalek king Agag, as well as some choice livestock. In vain did he pray for God's—and the prophet's—forgiveness. Too late did he summon his prisoner Agag to his tent and "hew him to pieces before the Lord" (15:33). Saul was doomed.

SAVONAROLA   DWH 1498   HERESY

An austere Dominican monk who passionately preached spiritual repentance and political reform in Florence, inspiring paroxysms of piety, which included "bonfires of the vanities," in which lewd pictures and/or playing cards were immolated. After the corrupt ruling Medici were driven from the city by the invading French king, Charles VIII (whose arrival and victory the preacher had prophesied), Savonarola *ruled* Florence. He did not, however, rule Italy—or the world. Pope ALEXANDER VI did. And when neither flattery nor bribery convinced the reformer to commit Florence to his "Holy Alliance" against the French, Alexander had Savonarola excommunicated, tortured, and burned at the stake.

SCARAPINO

A tiny, silly Italian imp named in the Tuscan epic *Orlando Innamorato*.

SCARMIGLIONE

A disheveled (so his name signifies) member of the team of Dante's demonic guides in canto 21.

SCHLEMIHL, Peter

A schlemiel (from the Yiddish word *shlemil*) is a fool, a man easily duped (the biblical—Numbers 2—Israelite general Shlumeel was a consistent loser). In an 1814 fable by Chamisso, a desperate character named Peter Schlemihl sells his shadow—and therefore his soul—to the DEVIL.

SCOT, Michael   DWH 1232   SORCERY

Michael Scot of Balwearie, Fifeshire, was a traveling scholar, active in the court of FREDERICK II. He translated the works of Aristotle from Arabic sources, which led to rumors (evidently believed by Dante) that he was a magician.

SCOX

A duke of Hell, Scox steals your money but promises to return it . . . in two centuries.

SEALIAH

Before his fall, Sealiah was an angel of the order of Virtues. As a demon, he is said to have great power over vegetables.

SEERA

A demon who controls time, possessing the ability to slow it down or speed it up.

SEMIRAMIS DWH 807 B.C. LUST

Blown about by dark winds in the Second Circle of the Inferno, where the lustful and gluttonous are punished, she is the first of the *Inferno's* damned to be identified by name—the Assyrian empress Sammuramat, whom Dante calls Semiramis. He knew her only by her reputation for brutal tyranny and monstrous perversion. His sources were the fifth-century Christian propagandist Paulus Orosius and the first-century B.C. Roman hack Diodorus Siculus, who between them alleged that Semiramis had betrayed her first husband, murdered her second, seized power, built the wondrous Hanging Gardens of Babylon, and declared incest legal in order to marry her own son. Thus she is in Hell, as Dante is informed by his tour guide Virgil, for being "so corrupted by licentious vice, that she made every form of lust lawful, to cleanse the stain of scandal she had spread." Upon her scandalous legend are based an opera by Rossini and tragedies by both the Spanish dramatist Calderón de la Barca and VOLTAIRE.

In real life, she was the wife of King Shamshi-Adad V (better known as Ninus), who founded the city of Nineveh. Upon his death (in 811 B.C.) she ruled the Assyrian Empire for five years as dowager regent, until their son Adad-Nirari III (or Ninyas) attained his majority. Among her actual achievements were a series of flood-control levees ("remarkable" ones, according to the Greek historian Herodotus) and successful military actions against the neighboring Medes and Chaldeans.

But it is the invariable fate of highly visible female politicians to be slandered as despotic nymphos—consider the reputations of CATHERINE THE GREAT, CLEOPATRA, ELIZABETH I, Empress WU . . . or Hillary Clinton.

SEMYAZA

The leader of the Watcher angels, assigned to instruct newly created humans in the art of sex. Semyaza taught one of Eve's daughters so well that she gave birth to his giant twin sons, Hiwa and Hiya.

SERGIUS III DWH 911 BLASPHEMY

This pope spent much of his brief reign digging up and dismembering the body of his predecessor Formosus. His mistress was the beautiful whore MAROZIA.

SET

A very ancient Egyptian war god, Set gradually evolved into an evil spirit, the Lord of Confusion and god of darkness. It was said that he murdered his hero-brother OSIRIS, for which crime he was castrated by Osiris's posthumous son, Horus. The identification of the villainous Set with the Canaanite idol BAAL justified some early Egyptian anti-Semitism. Set is pictured with the head of a mysterious snouted animal, perhaps an aardvark. See also TYPHON.

SETEBOS   WITCHCRAFT
The explorer Magellan reported this to be the name of a Patagonian goddess-demoness.

SEXTUS   DWH 35 B.C.   CRUELTY
We know—Dante tells us, canto 12, line 134—that in Hell's Seventh Circle Sextus suffers forever, drowning in a river of boiling blood, among the cruel. But who *is* he? Some scholars identify him as Sextus Pompeius, the son of Pompey the Great, who became a pirate operating out of Sicily and once cruelly cut off Rome's grain supply from North Africa. Others claim he is obviously Lucius Sextus Tarquinius Superbus, the sixth-century B.C. king of Rome whose cruel rape of Lucrece was one day to be most poetically described by Shakespeare.

SHAJAR al-Durr   DWH 1257   MURDER
The caliph of Baghdad, in whose harem this Armenian-born beauty was a slave, made a present of her to al-Salih Ayyub, the sultan of Egypt. She soon became his favorite wife, his sultana. But Ayyub picked an inconvenient time to die, expiring in the palace in Cairo just as word reached Egypt that the crusade of King Louis IV of France was marching against the heathens. Shajar cleverly concealed her husband's death—for ten months she ran the Egyptian government while awaiting the return from Iraq of the Ayyub heir, Turan-Shah. Her forces not only defeated Louis but held him for ransom. But the new sultan proved less than grateful. So Shajar conspired to have him murdered—by Baybars, leader of her elite personal guards, the Mamluks. She then proclaimed herself not merely sultana of Egypt but "queen of the Muslims." To placate the far-off caliph, the neighboring Syrians, and the ubiquitous emirs—among all of whom there were few feminists—Shajar consented to marry Izz ad-Din Aybek, one of the Mamluks. But soon the fool misunderstood his figurehead role and began acting on his own authority, whereupon Shajar had him murdered in his bath by her eunuchs. She had gone too far. The slave girls of Izz ad-Din's other wife beat the sultana to death with wooden shoes.

SHAKA   DWH 1828   CRUELTY
His father didn't want him—hence his name, which signifies a beetle that causes menstrual disorders. But Shaka became the founder of the great Zulu Empire, which he created in ten years from a small Bantu clan. He was a brilliant, ruthless military tactician. One by one, he attacked sur-

rounding tribes without warning or mercy, afterward absorbing the survivors into his nation. Under his leadership, the Zulus dominated the vast area of South Africa now known as Natal. Then, in 1827, Shaka's mother, Nandi, died—and he went nuts. His mourning consisted of the slaughter of 7,000 of his own people—every pregnant woman, together with her husband. He forbade the sowing of crops and the milking of cows; all milch cows were butchered, "so the newborn calves would know how it feels to lose a mother."

Shaka was assassinated by his own half brothers.

SHAMDAN

The devil who mated with NAAMAH (seductive sister of Adam's grandson Tubal Cain). Their offspring was the demon ASMODEUS.

SHAX

A demon who deafens and blinds the enemies of his friends.

SHERIDAN, Gen. Philip Henry
DWH 1888   CRUELTY

A brilliant, fierce, and usually successful Union cavalry officer in the Civil War, Little Phil was appointed military commander of Texas and Louisiana after Lee's surrender. "If I owned Texas and Hell, I would rent out Texas and live in Hell," said he, and he enforced Reconstruction so harshly that he was removed by President Jackson and sent west to slaughter the natives. Even if he had lived an otherwise virtuous life (which he didn't), he still would be damned for coining the statement "The only good Indian is a dead Indian."

SHIBBETA

This ancient Jewish demon was in the habit of strangling children for eating food that had been touched by unclean hands.

SHMIDT, Konrad   DWH 1368   HERESY

He convinced the citizens of Thuringia, Germany, that the prophesies of Isaiah referred to the coming not of Christ but of Shmidt, and that (the usual story) the end of the world was nigh. Naturally, they acclaimed him king of Thuringia and demonstrated their loyalty by acts of mass flagellation, whipping themselves and one another raw under the approving eyes (so they believed) of an angel named Venus. The Inquisition eventually took an interest in these goings-on and burnt at the stake the king of Thuringia, along with many of his subjects. They probably enjoyed it. See also DAVID KORESH.

SIMON MAGUS   DWH 1st century   SIMONY

Dante begins canto 19 of the *Inferno* with a burst of invective: "O, Simon Magus, and you wretched scum that follow him! You rapacious creatures who prostitute for gold and silver the things of God!"

The always mortal sin of simony—the buying or selling of spiritual things, including ecclesiastical office—is named after this famous "sorcerer" of Samaria, who converted to Christianity and was baptized by the apostle Philip. When Peter and John arrived to "lay hands on" the newly baptized, Simon offered them money if they would teach him the trick of invoking the power of the Holy Spirit, and he was strongly rebuked by Peter (Acts 8:9–24). In legend, the story continues: Simon traveled with a stunningly beautiful whore named HELEN. He challenged Peter to a magician's duel and conjured up fierce devil dogs, which Peter made vanish with holy bread. Simon next attempted to fly (off the top of the Forum in Rome) and crashed. Or had himself buried for three days but failed to be resurrected. Or was captured by the Romans but hypnotized his executioner into cutting off a ram's head instead of his, thereby convincing the emperor NERO of his ability to rise from the dead.

SIN   🐝

Milton, in *Paradise Lost* (book 2), personifies Sin as a woman to the waist, a serpent below. Hmmm. She sprang, he says, full-blown from SATAN's head and guards the gate of Hell.

SINON   DWH circa 1200 B.C.   DECEIT

The archetypal double agent or mole, this Greek soldier, on instructions from the crafty ULYSSES, sought and gained asylum in the besieged city of Troy and later convinced Trojans to accept the "gift" of the wooden horse. Dante, observing him in Hell (canto 30), comments on the awful stink. Homer maintained that Sinon was the son of SISYPHUS.

SISYPHUS

The patron saint, so to speak, of existentialists. In Hades, Sisyphus labors without respite to roll a heavy stone to the top of a steep hill, whence it always rolls back down—an image which to Albert Camus, at least, epitomized the human condition. Sisyphus was a clever fellow, a rascal, a trickster—some say he was the true father of the crafty ULYSSES. His mistake was revealing to the river god Asopus the affair between his daughter Aegina and Zeus.

SLADE, Joseph ("Jack")   DWH 1864   CRUELTY

Mark Twain met Slade once, in a stagecoach station. "Here was romance, and I was sitting face to face with it!" he wrote. Slade was an alcoholic gunslinger. The baddest man alive when he was sober, he was worse when drunk. He shot to death—sometimes tortured and then shot to death—dozens of men. He wore the ear of one of his victims as a watch fob. After Slade was lynched by vigilantes in Montana, his widow conducted his body back to his native Illinois in a tin coffin filled with alcohol. Slade offered Twain a cup of coffee. Recounted Twain, "I politely declined. I was afraid he had not killed anybody that morning, and might be needing diversion."

SOCRATES   DWH 399 B.C.   BLASPHEMY

This philosopher has been canonized by two millennia of secular humanists. Dante puts him in Hell's benign First Circle, or Limbo. But let's face it. Socrates was legally tried for, and convicted of, both blasphemy and "corrupting youth": He was a pederast. Not only was he perpetually unemployed but he squandered his inheritance, so that his wife and children were nearly destitute. Unless he was "just kidding"—the famous Socratic irony—he advocated the censorship of literature and a rigidly stratified society, and he discouraged participation in democracy. He may not have been a totalitarian, but he was certainly a snob. And, lest we forget, he committed suicide.

SOLAS

Demon who teaches astronomy.

SONNEILLON

Formerly an angel of the Fourth Order (Thrones), now a fiend with the cushy job of tempting humans to be angry with their enemies. Sonneillon has as his Heavenly adversary the forgiving martyr St. Stephen.

SOUTHCOTT, Joanna   DWH 1814   HERESY

A devout English Methodist spinster and a prophetess with a large following, Southcott announced (at the age of sixty-four) that she would be giving birth to the Messiah on October 19, 1814, and that his name would be Shiloh. This did not come to pass. Instead, Southcott died, on October 26, but left behind a sealed box "to be opened, by 24 archbishops, in time of national crisis." It was opened in 1927. It contained a lottery ticket.

SOUTHEY, Robert   DWH 1843   TREASON

A prolific poet, friend of such liberals as Wordsworth and Coleridge, author of the radical utopian call to arms *Wat Tyler,* Southey took a tour of Europe, where, said he, "I learned to thank God I was an Englishman." He returned an outspoken Tory and became the stern critic of his formerly fellow Romantics, whom he called "Satanic." He was awarded with the laureateship. When he published his "Vision of Judgement," celebrating King George III's triumphal entry into Heaven, BYRON issued a counterblast, his own "Vision of Judgement," in which the bored gatekeeper St. Peter eventually slugs the long-winded bard with his keys.

On Southey's behalf, it must be admitted that, before he went completely mad, he wrote "Goldilocks and the Three Bears."

STALIN, "Uncle Joe"   DWH 1953   TYRANNY

Josif Vissarionovich Dzugashvili's pious washerwoman mother wanted a priest in the family, so he briefly attended the Tiflis Theological Seminary in his native Georgia. Only God knows whether this is a mitigating factor.

STARKWEATHER, Charles   DWH 1959   MURDER

Starkweather was only doing his James Dean impersonation when he went on his interstate spree, killing nine people with his fifteen-year-old girlfriend, Caril [*sic*] Fugate, in tow. Their odyssey has become the stuff of legend—and of screenplays. He wrote his father from death row, "I'm not sorry for what I did cause for the first time me and Caril had some fun," and refused to donate his eyes to the blind: "No one ever did anything for me. Why in Hell should I do anything for anyone else?" thus establishing himself as a role model for neoconservatives.

STARR, Belle   DWH 1889   INCEST

The "dazzling beauty" and "female Robin Hood" of dime-store novels was actually a homely criminal named Myra Belle Shirley, who beat her children and her mare, Venus. She did *not* ride with the James gang as the *Police Gazette* claimed; in fact, her only connection with them was to have an illegitimate child (Pearl) by member Cole Younger. Jilted by Younger, she looked around for her next lover and seduced the nearest horse thief—who happened to be her son. He mustn't have returned her lust, since he shot her to death and put a picture of her horse on her tombstone.

STRANG, James Jesse   DWH 1845   HERESY

No sooner had Mormon founder Joseph Smith been assassinated in Illinois than Strang, a recently reformed lawyer and newspaperman, produced a letter, signed by Smith, naming him his successor. It was, in the great Mormon tradition, a forgery. Brigham Young somehow established that he—not Strang, nor Smith's own wife and son, nor any other of the many claimants (all waving dubious documents of their own)—was to lead the Latter-day Saints. He had Strang expelled from the church and, with most Mormons, lit out for the promised land in Utah. Strang headed for Wisconsin, accompanied by, among others, Joseph Smith's brother William. In 1845, Strang (like Joseph Smith before him) was visited by an angel, who presented him with a set of ancient plates and a pair of magic goggles to read them by. The plates were nothing less than "The Book of the Law of the Lord," and they proclaimed that Strang and his disciples (of whom there were now 5,000) were divinely instructed to arise and occupy Beaver Island, Michigan, there to practice polygamy. What choice had Strang, now and henceforth King James I in Zion, but to obey?

Before he was shot by disgruntled ex-disciples, Strang was twice elected to the Michigan legislature.

SUCCOTH-BENOTH

One of the rare—to judge by the usual artistic representations—demon eunuchs, he is employed in Hell as the keeper of SATAN's harem. On earth, he tempts mortals to jealousy.

SUKARNO   DWH 1970   TYRANNY

The leader of the Indonesian independence movement and self-declared lifetime president of the republic, who was known as Bung Karno, was—if ever anyone was—an "evil genius." He was a spellbinding speaker in a dozen languages and a great lover of women, any number of whom he married. Jailed and exiled for his opposition to the Dutch colonizers of his homeland, Sukarno welcomed the invading Japanese, to whom he offered his services—supplying them an abundance of propaganda, slave labor, and whores. After the war, as president of the republic, he moved into the Dutch governor's palace and took up the good life. Recognizing a "friendly dictator" when they saw one, the United States contributed a billion dollars to his lifestyle; Sukarno then denounced the imperialists and collected another billion from the USSR.

Rebellions and assassination attempts were features of his regime. In 1965 he hit upon the brilliant tactic of staging a coup against himself, in the course of which his USSR-financed army slaughtered a million "Communists."

SURGAT

This demon appears only on Sunday, between 11:00 P.M. and 1:00 A.M. He must be given a hair.

SUT

A Muslim demon, the Father of Lies, Sut is one of the sons of IBLIS.

SYLVESTER II   DWH 1003   SORCERY

He ascended the papacy after making a pact with the Devil, and being pontiff didn't stop him from continuing his relationship with MERIDIANA, his demon-mistress. Besides satisfying his carnal needs, Meridiana bestowed upon him wealth and a bronze head containing a spirit who could predict the future. When Sylvester asked the head questions about his mortality, the spirit inside assured him he would not die "except in Jerusalem," a city the pontiff then religiously avoided. However, one day while saying mass in Rome, the pope felt queasy and asked the altar boy the name of the church. When he heard it was the Holy Cross of Jerusalem, he dropped dead. He was buried in the Lateran, and for centuries his tomb would "sweat" before the death of a prominent person; if a pope were going to die, the tomb would sweat even more profusely, leaving a large puddle.

SYTRY

A foul fiend who encourages female nudity.

The bells of Hell go ting-a-ling-a-ling
For you but not for me.

—Traditional children's rhyme

The only thing to be said for this foul doctrine is that it made sin creative; that is, humanity owes infinitely more to the sinners who went on sinning in spite of it than it does to the preachers who tried to restrain sin by threatening it.

—NORTHROP FRYE, *The Great Code*

Thus spoke the devil unto me, "Even God has his Hell: it is his love for man."

— FRIEDRICH NIETZSCHE, *Thus Spake Zarathustra*

TABLIBIK
One of the demons of the fifth hour, the genius of fascination.

TABRIS
One of the demons of the sixth hour, the genius of goetic magic.

TAGRIEL
A demon who rules a lunar mansion.

TAMAIEL
One of the fallen Watchers—the "angel of the deep" (I Enoch).

TAMERLANE (aka Timur the Lame; Tamberlane)   DWH 1405
CRUELTY
Like his idol GENGHIS KHAN, whom he claimed (falsely) was an ancestor, Tamerlane never lost a war. In his lifetime, his armies conquered over 2 million square miles and were responsible for the deaths of hundreds of thousands in Russia, Persia, India, and central Asia. Although his vast empire crumbled after his death, he left this life on a philosophical note, observing, "Never yet has death been frightened away by screaming."

TAMMÜZ ·

A Syrian fertility god who yearly dies and is reborn. We read, in Ezekiel 8:14, of the heathen "women weeping for Tammüz" and, in *Paradise Lost* (1.446) of "Damsels" lamenting his fate "in amorous ditties." As a Christian demon, Tammüz is the Devil's ambassador to Spain and is known to be at his most powerful during the month of October.

TANCHELM DWH 1115 HERESY

This monk of Antwerp, a wandering preacher condemning the lax local clergy, went too far when he urged folks to withhold tithes, then declared himself possessed by the Holy Spirit, next proclaimed his own divinity, and finally married a statue of the Blessed Virgin Mary. The faithful brought presents and partook of a curious sacrament—drinking Tanchelm's bathwater. After the egomaniacal heretic's death (he was stabbed by a priest), the efforts of the great St. Norbert were required to win Antwerp back to the Faith.

T'AN-MO ·

Chinese archtempter, the counterpart to SATAN; T'an-mo fills humans with covetousness and desire.

TANTALUS ·

From his name, and his punishment in Hades, we derive our word *tantalize*—for this erstwhile demigod spends his hungry, thirsty eternity standing in a pool of cool water from which he cannot drink, beneath a fruit tree from which he cannot eat.

There is some question as to what Tantalus did to deserve such torture, but his sin certainly involved comestibles. Some say he shared a portion of Heavenly ambrosia, the food of the gods, with mere mortals. Others claim that he invited the gods to dinner and, in order to test their omniscience, served them a dish composed of his son.

TAPHTHARTHARETH ·

Demon of the sphere of Mercury who is assigned the magical number 2,080.

TARAB ·

A demon of the twelfth hour who is the genius of extortion.

TARAKA ·

An Indian demon who threatened the gods by means of his yoga austerity. He is known as the Danava Demon.

TARNOWER, Dr. Herman (Hi) DWH 1980
CRUELTY

His picture on the cover of his famous diet book reveals that "Hi" resembled a devil even before he went to Hell. Ugly, yes, but that didn't stop the unflappable Hi: He was a society doctor, gourmand, snob, millionaire, snappy dresser, and, most incredibly, a ladies' man. His servants were kept busy shuttling the negligees of rival mistresses in and out of his bedroom, depending on which one was heading to Hi. He addicted his girlfriend of fourteen years, Jean Harris, to amphetamines, refused to pay her for editing (some said, writing) his best-seller, and, confirmed bachelor that he was, reneged on his marriage proposal. The proper Harris returned the engagement ring, which Hi then sold, using the cash as a down payment on a house for his other, much younger galfriend. When Harris was indicted for his murder, millions of women wondered what her crime was.

TARTARACHUS

The Keeper of Hell, Tartarachus first appears in the apocryphal (third-century) scripture *Vision of Paul*, in which he is an angel "appointed over punishments." It is his task to torment sinners between the time of their deaths and the Last Judgment.

TASH

A demon with the body of a man and the head of a bird with a curved, cruel beak. Tash holds his four arms high, stretching them northward. When he floats over grass, it withers beneath his feet.

TAWISKARON

A Native American evil spirit, Tawiskaron encourages toads to drink up the fresh water needed by humans.

TCHORT

The Russian SATAN, known as the Black God.

TEACH, Edward   DWH 1718   PIRACY

Blackbeard, they called him—he wore it tied up in ribbons. With five ships crewed by 500 cutthroats, he preyed for ten years on commercial shipping from New England to the West Indies, under the protection of the governor of North Carolina, with whom he shared his swag. The town of Bath, N.C., turned out to celebrate his wedding to his fourteenth bride, a local fifteen-year-old. Finally, a ship commanded by Lieutenant Maynard of Virginia engaged Blackbeard at sea; it took twenty-five cutlass strokes and five bullets to do the pirate in. This "bloody pirate" serves on the jury from Hell in Stephen Vincent Benét's story "The Devil and Daniel Webster."

TEFNUT

Tefnut lives in the Egyptian Underworld with her twin sister, Nut. Because she feeds on blood sacrifices, her face is always red.

TEGGHIAIO, Aldobrandi   DWH circa 1260   VIOLENCE

A military leader of the Guelfs of Florence who attempted in vain to call off the disastrous attack on Siena in 1260. He now scampers barefoot across the burning sands of the Third Circle.

TELCHINS

These demons work in metal, use the evil eye, and occasionally appear in the sea as mermen.

TEN-GU

These Japanese forest goblins have long noses and like to live in hollow trees.

TEPES, Vlad   See DRACULA.

TERLY

In the *Grimorium Verum,* Terly is mentioned as an imp who will, on command, fetch a woman's garter.

TERMAGANT 🦌

A demon whose idol was supposed—by the Crusaders—to be worshipped by their enemies, the Saracens. This seems unlikely, since graven images are forbidden in Islam; nonetheless, Termagant became a featured ranting, raving villain in the so-called morality plays. Since he appeared onstage clad in flowing eastern robes, the peasant audiences assumed that he was a woman—and his name came to imply a shrew or scold.

TERRAGON 🦌

The familiar and favorite demon of King HENRI III, who once procured a prostitute for Terragon.

TERVEGAN 🦌

A cannibal demon, featured in the thirteenth-century French farce *Salut d'Enfer.*

TETZEL, Friar Johann   DWH 1519   SIMONY

When he launched his great indulgence sale in Germany, Tetzel claimed to proffer an indulgence so powerful it could absolve any sin—even that of raping the Blessed Virgin Mary! He entered towns with much fanfare and in his booming voice went into his impersonation of souls in Purgatory: "Pity us! Pity us!" He even composed a little ditty, which may have been the first commercial jingle:

As soon as the coin in the coffers rings
A soul from Purgatory springs

TEZCATLIPOCA 🦌

The Aztec god of Hell. When he vanquished Chaos, Tezcatlipoca tore her in two, so the universe could be differentiated.

THAGRINUS 🦌

Demon of the fourth hour, the genius of confusion.

THAÏS   DWH 4th century B.C.   FLATTERY

History's most famous courtesan, Thaïs traveled with ALEXANDER THE GREAT into Persia and there persuaded him to burn down the city of Persepolis. Her name became generic for *prostitute*—there was even a reformed Christian hooker named St. Thaïs. Dante, for some reason, thought her a flatterer and describes her in their malodorous afterlife company (canto 18), sunk in a river of excrement: "that repulsive and disheveled strumpet scratching herself with shitty fingernails, spreading her legs while squatting up and down."

THAPHABAOTH

A Gnostic demon who appears in the form of a bear.

THEODORA   DWH 548   LUST

The beautiful, wise, and politically powerful wife of the Byzantine emperor Justinian was a feminist. As coregent, Theodora passed divorce laws favorable to women, outlawed the traffic in young girls, and out-maneuvered the regime's opponents. She was also a sex maniac.

Procopius, the official court historian, also kept a gossipy diary, now known as the *Secret History*. He tells us that Theodora's father was a circus bear trainer and that in her youth she had been both a striptease dancer and a prostitute with a specialty—"she appeared to have her private parts not like other women in the place intended by nature, but in her face."

THEODORIC   DWH 451   VIOLENCE

The Romans hired Theodoric, king of the Visigoths, to rid them of German invaders. The homely, barbaric king soon became en-amored of their culture and, poignantly, wanted more than anything to be Roman—a wish that was clearly not granted, since his ascension to the throne of Rome marked the end of the Roman Empire. He was trampled to death by his own men during a battle with ATTILA THE HUN. In his *Dialogues,* Pope Gregory the Great recounts that a monk on the isles of Lipari saw the ghost of Pope John hurl the bar-barian interloper-king into a volcano.

THESEUS

For shamelessly and selfishly abandoning the princess Ariadne, the poet Ariosto condemned this hero to Hell. But in canto 9, at the gates of Dis,

Dante is threatened by the guardian ERINYES (or Furies) and hears them regret "letting Theseus get away." Theseus, it seems, had once raided Hades on a reckless mission to rescue PERSEPHONE. He himself was captured and imprisoned by PLUTO but was rescued and returned to the Upper World by the mighty Hercules.

THESPIUS'S FATHER   MURDER

The esteemed Roman historian Plutarch (who was actually a Greek) composed *The Vision of Thespius,* a travelogue of the Underworld ruled by DIS. The traveler, Thespius, beholds his own father among the damned, for the crime of poisoning some rich dinner guests.

THOTH   🐾

The Egyptian god of magic, whose early followers believed he hatched the earth in the form of a giant egg. A latter-day disciple, ALEISTER CROWLEY, named a best-selling tarot deck after him. Thoth was known for his creative powers; he it was who instructed the dismembered OSIRIS how to reconstitute his body.

THURSAR   🐾

Crude German demonic beings with big ears covered with rough hair.

TIBBALD   DWH circa 1290   TREASON

On the morning of November 13, 1280, Tibbald opened the gates of Faenza, admitting a war party of Bolognese Guelfs who slaughtered the entire (Ghibelline) Lambertazzi family. His motive for this dastardly deed was a quarrel he had with the Lambertazzis over a prize pig.

TICCHI-TACCHI   🐾

A playful Italian demon.

TIPPU TIP   DWH circa 1902   CRUELTY

A black (African) Arab, by repute "the greatest slaver of them all," in the employ of Said Barghash, the sultan of Zanzibar. Tippu, who claimed to be "named for the sound of rifles," was a businessman, pure and simple; he dealt slaves and had a monopoly on the ivory trade. He was not above collaborating with the minions of the Belgian king LEOPOLD II.

TIR   🐾

In Islam, one of the sons of IBLIS. Tir is the demon who causes accidents.

TIRESIAS   SOOTHSAYING

He is the first "shade" encountered in Hades by ULYSSES, and he thirstily drinks a bowl of blood before addressing the hero. Virgil points him out to Dante in the fourth bolgia of the Eighth Circle as "the one who changed his shape." He is alluding to the legend that Tiresias was once briefly transformed into a woman; by virtue of this experience, he was able to settle a bitter argument among the gods as to which sex takes more pleasure in sex. ("Woman," he firmly declared.) Tiresias's gender bending was the result of his watching snakes mate—which seems odd, given that he had previously been struck blind by the goddess Athena for spying on her at her bath.

TISIPHONE

One of the pitiless ERINYES (Furies), Tisiphone is snake haired and wears a living snake for a belt.

TITUS   DWH 81   BLASPHEMY

After his legions destroyed Jerusalem and very nearly obliterated the Jewish nation, this emperor personally burned the temple, ransacked the Holy of Holies, and took the golden menorah back to Rome. The Arch of Titus was created in memory of his great victory, and it is said that after a Jew walks under it, he is no longer a Jew.

TITYUS

Leto was a beautiful Titaness by whom Zeus fathered—among other gods—Apollo. When she was nearly raped by the giant Tityus, Apollo killed him, and Zeus condemned him to Hades. There he is spread-eagled and pegged out (his body covers nine acres), and vultures, which nest in his guts, eat his liver. All this is attested to by eyewitnesses AENEAS, ULYSSES, and Dante (canto 31).

TLAZOLTEOTL

An Aztec witch who rides around on a broomstick, holds Sabbats at crossroads, and causes thunderstorms.

TOGLAS

A demon of the eighth hour, Toglas is the genius of hidden treasure.

TORQUEMADA, Tomás de   DWH 1498   CRUELTY

This Dominican friar was named grand inquisitor in 1487. By the time he finished, the Spanish Inquisition had claimed over 300,000 victims—not including the 160,000 Jews he exiled for the sin of not converting. Torquemada felt he was too sensitive for his job: He would cry bitter tears over those lost to SATAN and often had to leave the room when the torture of a heretic began. His sole comfort, he claimed, was the knowledge that what he did was "for the greater glory of God." He was a vegetarian who fasted constantly and an ascetic whose only concession to his great position was his palace, with 250 servants and 50 bodyguards. Once, when he heard King Ferdinand and Queen Isabella were letting some rich Jews remain in Spain for a price, he held a crucifix in front of them, shouting, "Judas sold Jesus for thirty pieces of silver. Will you sell him for more?" It is to be hoped that the chastened royals never found out about Torquemada's Jewish grandmother.

TORVATUS 🦇

One of the demons of the second hour, the genius of discord.

TRISTRAM   DWH circa 600   ADULTERY

The tragic hero of popular medieval romance, whom Sir Thomas Malory made a knight of the Round Table, Sir Tristram of Lyonesse is among the sexual offenders Dante sees in the Second Circle of Hell. Tristram had the misfortune to fall in love (in Ireland) with a married woman named Iseult and then to compound his problems by marrying (in Brittany) another woman of the same name. RICHARD WAGNER's opera *Tristan und Isolde* tells the whole, messy story.

TUKIPHAT 🦇

A demon of the eighth hour, the genius of the shamir.

TUNG YUEH TA TI 🦇

In Chinese mythology, the "Great Divine Ruler of the Eastern Peak." A grandson of the Jade Emperor, Tung Yueh Ta Ti judges the dead, assisting YAN LU WANG.

TUNRIDA 🦇

A Scandinavian female devil.

TUTIVILLUS (aka Titivil) 🦇

This nasty demon distracts the faithful at prayer and collects all the words omitted or slurred by priests while they are saying mass. He was sufficiently well known to be featured as a comic villain in the English morality play *Mankynde,* circa 1470.

TYDEUS

One of the rebellious Seven against Thebes, Tydeus slew Melanippus in combat but was himself wounded. As he lay dying, he called for his enemy's head and ate it.

TYPHOID MARY (Mary Mallon)   DWH 1938   MURDER

She was an immunological marvel—someone who carries a deadly agent without ever being or feeling sick. The stout Irish cook caused at least twelve typhoid epidemics, including one that alone claimed 1,400 victims. As she and her deadly stool moved from city to city, Mary realized it wasn't a coincidence that typhoid broke out whenever she started cooking. She changed her name whenever she relocated and hid when authorities dropped by. It took a health inspector with the skills of a detective to track Mary down in her latest kitchen. He demanded a stool sample, and she responded by lunging at him with a meat cleaver. When the controversial sample was finally extricated, a microscope revealed it to be teeming with typhoid salmonella, sending Mary, the greatest microbe carrier in history, into lifetime quarantine.

TYPHON

Visiting Greeks for some reason identified the Egyptian god SET with this Titan, despite the fact that Typhon was known to have 120 heads. He was the son of the god Tartarus and the father of the Hell hound CERBERUS. Zeus imprisoned him, along with TITYUS, under Mt. Etna, which accounts for its restlessness, i.e., its tendency to tremble and erupt. Typhon lives there with his bride, the hideous giant Echidna. Since he belches flame and lives underground, and since his body, from the hips downward, consists of two serpents, some authorities see Typhon as the prototype of our own Devil, and he has been a favorite of magicians from classical times.

TZ'U-HSI   DWH 1908   TYRANNY

The empress dowager of China was the original Dragon Lady. With four-inch-long fingernails and six-inch-high heels, Tz'u-hsi teetered around her lavish palace trailed by a retinue of eunuchs and informers. A concubine of the emperor at age seventeen, she seized control of the government when he died and a few years later made her son emperor. When her son died, Tz'u-hsi eliminated her two daughters-in-law, one with an opium overdose and the other with a poisoned milk cake. Then she put her nephew in power, but when he started exhibiting humanitarian tendencies (such as the Hundred Days of Reform), she threw him in prison and left him there. Even though she slept next to a picture of her idol, Queen Victoria, Tz'u-hsi encouraged the Boxer Rebellion and declared war on Great Britain.

When dying, she refused prayers for her recovery, saying, "No, I have sinned enough. I will die." Then she sat up and gave a final warning about the dangers of involving women and eunuchs in government.

Under modern conditions any effective invitation to Hell will certainly appear in the guise of scientific planning.

—C. S. Lewis, *Of Other Worlds*

Upon the deathbed subject, the clergy grow eloquent. When describing the shuddering shrieks of the dying unbeliever, their eyes glitter with delight. It is a festival.

—Robert G. Ingersoll, *The Great Infidels*

UDU

An ancient Mesopotamian demon.

UGOLINO della Gherardesca, Count   DWH 1289   TREASON

This treacherous nobleman betrayed his sometime ally Archbishop RUGGIERI DEGLI UBALDINI and ordered him starved to death. In Hell, the two are frozen in holes—but the archbishop's prison is positioned so that he can gnaw his enemy's skull.

ULLIKUMMI

An Anatolian demon who was created when King Kumarbi made a stone pregnant.

ULYSSES   DWH circa 1200 B.C.   EVIL COUNSEL

The Greeks called him Odysseus, the Romans—and, following them, Dante and James Joyce—Ulysses. In Homer (whom Dante never read), he is a hero, both brave and cunning, but in medieval legend he is unscrupulous and cruel. Thus, in the *Inferno* (canto 26), he and the treacherous DIOMEDES burn but are not consumed together in a single flame. At Dante's request, Virgil interviews Ulysses, who recounts a different end to his adventures than the one told in the *Odyssey:* Ulysses and his crew do not return to Ithaca but sail through the Strait of Gibraltar and across the western ocean, perishing, after five months, within sight of a "mountain shape"—possibly the first reference in literature to America.

UPHIR

A medical demon, Hell's official physician.

URBAN VI   DWH 1389   WRATH

A pope somewhat given to drunken rages, he excommunicated Charles III of Naples to counter a power play by the Frenchman and was in turn attacked by him. The plastered pontiff would climb to the battlements of his besieged castle and, while arrows fell around him, employ bell, book, and candle to excommunicate the entire army below. Pressured by the French, the cardinals convened and elected a second pope, a Frenchman who styled himself Clement VIII. This Western Schism at least provided Christendom with a subject for jokes. The English reformer JOHN WYCLIFFE cracked, "I knew the pope had a cloven hoof, now I see he has a cloven head, as well." The wise St. Catherine of Siena observed, "We already have one fake pope—why do we need two?" Urban excommunicated Clement's supporters: the French, Spanish, Scots, and Neopolitans. Clement in turn excommunicated Urban's adherents: the English, Portuguese, Romans, and Venetians. The finally

victorious Urban tortured his captive foes with even more than the usual severity and enjoyed it too. He died by poison.

URBAN VIII DWH 1644
SOWING DISCORD

He was a famous builder, of palaces and fortresses. The construction contracts went to members of his family, and the bronze they employed was stolen from the Pantheon. Urban VIII was a friend of Galileo, and kindly offered to write the preface to the old scientist's new work, *Dialogue Concerning the Two Chief Systems,* but he was deeply insulted when he read it: His own often-expressed orthodox views concerning the relationship of the sun and the earth were therein maintained by a moron named Simplicius. He summoned Galileo to Rome and, under threat of torture, ordered him to retract

and recant. A recent pope has apologized.

URIAN

A demon, the "Lord of the Sabbat," invoked in Goethe's *Faust*.

URIEL

An unfallen Archangel, Uriel is assigned by God to guard the gates of Hell.

USIEL

A demon with twenty servants who finds buried treasures. Although Milton identifies him as a lieutenant in Michael's victorious Heavenly army, the Cabala informs us Usiel is one of the "unholy Sefiroth," who mated with a mortal woman and by her begat giants.

UTNAPISHTIM

The name, in the epic of Gilgamesh, for the Babylonian Noah. Utnapishtim was the only righteous human and thus survived the Flood. He now lives eternally among the dead.

VLADIMIR: Go to Hell.
ESTRAGON: Are you staying there?
VLADIMIR: For the time being.
　　　　　　　—SAMUEL BECKETT, *Waiting for Godot*

VADATAJS

A Latvian demon who leads travelers astray at crossroads.

VALAC

A president of Hell who comes disguised as a little boy with the wings of an angel. Valac rides a two-headed dragon and will give true answers to questions about hidden treasures. He specializes in delivering serpents.

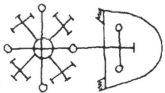

VALFAR

A demon who appears as a many-headed lion and is invoked for the protection of robbers and brigands.

VANDERBILT, "Commodore" Cornelius

DWH 1877   THEFT

He built his $100 million steamship and railroad empire through graft and bribery, openly declaring, "What do I care about the law? I got the power!" What the former Staten Island ferryman did care about was throwing vulgar parties, at which he invited his many lady friends to dig in a trough for jewels.

The Commodore became a follower of those famous spiritualists the Woodhull sisters. He set them up in their own brokerage firm, allowing them to use the substantial profits to publish a "free love" weekly. Once he asked the sisters to contact the spirit of his dead business associate and fellow crook Jim Fisk, but during the séance Vanderbilt's recently departed wife, Sophia, appeared instead. Vanderbilt was not pleased, snapping, "Business before pleasure. Let me speak to Jim."

VANINI, Lucilio   DWH 1619   ATHEISM

An ordained priest, Vanini was discovered preaching atheism, an offense for which he was strangled and burned. He also had his tongue cut out, but not before he got in the last word: "There is neither God nor devil; and if there were a God, I would pray for Him to send a thunderbolt on this Council."

VANNI Fucci   DWH 1300
THEFT

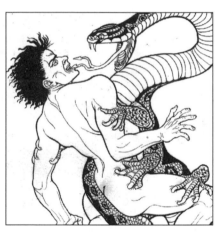

A bastard in every sense of the word, this illegitimate son of a Pistoian nobleman was a murderous bully. But to Dante's surprise and his own eternal shame, Vanni suffers not among the wrathful but in the company of thieves—because, in 1293, he had robbed the sacristy of the church of San Zeno.

VANTH

An Etruscan demon, Vanth has a large eye on the inside of each of her wings.

VASSAGO

Yet another demon gifted with the ability to foretell the future.

VELES

Slavic god of the Underworld.

VENEDICO Caccianemico   DWH 1297   PANDERING

An ambitious politician, leader of the Guelf party of Bologna and sometime mayor of Milan, Caccianemico now resides in Hell's Eighth Circle, "in a pickle," says Dante. There he cringes eternally under the lash of devil guards, as they quite properly torture him for the sin of pimping his sister to a powerful marquis.

VEPAR

A demon who can assume the form of a mermaid, Vepar guides battleships, causes storms at sea, and can create the illusion that the sea is full of ships. He causes death by worm-eaten wounds.

VERDELET

The master of ceremonies in Hell. When Verdelet visits earth, he uses pleasant sounds to seduce females but causes maggot infestation in males.

VERRES   DWH 43 B.C.   CORRUPTION

Governor of Sicily under the emperor Sulla, Verres established a regime that was a nightmare of cruelty and extortion. Finally brought up on charges, he expected to be exonerated, thanks to his well-placed bribes and influential friends, but he did not reckon on the prosecutor, Cicero, whose brilliant, vitriolic summation exposed Verres as a paradigm of the corrupt and repressive ruler.

VERRIER

A demon, formerly a prince of Principalities, who tempts men against the vow of obedience by making the neck stiff and incapable of bending to another's will. Verrier's adversary is St. Bernard.

VERRINE

A former angel of the order of Thrones, Verrine in Hell is next in place to ASHTORETH. That he specializes in tempting mortals to the sin of impatience we have on the authority of Sister Madeleine of Loudun, who was briefly possessed by him. His adversary is St. Dominic.

VETALAS

Evil spirits in Indian folklore, they haunt cemeteries in order to reanimate corpses. The vetalas look almost human, except their hands and feet are turned backward. They live in stones scattered about the hills.

VICIOUS, Sid   DWH 1979   SUICIDE

This British punk rocker, whose art consisted of slashing himself with a razor and vomiting while performing, in one year survived an overdose of heroin, a suicide attempt, and killing his pathetic American girlfriend, Nancy Spungen. He then died of a heroin overdose one day after he was released from a detox program. A true working-class hero, Vicious hailed bourgeois taxicabs with the use of his middle finger.

VICTOR EMMANUEL I   DWH 1824   TYRANNY

The reactionary king of Sardinia, Victor Emmanuel was sent to France to observe their government, but he only noticed that French women did not wear underpants. He refused to grant his country a constitution but did give away his toenail parings as Christmas presents.

VINE   ⚘

"Something there is that does not love a wall," wrote the poet Robert Frost. Vine was the name medieval demonologists had for this wall-destroying spirit. In addition to destroying walls and barriers, Vine causes storms at sea and reveals to witches the names of magicians.

VINTRAS, Eugene   DWH 1875   HERESY

He was the humble foreman of a cardboard factory in France until the day he received a letter from none other than John the Baptist. It said that since Vintras was the living reincarnation of the Baptist (something he hadn't even suspected!), he should go forth and proclaim "the Age of the Holy Ghost." In the same year he received another letter, this time from the Archangel Michael, who revealed that someone named Charles Naundorf was the real king of France. These wondrous events inspired Vintras to found a cult, the Work of Mercy, and the Church of Carmel, but in 1846 he was arrested for conducting black masses and masturbating at the altar. Eyewitnesses said that during a black mass Vintras could make blood, later determined to be genuine, appear on the host. It came as no surprise when Vintras reported that the Blessed Virgin Mary had personally visited him to confirm that he was damned. He passed leadership of his movement to the even more disreputable Abbé BOULLAN.

VIR   DWH 1966   SOWING DISCORD

Byname of V. D. Savarkar, founder of the Mahasabha, an Indian Hindu organization devoted to celebrating and enforcing their superiority to Muslims. Vir was personally cleared of any responsibility for the murder of Gandhi by a Mahasabha member.

VITALIANO dei Vitaliani   DWH after 1300   USURY

A Paduan loan shark, still living at the time of Dante's tour of the Inferno, for whom the poet is assured by another usurer, RINALDO DEI SCROVEGNI, that a place is reserved in the Seventh Circle.

VJESHITZA   ⚘

A beautiful succubus with flaming wings, Vjeshitza drives men mad with desire.

VLAD the Impaler See DRACULA.

VODNIK 🦇

Polish water demons, believed to be the souls of unbaptized children. It is advisable to sacrifice the odd chicken to these malevolent sprites.

VOLPULA 🦇

A demonic science teacher.

VOLTAIRE (François-Marie Arouet)
DWH 1778   ATHEISM

At the height of his fame, Voltaire drove around in a luxurious carriage preceded by mounted heralds blasting trumpets. Perhaps he was compensating for his five-foot-one stature. The great libertarian was less than generous: He once had a fellow poet thrown into the Bastille, and when he won the lottery (employing his considerable mathematical skills), he hoarded the winnings. He did, however, invite the husband of his mistress, the marquise du Châtelet, to live with them in their love nest.

Voltaire despised all religion, against which he wrote blasphemous satires. But he called himself a "naturalistic deist." One morning he asked a friend to view the sunrise with him and, overcome, prostrated himself, crying, "I believe in you, Powerful God! I believe!" Then he stood up, dusted himself off, and quickly added, "As for Monsieur the Son and Madame his Mother, *that* is another thing."

As he lay on his deathbed, he was approached by a priest. "Who sent you?" asked Voltaire. "God," replied the priest. Voltaire dismissed him, saying, "You'll have to present better credentials than that." His last words, as the nurse lit the bedside lamp, were "What? The flames already?" Maybe he was joking.

VON MOSSAU, Maria Renata Saenger DWH 1730   SORCERY

At the tender age of seven, she vowed herself to SATAN and at thirteen was a master herbalist, maker of venomous drugs, and mistress of a rich old man. Scheming to take over the convent at Munich, von Mossau posed

as a virtuous maiden and was admitted as a novice. She was always punc-
tual for mass, became a member of the choir, and eventually ascended to
the rank of subprioress. Once in control, von Mossau arranged for a host
of demons, disguised as handsome young men, to seduce and possess the
nuns. The demons made their debut at the Feast of the Holy Innocents,
when they emerged from the possessed nuns, cursing and identifying
themselves: Aatalphus, DATASCALVO, DUSACRUS, Elephantan, NABASCURUS,
and NATASCHURUS. When she was uncovered as the instigator, Maria, unrepentant, announced that she was changing her name to Emato in an effort
(quite unnecessary) to further disassociate herself from the Blessed Virgin
Mary.

VOVAL

A demon in charge of love potions.

VUAL

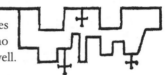

Another demon of lust, Vual "procures
the love of women" on behalf of those who
invoke him. He speaks Egyptian, but not well.

What fresh Hell is this?
                                        —DOROTHY PARKER

*What we believe about Hell remains . . . the touchstone of what we believe
about politics.*
            —JAMES V. SCHALL, SJ, *The Politics of Heaven and Hell*

Whenever God erects a house of prayer,
The Devil always builds a chapel there;
And 'twill be found, upon examination,
The latter has the largest congregation.
            —DANIEL DEFOE, "The True-Born Englishman"

*Who has the most reason to fear Hell: he who is in ignorance whether there is
a Hell, and who is certain of damnation if there is; or he who certainly believes there is a Hell and hopes to be saved?*
                                        —PASCAL, *Pensées*

Who would sell his friends, his country sell
Do other deeds too base to tell,
Deserves the lowest place in hell—
Van Buren!!!!
            —Song during the 1840 presidential race

*Why, yes, Sir, the worst licentious man, were Hell to open before him, would
not take the most beautiful strumpet in his arms.*
                                        —SAMUEL JOHNSON

WAGNER, Richard   DWH 1883   CRUELTY

To avoid contamination when conducting the work of Mendelssohn, a
Jew, Wagner found it necessary to wear white gloves, which he stripped off
and dropped on the floor the minute he finished. No wonder he inspired

the young HITLER, who when listening to
his music claimed to be "transported
into the blessed regions of German
antiquity, the ideal world." The
composer, chronically in debt—
no doubt due to his penchant
for fur bathrobes and silk dress-
ing gowns—was saved from
debtors' prison by his mad
benefactor, King Ludwig II,
who commissioned him to set
German legends to music. That
kept Wagner busy for the rest of
his life . . . along with his extramar-
ital affairs with the wives of his friends
and his personal toilette. He soaked for
hours in a hot tub scented with Milk of Iris per-
fume so he could smell himself while he wrote. On the frequent occasions
when admirers compared him with Christ, Wagner would always respond
with a polite "Thank you."

WALL 🐾

Once an angelic Power, now a grand duke of Hell, who appears as a
camel.

WAMBEEN 🐾

Demon of the Australian aborigines, Wambeen sends fire and lightning to kill travelers. He stinks.

WARNER, Jack L.   DWH 1978   SOWING DISCORD

The brothers who were Warner Bros. were the toughest, cheapest
(Jack was said to have oilcloth pockets so he could save soup) employers in
town, despised by everyone who worked for them. Jack and Harry despised each other as well, each avoiding the commissary when the other
was there. Harry once chased Jack around the studio brandishing a lead
pipe.

Actually, Jack hated pretty much everybody, except his masseuse, but
including his son, Jack, Jr., whom he disowned. Much of Jack's wrath was
directed at his writers. He hired spies to listen outside their doors for typ-
ing sounds and make sure they didn't sneak off the lot for coffee. He offered the writers of *Casablanca* up to the House Un-American Activities

Committee in the eager, reactionary speech to the committee that made him the only Hollywood mogul who voluntarily "named" employees.

Boorish even by Hollywood standards, he once greeted Mme. Chiang Kai-shek and a group of Asian dignitaries by saying, "Holy cow! That reminds me! I forgot to pick up my laundry." When *Casablanca* won the Best Picture Oscar, Jack had the producer, Hal Wallis, physically restrained from getting out of his seat so he could bound up to the stage, smiling, to accept the award . . . alone. He played tennis daily until he went to Hell at the age of eighty-six.

WEI Chung-hsien   DWH 1627   TYRANNY

The antepenultimate Ming emperor Chu Yu-chiao preferred do-it-yourself carpentry projects to statecraft and was pleased to let his mother's eunuch butler run the government. For three years, Wei's eunuch forces—soldiers and spies—fanned out across China, extorting taxes from the populace, selling offices, and purging their reform-minded Confucian opponents. Wei himself became the object of a cult, to whom temples were dedicated. Upon the emperor's death, Wei fell from power and, to avoid trial, hanged himself.

WEST, Mae   DWH 1980

LUST

A professional vaude-villian at age six, West became sexually active at twelve—as she put it, "I used to be Snow White, but I drifted"—and she stayed active well into her eighties. She was over forty when she landed in Hollywood to become, according to W. C. Fields, "a plumber's idea of Cleopatra," and her double entendres ("Is that a gun in your pocket or are you just glad to see me?") saved Paramount Studios. She loved Hollywood hunks but hated all blond actresses (Dietrich was to her the "Kraut cunt") except Marilyn Monroe, and she only liked Monroe after she was dead.

The scripts she wrote for the plays *Sex* and *Drag* (a sympathetic view of homosexuality) caused her to be driven out of New York by local moralists. She became a devotee of the spiritualist Sri Deva Ram Sukul and found herself the channel for a spirit called Julie, who operated from the actress's solar plexus. But when the talky spirit started to interfere with her sleep, Mae told her to scram.

WHIRO

A demon of the Maori in New Zealand.

WILHELM II, Kaiser

DWH 1941　　**CRUELTY**

It was long believed that Queen Victoria's Prussian grandson was an autocratic, bellicose bully who started World War I. Historians have recently concluded that he was a weak, vacillating momma's boy who merely let it happen.

WILKINSON, James　DWH 1825

TREASON

A real skunk. After honorable (if noncombatant) service in the U.S. War of Independence, Wilkinson settled in Kentucky, where, in 1787, he took an oath of allegiance to Spain. As a paid Spanish agent (Number Thirteen), he attempted to sell the Kentucky settlements to Spanish Louisiana authorities—while simultaneously receiving a U.S. Army commission and becoming governor of the territory. His ambitions foiled by history, i.e., the Louisiana Purchase, Wilkinson next schemed, with AARON BURR, to conquer and rule an independent state—the entire American Southwest. For reasons of his own, he then betrayed Burr to President Jefferson; a trial followed, and Burr was acquitted, but Wilkinson—a traitor who had betrayed a traitor—somehow emerged as the major general in command of New Orleans. His final military maneuver was a fiasco of a raid on Montreal in 1813, after which he retired to his Mexican estates.

WILLIAMS, William (Old Bill)   DWH 1849   CRUELTY

The town of Williams, Arizona, is named for this mountain man, trapper, army scout, and scalp hunter. In the 1830s, when the U.S. government was paying a bounty for Indian scalps ($100 for a male's, $50 for a female's, $25 for a child's), it was the wily Williams who discovered that the easiest way to gather them was to raid villages while the braves were away and steal *their* scalp trophies. This hero later joined a gang of California horse thieves, and, while acting as a scout for Gen. John C. Frémont, devoured the frozen bodies of eleven railroad surveyors he had led into the impassable La Garita Mountains.

WINDSOR, Duchess of (Wallis Warfield Simpson)   DWH 1986
TREASON

When Wallis heard her boyfriend, King Edward VIII (see DUKE OF WINDSOR), on the radio, giving up the throne "for the woman I love," she went into a rage, smashing everything in sight. She had wanted to be queen or mistress to the king, not the wife of an . . . exile. Even so, their exile demanded little in the way of self-sacrifice: The elegant couple traveled through war-torn Europe with 222 suitcases (not counting her jewel cases and hatboxes) and an entourage that was likened to an "unaffiliated army." But, in truth, the duchess was hardly unaffiliated, since it has been revealed that during the war she leaked official government secrets to the Nazis. Even at the height of the London Blitz, she felt no sympathy for beleaguered England: "After what they did to me, I can't say I feel sorry for them—a whole nation against a lone woman!" England did, indeed, hate her, especially Churchill, who called her "that bitch"—but HITLER was a staunch fan. In his view, "She would have made a good queen."

She did live like a queen, with a twenty-two-carat-gold bathtub, lap dogs, and a butler who knelt before her to put on her bedroom slippers. The duchess, who once bought fifty-six pairs of shoes in one afternoon, was never known to have left a tip. After her death, at the sale of her jewelry (which netted more than $50 million), several gems showed up that the duchess had years before claimed stolen—adding insurance fraud to her lengthy list of sins.

WINDSOR, Duke of (King Edward VIII)
DWH 1972   LUST

Cruel girlfriends used to make reference to his sexual shortcomings, calling him "little man," and even his wife (see DUCHESS OF WINDSOR) once quipped, "My husband was never heir-conditioned." While she was still his mistress, Wallis Simpson, who was allegedly versed in the Chinese sexual art of Fang Chung, won the heart of the kinky king by indulging both his foot fetishism and his desire to dress up in diapers and be wheeled around in a baby carriage.

It was odd that he spoke English with a cockney/American accent and odder still that the only language he spoke with perfect modulation was German. This must have come in handy when the duke made his triumphant tour of Germany just before World War II, cheered by cries of "Heil Edward" and "Heil Windsor," to which he eagerly responded with the Nazi salute. He told his idol, ADOLF HITLER, that "the German and British races are one" and blamed any "tension" on "Roosevelt and the Jews."

He devoted his remaining years to setting the standard for the Eurotrash generations to come, wandering with his wife, disco dancing, receiving sheep embryo injections, and charging a hefty fee to be the weekend guest of rich, pretentious Americans.

WORMWOOD

The bitter herb *Artemisia absinthium* first sprang up in the track of the serpent SATAN as he slithered out of Eden. In Revelation 8:11, Wormwood is the name of the "star that fell from Heaven," sometimes identified as LU-

CIFER. In *The Screwtape Letters*, by C. S. Lewis, Wormwood is a feckless apprentice "junior devil."

WU CHAO, Empress   DWH 705   VIOLENCE

Only one woman has ever ruled China. One was enough. Her sins were many. At age thirteen, she became a concubine of the T'ang emperor T'ai Tsung. After his death, she became the favorite of his son and successor, Kao Tsung. This is a sin usually referred to as incest. She bore Kao a son, strangled him (infanticide), and placed the blame on the empress (false witness). No sooner had she become empress than she ordered the mutilation and murder of both her predecessor and her mother-in-law, which was treason. Haunted by their ghosts (superstition), she built and moved into a new palace. The young emperor soon took sick, and for decades Wu ruled in his name. Enemies, real, potential, or imagined—including three of her own sons—were executed (cruelty). Her armies invaded and conquered Korea (tyranny).

The emperor died in 683; in 690, Wu declared herself empress, which was usurpation. That year she also proclaimed herself Holy Mother, Divine Sovereign, and a reincarnated Buddha, which was blasphemy. Only then, at age sixty-five, did she turn to lust. Her first lover was a giant wrestler named Feng, whom she called Little Precious. Her last years she devoted to pampering the Chang brothers, a pair of pretty perverts.

WYCLIFFE, John
DWH 1384
HERESY

This highly esteemed First Reformer, the first translator of the Bible into English, started out as an ordinary corrupt scholar-priest, drawing a salary from a parish in which he did not reside.

Like many a "reformer" since (see, e.g., JOHN KNOX), Wycliffe had the courage to defy the faraway pope (in this case, Gregory XI) but was wonderfully subservient to the local authorities (such as his patron, Prince John of Gaunt, on whose behalf Wycliffe even waived the right of sanctuary, so that his henchmen might murder a man in Westminster Abbey).

Xerxes did die
And so must I.
—*The New England Primer* (1737)

Xilquxilqu besa besa. (Charm against a horde of demons)
—from *The Necronomicon*

XAPHAN

One of the original rebel angels, now a mighty demon. During SATAN's war against God, Xaphan suggested arson as a tactic: He proposed burning down Heaven. Fittingly, he now tends the furnaces of Hell with his bellows.

XARMAROCH

A demon, "Ruler of the Tenth Dungeon," with seven dragon heads.

XASTUR

Foul demoness who slays men in their sleep and devours what she will.

XEBETH

The demon of overactive imaginations—author of lies, miraculous tales, and fancies.

XERXES   DWH 465 B.C.   TYRANNY

A despotic ruler of Persia, he appears in the Bible (the Book of Esther) as King Ahasuerus. Having decided, for no apparent reason, to invade Greece, he ordered the construction of two pontoon bridges across the Hellespont; when a storm destroyed them, he personally administered 300 lashes to the sea. His vast army did manage a victory over the small but valiant Spartan force in the pass at Thermopylae (see EPHIALTES) and proceeded to sack the city of Athens. But after his navy was destroyed at the Battle of Salamis, Xerxes went home and spent the remainder of his life building colossal monuments to himself and participating in unseemly harem intrigues, one of which the Jews commemorate to this day on the feast of Purim. He was assassinated, finally, by the commander of his palace guard. According to the Roman satirist Lucian (in *Conversations with the Dead*), the once mighty Xerxes is a ragged beggar in Hades. Rabelais (in *Gargantua and Pantagruel*) at least gives him a job there—he is described as hawking mustard and "pissing in his bucket, the way the mustard sellers do in Paris."

XOBLAH

A demon who is represented in the secret alphabet of demonic texts.

You who now hear of Hell and the wrath of the Great God and sit here in these seats so easy and quiet and go away so careless, by and by will shake and tremble and cry out and shriek and gnash your teeth.

—JONATHAN EDWARDS, sermon,
"The Future Punishment of the Wicked"

YAGODA, Genrikh Grigoryevich   DWH 1938   TYRANNY

An early, eager member of STALIN's secret police (Cheka), Yagoda became deputy chairman of its successor organization, the OGPU. From 1930, he was in charge of the USSR's system of forced labor camps. In 1934, he became head of the newly formed NKVD and began preparing the first sequence of infamous "show trials," in which decent Communists publicly accused themselves of astonishingly wicked crimes, after which they were "purged." In the third of these tragic courtroom farces, Yagoda found himself charged with, and found guilty of, being a "Trotskyite saboteur," and he was soon, and quite properly, shot.

YAHO

In the lore of the Australian aborigines, a hill-dwelling cannibal monster who kills, roasts, and eats women.

YAKSHAS

Indian demons who, as soon as they were created by Brahma, wanted to devour (*yaksh*) him.

YALE, Frankie   DWH 1927   MURDER

Brooklyn-born president of the Unione Siciliane, "the Black Hand," a crime cartel. AL CAPONE got his start as a bouncer in Yale's New York saloon. A thief, pimp, killer, and bootlegger, Yale not only ran a protection racket on New York tobacco store owners but had his face printed on the cigar boxes. (Thus, in Brooklyn slang, "Frankie Yale" came to mean anything expensive and crummy.) Capone, now in Chicago, suspected (rightly) that Yale was hijacking his shipments of liquor and selling them back to him. Scarface ordered a history-making hit—Frankie was the first (but hardly the last) mobster to be mowed down by a submachine gun. At his funeral, twenty-eight trucks of flowers followed his $12,000 casket.

YAMA

The Adam of the Zoroastrian system, Yama was the first human created and the first to die; he is now the ruler of Hell. Yama is also (by no coincidence) the name of the Hindu judge of the dead. He is green, with red eyes, and rides a buffalo.

YAN LU WANG

A Chinese demon god, Yan Lu Wang presides over *kuei*—all the damned—at T'ai Shan, that is, in Hell.

YANG Kuei-fei   DWH 756   SOWING DISCORD

The subject of many poems and plays, she was the beautiful and ambitious concubine of the T'ang emperor Hsuan Tsung. She was also, curiously enough, obese. She entered the court by marrying the son of the sixty-year-old emperor, but Hsuan became so infatuated with her that he obliged his son to divorce her. The emperor could refuse her nothing—soon her sisters were added to his harem and her brother to his government, as first minister. Yang next "adopted as her son" a dashing young general, An Lu-shan. He led a rebellion, forcing the emperor's disgraceful resignation and flight—during which Yang and her brother were killed by indignant imperial troops.

YAOTZIN

Aztec god of Hell.

YESENIN, Sergey   DWH 1925   DESPAIR

A peasant poet newly arrived in Moscow, Yesenin welcomed and sang the praises of the recent Bolshevik Revolution, which he believed would value and defend "little wooden things"—the soul of Russia—against materialistic progress—machinery, iron, stone, and steel. He was viewed as useful to the Party and became something of a poetry-reading pop star in Moscow. There, in 1922, he met and married the flamboyant, barefoot, scarf-waving American dancer Isadora Duncan. Together they toured Europe and America, drunkenly trashing hotel rooms to the delight of the tabloids, and the poet added a cocaine addiction to his alcoholism. He returned to Russia full of self-loathing and to his native village, where his beloved "wooden things" had been replaced by a factory. Although he had read "not five pages of Marx," he attempted a volume of propaganda verse—then hanged himself in a Leningrad hotel room, leaving a last poem written in his own blood.

YOKO

Among the texts unearthed at Nag Hammadi in Egypt is an early (pre-185) Gnostic-Christian scripture, *The Apocryphon of John*. It describes a female God—or at least a "consort" of ARCHERON, the Tempter. Her name is Sophia. She it was who begat the female archdemon known as Ouch epipto, under whose control are the four chief tempter demons, the enemies of humankind: Blaoman (fear), Ephememphi (pleasure), Nenentophi (grief), and Yoko (lust).

Lusters suffering the wages of their sin.

YOMAEL

Yet another of the Enochian Watcher angels—a prince of the Seventh Heaven—who rebelled against God by falling in love with a mortal woman.

YSHIEL

Demon in the secret alphabet of demonic texts.

YUKI ONNA

A female ghost of Japan who frequents snowstorms, putting her victims to sleep and then freezing them to death.

Zen Master Hakuin was asked by a Samurai, "Is there really a paradise and a Hell?"

"Who are you?" asked Hakuin.

"I am a Samurai."

"You a Samurai? What sort of lord would have you as his guard? You look like a beggar!"

The Samurai became so angry that he began to draw his sword.

Hakuin continued, "So. You have a sword. It is probably too dull to cut off my head."

As the Samurai lifted his sword to strike, Hakuin said, "Here is the gate of Hell."

At these words, the Samurai sheathed his sword and bowed.

"Here open the gates of paradise," said Hakuin.

> —Traditional koan

Zodacare od Zodameranu! Odo cicale Qaa! Zodoreje, lape zodiredo
Noco Mada, hoathahe Saitan!

*(Open the mysteries of your creation! Be friendly unto me, for I am the same,
the true worshipper of the highest and ineffable King of Hell!)*

> — Seventeenth Enochian Key, from *The Satanic Bible*

*Zirel, daughter of Roize Glike, missed me, and her eyes were sad. She is mine,
mine, I thought. The Angel of Death stood ready with his rod; a zealous little
devil busied himself preparing the cauldron for her in hell. . . . But what is
Eve without a serpent? And what is God without Lucifer?*

> —ISAAC BASHEVIS SINGER, "The Mirror" from *Gimpel the Fool*

ZABULON 🦎

A demon who, in the seventeenth century, entered the convent of
Loudun on a bouquet of roses thrown over the wall.

ZAGAN

A great king and president of Hell, Zagan appears first as a bull with the wings of a griffin and then assumes human form. He makes slow men witty and fools wise, turns water into wine, blood into oil, and oil into water; he can change any metal into the coin of the realm.

ZAHAROFF, Sir Basil   DWH 1936   SOWING DISCORD

An international arms dealer and financier, Zaharoff was known as "the mystery man of Europe" and "the merchant of death." At age twenty-three, he left England (deserting his wife) when accused of embezzling funds from his Turkish uncle's dry goods firm. Living in Athens under an assumed name, he fell among diplomats and, in 1888, formed a partnership with Hiram Maxim, inventor of the machine gun. Zaharoff began selling these and other weapons, first in the Balkans and then to other interested parties throughout eastern Europe, and he found love with the wife of a deranged Spanish duke. During the First World War, he supplied (retail) the means of slaughter (wholesale) to French and English forces—for which service he was awarded membership in the Legion of Honor, a knighthood, and enough money to become one of the world's richest men. He retired to operate a casino in Monte Carlo.

ZAHUN

Demon of the first hour, the genius of scandal.

ZALAMBAR

An especially nasty Islamic demon, the offspring of IBLIS, Zalambar is the "author of mercantile dishonesty."

ZALBURIS

Demon of the eighth hour, the genius of therapeutics.

ZANGARA, Joseph   DWH 1933   MURDER

After his emigration from Italy to New Jersey, Zangara made no secret of his politics: hatred of "kings and capitalists." After he opened fire on a car in which President Roosevelt was riding, he confessed, "Make no difference. Presidents just the same bunch, all the same. I see Mr. Hoover first, I kill him first." Nevertheless, because the man he actually killed was the crime-busting mayor of Chicago, who was sitting beside FDR, Zangara is reputed to have been a hired Mafia assassin.

Seated in the electric chair, Zangara sealed his eternal fate. He sneered at the witnesses, "Lousy capitalists," and declared, "There is no God."

ZAQQUM

This is the name given, in the Quran (37.62–68), to a tree that grows in deepest Hell. Its flowers are serpent-headed demons.

ZAR

Muslim demons who possess wives and make them demand beautiful clothes and perfume.

ZAREN

Demon of the sixth hour, the avenging genius.

ZAROBI

Demon of the third hour, the genius of precipices.

ZAZEL

One of the fallen-angel demons named in the Book of Enoch, Zazel is invoked in casting love spells. Agrippa von Nettesheim lists him as one of the demons of Saturn, where he lives in a cave with his sons.

ZEPAR

A great duke of Hell, Zepar appears in red apparel, armed like a soldier, and inflames women with love for men—but some accounts say he also makes them barren. In addition, he causes women constantly to change their minds, hence inspiring men to resort to pederasty.

ZEVEAK

A demon of the moon.

ZEVI, Sabbatai DWH 1676 HERESY

In the city of Salonika, in 1648, a handsome, twenty-two-year-old Turkish Jew of Spanish descent, a student of the mystic Cabala, announced that he was the Messiah. To substantiate his claim, he publicly pronounced the name of God and married the Torah. He traveled to Jerusalem and thence, in 1662, to Egypt, where he won the allegiance of the

The column of Heresy

Turkish governor's influential Jewish treasurer. In Cairo he also met and married Sarah, a Polish ex–convent girl and practicing whore. When he returned to his hometown of Smyrna, he was hailed by crowds as the King of the Jews. Word of their deliverance spread to Jews across Europe, from Venice to London, where the stock exchange established ten-to-one odds that the Jews would establish a homeland in Palestine, where Zevi was waiting to greet them. Pilgrims by the thousands sold their earthly goods for a song and flocked to his kingdom. It seems that the secret of Zevi's success was his doctrine—and practice—of "Sacred Sin": The way to get rid of temptation is to yield to it; one can only triumph over evil by practicing it. Thus, on fast days, his followers feasted—on pork, yet! Needless to say, there was also plenty of unrestricted sexual activity. Since the Holy Land was a Turkish possession, the Messiah and his followers marched to Constantinople, to demand recognition from the sultan. That worthy received the king of the Jews most graciously, and made him an offer: Put a turban on your head, or lose it. Zevi and Sarah were thenceforth known as Mehemet Effendi and Fatimi Radini.

ZHONG-KUI

Zhong-kui became a popular Chinese demon after committing suicide when he failed to take first place in a civil service examination.

ZHSMAEL

Demon invoked to separate married couples.

ZIMIMAR

King of Hell's northern regions.

ZIZUPH

Demon of the eighth hour, and the genius of mysteries.

ZOPHAS

Demon of the eleventh hour, and the genius of pentacles.

ZOPHIEL

An angelic double agent, Zophiel was first employed as God's spy, infiltrating the Satanic side during the War in Heaven—but all the while, he was actually on the side of the rebels. His cover blown, he was cast down with the rest. He now holds the position of "herald of Hell."

ZU

A demonic storm bird in Babylonian mythology.

ZUBATOV, Col. Sergey   DWH 1917   SUICIDE

He created Police Socialism when, as chief of Okhrana, the czar of Russia's secret police, he resorted to the finky strategy of founding and funding several "workers' organizations" in order to spy on them. When the *real* revolution began, Zubatov shot himself.

ZULEIKA   DWH circa 2000 B.C.
BEARING FALSE WITNESS

This is the traditional name given to the randy wife of the Egyptian pharaoh Potiphar. She attempted to seduce the handsome and holy Joseph—he of the many-colored dream coat—employing the least subtle come-on in history: "Lie with me" (Genesis 39:7). Rebuffed, she then accused Joseph of attempted rape and had him imprisoned!

ZUPHLAS

A demon of the eleventh hour, Zuphlas is said to preside over the astrological sign of Libra.

ZWINGLI, Ulrich   DWH 1531   HERESY

Holding invariably the last name listed in the indexes of history books, Zwingli was the third member of the Reformation Trinity (with Calvin and Luther). This Swiss theologian was—like the great St. Augustine before him—given to repeated youthful bouts of frenzied fornication followed by periods of gloomy remorse. Unlike the saint, Zwingli was already an ordained priest at the time and never did manage to "keep it in his cassock"; maybe that's why his first proposed "reformation" of the Church was the abolition of clerical celibacy. Going from

ANNO AETATIS EIVS XLVIII.

bad to worse, he was soon denying the Real Presence of Christ in the Eucharist—and even the existence of Purgatory! When news of Zwingli's death (in a battle between his deluded followers and victorious Catholic forces in the War of Kappel) reached Martin Luther, his fellow reformer could only observe, "How well God knows his business."

PICTURE CREDITS

Authors' personal collection: pages 59, 167.

The Bettmann Archive: pages 61, 75, 81, 88 (bottom), 108, 128, 146 (top), 153, 174 (top), 185 (bottom), 207 (bottom), 217, 221, 241, 244.

The Dore Illustrations for Dante's Divine Comedy, **Dover Publications, 1976:** pages 31, 88 (top), 99, 229.

Ein Dantekranz aus hundert Blattern **by Paul Pochhammer, G. Grotefche Verlagsbuchhandlung, 1906:** pages 151, 230, 234.

New York Public Library Picture Collection: pages 7, 8, 9, 11, 12, 16, 18, 21, 22, 23, 24, 25, 28, 29, 30, 34, 36, 37, 38, 42, 43, 44, 46, 47, 52, 55, 57 (bottom), 58, 60, 69, 70, 73, 76 (bottom), 77, 82 (bottom), 83, 84, 85 (top), 89, 90, 100 (bottom), 104, 105, 110, 111, 112, 114, 115, 116, 117, 118, 121, 124, 125, 127, 129, 130, 133, 134, 140, 146 (bottom), 150, 155, 156, 157, 162, 163, 165, 166, 168, 174 (bottom), 175, 177 (top), 179, 180, 181, 182, 185 (top), 186, 187, 190, 191, 193, 195, 197, 198, 200, 203, 207 (top), 208, 209, 210, 213, 215, 216, 218 (bottom), 222 (top), 224, 231, 233 (bottom), 237, 240, 242, 245, 247 (top), 257 (bottom).

Picture Book of Devils, Demons and Witchcraft **by Ernst and Johanna Lehner, Dover Publications, 1971:** pages ii, 251, 255.

Symbols, Signs & Signets **by Ernst Lehner, Dover Publications, 1950:** pages 15, 17, 82 (top), 166 (bottom), 172, 208 (middle), 225.

Treasury of Fantastic and Mythological Creatures: 1,087 Renderings from Historic Sources **by Richard Huber, Dover Publications, 1981:** pages 53, 63, 100 (top), 141, 161, 177 (bottom), 222 (bottom), 250, 257 (top).

Turner Entertainment Co.: pages 76 (top), 85 (bottom).

ABOUT THE AUTHORS

SEAN KELLY has recently assured his own eternal damnation by co-writing *HERstory: Lisa Marie's Wedding Diary* for Villard Books.

ROSEMARY ROGERS, co-author of *Saints Preserve Us!,* is currently writing a comedy screenplay about the ongoing battle between saints and demons. Even though she's lived in New York City her entire life, she still believes that good will triumph over evil.